Venetian Moon

CLARISSA ROSS

CRIMSON
ROMANCE

F+W Media, Inc.

This edition published by
Crimson Romance
an imprint of F+W Media, Inc.
10151 Carver Road, Suite 200
Blue Ash, Ohio 45242
www.crimsonromance.com

Copyright © 1980 by W.E. Dan Ross

ISBN 10: 1-4405-7285-2
ISBN 13: 978-1-4405-7285-2
eISBN 10: 1-4405-7286-0
eISBN 13: 978-1-4405-7286-9

Chapter One

ON A late afternoon in March, 1822, Betsy Chapman stood staring out the great drawing-room windows of Malworth Castle, the home of her family for more than two centuries. This huge stone castle sat proudly on a small hill near Maidstone in the county of Kent. Betsy, a slim blond-haired beauty with large dark blue eyes, had grown up in an England ruled by the corpulent Prince Regent. And from childhood she had known the threat to England of the Emperor Napoleon.

That threat no longer existed; only a year earlier the exiled emperor had died on the island of St. Helena. Sadly she had lost her only brother, Richard, in the decisive battle of Waterloo in which Napoleon had met his final defeat. Now she lived in this great castle with her mother and her new stepfather, Sir John Cort, a man whom she detested not only because he wantonly gambled away her late father's money but because of his infidelity and cruelty to her weak mother.

And now Sir John Cort had behaved more odiously than ever in arranging a marriage between her and his crony and companion in lust, Lord Alfred Dakin! A dreadful match from the point of age alone since Betsy was only twenty-two and Lord Alfred was an emaciated sixty-one. He had daughters older than Betsy, and the scandalous whispers about him hinted of his liking for young women, even mere girls! It was also said that he had suffered a bout of the dread pox contracted from a Brighton whore.

Betsy was repelled by the sly, sniggering attentions of the old fop. She had angrily warned her mother and stepfather she would not marry him. But they seemed to hope he would win her over in time. Or perhaps they counted on breaking her spirit so that she would accept this unfortunate marriage.

Betsy, lost in thought, continued to gaze grimly out the window at the winding gravel roadway which led from the main road to the entrance of Malworth Castle. Lord Dakin was coming for dinner that evening, and from what her mother had said, Betsy feared the old roué might be going to choose the occasion to propose to her.

She chafed at the situation in which she found herself. Her father, Sir Ian Chapman, had been an official of the British consular service. The family had moved about the world during her early years. She and her brother, Richard, had been taught by an absentminded old Church of England clergyman. This old scholar's health made it impossible for him to take charge of a church, but he managed to eke out a living by taking on the children of rich and titled families as private students. Old Father Warren had traveled halfway around the world tutoring them.

Her father had been an athlete and a horseman. He had made no distinction between her and her brother, so that she had grown up able to ride a horse and fence as well as any man. Her tomboyish period was fondly remembered by her now as perhaps her happiest time. With the death of her father four years earlier from a liver affliction her good days seemed to have come to an end. Her brother's death at Waterloo three years prior to that had been the start of the ill fortune which had hounded her since.

A comrade-in-arms of her brother had come to her with a troubling account of his death. According to this young officer her brother had died as the result of a Major Eric Walters regrouping his collapsed infantry company against official orders and sending them on a needless suicide mission.

Betsy, still grieving for the dead Richard, had been shocked at this grim tale. And she had only recently sent a complaint to Lord Gray at the War Office. She hoped to somehow make this Major Eric Walters pay for his reckless act which had caused the death of so many of his men. The young officer had told her that Major Walters was still alive and well in London.

Only a few days ago she had received a rather strange reply to her letter. It was on War Office stationery but not from the office of Lord Gray. Rather it was from a mysterious Felix Black of whom she had never heard before. His letter had noted her complaints, and he had written that he would be in the area of Maidstone on this day and would call at Malworth Castle to see her. She was waiting for his arrival now.

By a happy coincidence her mother and stepfather had found it necessary to journey to nearby Canterbury for a conference with the family banker—no doubt a direct result of Sir John's folly at the gaming tables. At any rate it meant they would be away from the castle when her visitor arrived, and she would be able to interview him alone.

Betsy felt it important that the interview be private for several reasons. She did not think her mother cared a great deal whether Richard's death had been caused by negligence or not. Lady Cort was a vague, shallow-minded woman who she sometimes felt could not truly be her mother. It was from her father that Betsy had inherited her sharp intelligence. And she intended to get to the truth of her brother's death.

She was certain her stepfather would only make light of her concern: try to prove it was all imagination on her part, that she had listened to a half-baked story of some young officer and acted on it too swiftly. She was used to his overbearing, arrogant ways and was grateful that he and her mother would be absent all the afternoon.

Clouds made the sky gray; the day was as somber as her own mood. She speculated on what sort of person this Felix Black was and whether he had taken the contents of her letter seriously or not. There had been no hint of his attitude in his reply. He had merely informed her that he would call on her.

As she watched, she suddenly became aware of a carriage coming down the gravel road in the distance. Her heart began to beat a little faster, and she tried to keep herself firmly in control as she watched the vehicle approach. And she could not help but notice a certain strangeness about it. It was a high black carriage; the single horse drawing it was also jet black, and the coachman perched on the front seat wore black and had a black stovepipe hat!

She could not help thinking that the carriage might have dropped out of some funeral procession. As it came slowly to the entrance of the castle, it halted. The coachman tied the reins around the end of the seat and then jumped down to open the carriage door for his passenger.

Betsy watched tensely. For a moment no one appeared, and she wondered if it were all some macabre joke, that the carriage might be empty. But then a black top hat came in sight and following it a thin figure of a man dressed in black! The man was slightly stooped, and he hesitated to say a few words to his driver. Then he moved on to the door.

Betsy prepared herself and was standing calmly in the middle of the drawing room when Hobbs, the butler, marched in and announced her visitor in his booming voice, "Mr. Felix Black, miss!"

"Thank you," she said. And she went forward in her brown velvet dress specially chosen for the occasion and held out her hand for her visitor to take. "How do you do, Mr. Black!" she said.

The bent, thin man had removed his top hat, and she saw that only a few sparse black hairs were plastered across his bald head. He had a thin face with deep-set eyes and high cheekbones, his mouth was thin lipped, and his shoulders were narrow.

"My greetings, Miss Chapman," he said in a dry rustle of a voice as he took her hand in his clammy weak grip.

"You must be tired after your journey from London," she said.

His deep-set eyes were fixed on her with interest, and they naturally were also black. He said, "I paused along the way for food and drink, thank you."

"May I not offer you something?" she wanted to know.

The thin man couldn't seem to keep his eyes off her. Continuing to embarrass her with his fixed stare, he said, "A sherry perhaps."

"Of course," she said. And she rang and asked Hobbs to have a maid serve some sherry. Then she indicated two nearby chairs and said, "Let us sit for our talk. You must be surely tired from your long ride."

"Thank you, Miss Chapman," he said in his dry way. He glanced around at the spectacle of elegance surrounding them— from the fine old furniture to the paintings and tapestries on the walls. "This is a true mansion."

"We are rather proud of it," she said with a small smile. "My father's family has owned this property for several centuries. Not this house, of course; it was built later. But the land."

"Yes," he said, staring at her again. "I know you are one of England's oldest families."

She sat in a high-backed chair and primly folded her hands on her lap. She said, "That is why it seemed so tragic that my brother, the only male heir, should have perhaps died needlessly."

"Ah, yes," he said with disinterest as he carefully sat opposite her.

The maid came hurrying in with a tray holding a decanter of sherry and glasses. The tray was placed on a table beside Betsy, and she poured a drink for her visitor and passed it to him and then poured one for herself. All the while she was trying to decide what sort of person he might be. He was from the War Office, but surely he had never been a soldier who had seen active service. His bent figure was so frail looking and his skin color was pasty white in contrast to his black clothing.

She said, "It was good of you to come."

"Your letter interested me," he told her as he took a sip of the wine.

"I appreciate your paying so much attention to it. You could well have considered it the ravings of some female lunatic."

"Not at all," he demurred. "It was well written, and I could tell it was from a lady of some position even before I read the signature and realized who you were."

"Really?" She could see that he was extremely sharp along with being discreet.

He told her, "Your late father, Sir Ian Chapman, had a long and outstanding career in our diplomatic service. Until his death, so regrettable, he was a member of that service."

"It was his pride," Betsy said. "He wanted nothing more than to serve his country. The same could be said of my brother, Richard."

"And of you, young lady, I'm sure of that," he said in that same rasping voice.

"Unfortunately, because of my sex, I have not had the same opportunity to stand forward for my country. But I promise you I feel as strongly."

The thin man's narrow face showed interest. "I'm glad to hear that."

She said, "That is why I wish to learn the truth about my brother's death. And if his commanding officer was at fault, I would want to see him punished."

"A rational enough wish," the thin man in black said quietly.

"So I was not only grief stricken but frustrated by this word that Richard's death mightn't have been necessary." And she again recited all that she had written in the letter to him. He sat there listening and showed what appeared to be interest.

When she had finished, he put aside his empty wine glass carefully. Then glancing at her, he said, "Yes. I'm very well acquainted with the manner of your brother's death, miss."

"And what, pray, are you to do about it?"

"The battle of Waterloo is history now, young lady. No act of mine can change what happened on that eventful day."

She protested. "I fully realize that, sir. But if my brother was needlessly sacrificed, I wish the one responsible to be punished."

The man nodded his almost bald head and suggested, "You bear an undue hatred for this man, a man who may have done his best. His worst offense might be that he temporarily lost his head in the midst of that awful battle!"

Her eyes opened wide and her cheeks warmed as she asked of him, "Are you reproving me for my stand?"

"It has perhaps become an obsession, has it not?"

"No more so than is natural," she flung back. "I loved my brother, Richard, as I have rarely loved anyone!"

"I know," her black-clad visitor said quietly. "You were both on Saint Helena together."

Betsy gasped. "How do you know that?"

The thin man offered her a bony smile which gave his face a more skeletal look than ever. He rasped, "I know all about you, young lady. Your entire history! The history of your family!"

She stared at him in dismay, wondering what sort of person he was and why he had taken this trouble to visit her if he were not sympathetic to her complaint. She said, "Are you telling me my complaint to the War Office was unreasonable?"

"Not at all," he said. "I only am trying to point out that there may well be no villain in this drama of the battlefield, that the man who gave the order resulting in your brother's death was confused and not evil intentioned. That he perhaps regrets what happened to this very hour."

She sat up very straight. "You are making a plea for the man I consider my brother's murderer. Why did you bother to come see me at all?"

He coughed, a dry, racking cough, and produced a white handkerchief and pressed it to his mouth for a moment. Then he drew it away and stuffed it in his pocket as he told her, "I have come to visit you for quite another reason."

"Another reason?" she echoed in bafflement.

"Yes." He was studying her with an odd look of satisfaction.

"Pray tell me what it may be," she begged him. "You are from the War Office, are you not?"

"I am," he said. "How else could I come by your letter?"

"Please continue!"

He stood up. "I will move about," he told her. "It is easier for me to think on my feet."

"Whatever you like," she said.

He gave a deep sigh. "Until recently I have been head of a division of the War Office. Now I have been told to retire, that my usefulness is at an end. I'm spending my last few weeks in the office I have occupied so long, being forced to retire to my dark and unhealthy London house, ignored by those I have served so well, including His Majesty."

"That is too bad, sir," she said. "But what has it to do with me?"

He moved away a little and made a gesture of his thin hand. "If you will be but patient, you will hear."

"I'm sorry," she said, beginning to think she was entertaining a madman.

He swung around to face her and said, "I'll venture that until you received my letter, you never had heard the name of Felix Black."

She stared at the odd, shabby figure. "That is true."

"And yet for years I have been one of the most powerful forces in the War Office. I have been chief of espionage."

"Espionage!"

"And before that I was the foremost spy of the service," the thin man ranted on. "Yet today I am discredited and soon to be discarded."

"Why? And what has it to do with me?"

He came close to her and pointed a thin forefinger close to her lovely face. "Your father was stationed on Saint Helena just after Napoleon was exiled there."

"Yes."

"Soon after your family had word of your brother's death in the battle of Waterloo, you along with your father and mother and an ancient Anglican priest all arrived on the bleak island. Your father was sent there as assistant to Admiral Cockburn."

"Yes," she said almost in a whisper. "I was beside myself with sorrow and anger at first. Dear old Father Warren tried to remove the rancor from my heart."

The cold, sharp eyes fixed on her. "You were often a guest at Longwood, the estate of the Balcombe family on Saint Helena."

"I was."

"And it was while you were there that you met the former Emperor Napoleon who was temporarily living in their garden house. You were only sixteen but lovely, as you are now. You, along with Betsy and Jane Balcombe, became good friends of the man who had changed the face of Europe."

She said, "Are you making some sort of charge against me? That was long ago. Napoleon is dead!"

Felix Black regarded her with one of his cold, superior smiles. "You hated the emperor at first! And when he asked you why you were so bitter, you told him. And when you said your brother had died at Waterloo because of him, he was full of sympathy for you. And he told you that to all intents he had died there as well."

She stared at him in amazement. "Almost his very words! How could you know that?"

"Napoleon had great charm," the man in black went on relentlessly. "He won you over. You soon became as friendly with him as the Balcombe girls. The gossips on the island whispered about the scandal of this middle-aged conqueror at last being conquered by a beautiful English girl."

"I will not have you tarnish the friendship," she told him. "My father and mother approved. For a time I felt less bitter about Richard's loss. It was not until later I heard the story about garbled orders and realized he had been the victim of one of our own British officers—not the enemy."

The thin, nearly bald man showed a wry smile. "You wished to believe that. For since that sunset eve on Saint Helena, when you and Napoleon wandered off to stand on the cliff's edge hand in hand, you have always revered the memory of that fat Corsican!"

"Do not speak of him like that!" she cried, springing up. "He was a noble figure, and I cared for him deeply. Call it treasonable if you will. Charge me as you like!"

The stooped man came close to her and said, "I blame you not at all. I did not come here to charge you or condemn you."

"Then why?"

"I wanted to find out if you remembered."

"How could I forget?" she asked brokenly as she turned away from him. "It was my first true love affair. I was a child and he a man of much experience. Yet it was beautiful and he, the ogre of my childhood memories, was tender and loving to me. When I learned that because of my father's illness we were to leave the island, I thought my heart would break. My only consolation was his promise that he would never forget me."

"If it is of any small value to you, he never did."

She wheeled around to stare defiantly at the weird figure in black. "How can you know all this? You unhealthy man!"

He smiled. "Do you remember Dr. Barry Edward O'Meara?"

"Of course. He was the British medical officer appointed to look after the former emperor."

"He was my man. A member of the British Intelligence. Unhappily I also had to later recall him. He came under the spell of Napoleon to the extent that he now spends his time writing books in his defense. Needless to say he is no longer one of His Majesty's spies."

"Barry O'Meara!" she exclaimed, a look of days past recalled in her blue eyes. "I always liked him. I never guessed. So he was the one who told you about me."

"He and others," the master spy said. "I have always conducted an efficient department."

She sighed. "With all the guards and small freedom left to him, I knew there had to be spies. But I did not guess that Dr. O'Meara was one of them. He was Napoleon's friend."

"He still is," Felix Black complained. "If he keeps on writing his infernal books, he's going to wind up in prison."

She said, "So you have not come here to help me about my brother's being sacrificed. Why have you made this visit?"

He faced her in silence for a moment. "Can I trust you implicitly? Have I your sworn word that what I'm about to say to you will never be repeated?"

Betsy was upset. "What are you talking about?"

"Do you swear to remain silent?"

"Yes," she said. "As long as it means no harm to anyone." She was beginning to suspect that he was about to enlist her in some plot against her former friend Dr. Barry O'Meara. It was evident they wished to silence the former spy.

Felix Black frowned. "Because of what I'm going to tell you, I'm being driven from my office. Reviled! Scoffed at as an old fool living in the past! No one wants to believe me!"

"Explain," she said.

He seized her by the arm and fixed his fanatic's bright eyes on her. "Napoleon lives!"

"What?"

"He lives! He was successfully rescued from the island of Saint Helena, and he is somewhere in Europe in hiding at this very moment."

"Preposterous!" she gasped.

"That is what they are all saying," Felix Black said, still clenching her arm so that it pained. "They ignore all my years of being mastermind of the world's greatest spy network."

She said, "It is common knowledge that Napoleon died of a liver afflicton that came from his being held on that dread island. My father contracted the same liver ailment, and it killed him."

"A man died of a liver affliction in Napoleon's bed, but it was not Napoleon," the thin man in black said with passion. "And now the former emperor is virtually a prisoner of one of the great criminal minds of our day, a political upstart named Valmy. This Valmy is the head of a group of ex-military men and others who wish to seize power from the new king of France. Later it is Valmy's plan to see that Napoleon, once in power again as a puppet leader, is murdered. Then Valmy will become the new ruler of France and be on his way to conquer Europe. His particular hatred is for England and all things English!"

She listened to the trembling old man in awe, not sure whether all that she heard were the ramblings of a mind which had broken under long years of strain or the stunning information gathered by one who was still a mastermind of espionage. Somehow she felt what he was saying might at least have some truth in it.

In a hushed voice she asked, "Why have you told me all this?"

He had released her arm, and now he twisted his hands in nervous fashion and said, "Because I need your help."

"My help?"

"Yes," he said. "I have been discredited at the War Office. I shall be leaving shortly. But I'm going to conduct this campaign on my own. My house shall be my headquarters, and I shall enlist my own agents to try and rescue Napoleon from this Valmy, warn him of the fate in store for him, and have him take an armed vessel to the United States."

"The English betrayed him before when he could have made his escape to America easily," she reminded the man in black. "Why should he trust us again?"

"Not the nation, but me," the thin man said excitedly. "He knows of me. There is a house built for him in Louisiana, funds aplenty for a life of ease, and safe passage on a United States armed vessel."

"Why should you care what happens to him?"

"I don't! But I want to save Europe from the madman Valmy. The nations cannot stand another senseless war, and there will be one if Valmy succeeds with his scheme. The ace card is in his hand—the former emperor."

"I find it all impossible to believe," she said.

"So do the others," he told her. "But if I bring this off, the fat oaf we call His Majesty will invite me to the palace for honors. I shall have my revenge. Those that call me mad now will bow to me in gratitude."

"What do you want of me?" she asked.

Felix Black gazed at her grimly. "I need you to be my chief agent. You know Napoleon, and he trusts you. If you tell him what Valmy is up to, he will believe you."

"I know nothing of such things," she said.

"You are an excellent shot, you fence as well as any man, and you ride horseback like a trained cavalry officer," he said.

"You have been well informed."

"Always," he agreed. "It is my strong point. There are only a few tricks to be learned and I can soon teach them to you. A matter of codes, techniques for getting information, a knowledge of picking locks, and a familiarity with needed poisons."

She said in disbelief, "You wish to enlist me to go to France in search of a returned Napoleon and save him from this Valmy?"

"Exactly," he said. "You would not be alone, of course. I shall direct this strictly private group. I hope to enlist O'Meara as a member, and I would have you work in conjunction with a trained male spy who has gained a reputation under the code name of Robin. It would be his duty to protect you."

"I'm afraid I must refuse you," she said. "I am happy to be living a quiet country life here with my mother and my stepfather."

The man in black smiled at her coldly. "Did you say you are happy here?"

"Yes," she said in weak defiance.

"I wish it were true," he said. "But it is not so. You are chafing under the indifference of your mother and the cruel arrogance of your stepfather!"

"Please!" she protested.

"Let me finish," he said sharply. "Your blessed stepfather is cutting deep into your father's estate. At this moment he and your mother are in Canterbury further mortgaging this house and the land it is on to pay his latest gambling debts!"

"No!" she pleaded, shocked but aware that it was all too likely to be so.

"And you know how he plans to repair his fortunes?" the man in black asked. "He plans to sell you in marriage to his repulsive friend, the elderly Lord Dakin! A lustful old man rotten with syphillis and still reaching out to taint someone of your youth and beauty!"

"Go, Mr. Black," she said in a broken voice "You have said enough."

"I could tell you more," the man in black said "But I have already caused you more pain than I wish. For your own sake you should escape from this house. For the sake of a man you once cared for deeply, you should enlist in this crusade with me. And for the sake of the England for which your brother gave his life, save it from another war! For make no mistake, once in power, Valmy will strike against England."

She shook her head. "I'm sorry. I believe you are mad, Mr. Black."

"I hear that often," the man in black said with a shrug of his narrow shoulders. "Yet I swear all I have told you is true."

"Fantasy!" she said.

"So they say," he said with a bitter smile. "They think it is a product of my own mind, put forward so I may hold onto power. So they are removing my power. But I will fight this menace if I have to fight it alone."

"Good day, Mr. Black," she said firmly.

He bowed. "Good day. If you come to agree with me, you may find me at my house in Fetter Lane. The number is Twenty. I need you badly. So does the man who was your first love."

He bowed again and went on out. She stared after him and then crossed to the window where she had been standing when he arrived. She saw him in a his black top hat and suit make his way to the carriage. He gave the coachman some instructions and then stepped inside and vanished. After a moment the black carriage and horse vanished up the gravel roadway, lost among the trees at the turn.

She stared out at the sullen day and wondered if it had all been a strange trick of her mind. Had she imagined the weird black coach and the visitor who came in it? Had the tall tale which she'd listened to been a hint of her own approaching madness? Surely it was the strangest experience she'd known in a long while.

A genius of evil! That was how he had struck her. His knowledge had made her think of an all-knowing Satan spying on his unwary subjects and reporting their misdeeds with unholy glee. Tears sprang to her eyes, and she fled up the stairway to her bedroom. There she threw herself on her bed and sobbed.

Remembrance of St. Helena came back to her all too vividly. Her kindly father had stood up for her when her mother reproached her for her friendship with Napoleon. So she had enjoyed her short stay on the bleak island and spent much time with the exiled emperor.

He had talked to her of his son, the king of Rome. And he'd said wistfully, "I have no fear whatever about my fame. Posterity will do me justice. The truth will be known, and the good I have done with the faults I have committed will be compared. Although I have failed, I shall be considered an extraordinary man."

Only six years ago! How close they had been! Since then she had lost her beloved father. Next Napoleon had died of apparently the same illness brought on by the difficult island climate. At the moment she was in a state of despair, frantic that she might somehow be forced into a hideous marriage with old Lord Dakin.

And because she'd written about Richard's death to the War Office, this fantastic man and his utterly insane story had come to her. His invitation to join him in London as one of his private secret agents might seem more reasonable if she could make herself believe what he'd told her. The trouble was that she could not.

When Betsy went downstairs to dinner, her mother and stepfather had already returned and were having sherry in the drawing room. As she joined them, the big bulldog-faced Sir John Cort was haranguing her mother about something. He stood before the fireplace, his back to it, as he uttered a tirade of abuse at his unfortunate spouse. Maria Cort sat dejectedly in her chair, her glass of sherry held loosely in her hand as she listened to her husband.

Her thin, lined face lighted up a trifle at the arrival of Betsy since it would mean that some of the attention would be temporarily taken from her. "How nice you look, my dear," Maria said. "The white gown becomes you nicely. I'm sure Lord Dakin will be taken with it."

Almost angrily she replied, "I did not wear it to please Lord Dakin. In fact I wasn't at all sure he was coming tonight."

Her stepfather, resplendent in blue jacket and fawn trousers, scowled at her, and in his booming voice told her, "I'm sure I made that quite clear. Alfred is coming to stay overnight with us, and it is his hope, and ours, that you will come to some arrangement whereby your engagement can be announced."

"Never!" she said, defiantly facing her stepfather.

"Don't be rash, my dear!" her mother counseled her.

"You should consider yourself a fortunate young woman to be picked out by a man like Lord Dakin for marriage. As Lady Dakin you will rule London society," Sir John Cort said.

"A groom of sixty-one with an odious reputation," she said angrily. "All London would either pity me or laugh at me!"

Sir John Cort's ugly face took on a purplish shade, and he turned to demand of the hapless Maria, "Is this the respect you get from your ungrateful daughter?"

Maria, pinched looking under the lace cap she wore, pleaded with the burly man. "Do not be too hard on her, John. She has lost both a brother and a father, each of them dearer to her than I."

"Another disgrace!" Cort snapped, his jowls flapping over his tall, hard collar. "The girl was ruined by her father! His bad judgment was exemplified while you lived at Saint Helena—to allow his daughter to become a friend of Napoleon!"

Betsy exclaimed, "Do not speak against my father!"

"Ha!" Her stepfather snorted with disdain. "Next you will be warning me to proceed easily with the name of Napoleon!"

"I do warn you," she said with defiance. "Napoleon was my true friend!"

"Listen to her!" her burly stepfather exclaimed. And to Betsy he cried, "I vow you had no scruples of being in the company of an older man then!"

"Napoleon respected me," she said. "He did not want to ravish me as your lecherous friend does!"

Sir John Cort told her angrily, "If Lord Dakin marries you, it will be as close as you can ever expect to your becoming a lady. If only in name!"

"Lord Dakin is a fine gentleman, my dear," her mother said in a frightened voice.

Betsy smiled bitterly and told the two, "I suspect you need the match to replenish the family fortune. It is widely known that in your jaunts to London gaming houses you have squandered most of the fortune left by my father!"

"You hear that, madam!" her irate stepfather roared at her unfortunate mother. "This girl has no respect for me!"

"John!" Maria wailed pitifully.

At that moment Hobbs came into the room and cleared his throat to announce, "Lord Alfred Dakin's coach is in the drive, sir!"

"Thank you, Hobbs, I shall go at once to greet him," her stepfather said. And to them he went on scathingly, "It is not your daughter's fault that he has not caught us all quarreling like drunken fishwives!" And he strode off to welcome his old friend.

Maria looked up at Betsy sadly as soon as they were alone. "I do wish you would try to get along with your stepfather."

"I hate him!" Betsy said angrily. "I cannot conceal it!"

"He is only trying to arrange a suitable match for you. It is time you were married! Most of your friends are already raising children!"

"I can wait for marriage until I meet a man I love," she told her mother.

"You may wait a lifetime without finding such a person," Maria Cort lamented.

She knelt by her mother and said, "You above all people ought not to say that. I have such fond memories of your happy life with my father. Why did you have to marry again? And marry such a bounder as Sir John!"

Her mother whimpered, "I thought all men were like your father. Sir John flattered me and made so many promises—none of them which he bothered to keep. My only happiness rests in you!"

"And would you have me married to that old reprobate?"

"No," her mother said. "But Sir John is so forceful. I cannot seem to prevail against him."

"Then I promise you, I shall," Betsy told her mother grimly. She stood up again as she heard the voices of her stepfather and Lord Alfred Dakin approaching.

Lord Dakin came strutting into the room resplendent in a pale yellow silken jacket and dark blue trousers. He wore a wig too black to look natural and somewhat ill fitting. His thin fece was powdered and rouged, and he studied her with his lorgnette held up to his watery blue eyes.

"Damme, you never looked more lovely!" he said in his high-pitched voice, ending with a giggle.

"My daughter has been looking forward to your visit," Sir John Cort said, his eyes at the same time flashing a warning to Betsy not to deny this flagrant lie.

Her mother was on her feet and smiling at the ancient fop. "May I say how well you look, Lord Dakin. Your youthful appearance is the talk of London society. I have heard matrons whisper behind their fans that while their birth dates are the same as yours, you appear young enough to be their son!"

"Thank you, dear lady," Lord Alfred Dakin said. "Perhaps it is because I prefer the company of the young, particularly in my bed, that I have retained my own youth!" He guffawed at his distasteful joke.

They all, with the exception of Betsy, joined in laughing at his sally. Sir John turned to her with a frown and asked, "Have you no word of greeting for Lord Alfred?"

"I'm sure he knows he is welcome enough here without my adding to his greeting," she said quietly.

"True!" the old roué said, waving his jeweled lorgnette. "I need no reassurances from one who may soon share my love. A true Juliet and her Romeo, determined to be eternally youthful!" He giggled once again.

Even Sir John looked slightly disgusted at his performance and said, "Let us proceed to the dining room! I have your favorite pheasant and a bushel of fine oysters for your pleasure!"

So they proceeded to the dining hall. There at the elegant candlelit table a feast was served. Betsy tried to remain silent while the others kept up an unending conversation. The tales of the latest London scandals and the bon mots of the town gossips were repeated at the table with glee. Betsy tried to ignore the giggling and braying of the old man who would be her Romeo.

Shortly after the meal, when he approached her and made attempts to fondle her breasts covertly as they stood alone for a moment in the drawing room, she complained of a headache to him and hurried off to her room. She knew that her stepfather would be in a rage, but she did not care.

As she undressed for bed, she again thought of her visitor of the afternoon and his offer. Escape to London even in the pursuit of what might turn out to be a mad fantasy did not seem so farfetched to her now.

She had carefully locked the door to her bedroom, and so she fell asleep without any apprehensions. This made it all the more terrifying when she awakened in the middle of the night to hear a key being turned in the bedroom door. The moon shone into the room, flooding it with a cold blue light as she gazed at the door in consternation!

Chapter Two

BETSY DREW the sheets up over her lightly covered rounded breasts as she watched with a feeling of horror as the door opened. She immediately guessed what was happening. Her stepfather had provided his lecherous friend with a duplicate key to her room! She was being offered to Lord Dakin as a tasty treat along with the pheasant and the oysters.

Now the door was opened, and the skinny Lord Alfred Dakin, clad only in a nightshirt which barely came to his hips, stood revealed before her. A mad, lustful smile was on his ugly old face as he closed the door behind him and began advancing to his bedside.

"My lovely!" he croaked.

She pulled away to the other side of the bed, crying out, "Don't dare come near me!"

His answer was a throaty chuckle. He knelt on the bed, his nightshirt riding up so that the revolting ugliness of his dangling private parts was thrust toward her. She let out a cry of revulsion and got to her feet on her way to the door and escape!

With an agility surprising in one his age and probably produced only by his heightened state of lust, he scrambled across the bed like a schoolboy and then ran after her. He caught her before she reached the door and clasped one hand over her mouth and held her struggling body with the other arm.

All the while he crooned foul suggestions in her lovely ears. And as she struggled with him, he managed to tear at her thin nightgown until shortly she was completely naked. The awareness of her nudity seemed to spur him on more. With a mad strength he swung her around and flung her on the floor by the side of her bed!

Gasping from his exertions and giggling with glee, he held her down as he mounted her and prepared to ravish her. She was stunned for a moment after hitting the floor, but as her mind began to work again, she groped out wildly with her one free hand, seeking a weapon!

With a rush of inner exultation she found one! She grasped the handle of her chamber pot and swung it out and brought it down over his balding head, no longer protected by his wig. The pot made a thud, and he relaxed his grip on her. It was her cue to bring it down on the bald head a second time. This time blood spurted forth, and he fell to one side unconscious.

She dropped the chamber pot. Lying there breathing heavily, she studied him with disgust. It was possible she had killed him, and if so she did not care. All she could think of now was escape. Escape from the ugliness of this scene, escape from the old house which was no longer a haven for her, escape to London and whatever Felix Black might have to offer!

This resolved, she lost no time in dressing and hastily packing a single bag with the necessary things she would need for travel and a few days in London. She could buy other things later. She had money hidden in one of her dresser compartments. She put a few notes in her dress pocket and the rest in her bag.

As she hurried about her preparations for running away, the old roué lay motionless on the floor. She knelt by him to see if he were still breathing. And he was, though it was slow and labored. A grim expression on her face, she put on her cloak and bonnet. Then bag in hand she quietly let herself out of the room.

She made her way downstairs and out into the cool air of early morning with the same caution. It was too early for even the humblest of their servants to be awake yet, and she knew she could not hope to take a horse from the stables without being heard. Her only chance was to walk to the main road and wave down the stagecoach on its way to London. It was the usual custom to pick up fares along the highway if there was any empty space. She could only pray that one would soon come along to pick her up.

She did not halt until she reached the main highway about a half hour later. Dawn was starting to break, and she glanced behind her and wondered what was happening at the castle. When morning came and Lord Dakin did not appear and was not found in his room, they would search for him. Whether they found him alive or dead depended on fate. He was an old man and the chamber pot a heavy weapon. She had not spared him at that moment of crisis. She had struck him hard!

Her ruminations were interrupted by the sound of horses' hooves and the creaking wheels of a stagecoach approaching and approaching in the right direction! Headed for London! She at once took a stand in the middle of the rutted road and began to wave her arms frantically.

The red and gold stage came bearing down on her, drawn by four magnificent horses. The driver reined them sharply and called out to them; they came to a restless, neighing halt! A stout man in cape and stovepipe hat seated with the driver jumped down and confronted her.

"What do thee want?" he asked, his bronzed fece surly.

"Passage to London," she said.

He eyed her suspiciously. "Do you have the price?"

She held out a note. "Will that be enough?"

" 'Twill do," he said shortly and stuffed it in his pocket. She knew that it was more than enough to pay for a half dozen fares, but she wasn't in a mood to argue this with him. She wanted to get on to London as quickly as she could.

The man opened the door of the stage and helped her up the big step. Inside there were three men, an old woman, and a young girl with a child in her arms. All of them were still in a sleepy state, their rest interrupted by her arrival. The air in the stage was heavy and smelled of strong spirits as well.

She was pleased to see an empty space next to a heavy man wearing a clergyman's black suit, clerical collar, and flat clerical hat. His oval-shaped face wore a benevolent expression, and he seemed the only one of the several passengers fully awake. He at once offered her a smile and moved a little to make room for her.

No sooner was she seated than the stage started on its way once again. The other passengers closed their eyes and attempted to sleep again. Only the stout clergyman remained awake. Now he beamed at her with his kindly eyes and in a low voice informed her, "I am Parson Midland."

"How do you do, reverend sir," she said a little stiffly.

The friendly man said, "May I presume by saying it is odd to have a young woman alone flagging the stage in the small hours of the morning. Are you in some sort of trouble?"

She shook her head. "No. I decided I wished to visit some friends in London."

The clergyman raised his eyebrows. "And you did not take a carriage to the nearest inn and wait for the stage there?"

"No," she improvised quickly. "There is illness at home, and I did not want to put anyone to a bother."

"That is truly Christian of you," the middle-aged portly clergyman said with pleasure. "There is talk of the young not being properly pious. I do not agree. And I think you are a prime example of the good that can be found among our youth."

"Thank you," she said with a sigh. "I fear I am not all that good."

"I'm sure you are," Parson Midland said. "And now I must be completely honest with you. I know who you are."

Her eyes widened. "You do?"

"Yes," he said. "You are the daughter of Sir John and Lady Cort. I saw you together at a fair in the marketplace of Canterbury."

"I think you have made a mistake," she faltered.

"No," the clergyman said with a reassuring smile. "You were pointed out to me. Also I was told Sir John was merely your stepfather."

"I see," she said, feeling trapped.

The stout man told her, "You have no reason to fear me. You can be quite honest with me. I wish only to befriend you."

"You are kind," she said. "And it is true I am Betsy Chapman. I have left the castle because of an intolerable situation there!"

"Ah! You are running away."

"You could hardly call it that. I am of age."

"Let me phrase it differently. You are running away from home without informing your parents or asking their approval."

Her eyes flashed angrily. "I do not need my stepfather's approval. He is a beast who would pander me to a lecherous old man."

The clergyman closed his eyes for a moment and in a low voice murmured, "The sins of the flesh! How vile some humans are!"

"Sir John is among the vilest. And so is his friend, Lord Dakin, whom he would have me wed!"

"That broken-down old roué," Parson Midland said with dismay. "I cannot believe it!"

"Yes," she said. "It is all too true. I have escaped from their trap, and now I'm on my way to the house of a friend in London."

"Thank the Good Lord you have such a friend," Parson Midland said piously. "For if you found the countryside corrupted by wickedness, I can only warn you London today is a veritable cesspool of sin!"

She gazed out of the window at the passing countryside. Dawn had come, and everything now stood out clearly. She said in a forlorn voice, "I have no choice but to go to London."

The clergyman at her side said, "May I offer a suggestion?"

She glanced at him. "If you like."

"You are new to the city," Parson Midland said. "I am well versed in its ways. When we arrive in the great metropolis, let me look after you until I have safely delivered you to your friends."

"That is most kind of you," she said. "But I'm sure there is no need."

"But there is!" he insisted. "London is a dangerous place even for a young woman of some experience. There are wicked men and women waiting at the inns to prey on new arrivals. Wicked characters who will kill for a small amount or lead the unwary into a life of sin."

"I shall be careful of such people," Betsy said. "Thank you for your warning."

"To rest my mind, let me do more than that," Parson Midland said earnestly. "Let me escort you from the stage, share a light meal with you, and then hire a carriage and accompany you to the residence of your friend. When I see you safely there, my mind will be at ease and I will bid you good-bye."

She smiled at him. "You are one of the kindest men I have ever known."

The stout clergyman looked pleased. "I am of the cloth, my dear. I must strive to be worthy of my calling."

As the stage reached the outskirts of London, the friendly clergyman continued to talk to her. She found him an excellent traveling companion, well versed in almost everything. He spoke of having done chaplain duty at Waterloo, and she mentioned Richard's death. He was properly sympathetic and told of seeking out a small church near Canterbury but finally giving up and going to London because he felt his calling was to help those poor creatures lost to the city's slums.

"So here I am returning to mission work among the lowest of the low," he told her.

"Surely the police must try to keep crime down," she said.

Parson Midland sighed. "The police are poorly organized. And there are an unbelievably modest number of them. Also their wages are far too small. The result is that these underpaid and overworked men often themselves become dishonest. Beadles, constables, street keepers, and watchmen are all too often in league with criminals."

"That is distressing," she said, alarmed.

He looked somber. "Corrupt police and numerous criminals. There are what are called flash houses. In these places hundreds of young people sleep nightly. There they are boarded and trained in crime. The boys become thieves and pickpockets; the girls in their earliest teens become prostitutes. These poor girls are taught where to go and what to do. Often they sleep with the flash-house boys for companionship, but their business is among strange males in the streets."

"Surely there is some other choices for them?"

"None," the parson said sadly. "No hope but in thieving and whoring. Unless they are prepared to sleep in sheds or under stalls and live on garbage, there is no means of livelihood for them but crime. These are the children I hope to help by establishing a mission."

"I pray you are successful," she told him. "I had no idea there were young people faced with such choices."

He nodded. "It seems to transcend classes. Your wicked stepfather attempted to make you the slave of that despicable roué, Lord Dakin!"

"True!" she said with a shudder. "It was like forcing prostitution on me!"

"It was truly," the clergyman said. "And I know that men like Lord Dakin, elderly rakes often suffering from venereal diseases, prey on the children of the streets. The procuresses who watch over these unhappy young girls keep a vigil to prevent their reformation. They follow them on their daily and nightly rounds and take most of the wretched money the girls make. They keep them in a state of inebriation if not complete intoxication until they are too addicted to the bottle to have any other interest. Completely degenerate, falling lower and lower in the scale of prostitution, finally they die in the gutter or some other foul place, prematurely aged and riddled by disease!"

"You should preach widely for funds and put all this in your sermons," she told him.

"I intend to do just that," the stout man said, brightening a little. "So now you understand why I worry about you."

The interesting and informative conversation came to an end as they arrived in the busy streets of London. Even at an early hour wagons and carriages fought for a place in the crowded thoroughfares. The poor houses of the outlying district gradually gave way to stone and brick mansions and the great stately emporiums of business and government. The noise grew as they penetrated the bustling city.

All the others in the carriage came awake and reacted to their arriving in London in various ways. The baby cried lustily as its mother attempted to quiet it. The stage slowed down and finally drew to a stop in the courtyard of one of the largest inns which Betsy had ever seen. She had been to London several times before but never on her own. Alone the loud, busy city was more than a little frightening.

But fortunately she had Parson Midland at her side. He not only kept her close by him, but he also carried her bag. She considered it a good omen of her adventure that she had met up with such a person. At least she would be safe until she reached the house of Felix Black in Fetter Lane. And then she would discover if the story he had told her was the product of a mind gone mad or the most exciting event of the century!

Parson Midland warned her, "I do not advise we enter the inn for food and drink. There is much drinking of spirits in these places, and vile language is used openly—not fit for your innocent ears."

"I suppose we should have something to refresh us," she said.

"I fully agree," the parson said good-humoredly. "I always have a full breakfast, and I'm extremely hungry. Before we proceed to your friend, we must halt and refresh ourselves and have some food."

"What do you suggest?"

"I was about to tell you," he said. "A few blocks ahead there is a tiny tea shop run by a matron who is a friend and former parishioner of mine. I'm sure she will allow you to use one of her rooms to wash and refresh yourself. And we can then have breakfast in peace in one of her private dining rooms, our ears safe from violent and vulgar profanity!"

Betsy was again convinced of her good luck in finding such a friend. She said, "I'm sure you know what is best."

As it turned out, he did. The shop was clean and quiet. The elderly woman in charge of it greeted the parson with respect and warmth. She declared, "Parson Midland, the city has not been the same without you!"

The stout man beamed at the woman. "That is good of you to say."

"So many have come by and inquired for you," the matron said. "They feared you might have left us for good. But I told them, no, that you would be back. I said, Parson Midland is as much a part of London as the Covent Garden!" And she chuckled.

"Thank you, dear lady," the clergyman said. "I have taken Miss Chapman under my wing. I'm escorting her to friends. In the meanwhile may she freshen herself up here and have breakfast with me?"

"My house is always at your disposal, Parson," the old woman said. And to Betsy she confided, "You can consider yourself a lucky girl he's taken a liking to you."

"I know," she said. "I'm afraid I don't deserve it."

The old woman smiled. "Don't you worry, dearie. You deserve whatever the parson may do for you."

The matronly owner of the teahouse showed her to an empty bedroom, and Betsy repaired the damages of the journey. When she had washed and looked at herself in the mirror, she decided that she looked reasonably well under the circumstances. There were lines of tiredness at her eyes, but these would vanish once she had a proper rest.

Downstairs the pleasant Parson Midland greeted her and led her to a small room directly behind a larger dining room. He explained, "We can have complete privacy here."

"And it will give me a chance to rest before I go to my friend's house," she said.

As the old woman served them breakfast, the clergyman asked her, "Where does your friend live?"

"In Fetter Lane," she said. "Number Twenty."

He paused over his oatmeal. "I don't know anyone in Fetter Lane. But it is a good street."

"My friend is a rather important man," she said.

"May I inquire his name?" Parson Midland said. "I may know him by name though not knowing his address."

"His name is Felix Black," she said. "That is all I can tell you. I'm sworn to secrecy about the other facts concerning him."

"Ahha!" the stout parson said. "It has the sound of mystery and adventure."

"It could offer both," she said, "though I cannot be sure."

He sighed. "Of course your parents would not approve."

"My stepfather wouldn't," she said, "since he tried to sell me to that lustful Dakin."

"A dreadful business. Yet your mother would wish you back. What about her?"

"She is weak. I'm sorry for her," Betsy said. "But I will not be her victim."

"You should not be," he observed. "Yet you must be wary. If they know where you have gone, they may come in search of you."

"They will not know."

"I see," the clergyman said. "This Felix Black is known only to you."

"Yes," she said. "A link with my father from the old days. They were not even in the house when he came to visit me."

"So you will be safe from them and any reward they might offer for your return," Parson Midland said.

"I'm sure I will be," she said. "I do not suppose you will ever be questioned by them. But if you should be, I shall rely on you to keep silent."

"Be certain of it."

The old woman came in with a warm smile on her round rosy face. "I have brought you a good pot of tea. Made special to ease your weariness. Drink it up, my dear." And she poured out a full cup for Betsy.

Betsy drank the steaming brew and relaxed as the parson talked on in a friendly tone. She thought what a warm and pleasant retreat this was from the noise and bustle of the London streets. Again she complimented herself on her great fortune in having found such a mentor. She was about to tell the stout clergyman this when to her amazement she found her tongue had thickened. She could no longer form words, and as she made this discovery, a great lassitude came over her, and she closed her eyes and slumped back in her chair.

The sound seemed vaguely like the crowing of a cock at dawn! But it was not dawn; there was pitch blackness all around her! Betsy's head reeled as she raised herself on an elbow. She was stretched out on a cold, damp earthen floor. And then the crowing sound came again, and she was able to sort it out as a wild kind of laughter!

Where was she? And what had happened? Terror surged through her as her memory slowly returned. She had been at a table in the teahouse talking with the kindly Parson Midland when she had fainted! And how had she come to this dark, menacing spot? With a tiny moan she raised herself further to a sitting position.

Then a door opened, and a big woman in some kind of drab clothing and apron came into the room with a plate and a tin cup in one hand and a candle in the other. She was of middle age, her hair graying, and her face, which might have been pleasant once, bloated and sallow. She was generally unkempt in every detail.

Giving Betsy a wary look, she placed the plate of fish and chips and the tin cup of water down on the floor beside her. Then she backed away.

"That's some food for you," the big woman said roughly. "Don't you try any tricks! I'll be back for the plate and cup later."

Betsy struggled to her feet. "Where am I?"

The woman gave her a sardonic glance. "That don't matter to you!"

"I demand to know where I am and who brought me here. Surely not the Parson Midland!"

The woman let go that wild screeching sound which was her way of laughter. "The Parson Midland! You mean my Jim?"

She tried to think clearly, her head still reeling. "I don't know any Jim!"

"Yes, you do," the big woman said mockingly. "Jim is my man! He was a parson once before he went on the gin!"

"What are you talking about?"

"I'm telling you straight who your friend Parson Midland is," the woman said sharply. "That's what he calls himself now. Lost his calling when he was caught in the beds of too many of his church ladies! Ladies, indeed!" And she let out a hoot of that eerie laughter again.

Betsy said, "I don't believe you!"

"It don't matter to me," the big woman said. "But it happens to be the truth. He went on the gin after they put him out of the church. For a while they had him on show in a barrel at the fairs. A penny a look at the parson who poached on his female parishioners! A proper disgrace! Then I met him."

The enormity of it all was beginning to get through to her. She gasped, "Are you telling me Parson Midland was defrocked for adulterous relations with women?"

"You've said it all, dearie," the big woman agreed. "He was what you might say at the bottom of his barrel when I found him. I brought him here and set him up in a respectable business left me by my late husband! But that's not enough for Jim. He's ambitious. Likes to go off into the country where no one knows he's been defrocked and carry on as Parson Midland. Makes a good bit of cash on the side with some of his schemes!"

"He's a criminal!" Betsy said in despair. "And he drugged me and brought me here! Why?"

The woman winked at her. "Let him tell you that. He'll be by shortly to have a word with you."

"You dare not hold me a prisoner here!" she cried, advancing on the woman.

"None of that!" the big woman said. "There's no one to hear you or know you are locked down in this cellar. You'll do best to give us no trouble and make no fuss."

Angered, she warned, "You and your Jim will pay for this and dearly!"

"You tell Jim that!" And with another cynical hoot of that odd laughter the woman went out and locked the door after her, leaving only the lighted candle between Betsy and the grim darkness.

Now she began to take stock of her surroundings. She picked up the candle holder with its small, flickering candle and explored the narrow limits of the tiny cellar in which she had been imprisoned. Damp earthen walls and an earthen floor, only the one door leading into it. And that door securely locked.

She returned to the plate of food and tin cup. The food looked messy, and she could not eat it. But she did greedily gulp down the tepid water in the cup and wished she had more. And she thought how gullible she had been. She'd allowed herself to be tricked even before she reached the sinister back streets of the great city.

But how could she have suspected the jovial, kindly clergyman was a criminal? She was in no way prepared for the deception. And he had the ring of sincerity about him because once he had actually been a parson. Acting out the role had to be second nature to him.

So now she was a prisoner in this dark hole, with no idea of what might happen to her next. She tried to recall the conversation she'd had with the fat man, searching for some clue to his thinking.

Then the door was thrown open again, and the figure of the stout Parson Midland appeared in the doorway. He staggered slightly, and she saw that without his black suit and neat clerical collar he looked a good deal more like a drunken Jim. A stubble of beard covered the lower half of his face, and he stood there gazing at her with drunken dignity without saying a word.

She faced him angrily and demanded, "How could you do this to me?"

He nodded and in a slightly slurred version of Parson Midland said, "Child, how often I have asked that same question of an unthinking universe, about myself. We live in a cruel world."

"You deceived me!" she declared brokenly. "Took me in completely!"

"That is a feat," he said, rubbing his chin. "You can most gain from it by allowing it to be a lesson for you in the future."

"What do you want with me?" she demanded.

A smile of cupidity crossed the fat face. He patted the side of his nose with his forefinger and smiled. "You, dear girl, will make me rich!"

"Are you mad?"

He shook his head. "I'm possessed of the devil, but I am not mad! I'm holding you for ransom, my fine young lady. I know Sir John and your mother will pay a pretty penny to have you back safely. Right now a messenger is on his way to them to demand five thousand pounds!"

"They'll never give it to you!"

He chuckled. "I think they will. And if they won't, that old fool Lord Dakin will put up the money. He has plenty of it, and from what you told me, a powerful lust for you!"

She was horrified, knowing that he could all too well be right. Her mother would be upset beyond belief, and her corrupt stepfather would undoubtedly try to talk Lord Dakin into rescuing her with a ransom—if she hadn't finished the lecherous old lord with her heavy blows with the chamber pot. Returned, she would be expected to go through with the truly scandalous marriage out of sheer gratitude! It was a most unpleasant plot, and it might work!

She told the fat man, "You are a scoundrel!"

He said, "I have never denied it."

"Let me go and I will see you are paid well," she begged him.

"Not a chance. I know how to play this game. I need no help from you," he said.

"They'll send the police after you and let them rescue me!"

The fat man winked. "First they'd have to know where to look and they don't. I have that all arranged. I get the money first and turn you over later."

Betsy said, "It is not human to keep me in a place like this."

"It's dry and it's quiet," he said sanctimoniously. "It gives you a chance to contemplate. And if those parents of yours pay up as I expect, you won't be here for long!"

As he finished speaking, there was a sudden clamor of fierce barking from outside. She listened and turned to him with a strained expression on her lovely face. "Are you having me watched by guard dogs?"

He laughed. "No. But it's not a bad idea. What you heard is my employee, Gimpy, who you'll be meeting, feeding the dogs. Bull mastiffs they are. Hannah, my common-law wife, was operating this den when she lifted me out of the gutter. And I have helped her with it since. We stage the most ferocious dog fights in all London! All England, if you like! And most of the time the decision is death for the loser! Many a challenger has come here to be torn to bits!"

"Horrible!" she declared, sickened at the thought of it.

"Not at all," the fat man said, shifting his weight from one foot to another and going on to explain. "You see you must look at it as a sport! Better than the Romans' game of throwing Christians to lions! We just put two dogs in the ring and let the better one win!"

"What satisfaction is there in allowing poor dogs to tear each other to death?"

"Its the betting that pays," he said with a wink. "The gentry come and place their bets and watch the fights. A good lot of money changes hands some nights, and the house always gets its share. I've been told that some years ago the prince regent himself and some of his cronies came here to see one of the fights. Hannah's husband was in charge in those days and real proud of it!"

"I call it a scandal!"

"You'll be hearing a bit of noise now and then," the fat man warned her. "The fights go on every night. And the dogs get noisy every so often in the days. You can come out to the pit with me if you like. See what goes on. Don't try to escape. There's no chance. The door to the pit is locked on the other side."

He went out rather unsteadily, and she followed him if only to get out of the cell in which she'd been imprisoned. She found herself in a large cave of a room with a wooden walled square in the middle of it. At each end of the square there were gates to allow the dogs into the ring. And spectators could watch safely outside the five-foot fences.

The fat man went over to another fenced area in which a huge, ferocious-looking brown dog stood growling. Its hackles raised as the spurious parson approached the cage. On the other side of the fenced-in dog enclosure was a thin boy wearing a cap with a crutch under one arm. His back seemed strangely deformed so that one side of his poor twisted body was taller than the other. The crutch was under the armpit on his tall side.

The boy smiled and called out, "He's in a right mean mood today, he is!"

The fat man smiled at the angry big dog who was gazing up at him in a menacing fashion with small red eyes full of hatred. "Do you think so, Gimpy?"

"I do, sir," the crippled lad said. "He'll do well this night! I'm sure of that!"

"Maybe I'll just rouse him a little to show the lady," the fat man said with a smirk on his beard-stubbled face. And he reached down and brought up a whip and began flailing the huge animal with it. The reaction of the tortured beast was fearsome. He leaped into the air, almost getting at the man, but the fence was too high and the ex-parson beat the animal back!

Betsy could stand it no longer. She placed her hands over her ears and ran back into the other cellar where she'd first awakened. The snarling and howling of the mastiff followed her, mixed with the brutal laughter of the ex-parson. She sank down on her knees and wept.

The fat man did not return. It was Gimpy, the crippled lad, who finally came to pick up her dish of food and the tin cup. He stared at the plate of food in amazement. "You didn't eat any of it," he said in his piping childish voice.

She shrugged. "No. You can have it."

"Thanks!" he dropped down on the floor, put the crutch aside, and greedily devoured the contents of the plate.

She said, "Are you to be my jailer?"

"Righto!" he grinned at her. "But you won't find me too hard to deal with."

"How do you come to be here?"

"Working for Jim and Hannah?" he asked, still sitting on the floor by her.

"Yes."

"Well, you see, when I was a lad, I was sold to a sweep by my old dad. The way it was he had seven mouths to feed, and he couldn't manage one more. So I had to go."

"You're no more than a lad now," she chided him.

"I'm twelve years old," he said as if that were old age. "I were only five when I was sold."

Her eyebrows raised. "Sold? Do you really mean sold like a slave?"

"What other way is there?" Gimpy asked in wonder. "Crikey, lads are sold all the time! Gels as well, though they don't bring much until they're a bit older, if you know what I mean."

"Go on," she said, stunned by the candid way he revealed all this. It was quite ordinary to him, part of his world.

"Well, this sweep bought me, and he put me to work at once. Taught me the trade and made me do the climbing by the time I was six. And I was real good except when I had too much gin!"

"Too much gin! Did he let a child of six drink?"

Gimpy laughed. "You don't know much, miss. He fed me the gin to stunt my growth, see? He didn't want me to grow too quick, and gin was the answer. But I got to like it too much, and that was me ruination!"

"Did you become too drunken to work?"

"No. I did me work, but I wasn't as steady as I should be come an early morning. We were in this big castle like and he sent me up and I got near the top when I lost me footing. I tried to stop me fall, but I couldn't. I came all the way down and twisted me spine and broke me hipbone! From that day on I couldn't move without pain, and I was finished for climbing."

"It's a wonder you didn't kill yourself!"

"Chimney sweeps are tough," Gimpy said, grabbing his crutch and lifting himself up nimbly. "That was when Hannah took me in to help with the dogs. I've been here ever since."

"Don't you hate it! The way he abuses that poor dog!"

"Toby," the lad said. "Well, he doesn't abuse the other dogs like that. He happens to hate Toby because he took after him one day. Only Hannah coming along saved him. Since then old Jim has taken a liking to tormenting Toby. Made him the best fighter we ever had. Not that this is what he meant to do."

She listened and said, "You're saying there's a special hatred between that dog and the fat man you call Jim."

"Yes," Gimpy said. "But it won't last long. One night a dog will come along who'll tear Toby to pieces, and we'll have to get another fighter."

She said, "Do you understand that I've been kidnapped and I'm being held here for ransom?"

Gimpy nodded. "It means a nice bit of profit for Jim and Hannah. And I owe them everything. So don't expect any help from me."

With that he limped out and locked the door after him, leaving her alone in the dark cellar. She knew that somehow she must escape this dreadful place, but she could not think by what means.

Chapter Three

BETSY SUFFERED alone in the dreadful place for what seemed like hours. Then the woman Hannah returned carrying a washbasin, a pail of water with a dipper in it, and a battered tin chamber pot with a square of wood for a cover. She put all these things down inside the door.

She said, "There's a bit of soap in the washbasin. Mind you're careful with the water, it has to do for both drinking and washing up. And don't expect me to empty the pot more than once a day."

Betsy stood facing her, angry now. "You are pampering me too much, aren't you?"

The unkempt big woman sneered at her. "You think because you have a pretty face and figure you're something special! Well, listen to me, my lady, you're not! I've seen girls just as lovely as you go on the streets and in a year or two they're battered and bloated and don't look any better than me!"

"Are you threatening me?" she asked.

"I'm warning you," the woman said coldly. "Don't be too high toned! If we don't get the money from your parents, we may make you earn it by entertaining gents in here. Then we'll see how long your beauty lasts!"

Fear tightened her insides, but she refused to let the arrogant woman see it. She said, "You dare not harm me! You will pay for all you have done!"

"You're wrong!" the woman jeered. "We're the ones who will be paid. And with notes of the realm! That's what!"

Betsy drank a dipperful of the water and then used a little of it to wash. She was determined to keep herself in as good a condition as possible since this might build up her spirits. After that she sat thinking about her plight for a long while and wondered how long before the man with the ransom demand might return with some answer from her parents. Not too long. Perhaps by the end of another day.

Would these villains release her even if the ransom money were paid? She very much doubted it. They would find some way to be rid of her, if they didn't kill her, perhaps ship her over to a brothel in France. She had heard of such cases. It was not pleasant to think about.

Would Felix Black decide she had turned down his plea for assistance in his strange project and go ahead without her? Was the spy master mad, his mind finally turned by the strain of the years battling Napoleon? Or had he really fallen on to some important facts? It wasn't likely she'd ever know, not with all the odds against her of escaping frrom this place.

She fumbled in her pocket and found some coins. She counted them out, and it amounted to only a few bob. Hardly enough to bribe anyone. No wonder the fat Jim had not taken the coins from her.

Outside she heard Toby barking furiously and knew that he was probably being fed. Only when the fat man whipped him did he snarl and howl. It would be Gimpy tending to him.

A little later her door was unlocked, and Gimpy came in with a plate of food for her. He put it down, "Better eat it, miss. It's good enough, and you need your strength."

"Thank you, Gimpy," she said. "I'll try. You're kind."

He had put aside his crutch and was sitting, gazing at her as she ate. He said, "You're a proper pretty gal!"

She smiled. "Thank you."

"I'd let you go free if I had the say."

"Then I wish you had the say," she told him. "Where is this place?"

"Whitechapel," he said.

"Tell me about the dog fighting."

"You'll be hearing them at it tonight," he promised. "Old Toby has to fight again tonight. Hannah taught him herself, put him in the ring with a gummer first."

"A gummer?"

The boy nodded solemnly. "A gummer is an old dog who has fought a long time and has lost his eye teeth through age or had them pulled out. He fights with the dog in training, and the new dog learns from him the moves and how to protect himself."

"Then what?"

"Toby was put in with some mongrels who'd been toned up to fight. But before they were put in the ring with him, they had the parts most easy to attack shaved. That way Toby learned to go after them in those places. Once Toby fought a few of those curs and tasted their blood, he was made. Ready to fight like a champion!"

"Terribly brutal!" she said, shuddering.

"There's much that's brutal and little to do about it," the boy said. He picked up his crutch and prepared to go.

All the time he'd been telling her about the training of Toby, she'd been doing some quick thinking. Now before he could leave her, she said, "Gimpy, one minute."

"Yes," he stood, leaning on his crutch, his thin face pathetically wistful.

"If you had one wish you'd like to fill, what might it be?"

Gimpy looked behind him furtively and then leaned forward to her. "It's the gin! I miss it fearful, and they won't give any of it to me!"

"Why?"

"They don't trust me to drink!"

"I trust you, Gimpy."

"Thank you, miss."

She put her hand in her pocket and pulled out the coins and held them out to him. "Is that enough to get you some gin?"

His eyes opened wide. "Crikey! That will get me a bottle or two!"

"Then make your dream come true," she told him. "Take the money and bring the gin here and hide it. I won't tell on you, and you can drink it while you're here watching me."

He reached out and clawed for the coins and thrust them in his pocket. His thin face was glowing with anticipation. He said, "You won't regret this, miss. I promise you that!"

She nodded. "I want you to enjoy yourself, Gimpy." She knew she was doing wrong, but she steeled herself to it. If she were to survive, she had to learn to play the game.

Night came! She knew it only because Hannah told her when she came with another bucket of water. She sat alone in the dark, and a new ordeal began. She first heard the rumble of male voices growing louder in the adjoining cellar where the dog fights were held. Then came the fury of the fight itself and the snarling and howling of the battling animals as they fought for their lives.

Again she covered her ears, but she could not blank out all the sounds. The last pitiful howl of the dog that met its end in the ring came to her with heartrending clarity. There was a rumble of voices again and then silence as the crowd dispersed.

She was sitting thinking about attempting sleep when the door was furtively opened. She started and uttered a gasp of fear.

"It's only me. Gimpy!" came a whisper.

"Oh!" she said. "The fight is over."

"Yes. Toby won again. But it was close. The other dog near tore his eye out!"

"Don't talk about it!"

"I came by to hide it here," the lad whispered, limping over to her. "I want you to keep it for me."

"All right," she said. "But it will be bad for me if they find out."

"They won't," he said. "I'll come by when I bring your food around noon time. I'll stay awhile and have some of it then while I'm waiting for your empty plate."

"Very well," she said. And she took the gin bottles, and he went limping out and locked the door behind him.

Betsy hid the bottles in a far corner, placing them on their sides and brushing some debris over them. Then she tried to sleep, her mind disturbed by the events of the evening and the frantic knowledge that if she were to escape, it must be soon.

Her first visitor the next morning was the fat man. He was sober and in a bad mood. He said, "What a pretty vixen you have turned out to be!"

"Why do you say that?" she asked, playing along to find out as much as she could of what was happening outside.

"You all but killed that old blister of a Dakin," the fat man said angrily. "Still not able to talk! His doctors don't know whether he'll live or not!"

"Do you expect me to feel sorry?"

"You may have reason to," he snapped angrily. "Your precious mother is in hysterics, and your blundering stepfather cannot raise five thousand pounds! The only one who can pay up is Dakin, and no one can consult him about it."

"I doubt very much if he'd pay now anyway," she said dryly.

"We've given your parents an ultimatum," Jim warned her. "Either they find the money from some other source, or they will never see or hear from you again!"

She said, "Will they, even if they pay up?"

A nasty smile crossed the fat man's face. He said, "That is something to be decided after the money comes in."

"And I think I know how it will be decided," she said.

He nodded his approval. "You're beginning to think more sharply. Pity you didn't get on to it earlier."

"Yes," she said. "I might have been better able to deal with a certain man of the cloth!"

He made no answer but went out and locked the door. The future suddenly looked bleaker than ever. She knew the state of her family's finances, and she was almost certain they could not raise the ransom money. Lord Dakin was apparently still in a critical state. The ransom would not be paid. Jim, in his rage, would invent some especially evil punishment for her.

The morning dragged by, interrupted only once when she suspected that the fat man came by to torment and whip the dog Toby. She heard the animal snarling and howling along with the hoarse laughter of the drunken ex-parson. It made her feel ill.

Promptly at noon Gimpy appeared with her food. As soon as he set the plate down, he asked, "Where is it?"

She indicated the corner. "Over there!"

He limped over and came back with a bottle. Putting his crutch aside, he struggled with his thin hands shaking to open the bottle. When he'd managed, he held it up to his mouth and gulped down the strong watery liquid until he choked and it ran down his chin. He put down the bottle and rubbed his mouth with the back of his hand and blinked his eyes.

"Months since I had a drop," he told her in a hoarse whisper.

"Is it good gin?" she asked, feeling guilty.

He winked at her. "Good enough," he said. And he drank from the bottle again.

"Aren't you taking too much?" she worried.

"Mother's milk!" he said. "I can handle it!"

"Save some for tomorrow!"

He nodded to the corner. "There's still the other bottle."

"You're so small," she said. "Won't it make you drunk?"

"I'm used to it," Gimpy told her happily. "I never felt better. I'm floating on clouds!"

She begged him, "Be careful! We don't want to let Hannah find you drunk!"

He had consumed a major part of the bottle and now his eyes were glazed, and in a slurred voice, he declared, "Hannah is an old blister! She cheats at cards!"

"I know," she said. "Do give me the bottle. You've had enough. We must be careful!"

"God bless His Majesty!" Gimpy said drunkenly and lifted the bottle to his lips again. She was about to seize it and take it from him when the crippled boy suddenly went limp, let the bottle drop with its precious contents draining out onto the earthen floor, as he fell backward dead drunk!

Betsy stood up in alarm, staring at what she had wrought. She didn't know what to do next. But the instinct for survival told her she must get away from the drunken lad and quickly. She went out to the big room where the dog fights were held. Then she heard Toby growl suspiciously in his cage. She summoned all her courage and went over by the cage fence. The dog glared at her with his angry red eyes, and she saw the torn flesh around one of them.

"Good boy!" she said in a low voice.

The big brown dog growled again and showed its great yellow teeth. She was carefully observing the cage and saw there was an entrance to it at one end and an exit to the ring at the other. Each of these was held in place by a heavy push bolt. To open the gate, one had only to draw the bolt and swing the gate outward. Very cautiously now she pulled back the bolt as an aroused Toby began to bark furiously at her!

She stood there trembling, holding the gate in place manually now that the bolt on it had been drawn. The door from the front opened and an angry Jim showed his fat self.

He shouted down, "Toby! You beast! Stop that row!"

And then she deliberately stood up from where she'd been crouching so that he might see her, still holding the gate in place. The fat man saw her and let out a cry of outrage!

"What are you doing there? Where is that little fool, Gimpy! I'll kill that boy!" And he came unsteadily down into the big cellar.

He had been drinking, and it showed in his awkward movements as he came after her.

She waited until he was almost upon her, his hands reaching out for her, and she played her trump card. She jumped back and swung the gate open. It took the ferocious Toby but a second to know there was nothing between him and his tormentor. With a great snarl he leaped straight at the fat man's throat!

The ex-parson screamed in the manner of one who knows his death is at hand! He kept screaming as the great dog tore at his throat and worried him about. Betsy ran for the door leading upstairs.

The screaming grew weaker and the snarling continued as she reached the door only to be confronted by a white-faced Hannah! The big woman was about to tackle her when she saw what was happening down by the dog pit!

"God save us!" she screamed and ran down toward the now motionless man and the dog snarling over him.

Betsy did not wait to see what happened. She no longer cared. She pressed her way up the narrow stairs to the squalid house above. She raced through the house and out onto the street. There she nearly knocked over a startled fishmonger and his cart.

He cried, "All right now, miss. A little care, if you will!"

"I'm sorry," she gasped "Where can I find a law officer?"

"Let me see," the man said in wonderment. "I passed one about two blocks back that way!"

She didn't even pause to thank him but ran through the slum streets, ignoring the stares of the battered and dirty-looking humans whom she hurried by. At last she saw a moustached street keeper, his trusty stick in hand—old, but with a face that showed he put up with no nonsense.

Gasping, she ran up to him and managed, "Save me! I've just escaped from being kidnapped. My name is Betsy Chapman, and

I wish safe escort to my friend's house at number Twenty Fetter Street."

The man studied her with astonishment. "Come now, what is this all about, miss?"

"Please don't ask questions," she begged him. "Just take me to Mr. Felix Black at Twenty Fetter Street."

The street man although clearly a veteran was not too bright. Hired for a pound or less a week to keep peace in alloted streets during the daylight hours, these were usually honest fellows but only marginally intelligent. He removed his cap and ran his fingers through his long, thinning gray hair.

"What's this, now?" he wanted to know.

"I'm fleeing from kidnappers," she gasped. "I must get away from here at once!"

He replaced his cap and stared at her. The uncanny appearance of this well-spoken frightened young woman was something he did not feel equal to cope with. He said, "Now if you wish to place a charge against someone, you must see a beadle."

"I'll be placing no charges," she promised. "I only wish my freedom!"

"You're free as day now, miss," the old man said, totally confused.

She looked behind her apprehensively, expecting to see Hannah coming along the street in pursuit of her at any moment. She tried to make him understand. "It is dangerous for me here. I must get to my friend!"

Now a new voice from behind her joined in the one-sided exchange, a loud, booming voice demanding to know, "What is going on here?"

She swung around to find herself facing a loudly dressed man in a checkered brown jacket and light fawn trousers. He carried an ebony walking stick with a silver head. He used the walking stick to bar the street man from getting nearer her. He said with authority, "One moment, my man!"

Almost automatically Betsy poured her tale of woe out to him, ending with, "I'm afraid they may come after me again!"

The man so extravagantly dressed stared at her in wonderment. "It's an amazing tale," he declared. "It would go well on the boards even if it has no truth!"

"But it has!" she protested.

The man patted the street keeper on the back and told him, "I shall take this girl under my wing! Or perhaps one might say under my cloak!" He smiled at this since he was also wearing a short black cape.

The street keeper hesitated. "I want her seen to safety."

"I shall do that," the man in the extravagant outfit promised. "I'm George Frederick Kingston, member of the Covent Garden company, honored member of an honored profession; I am in short a well-known actor, and I shall take this girl to her friends at Fetter Street."

The old street keeper looked relieved. "Very well, since you've identified yourself. But mind I shall hold you responsible for her welfare."

"Depend on it," the actor said with a flourish of his walking stick, and he took Betsy by the arm and led her away.

She reluctantly went with him, worrying, "Can I trust you? No one seems quite what they appear to be in London!"

"Ha!" he said grandly. "That is the reason I have often been at the peak of my profession. My business is make-believe. I must always be somebody else and do it well. Yet in true life I'm a rather simple fellow!"

She was so bewildered by his sudden appearance and his flamboyance that she had taken small stock of him as an actual person. She saw now that he was a slim man of about forty with brown hair and long sideburns and a plain if pleasant face—the sort of face one saw again and again and hardly remembered.

She pleaded, "You will see me safely to Twenty Fetter Street?"

"I have given my word!" he said in his theatrical fashion. "The devil of it is that it happens to be on the other side of London and we shall require a carriage." He gave her a questioning glance. "Can you supply me with the money to pay for a carriage?"

"No. Those villains took everything from me!" she said unhappily.

"Not everything, my dear," he said loftily. "He who steals my purse steals trash and all the rest, if you follow me." He paused and frowned as he searched the street for a carriage. "It so happens that I'm between engagements and so also have no funds!"

"You don't need any," she said. "My friend will gladly pay for my transport! We can collect it from him!"

George Frederick Kingston came to life again at once. He took her by the arm and moving more quickly headed for a wider and more busy thoroughfare where a carriage might be located. He said, "You shall be at the door of Twenty Fetter Street in a flash!"

They did not arrive there in a flash but soon enough. The carriage they located was somewhat decrepit and the horse ancient, but they made their way through the clogged traffic of the great city's streets with all the speed which might be expected. Betsy sat beside the actor, weary and stunned, barely hearing his descriptions of the various sights which they passed along the way.

Fetter Street proved to be a cul-de-sac of modest two-story brick houses, and number Twenty was at the very end. She remained seated in the carriage while the actor went to the door of the house to inform Felix Black that Betsy Chapman had arrived and needed the money to pay for her carriage.

She watched as the flamboyant Kingston waited at the door. Then the door was opened by a prim thin woman in white lace cap and jabot with the inevitable black dress which Betsy would have expected. The woman listened to Kingston's story and quickly shut the door on him.

The actor, who now had his top hat in hand, turned to Betsy seated in the carriage and indicated that she should be patient. Next the door opened again, and this time she recognized the bent, spare figure of Felix Black. He slowly counted out the cab fare and gave it to the actor.

Kingston returned and paid the carriage driver and helped her down and over to the front door where Felix Black still stood waiting for them. The elderly spy looked more sallow and thinner than when she'd seen him only a short time before. He said in his dry voice, "I had almost given up hope of your arrival. Do come in!"

He led them along a dark hall which had a musty smell and into a large study. The walls were lined with bookshelves, and there was a huge desk with a clutter of various items and papers on its broad surface. Several chairs served for visitors while the old man had a comfortable swivel chair behind the desk.

He went slowly over and seated himself and waved them to seats opposite him. George Frederick Kingston looked much impressed by the surroundings and sat there in dignified silence.

Felix Black said, "Tell me what decided you to join me and what brought you here in your present state, without proper clothing or luggage."

She ignored her weariness and quickly gave him an account of the events which had led to her running away and then her series of harrowing experiences in the custody of Parson Midland. She said, "I only barely managed to escape."

The thin, lined fece of the master spy wore an approving look. "But you did manage it. You were resourceful. It was a good test of your ability."

"I escaped with nothing," she lamented. "They took all my money and things."

"That is no problem," he told her. "I can look after your needs, and you will be paid by me from this day." He glared at Kingston. "But who is this fellow?"

"I can tell you but little of him, but he has been a good friend in helping me get here," she said.

The old man behind the desk fixed his piercing eyes on Kingston and snapped, "Well, man, speak up for yourself!"

George Frederick Kingston leaned his hands on the silver knob of his cane and said pleasantly, "I'm an actor, sir. Not unknown in the provinces but confined to occasional supporting roles here at Drury Lane in London. I'm presently waiting a summons from Kean to play Bassanio in a new production of *The Merchant of Venice*. He vows he will never play Shylock without my support as Bassanio!"

"You are, in fact, an out-of-work actor," was Felix Black's sharp comment.

Kingston showed all his charm. He smiled. "Well, that is surely one way of looking at it. I prefer to regard myself as resting between engagements."

"Yet you hadn't a sou to pay for the carriage," the old man said.

"True," the actor said with a sigh. "There are times when one might wish one had been better endowed financially by one's family. And yet I am a direct descendant on my mother's side of the famed Captain Cook!"

Felix Black was studying him. In his dry voice he said, "I'm not interested in your family history. I'm trying to judge your ability."

"My theater appearances have been well accepted," the actor said. "Yet I always find it difficult to praise myself."

"Aha!" the man behind the desk said. "Have you heard of me before?"

"I can't say that I have," Kingston told him. "We theater folk know few outside our profession."

Felix Black offered a dry cackle of laughter. "The same may be said to be true about my own profession. Have you heard of the secret service?"

Kingston looked impressed. "I have, sir. I have even acted in several productions based on the experiences of His Majesty's secret messengers!"

"Trash written by hacks," Felix Black snapped. "I'm talking about the real thing. I have just now retired from the service, and I'm setting up my own espionage group for a dangerous assignment. I still have a few openings. An actor could be useful to me. Would such work interest you?"

Kingston crimsoned and glanced at Betsy. "It pains me to say this before the young lady, but I have been out of work so long, despite my ability, that I am ready to grasp at any job opportunity. Take any risk!"

"Very well. I propose to test you," Felix Black said. "While I'm getting this young lady settled in, I want you to go out and find someone for me."

"I shall try," Kingston said. "Who, sir? And where may I find him?"

"In the nearby marketplace," the master spy told him. "The fellow I want to locate is a good deal older than you, has a short white beard, walks with a limp and deals in stolen meat at bargain prices. I have a score to settle with him. If you can find him and present him to me, I can use you in my new organization."

Kingston stood up, looking a trifle baffled. "I have made note of all the fellow's particulars," he said, "and I shall do my best."

"Then off you go!" Felix Black said.

Kingston bowed to him and then to her. In his pleasant fashion he said, "I have enjoyed our meeting, Miss Chapman. I hope I may see you soon again."

"Thank you for your kindness to a stranger," she said.

"But such a lovely stranger," the actor said. And with a last bow he left them.

When he had gone, Felix Black asked her, "Do you think I can trust him?"

She smiled thinly. "After the way I was taken in by that awful ex-parson, I can hardly put myself up as a judge of character. But in the short time I've known him, I would say George Frederick Kingston is a man of honor."

"Exactly my own conclusion," the master spy said. "The big question is whether he has talent and intelligence. We shall see."

She fixed her eyes on the old man and asked, "Are you still convinced that Napoleon is alive and hidden somewhere in Europe?"

"Yes," he said grimly. "More than ever. It cost me my post at the secret service office, and now I shall be gambling my reputation and my personal wealth on my being right."

"It is a large gamble."

His eyes showed the fire of a fanatic as he leaned forward and said, "But if I succeed, I will be assured a place in history. My name will go down with Napoleon and Wellington as one of the great figures of this age! And I shall destroy Valmy and save Europe from another round of bloodshed!"

She said, "I must get away from England, or my mother and stepfather will try to find me and make me return to them."

His smile was sour. "And a marriage to your Lord Dakin if he recovers?"

"I would drown myself first," she said. "What can I do about clothing?"

"You will live here until you leave," Black said. "I shall have a dressmaker come in tomorrow morning. She will make you a new wardrobe and order the things you'll need otherwise. I shall deposit a hundred pounds to my bank in your name, an advance on your salary, which you may draw on as you like."

"You are too generous!" she gasped.

"Not at all. You are invaluable to me. Much more so than an ordinary agent. You have known Napoleon. You were staunch friends despite the difference in your ages. If you are able to contact this supposed Napoleon, you can shortly tell whether he is a fraud or not. Only he and you would know the subjects you discussed and the spots you visited together. A few clever questions from you, and we will have established whether this man is genuine or not. That is why I need you, why you can do what is impossible for any other agent, no matter how clever he may be."

"I see," she said quietly. "And if I do confront this man and decide he is Napoleon, will I not be using our friendship to destroy him?"

"Not destroy him but save him," the man behind the desk corrected her. "If he falls under the influence of the political scoundrel Valmy, he will be used and then murdered. I offer him escape from France and a safe passage to America to live in a proper style for the rest of his life. He will be a hero over there."

"He could have been honored in England as a defeated and gallant enemy," she pointed out. "But they lied to him and sent him to needless exile in Saint Helena."

"I do not intend to lie to him," the thin man in black promised. "This is to be the high point of my life."

"I believe your sincerity," she said. "And I will do as you order."

"Now you are talking sensibly, my girl," he said. "I shall have Mrs. Glenn show you to a room upstairs. Freshen yourself and rest. Join me down here at dinner. I will have another of my agents here whom I wish you to meet."

"Oh?"

"One of our trusted agents," he said. "And he has decided to throw in his lot with me."

"Then I shall be working along with him?" she said.

"You two will be among the dozen or so of the network I'm building," he agreed. "This young man goes under the code name of Robin. We shall find a code name for you as well. But in the meanwhile you will meet at dinner."

Mrs. Glenn showed her upstairs to a good-sized room with its own fireplace overlooking the street below. She was as dry in manner as her employer. "It has the best view and the least north wind," she said.

Betsy was studying the modest four-poster bed and told her, "It looks very good to me."

"Being a fine lady and all, it cannot be what you're used to," Mrs. Glenn said simply. "But Mr. Black is a man of simple tastes, and his wife was a woman without social ambitions."

"Is his wife alive?"

"Dead these five years and the only son was killed in the war with Boney," Mrs. Glenn said. "The master has known a great deal of sorrow."

"He seems completely dedicated to his work," she said.

The woman nodded. "It is all he has. Though things have taken a strange turn since he gave up his post at the War Office. All sorts of unusual people have been in and out of here!"

Betsy smiled. "I suppose I am one of them."

"No offense meant," Mrs. Glenn said. "There's water in the pitcher and coal for the fireplace. And I'll bring you some clean towels directly." With that she vanished, only to return a little later with an armful of fresh white towels.

Betsy rested for a while, and then it was time to go down to dinner. She looked out her window and saw that it had started to drizzle and there was also a heavy fog. She fixed her hair and dress to make herself as presentable as possible and went downstairs.

The drawing room was dimly lighted by ornate lamps on several tables scattered about the high-ceilinged room, and a warming glow came from the fireplace. But the room was empty, and she began to wonder if she should have waited to be summoned. She went and stood before the blazing coals of the fireplace for a moment.

Then her fears were put to rest by the sound of male voices approaching. And in a few seconds Felix Black came into the room accompanied by a tall, dark-haired handsome man with a fine military bearing even though he wore a black jacket and gray trousers.

Felix came to her with a smile on his wizened face. He said, "My dear Betsy, I would like you to meet my valued agent, Robin."

"How do you do," she said, impressed by his even good looks and manly dignity.

"I'm delighted," he said with a pleasant smile. "It seems we are destined to be partners."

"So I understand," she said.

The young man asked, "Do you speak French well?"

Felix Black spoke up. "As well as any native Frenchwoman."

The agent called Robin looked pleased. "That is something we need. An agent really proficient in French. Mine is so uneven I have to always pose as a Polish citizen or count. Anything to cover my accent and incompetence."

She said, "It has been a long while. My French is still a trifle rusty. Were you in the army?"

"Yes," Robin said. "I served under Wellington."

"So did my brother," she said proudly.

"Really? Perhaps I knew him," he suggested.

"I rather doubt it," she said. "He was killed over there."

"I'm sorry," the young man said. "Too many good men met the same fate."

She said, "But you were most fortunate."

"Yes," he agreed.

Felix Black had poured them sherries, and now he handed them their glasses. He said, "As we three know, the war with France may not yet be over. If Napoleon is brought out by Valmy and they are able to gather enough political strength, the new king will be forced to flee, and we will have an unstable France led by the political opportunist Valmy in the name of a worn and broken Napoleon."

The young man sipped from his glass. "I'm anxious to begin the assignment. If what you believe happened took place, then every lost day counts."

Felix nodded over his own glass. "A year has passed since Napoleon was supposedly buried. In the meanwhile Valmy has spirited his man to Europe and has been organizing an underground. When he gives the signal, these movements will come out in the open and make the previous insurrections look like children's parties!"

The young man turned to her. "Are you prepared for the danger you may face? It could cost you your life."

Betsy offered the young man a rueful smile. "If we are to work as partners, you will face the same risk, will you not?"

He nodded. "I'm prepared."

"Well spoken," the bent old man in black who was to direct all their activity said. "I shall try to reduce the danger to a minimum. But this is a kind of warfare. And people know they are often called upon to give their lives in time of war."

The handsome Robin turned to her again and said, "You have not yet told me the facts of your brother's being killed."

"No," she said quietly. "It is something that bothers me greatly. I feel he died in vain."

"Why do you say that?"

She sighed. "I have been told on reasonable authority that his commanding officer disobeyed orders from above and sent his company into battle when the odds were hopeless."

"That could happen," the young man agreed. "It is often a matter of quick judgments."

"This officer made a reckless decision, and so my poor brother died because of it," she said.

"What was his name?" the man known as Robin asked.

She glanced at the old man. "We have no secrets here?"

"None," Felix Black said. "I wish you two to know each other by your real names."

She turned to Robin and said, "I am Betsy Chapman. My brother's name was Captain Richard Chapman."

A strange look crossed the face of the handsome man as he said quietly, "I'm delighted to know you, Miss Chapman."

She said, "But you haven't told me your name?"

"No, I haven't," he said. "My name is Eric Walters, Major Eric Walters. I was your brother's commanding officer. So I fear you will not care to associate yourself with me."

Chapter Four

THE SPIDERY Felix Black's sallow face showed consternation as he gazed at the two over his sherry glass. He confessed, "Indeed I'm aware of that. I hoped by throwing you together, she would overcome her strong feelings on the matter."

The handsome Walters said, "I cannot blame Miss Chapman for wishing to blame someone for her brother's death. The utter stupidity of all war is beyond endurance! But I swear I only obeyed the instructions given me and had no choice in sending my men to battle."

Betsy was slowly recovering from the shock of this revelation. She had been greatly impressed by the good-looking Walters and felt she could come to genuinely like him. Now all that was spoiled. This handsome, courageous man was none other than the officer she had hated for so long.

She forced herself to say, "It does not matter. Let the past rest. I can work along with you and the others."

"Good girl!" the thin Black said with unusual warmth. "You are being sensible. I daresay someone told you this tale of confused orders in an unfortunate attempt to make you accept the death of your brother—turning your despair into anger at an imaginary villain!"

Eric Walters spoke up. "It was a day of unimaginable confusion! I recall it with torment even now. For a time it seemed we had lost the battle. But never did I give what could be interpreted as an order causing needless slaughter."

She avoided his eyes as she said, "I was no doubt wrong in making a judgment of something of which I really know nothing. It better be a subject avoided." Yet she knew she still doubted.

Felix Black said, "We shall not let this make any difference. We are now united in a cause as important as that battle at Waterloo. We shall press on in unity."

"To success," Eric Walters said, raising his glass. She made no comment but drank along with the two men.

The old master spy said, "Now I think we should move on to the dining room where Mrs. Glenn has dinner awaiting us."

The three started across to the dining room when there was a loud knocking on the front door. Felix Black halted and said, "I had better see who is there."

He went to the door and opened it. At once an old man with a white beard, a bulging stomach covered by a blue smock and wearing a peasants shapeless cloth hat came limping into the room. "You sent for me, master?" the oldster said loudly in a country accent.

The master spy stared at him. "You are the butcher? The one convicted of selling stolen lamb from good Kent farmers!"

The stout yokel laughed heartily. He had a large red nose which hung prominently over his white beard. "You be right, master," he said, slapping a hand on his thigh. "And when I heard that you wanted to see me, I brought along a quarter! It's outside in my cart!"

"You are a rogue!" the man in black told him.

The old yokel roared with laughter again. "Indeed, master, I am. But I've not seen the inside of a prison yet. And my meat is the best. That's why I have customers like you! All gentry!"

Black asked sharply, "Who told you I wanted you?"

"Grand dressed fellow!" the white-bearded yokel said. "Said he was of the theater. I told him the only theater I'd seen was Punch and Judy! And he told me to come straight here, and so I did!"

Felix Black turned to Betsy who had been standing watching this scene along with Eric Walters. The old man told her, "Your friend Kingston is pretty clever after all. I sent him out to find this man, and find him he did!"

"I think it remarkable," she agreed. "You gave him only a scant description."

"It was a test, and he has passed it with merit," the old spy master said. And then he startled her by turning to the old yokel and telling him, "You need pretend no longer, Kingston. I'm convinced I can use you."

"Thank you, master," came the reply in the yokel's loud voice. Then to her utter amazement the yokel pulled off his false nose and unhooked his beard to reveal the familiar face of George Frederick Kingston.

She went to him and exclaimed, "You fooled me completely."

"That is my profession," he said airily.

She gazed at his stomach. "You seemed so fat!"

"Some padding and the smock, tends to make you look properly stout," he said with a smile.

Eric Walters added his comment. "Masterly makeup!"

"I agree," Felix Black said. "Kingston not only made himself up to look the part, he acted the role. All of you remember that. Think your roles from inside."

George Frederick Kingston said, "I shall be going now."

"Very well," the old spy master said. "I shall want you here tomorrow afternoon at two for a briefing about your new job with me."

"I'll be here," the actor said, his nose and wig in hand. "And thank you. And you, Miss Chapman. It was you led me to this place and employment."

She smiled. "I hope you'll continue to feel it was a good turn."

"Never fear!" he said. And he bowed and left.

The three of them went on to dinner in the adjoining room. The dinner was as plain as the room. Cold mutton and not too much else along with weak tea and cheese for dessert made up the meal. Betsy decided she would not have to fear putting on weight with the fare.

She said little at dinner, but the two men talked a good deal. It was apparent that following the battle of Waterloo Eric Walters had switched from the army to the secret service. He and Felix Black had planned and executed a number of campaigns together. She tried not to eavesdrop, but she could not help hearing all they were saying, and they did not seem to mind. She was one of them!

It appeared that Eric Walters's special domain had been France and Germany. He knew a great deal about the new court of Louis XVIII and its many weaknesses. He and Black were both of the opinion that the new monarchy was ridiculously unstable, and it would take no great uprising to send the new king in flight to exile.

Dinner had ended long before, and still the two men were engrossed in their talk. At last Felix Black glanced her way and apologized, "Upon my word, I declare we forgot you were here! A thousand pardons! You look weary!"

She managed a tiny smile. "I am exhausted. May I be excused?"

Both men were on their feet at once, and Felix Black came and offered his thin arm for her to be escorted from the room. The handsome Eric Walters bowed good night, his expression sad.

Black saw her to the stairs and said, "You know the way. Try and get a good rest."

"It will be easy after where I've spent the nights prior to this," she said.

"The cell behind the dog ring," the master spy said. "Yes, I think we may call this an improvement." He paused and his keen eyes met hers. "Please attempt to overcome your hatred of Major Eric Walters."

Embarrassed, she held her head. "I have hated him so long without actually identifying him with a real person. It is deeply ingrained, it will take awhile."

"I expect that," he said. "But do try. You will face many dangers, and whatever happened at Waterloo, he is a good man."

"I'll try to keep that in mind," she promised. Then she bade the old spy master good night and went upstairs.

She slept the moment her head touched the pillow. It was not a good sleep, for she was tormented by horrible nightmares of her imprisonment in that Whitechapel cellar. It would take time to erase the terrors she had experienced there from her subconscious. So she twisted and turned in this clean, comfortable bed so far from that dread place!

She wakened to dawn and the shouting of a fishmonger peddling his wares in the street outside. The cries of "Fresh Fish! Cod and Haddock!" came again and again like a kind of morning mass being sung out there.

She quickly washed and dressed, realized how much a single night's rest had done to restore her. When she went below, she found the old master spy already having breakfast, and she joined him.

He helped her sit and then sat down again himself. He said, "Did you rest well?"

"Except for the nightmares."

"Yes," he said. "No doubt you'll have some bothersome ones for a little while."

"But I am rested."

Mrs. Glenn came and began to serve her an ample breakfast of cereal, smoked fish, and muffins. The tea was stronger than it had been the night before.

Betsy said, "Major Walters has not come down."

"He does not live here," Felix Black said. "You are the only one of my agents who will share my residence."

"I was not aware of that," she said.

The thin man in black nodded. "Your stay will be of short duration. I have sent out messages to the seamstress and a milliner.

They should both be here to give you attention this morning. The seamstress is a marvel. I guarantee she'll have your wardrobe ready within a matter of days."

"You are being very kind," she said.

"Not at all. You are a valuable agent. I want you to be satisfied."

They parted after breakfast, and she did not see him for the balance of the morning. But before he went to his study, he told her the name and location of his bank and explained how she could draw on her account there. She realized how thorough he was as he went over every detail.

Then the stout Mrs. Higgins arrived with two giggling young women helpers. Mrs. Higgins was of ample girth with a ruddy pleasant face. She had a shop on a prominent street which was looked after by her help.

She proudly told Betsy, "I reserve my own services for ladies of the gentry. I have my pick of them. And I'm pleased to be doing for you as the daughter of Sir John Cort."

"Stepdaughter," she said. "My father was also titled and my family name is Chapman."

"It does not matter," the stout woman said. "I shall fix you up with a wardrobe of which you'll be proud. Is that not right, girls?"

"Yes, Mrs. Higgins," the two young maids said in unison, bobbing and giggling.

"Off with your dress!" the big woman ordered in her authoritative way, and she went after Betsy with tape measure and pins as she fitted some material around her.

"I love the green silk!" Betsy said of one roll of material.

"And so you ought!" Mrs. Higgins said. And in a loud stage whisper she demanded, "Do you know who has a dress made of that very same cloth?"

"I can't imagine," she said.

"Mrs. Fitzherbert, that's who," the woman said. "Though I must say she took a good deal more material than you will. You have a pretty figure, my dear. And a pretty face!" She turned to her little helpers. "Don't you agree, girls?"

"Oh, yes, Mrs. Higgins, yes indeed," they chanted in unison once again.

Their business was to run fetch a roll of material, then fold it up neatly and put it aside. They sought out piping and ribbons and buttons to be tried. Mrs. Higgins barked out orders and kept them in a state of perpetual motion.

Midmorning she left Betsy standing in her shift while she slumped into an easy chair and enjoyed a cup of tea brought her by Mrs. Glenn. The two assistants sat silently by.

"Must have my tea," the stout woman said. "Backbone of the empire, I say. Take away an Englishman's tea and you've taken away his character!"

The ordeal went on with Betsy suffering more than one pin prick, but by the time Mrs. Higgins and her helpers had packed and were ready to leave, her entire wardrobe had been planned.

"Don't worry about the underthings," Mrs. Higgins assured her. "I shall pick out the best for you from my store. It's stocked with the finest."

"I'm sure I can depend on you," Betsy told her.

"Back the day after tomorrow for fittings," the woman said as she left with the two young girls trailing after her.

Betsy slumped down in the easy chair in a state of exhaustion. She could not help but wonder at the kind of place London was. It contained everything—more than its share of squalor, poverty, and misery! More than it should have of crime and cruelty! And in contrast there was this other city of wealth and power in which anything could be bought by merely seeking the proper person. A world as different from that other one as day from night.

She had barely revived from the odeal with Mrs. Higgins when the French milliner arrived. She was a tiny woman, and she had a single helper, a wizened old lady who carried a collection of striped round boxes in which were all sorts of bonnets, hats, and hairpieces.

The vivacious Frenchwoman fitted her out with hats and bonnets and then with an arch smile informed her, "It is the order of Monsieur Black that you must have wigs. One that is much darker than your own hair and one of some other color, I think perhaps red!"

"But why?" she protested. "My own hair is in perfect condition. Or at least it will be when I manage to get it washed."

"Ah, it ees not zat," the mademoiselle laughed.

"What then?"

"For the disguise!"

"The disguise!" she echoed in wonder, and then she understood. So there began another session before the big dresser mirror as the woman sought to select a wig which would enhance her and make her look different.

As Betsy stared at herself in a wig of jet-black hair with a different coiffure, she exclaimed, "This is not me! I wouldn't know myself!"

"That is exactly the point," said Felix Black who had come unnoticed into the room. "I find that one most useful."

"So I will often be required to change my personality," she told the thin man, turning to him.

He smiled bleakly. "There may come moments when it is necessary. Perhaps a moment when escape is only possible by taking on another identity. Then a wig is invaluable."

"I'm to have two," she said with a smile. "The other one a light auburn."

He bowed. "I have every faith in Mademoiselle. She will also fit you with several corsets and bustles. They will be for suggesting changes in your figure, and some of them will have built-in compartments for hiding secret papers and the like."

Betsy smiled. "I'm discovering that this espionage business is not as simple as I thought."

"I fear it is rather complex," Felix Black said, and he left them.

She was exhausted from her busy morning and welcomed a chance to rest before the afternoon session which the master spy had called. When she entered the office at the appointed time, she found the dedicated Felix Black seated at his desk and Major Eric Walters and George Frederick Kingston standing talking together. They all gave their attention to her as she joined them.

Felix Black told them, "Please sit down. This will take awhile."

She sat close by the desk, and Kingston, with a friendly nod for her, took the chair next to her. The handsome Walters seated himself at the other side of the room. He still seemed inclined to be aloof because of knowing her feeling toward him.

The old master spy began speaking to them in his rasping voice. "I cannot too strongly advise you of the magnitude of this undertaking. The War Office has dismissed me as a madman for my belief that Napoleon was rescued from Saint Helena and is now in Europe somewhere waiting the moment to start a fresh revolution in France."

Eric Walters spoke up. "It is well known there were such plans. The most ambitious of them of which I'm aware concerned a group here in London who was developing a submarine which could approach the shore and pick up the emperor from a small fishing boat. But they were spied upon, and all the principals arrested."

Felix Black's lined face showed amused reaction to this. He said, "That is no news, since I was in charge of the spy operation which apprehended this group. Unhappily the War Office decided this was the end of the rescue plan. And it wasn't."

"What actually makes you believe the man who died on Saint Helena wasn't Napoleon?" Betsy found the nerve to ask. "I had a letter from a young woman living in the house next to Sir Hudson

Lowe. She said she had glimpsed the emperor, and he had failed terribly. But he was still plainly recognizable."

The master spy said, "The plan budded in Marseilles. A wealthy shipping merchant living there, whose name was Jean LaFlenche, enjoyed a notoriety for being almost a double for Napoleon. He was also a stalwart admirer of the former emperor and believed that his hero had been cruelly duped into exile."

"Which is partly true," Eric Walters said. "He was in sight of Plymouth when he was first persuaded to step on board the *Bellerophon.* He in no way expected to be sent to that distant island."

Kingston nodded. "I was playing in a company at Plymouth at the time. I remember the natives were full of curiosity about the fallen emperor. A number rowed out to pass near the ship and saw him standing at the rail. He waved to them, and they waved back and some actually cheered him! I did not make the journey myself."

"A pity," Felix Black said in his dry way. "You would at least have caught a glimpse of him. To return to Marseilles. In late 1819 our man LaFlenche became ill. It was not long before his doctors advised him he was suffering from a terminal illness of the liver."

"Which is what Napoleon is supposed to have died from," Betsy said.

"That and certain other complications caused by the climate," the master spy said. "About the time of this diagnosis he was called on by two of the men most loyal to the exiled emperor, one a military man, General Vidal, and the other an Admiral Leblanc. I believe it was at this meeting that the scheme was concocted. LeFlenche, knowing he would soon die and that he resembled Napoleon enough to deceive even at close range, offered to take his hero's place. A last great adventure for him and an opportunity to give the man he devoutly believed in freedom."

"What then?" Eric Walters asked.

"Word was secretly sent to Saint Helena. Napoleon was not well, but he was not seriously ill. But he at once began to take measured doses of arsenic to simulate a grave gastric problem. The poison made him truly ill and confused the doctors attending him."

She asked, "Does Dr. O'Meara think this possible?"

"Yes," Black said. "He agrees this would be the ideal way of simulating the effects of illness. At this point LaFlenche is supposed to have died. No one aside from his only close relative, a spinster daughter, was at his bedside along with the doctor who had been his friend for years. The undertaker was a former employee at the shipyards owned by the LaFlenche family. No one was allowed to view the body, and it was placed almost immediately in the family cemetery outside the city. A gigantic marble stone marks the tomb today."

As the old man paused, Betsy said, "You are suggesting that LaFlenche was not buried but taken to one of his ships on which he journeyed to Saint Helena?"

Felix Black nodded, "We have a record that a four master, the *Juliette*, left for distant waters on the very day of the supposed burial. The captain was also a close friend of Jean LaFlenche. And most interesting of all, during a time when he'd been attached to the French navy, he had tried to invent a safe underwater warship."

"The submarine business again!" Eric Walters said, showing great interest.

"Exactly," Felix Black continued. "We know the ship sailed close to Saint Helena. And I believe that a small underwater craft took the dying LaFlenche to the shore where Napoleon was waiting in a rowboat. The men exchanged places, and Napoleon was taken back to the *Juliette* while LaFlenche took his place on Saint Helena for the great impersonation. The *Juliette* returned to Italy, and the supposedly ailing LaFlenche was put ashore in Naples. The story circulated among the crew, who had been kept in the dark about the exchange, that LaFlenche was about to die and wanted to die on land."

"So it is possible Napoleon may be alive in Europe," Walters said.

"With plenty of time to get over the effects of his taking the arsenic," the master spy said. "He may have kept in hiding as he awaited the coming of Valmy."

"Who is Valmy?" the actor, George Frederick Kingston, wanted to know.

"A man who will play a powerful role in all our futures," the old spy leader warned him. "Valmy is the leader of a small group of political misfits that has been gradually gaining much strength in the disillusionment accompanying the wretched reign of Louis The Eighteenth. By combining his group with the scattered supporters of Napoleon, he is sure he can march on Paris and take the city and the French nation by storm."

"And this is what we are to try and prevent?" Eric said.

"Exactly," the old man replied. "I need certain facts confirmed, such as the death and burial of LeFlenche. If the body of LaFlenche were found in that tomb, it would indicate that I have been in error. In this instance the rest of the operation would be halted. We would be reasonably sure that it was truly Napoleon who died on Saint Helena."

Eric Walters said, "So our first port of call will be Marseilles?"

"Yes," the spy master said. He asked Kingston, "How is your French?"

Kingston shook his head. "I fear I know just a word here and there!"

"It makes no difference," Black said. "You three shall travel as a group, and both Major Walters and Miss Chapman are adept at French."

"I'm certain I cannot match Miss Chapman in that respect," the handsome Eric Walters said.

"You will do," the master spy told him. "Kingston shall pose as your wealthy father, Walters, and the young lady will act as your fiancée. In that way you can travel without arousing any suspicion. When necessary you can break away and work alone."

Kingston asked, "Are there others involved in this, sir?"

The thin man in the dark suit nodded. "Yes. In all I will have about ten operatives. But I prefer that the others be unknown to you three, and you to them."

Eric Walters said, "That way if we are caught and tortured, we cannot reveal what we do not know."

"You are more aware of such an unhappy possibility than the others," the master spy agreed. He turned to Betsy and said, "I can excuse you and Kingston for a while. I wish to discuss the business of codes with Walters who is an expert in them."

Kingston stood up. "When will I be needed again?"

"We shall meet morning and afternoon each day until you depart for Marseilles," Felix Black said. "Tomorrow at ten."

Betsy and the actor left the study and went down the hall to the front of the narrow, dark house. She turned to Kingston and asked him, "Well, what do you make of it?"

"I'm excited," the middle-aged man said. "Perhaps I should have become a spy long ago. I had no idea it could be so close to playacting."

She smiled. "Nor I. It seems that I'm to be expected to be able to disguise myself as well as you. I have been supplied with wigs and other items for the purpose."

Kingston's plain face showed enthusiasm. "And we are engaged in something big! Something important! I've been an actor in small companies all my life, playing in towns you've never heard about. Now I'm being a part of a real-life drama which may be recorded in the history books."

She glanced back toward the study and said, "He makes it all sound plausible. But we mustn't forget the War Office let him go into retirement because they disapprove of his theory."

"Government!" Kingston said with disgust. "They're always the last to get on to anything."

"You might be right," she said. "At least it means work to you. And it will get me out of England."

He said, "What about having to be in the company of Major Walters?"

She sighed. "I do not look forward to it. I cannot forget he led my brother to his death, whether there was blame attached to his action or not. But I shall somehow manage."

"He seems a nice sort," the actor pointed out, "and certainly handsome."

She blushed. "I happen to be aware of that," she said. "But I cannot see that his good looks should be any key to his true character."

The actor nodded. "Quite so!"

Changing the subject as quickly as she could, she told him, "Meanwhile I want you to do me a favor."

"Anything that I can."

"You remember where I met you in Whitechapel?"

"Yes."

"Not far from there is a small cake shop. It is a front for a dog-fighting ring in the cellar under it. And it was in a tiny cellar room still further underground that I was kept prisoner."

He nodded. "You told me about it. When you left, the dog was attacking your captor."

"Yes," she said. "And Hannah, the ex-parson's wife, was running to try and rescue him. There was also a crippled boy, Gimpy, dead drunk in the back room. I want to know what happened after I escaped and if Gimpy is safe."

"You wish me to investigate?" Kingston said.

"If you will," she said. "Should the boy be alive and turned out by that woman, as I expect he must have been, I should like to help him."

Kingston said, "Do not worry about it, Miss Chapman. I will go to Whitechapel at once. I'll have some word for you tomorrow."

"Thank you," she said gratefully.

"Not at all," the middle-aged actor said, adjusting his cape and donning his top hat. "It will give me something to do."

She felt better once she'd arranged to learn about Gimpy. She was haunted by the memory of the pathetic lad and felt some guilt at having worked on his weakness and making him drunk. She wanted in some way to compensate him. She also was curious about what had happened to Parson Midland. It seemed all too likely that the ferocious Toby had finished him. As for Hannah, it was hard to say. She was a formidable woman who probably had somehow managed to save herself from the maddened animal tearing her husband's throat.

Again she rested, still weary from all she had gone through. Now she thought more about Malworth Castle and her mother and stepfather. She could not help wondering about the fate of Lord Alfred Dakin who had been unconscious when she'd last heard news of him. One thing was clear in her mind: she could never return there.

It was odd that through her letter to the War Office she should have come to meet the master spy, Felix Black. It was her friendship with Napoleon long ago on St. Helena which interested him, not any desire on his part to investigate the circumstances of Richard's death in battle.

And then it was through knowing Black that she had come face-to-face with the man she'd been blaming for her brother's loss. She had not been prepared for this, and she was still filled with confused feelings. She knew that she had no choice but to accept Major Eric Walters on a day-to-day basis until they had completed this task to which they'd been assigned.

The somber old house was especially silent when she went down to dinner. Then one of the wooden doors leading to the drawing room opened, and the bent master spy came out into the hallway to greet her.

His sallow face held one of his rare smiles, and he said, "I have a surprise guest for dinner. Someone you should be glad to meet."

"Really?" She wondered who it might be and felt unhappy that she had not received any of her new gowns.

"Do not be nervous," he begged her. "This is an old friend."

He led her into the drawing room, and there before the fireplace stood a familiar, robust figure. It was none other than Dr. Barry Edward O'Meara whom she had known on St. Helena when he'd been Napoleon's physician appointed by the British. He had grown a little heavier and his curly brown hair was graying at the temples, but he still had a wonderful smile.

"Miss Chapman!" he exclaimed loudly and came to take her hands in his. "What a pleasure!"

She stood facing the good-looking Irish doctor, and memories flooded back to her of those happy long ago days when her father had been alive and all the future seemed bright.

"Dr. O'Meara," she said with feeling. "I doubted that we would ever meet again."

Ever the gallant he said, "And I have continually wished that we would. You have grown up. No longer a girl but a lovely woman.'

She blushed. "I felt quite grown up when I knew you."

"You were enchanting," O'Meara said. And then his manner changed. "I'm sorry about your father. I only recently heard of his death."

"Thank you," she said. "I miss him sorely."

"You two were close," the Irish doctor agreed. "And so were you and the emperor."

"Yes," she said.

"That infernal liver disease!" Dr. O'Meara said, taking Felix Black into this as well. "I would swear that anyone remaining on the island long enough would be bound to contract it."

Black turned to her. "When Barry was on the island, he was acting for the British secret service under my direction."

"Much thanks I was given!" O'Meara exclaimed. "I complained when it was decided to move Sir Neil Campbell and I was also removed from the island."

"I acted on instructions from my superiors," Felix Black told the angry man. "I was only head of the department, not head of the government!"

"It was the beginning of all the trouble when Sir Neil was replaced by Sir Hudson Lowe. Everyone knew Lowe was a silly troublemaker. He treated the former emperor as no officer or gentleman ought to have been treated."

She said, "I had gone before all that."

O'Meara gave her a sad smile. "And I can tell you that the emperor missed you. You and your friends Betsy and Jane Balcombe. He used to joke about his two Betsys and his Jane. But there was little of the good humor of the old days after Sir Hudson Lowe arrived."

Betsy said, "I wrote him several letters, once when my father died and once before that. But there were no replies."

O'Meara grimaced. "That does not surprise me. He never received the letters. Be certain of that. Lowe chose to censor everything beyond the point of good sense. I also wrote and received no reply."

Felix Black said, "Sir Hudson Lowe took himself too seriously and also his role as Napoleon's chief warder. If he had been less stupid, we might not be faced with the situation as we are now."

Dr. O'Meara turned to her. "I hear you are to be part of Black's private organization."

"Yes," she said. "Are you not anxious to find out if Napoleon is alive?"

"I'm of two minds," O'Meara said. "I fear what this man Valmy may try and do with him if he is truly back in Europe and in his power. I would almost prefer that he be buried in his lonely grave on the island."

Felix Black explained. "Dr. O'Meara has taken up journalism and written a number of books explaining Napoleon's nature and quoting from his conversations with him on Saint Helena. He has done an interesting work of painting the former tyrant of Europe in sympathetic colors, making many of his actions understandable and even laudable."

"And so they were!" the Irish doctor said vigorously.

Black smiled. "I vow that only in this free England would you be allowed to publish such controversial writings."

O'Meara smiled bitterly. "Is it the freedom of England you're so proud of? Should you not look about you. What sort of land is this today? Or take yourself to Ireland and see what suffering is! English landlords in absentia do not make for happy tenant farmers!"

"That's bog talk!" Felix Black replied. "You are my good friend, O'Meara, but I cannot tolerate it. As for the state of England, I do not think it that bad."

The curly haired Irish doctor sneered. "Now is that true? Take your London! A city in which a nobleman can lose thousands of pounds in a night at Watier's! Yet little lads of five are forced to sweep chimneys, and girls of twelve parade the streets as prostitutes for little more than bread enough to keep them alive another day! His Majesty's staging wild orgies with his stays undone and tossed to one side as he ravages the wife of some grand gentleman of his circle. And the same grand ladies greet their sons and daughters and puzzle who fathered them!"

Felix Black clapped his hands. "Excellent! You've become a Christian orator as well as a pamphleteer! I vow you could also be a danger if you wished, O'Meara. Many a crowd could be roused by that speech."

Barry O'Meara turned to her, looking rather sheepish. "I'm sorry. I did rant on a bit. It must be my middle-class upbringing. I'm far too moral in my outlook. While on the other hand our friend Black has no morals at all. He surrendered them when he became chief of His Majesty's espionage service."

Black's thin face showed amusement. "You were one of us, O'Meara."

"So I was, to my everlasting shame," Barry O'Meara said. "So now I atone by trying to tell the truth about Napoleon as I knew him."

Betsy, impressed by his performance, said, "I must read some of your writings."

"I'll send you a copy of all of them," the Irish doctor promised. "If history remembers me at all, and I doubt it will, it has to be as the man who tried to help make Napoleon understood."

Felix Black raised an eyebrow and with a hint of sarcasm suggested, "Or more likely as the stubborn Irish doctor sent to spy on the emperor who ended up trying to serve two masters!"

"I was never the Judas you picture," O'Meara told the old man.

Black said, "If you two will excuse me, I shall see if Mrs. Glenn is ready to serve us dinner."

When they were alone, O'Meara came closer to her and said in a low voice, "I'm properly surprised to find you living here."

"I have had troubles since my father's death," she told him. "Things came to such a peak I had no choice but to flee to London."

"That is too bad. Your father would worry. He was a fine man," the Irish doctor said. "So now you have agreed to act as an agent for Black?"

"Yes. I seem to have no other course open. And it may be a chance to meet Napoleon again and perhaps be of help to him."

The burly emotional O'Meara glanced toward the door to be sure they were not being overheard, and in a low voice he said, "Do not count on seeing Napoleon or helping him."

She stared up at him and in a near whisper asked, "Why do you say that?"

"Because I fear that Felix Black may be mad!"

Chapter Five

BETSY'S LOVELY blue eyes opened wide with fear as she gazed up into the troubled face of the Irish doctor. In a hushed voice she asked, "Is that possible? That all this fine plan is madness?"

"I'm fearful of it," Barry O'Meara said. "I cannot believe it was possible for Napoleon to escape from that island."

"Then what does it mean?"

"A finely honed mind that has finally snapped," he told her. "I cannot see the War Office asking him to retire if all was well."

"He seems so sure," she worried. "And his facts to back up the story appear to be genuine."

The Irish doctor sighed. "Only time will tell. But I beg you to be careful. If you involve yourself with this and the facts are true, you are going to have to cross the path of one of the most dangerous men in all Europe."

"Valmy?"

"Yes. If Napoleon did escape, there is no question that Valmy was behind it. And he means the former emperor no good. He will use him and then destroy him."

She nodded. "That is what Felix Black says."

"In that he is surely right," O'Meara said. "As to the rest I'm not sure."

"That is why you will not take part in it?"

"Yes."

Felix Black returned and advised them that Mrs. Glenn was ready for them. Betsy noted the expression on his sallow face and felt he was secretly amused by something. And she had the odd feeling that he somehow knew that Dr. Barry O'Meara had warned her against the enterprise.

Dinner went well. There was no hint of rancor between the two men. Both were well read and familiar with the political situation, and she enjoyed listening to their discussions of the many colorful personalities of the time.

When dinner ended, Dr. O'Meara excused himself almost at once. He said, "I have a meeting to attend at one of the coffeehouses."

"I assume it has to do with Ireland," the old master spy said.

O'Meara smiled. "You know my interests too well."

"You must come again," Felix Black told him. "I have other aspects of Napoleon I would like to discuss with you."

"You know where to reach me," O'Meara said. And then he turned to Betsy and with great sincerity said, "It has been good seeing you again. I shall never forget the days on the island. Do take care of yourself."

She nodded. "I shall."

Felix Black saw him and out and then returned to her. The spidery man in the shabby dark suit said, "What did he talk to you about when I was absent from the room?"

Flustered, she said, "I'm not sure that I remember."

"I'll refresh your mind," he said. "He told you I was mad."

She gave the master spy a frightened look. "How could you know that?"

"I have learned to guess what people around me are thinking. You must also cultivate the gift. It may come in useful to you."

"I shall try," she promised. "As for Dr. O'Meara he is a very emotional person. I don't think you should hold his occasional rash judgments against him."

The thin man smiled bleakly. "He is Irish. That explains a good deal."

"He seems unable to believe that Napoleon is alive."

"Because he has been thinking of him as dead and writing of him in that manner," Felix Black said. "He has brainwashed himself."

"No doubt."

"The things that happen to us are often beyond our wildest imaginings," he pointed out. "When you were kidnapped by Parson Midland, it was beyond anything you could have conceived."

Betsy said, "Without a doubt."

"So it is in every phase of life. O'Meara has told himself that Napoleon is dead. He is sure of it. So he will not accept my story. He calls it fantastic! But much of life is filled with fantastic twists."

She said, "I have come to learn that. And he did not change my mind. I'm still eager to be part of this adventure."

"Good girl," the master spy said. "That is another thing I have learned: to be a shrewd judge of character. I counted on you from our first meeting."

The next morning Mrs. Higgins and her young ladies came again. There was another round of fittings and fussing, but happily it did not last as long this time. Also Mrs. Higgins brought her a number of underthings as well as a selection of nightgowns.

"Best from my stock, my dear," the stout woman said. "The dresses will be ready in a day or two. I may be able to deliver the first one tomorrow."

Betsy was pleased with this promise and the way the various outfits were shaping up. At ten o'clock she joined Kingston and Eric Walters in the study as Felix Black lectured them on the first section of their journey. They were taking a stage to Dover, crossing to Calais, and from there taking a coastal vessel to Marseilles. He told them the length of time it would take them and what they should bring with them.

When it was over, George Frederick Kingston took her out to the drawing room and told her, "I have some information for you."

Eagerly she begged him, "Please tell me!"

"First the parson is dead. Toby tore his throat open before Hannah finished the dog by stabbing it with a carving knife."

"I thought she would do something like that," Betsy said. "I must admit I shall be troubled by all this for a long while."

"She found the lad in a drunken state and threw him out into the street. A cobbler in the next building took him in."

"And?"

"Hannah has vanished. She locked the place up as soon as she made burial arrangements for the parson. No one knows where she went."

"And what about the boy, Gimpy?"

The actor looked sad. "I'm afraid it's the streets for the poor boy. The cobbler who kept him overnight can do no more than that. He has too many mouths of his own to feed."

She said, "If he's left to the streets, he will soon die. He is not well."

"That is plain to see," Kingston said.

"What can I do for the poor lad?" she wondered.

The actor said, "Would you resent a suggestion on my part?"

"Of course not," she said.

"I have a cousin who is a watchmaker," Kingston said. "He has a busy shop, and he's always on the lookout for smart lads anxious to learn the trade. Not only that but he and his wife give the apprentices room and board in their own lodgings over the shop."

She said, "It sounds ideal. Gimpy is too frail for any heavy work."

"That is what I was thinking," the actor said. "This is an occupation where he would be able to remain seated for long hours and only use his eyes and hands."

"Do you think you could persuade your cousin to take the boy on?"

"I could, miss," the actor said. "But he expects a fee of ten pounds for the apprenticing. He returns it later when the lad has proven himself and is able to turn in a proper day's work at the trade."

"That sounds fair enough," she said. "I shall give you an order on my account for the ten pounds, and you take Gimpy to him."

Kingston looked pleased. "You're making no mistake, miss. I promise you that. I'll go to him straight off. I know where to find him."

So this was settled, and she felt much better for it. Gimpy's poor twisted body and wistful face had haunted her more than she was willing to admit. While she wanted to put the rest of the horrible experience out of her mind, she could not forget the lad who had befriended her.

Felix Black came to her after lunch and said, "I should like to have some evidence of your skill with a pistol."

"I have not used one since my father's death," she admitted. "It was he who taught me how to shoot."

"I have a room in the attic designed for target practice and other tests of skill," the old man in black said. "You will follow me up there."

He led her slowly up two steep flights of stairs to the attic of the old house. There she found herself in a room empty of furnishings of any kind. There were two windows to let in light, and the walls were unfinished boards. He went down to one end of the attic and put up a board with circles on it. Then he returned to her and handed her a pistol which he took from his pocket.

He indicated the target and said, "I want to see what you can manage."

She weighed the small pearl-handled pistol. "It is just about right for me," she said.

"I thought it would be when I selected it," he told her. "You can begin whenever, you like."

He stood back and let her aim for the bull's eye on her first shot. She fired, and the bullet went far astray. It struck the outside edge of the target board.

She turned to him in dismay. "That was dreadful."

"I've known worse," was his encouraging comment. "I have had students whose first shots didn't land near the board. You try again and keep on trying."

Her second shot came much closer. She said, "I think I will come back to it after a little."

"I'm sure you will," he said. "You have a good eye."

But it wasn't until several shots later that she managed to hit the target next to the bull's eye. She turned to the old man who had continued to watch her. "I'd best end this now. If I keep on, I'll only get worse."

He nodded assent. "You are right. You've shown great progress today. By the time you leave, you'll be able to handle the weapon as well as you need to."

"I like the pistol," she said about to return it.

"No. Keep it," he said. "It is yours."

She looked down at it. "I'm not sure I could use it against anyone."

"Don't worry," he said. "Circumstances will take care of that." And they went back downstairs.

It was not until later that she realized the full meaning of his words. He had been telling her in a casual way that she would not hesitate to use the pistol if it meant her life. She was moving into a situation where weapons might well be directed at her, and she would be forced to defend herself. There would be no time for meditating on moral scruples.

She thought she had finished the period of testing, but she had not reckoned with the kind of instructor Felix Black was. When she and Major Eric Walters joined him in his study later that day, he had another surprise in store for her.

He told her, "This morning we tested your ability with a pistol. You did well."

"Thank you," she said.

"This afternoon I wish to find out if you are as expert a fencer as you have suggested," the master spy went on.

She blushed. "I made no claim of being an expert."

"But you do know how to handle a blade?" he asked.

"Yes. I have had fencing instruction."

"Excellent," Felix Black said. "Major Walters is also a veteran at fencing. He will judge your competence. For this test you had best wear trousers and a shirt to give you full freedom of movement. Mrs. Glenn has left these items in your room. You will go and change, then join Major Walters in the attic."

Eric looked embarrassed. "I promise you I'm only a very ordinary swordsman!"

She told him, "I will go to the attic as soon as I have changed."

The trousers and shirt were on her bed as the master spy had promised. She slipped off her dress and bustle. Then she put on the tight-fitting black pants and the shirt which she left open at the neck and loose at the wrists. She stared at herself in the mirror and was amazed at the great transformation in her. She looked like a lithe young boy!

Her hair was swept up, and she feared it might get in her eyes if it tumbled down, so she unpinned it and tied it back with a ribbon. This made her look younger and even more boyish. She smiled at herself grimly and wondered whether Eric Walters expected her to have any true fencing skill. Her teacher had actually been one of Napoleon's officers who had filled in time by working with her patiently.

Once the emperor had come upon them fencing and had actively encouraged her. Her father had also been proud of her skill in this field. But again she had not fenced for a long while.

When she reached the attic, Eric Walters was there alone, waiting for her. He had taken off his jacket and vest. His shirt was also open at the neck, and he had loosened his shirt sleeves. He was testing a blade when she joined him.

"You may have your choice," he told her, offering her the blade to test.

She held it, moved it about, and balanced it. Then she tried the other blade and decided. "I like this one."

He went to the corner and found masks and gave her one. As he fitted his own on, he said, "No use being without protection."

"No," she agreed, adjusting the straps on hers and putting it on.

He stood facing her, sword in hand, seemingly loath to begin. "I will take it at a slow rate," he promised.

She raised her eyebrows. "For my benefit?"

"Of course."

"But you mustn't," she protested. "Otherwise how will it be a proper test of my ability?"

"I'm a man," he said. "You're a mere slip of a girl."

"The blades do a good deal to even that."

He smiled. "I like your spirit. I hope you're still not feeling hatred toward me for what happened so long ago."

She said, "I will always think of it."

He still hesitated. "I'm sorry about that. I think it important for us to be friends."

"Why is that necessary?"

"We are moving into great danger—an expedition from which none of us may return."

"So?"

"We need a close alliance. A feeling that each can depend on the other."

She eyed him coolly. "As far as our work together is concerned, there is no reason why you cannot depend on me. My personal feelings are something else."

His handsome face took on a bitter expression. "You prefer to cling to your hatred as a drowning man clutches at a spar."

"I think we have discussed it long enough," she said.

He nodded. "On the ready!" And he bent a knee in fencing position.

"Ready!" she called back and took the same stance.

Each hesitated for a fraction of a second, then they moved in, their swords clashed, and the combat between them began. She was light on her feet and very sure. He had the advantage of strength in handling his blade, but he was not as quick.

Several times she darted back just as he had the advantage, and then she moved in again to engage his blade and further taunt him. Her style was cleaner than his, and he began to hack the air at times and assume dangerously careless postures.

The duel went on. They were both breathing heavily from the unusual exertion, and she could see the streams of perspiration running down the cheeks of her handsome opponent. His eyes kept fixed on her, and he tried to corner her with an aggressive motion of the blades, but she was able to free herself and engage him on her own terms.

The battle seemed equal since her superior skill was matched by his sheer strength and staying ability. She knew that she was tiring and soon must begin to falter. Then, when she least expected it, something startling happened! He was slashing at her in one second and in the next his knee buckled and he stumbled.

Her extensive training came to the fore. She could not help but take advantage of his faltering. With an expert twist of her blade she sent his flying to the floor beside him. In the next moment she was up to him, the point of her blade poised on his bare throat!

It was a moment neither of them would soon forget! Her eyes met his, and she saw both fear and admiration there. She held the blade point in that deadly position for a few seconds longer and then backed away.

He stood up and took off his mask. Staring at her, he said, "You could have killed me!"

She had removed her own mask, and now she nodded. "Yes. I found the moment frightening."

"It wasn't exactly pleasant for me," the young man said. "Especially knowing how you feel about me."

"I wasn't thinking of anything but our match," she said stolidly. "What happened to you?"

He looked embarrassed. "A souvenir of Waterloo! My right knee was injured. They thought I might have to lose the leg. But it healed. Every now and then it gives me trouble. Without any warning!"

She said, "I thought you escaped without any harm."

"I wasn't killed," he said, "but I was wounded."

"Knowing you have this weakness, it is rather mad of you to keep on fencing," she said.

He smiled grimly. "I thought I was up against an amateur. That I had nothing to worry about. You are better than good."

She said, "I had an excellent teacher. An officer who was an aide-de-camp to Napoleon on Saint Helena. He had plenty of time to take pains in teaching me."

"He did well."

"Thank you."

"Did the emperor ever see you handle a sword?"

"Many times."

"What did he think of you?"

"He told me I was an apt student and that he loved fencing. He had been an expert when he was a young officer."

Major Eric Walters said, "If you don't mind, I'll give you a better than passing mark with Felix. And I won't fence with you again."

She raised her eyebrows. "How else am I to keep in good practice?"

The young man picked up his sword. "You don't need to improve," he said grimly. "You're good enough."

She went to the window and looked down into the cobbled cul-de-sac far below. She said, "All this seems like a dream. I'm sure I'm going to wake up soon and find myself safely home in bed in Kent. That none of this can be real."

He came over to stand beside her. "I promise you it is real enough."

She glanced at him. "Until all this happened, I lived in a secure little world. I didn't know there were so many other worlds."

He smiled bleakly. "Perhaps you were wrong to run away. You should have stayed in Kent and married."

She eyed him angrily. "What do you know about it?"

"Nothing, I must admit."

She turned to stare out the window again. "After my father's death, I had no one. My mother is so weak. If my brother Richard had lived, it would have been different for me."

He said, "I know you blame me for Richard. But I had no wish to cost him his life. He was my friend."

She eyed him again in angry fashion. "I think that makes it worse. He must have trusted you, and you betrayed him!"

The young man shook his head. "I did not betray him. I followed my orders and sent him into battle. But I was at his side until I fell wounded."

"I'd rather not discuss it," she said wearily. "I'm going down to change."

She went back to her room and bathed her face and slowly changed back into her dress. She was trembling a little at the remembrance of what had happened in the attic. She knew, and she alone, that there had been that first second after she'd disarmed Eric Walters and pressed the point of the sword against his throat that she had the impulse to drive it on through!

The blood would have gushed forth, and he would have choked to death. She would have been hysterical, and no one would have blamed her. It would be put down as an unfortunate accident.

Perhaps Felix Black might guess, but he would not accuse her. He would perhaps be more satisfied with her and consider her better equipped for the business ahead.

When she went downstairs, Mrs. Glenn told her she was wanted in the study. She went down the hall and found the old man there standing looking out the window. On hearing her enter, he turned.

He said, "The fog is returning again."

"It seems you often have fog in London," she replied, feeling tense and wondering where Eric Walters had gone.

The master spy's thin face showed no expression. He said, "It is the time of year. We suffer most in the spring and in the fall. But I have a liking for it."

She smiled. "Perhaps because a thick fog offers easy concealment. Excellent for espionage."

"Yes, that frankly is one reason for my not minding it," he said. "Walters has left for the day."

"Oh?"

"You could have killed him, I understand."

"I think he exaggerates."

"He didn't act as if he were exaggerating," the master spy said. "I think he was badly unsettled."

"I had no intention of harming him."

"I wonder," Black said, studying her. "I think you have depths which most people don't perceive."

She tried to dismiss this lightly. "Mightn't that be said of almost everyone. Few wear their hearts on their sleeves."

"Certainly not you," he said. "I congratulate you on your fencing skill. And I have word for you from Kent."

Betsy gasped. "You have told them where I am?"

He shook his head. "Never fear that."

"What is the news from Kent?" she asked.

"You will be relieved to know that Lord Alfred Dakin has recovered sufficiently to return to his home. My informant says he left in a high dudgeon!"

"A horrible old man!" she said angrily.

"Yes," the master spy agreed in a dry tone. "I very much doubt that your stepfather will get the loan he requires so badly from him."

"I do not care," she said. "Surely there is enough land to sell to look after my mother. Let Sir John curb his gambling."

"I do not expect he will do that," the man standing by the desk said. "I know the pattern. He has likely approached the moneylenders again and is on his way back to the gaming tables."

"Surely his losses should teach him a lesson."

"Gamblers seldom reform. As a matter of fact I know that Sir John has returned to London. He was seen gambling at Watier's last night."

She at once felt uneasy. "I should leave the city as soon as possible. He mustn't find me."

Felix Black gave her a reproving glance. "There are times when you lack the spirit I expect in you."

"What do you mean?"

"You must learn to face danger if you are to be a secret agent. Learn to have confidence in yourself."

"This is different! It is a personal matter!"

"Not so different," he said. "It will be at least a week before you and the others will be leaving for Marseilles. In the meantime I want you to move about the city and be seen."

"I cannot!" she protested. "Not with my stepfather here and probably conducting a search for me."

"You will not appear as yourself," the master spy told her. "You will be the French mistress of Major Walters. In the black wig with a delicate black mole affixed to your cheek and suitable costume you will not be a simple country girl but a woman of the world."

She stared at him in amazement. "You expect me to go through with a charade like that?"

"I not only expect but I insist," the thin old man said. "You must learn to be able to face situations with confidence. This is the only way."

She took a deep breath. It sounded as mad to her as all the other business associated with him. Yet perhaps there was sense in this seeming insanity. It depended on one's outlook.

She said, "I had no idea becoming a secret agent could be so complicated."

"You're only at the beginning," he told her. "And by the way what are you feelings regarding young Walters now?"

Betsy hesitated. "Would you expect them to have changed?"

"You know him better."

"I still do not know the truth of that day at Waterloo," she said.

"So you do not trust him?"

"Not completely."

"At least you are frank," the old man said. "He thinks most highly of you."

"I cannot help that."

"I think you are doing him a wrong."

"Perhaps."

"However it does not matter as long as you can be civil to each other and work in harmony."

"I have no fear of that," she told him.

"You may go now," the old man said, seating himself at his desk.

The next morning when George Frederick Kingston arrived, he sought her out at once. He was in a jubilant mood as he told her, "I found the lad, and he's safe in my cousin's care."

"I thank you, Mr. Kingston," she said. "I have not been able to get the lad off my mind."

"He was inquiring for you," the actor told her. "He is truly grateful for what you've done for him."

"Without your help it would not have been possible."

"I played only a small role," Kingston said. "My cousin is of the opinion hell make an excellent apprentice."

"I sincerely hope so," she said. "And when I have finished with my work here, I shall look him up and give him encouragement."

Felix Black had the three of them in his studio for a brief lecture. His first information was, "I have received word from my agent in Italy that the man presumed to be Napoleon was taken to somewhere near the French border."

The dashing Eric Walters asked, "Does that mean Valmy is pushing ahead with his plan for an uprising sooner than you expected?"

"I think not," the master spy said carefully. "My feeling is that he wishes to keep his man on the move. That could indicate this Napoleon is an impersonator and not the genuine thing."

Walters nodded. "There is bound to be less chance of an impersonation being discovered if this Napoleon is kept on the go and out of reach of those who knew him well."

"Exactly," the master spy said. "And that is where Miss Chapman becomes so important. A short conversation with this man calling himself Napoleon should make it clear to her whether he is a fake or the real Napoleon."

"We are also to check in Marseilles," Walters said. "There is the question of whether the look-alike lies in the cemetery there."

"Your first task will be to make that investigation," Felix Black agreed. "At the same time my other agents will keep me informed of the movements of Valmy and his group."

Betsy spoke up. "I suppose it is reasonable to assume this Valmy has his own secret agents."

The man in black nodded grimly. "His forces outnumber ours by many. At the moment I think he is unaware of my plan, but once it becomes known, there is bound to be a battle between our forces."

"Sounds exciting," George Frederick Kingston enthused. "Rather like joining the army!"

Major Eric Walters gave the actor a look of scorn. "Not quite, my friend," he said quietly. "In this kind of war someone comes up on you from behind to slit your throat and leave you to die in some dark alley."

Felix Black said sharply, "No need to be melodramatic, Walters. You will discourage our recruits."

The handsome young man said, "I think it only fair they know the hazards, sir."

Kingston looked slightly upset. Glancing at Betsy, he asked, "Is this a proper field for a woman?"

"Do not concern yourself about me," she told the actor. "I'm willing to take the risks."

"And quite capable of taking them, especially when it comes to using a sword," the handsome Walters said with a grim smile. "I can still feel the cold steel on my throat."

"I wish to make the best use possible of your time before you embark for Marseilles," Felix Black said. "I want you to have some experience playing your roles. Kingston is to pose as your wealthy father, Walters. And Miss Chapman is to play the part of your mistress. Your French mistress while you are still here in London."

Betsy blushed. "Could I not be his sister?"

"No," the master spy said. "It is better this way. I want you to pretend to be very much in love. And as the boy's father Kingston will be caught between admiration for your beauty and disapproval at the idea of a French mistress having so much power over his son."

"By Jove you have it all worked out to the last letter," Kingston said with admiration. "The sort of role I can get my teeth into."

"You will be playing it for a long while, so you must be as perfect as possible," the master spy said. "You will need to whiten your hair, add a bit of paunch, and above all dress well but not with the flamboyancy of your normal dress."

The actor looked chastened. "I assume you will pay the bills for my costumes, sir."

"You may go to my tailor's and see if he can fix you up with some sort of rack suits," the man behind the desk said. "I want all three of you to make your first public appearance tonight."

"Tonight!" she exclaimed. "That seems very soon."

"I have a reason," Felix Black said. "My good friend, Sir Humphrey Wood, is having a ball and gambling at his new home in Regent Street. As a favor to me he has included you three on his list of guests."

Eric Walters looked slightly upset, "But look here. I know old Sir Humphrey. I have seen him often at my club."

"He has never met your father?" the master spy asked.

"No," Walters said. "My father chooses to bury himself in the country. He is a recluse. He never journeys to London."

"So Kingston can play your parent without any risk," the master spy said in his dry fashion as if it were all quite normal. "The fact you know Sir Humphrey makes it all the better. Most of London's society will be there."

Betsy said, "And I'm to wear my wig and play the French mistress? A rather unusual introduction to London society."

The handsome Walters gave her a warm glance. "I'm sure the town will approve of my choice."

Felix Black said, "Miss Chapman, I want you to allow Mademoiselle to dress you and make you up. When she finishes, you will look exactly like a French woman of easy virtue. A padded gown will enhance your curves, and you should be most convincing."

"What about answering questions?" she said. "That might be awkward."

The master spy said, "I think for this little escapade it would be best if you pretended not to know English."

Betsy wanted to know, "Suppose some buck speaks to me in French?"

"Answer briefly and always vaguely," Felix Black told her. "That is the style of kept women."

"I'm fortunate in having the benefit of your experience," she said with a rueful smile.

"You all know what you have to do," the man at the desk said brusquely. "A carriage will be here at seven to take you to the party."

After their dismissal George Frederick Kingston rushed off to the tailor to get some suitable clothes. Eric Walters lingered in the hallway to address her.

"Are you nervous?" he asked her.

"A little," she admitted.

"I'm sure you'll manage very well," he said.

"It is different for you," she told him. "You are playing yourself. My role is foreign to me."

"If you follow Black's instructions, you'll be all right. He is a master at this sort of thing."

"I'm beginning to realize that," she agreed.

The handsome Walters smiled. "Though I think it a shame to take a lovely creature like yourself and make her up as a painted French woman of ill repute."

"I do not mind at all," she told him. And not wanting to hear any more compliments from him, or get too friendly, she turned and went upstairs.

Mademoiselle arrived late in the afternoon, and the process of changing her into the French woman began. Betsy had to patiently allow the excitable Mademoiselle make her up. It all had to be exact, even to the dress with the extravagantly low-cut bosom—more daring than anything she had ever worn before.

"It is too revealing. And low in the back as well!" she complained.

"Not for the woman you are supposed to be," Mademoiselle laughed. "Those are the places you wish the men to focus their eyes on!"

By seven she was ready. And as she stood before the full-length mirror in her room, she was filled with admiration for the ability of Mademoiselle. She looked like quite a different person, while still retaining her own features.

Mademoiselle warned her, "You must walk so! Not like a little school girl but like a woman of experience!" And she moved slowly across the room showing her.

Betsy laughed and tried it and after a few minutes she was able to give a fair imitation of the mademoiselle. "Will I do?" she asked.

"But perfect!" Mademoiselle exclaimed. "Now we go down to Monsieur Black. He will have the final word."

Felix Black was in the lower hallway in earnest conversation with a well-dressed young dandy, Walters, and his richly clad and earnest-looking father, Kingston. All three men turned to watch her come down the stairway accompanied by a beaming Mademoiselle.

"Gad!" Eric Walters exclaimed. "I don't believe it! You're tormentingly beautiful!"

Felix Black stepped forward and took her hand. She bowed to him and smiled in a flirtatious manner. The master spy, with his usual dry understatement, said merely, "You will do!"

Kingston filled in generously with, "I have never had a more scintillating leading lady."

They left in the carriage which took them through the foggy cobblestoned streets. There was a somewhat embarrassed feeling among them that did not encourage conversation. So they sat in near silence.

After what seemed an interminable time to her, the carriage came to a halt by a mansion with torches burning on either side of its entrance. Pages in livery came running to open the carriage door and direct the driver where he was to take the vehicle.

Major Eric Walters, more handsome than usual in his evening jacket of blue, stepped down and took her hand to help her to the street. He smiled as he said, "The curtain is about to rise!"

Chapter Six

BETSY TENSELY clung to Major Eric Walters's arm. She was as nervous as she could ever remember as they mounted the stone steps and entered the vestibule of the great mansion. George Frederick Kingston was close behind them, and at the door he caught up with them and gave her a smile of encouragement.

"You'll be the hit of the party," he predicted.

Their wraps were taken by servants stationed at the door, and then they joined the reception line presided over by Sir Humphrey Wood and his wife, Lady Estelle. Major Eric Walters bowed to their host and hostess, who knew him well, and gave her introduction, "My fiancée, Mademoiselle Gaudet!"

Sir Humphrey Wood, a huge man of more than six feet, towered above her as he did over everyone else. He had a craggy face with a large, hooked nose, but his eyes were friendly, and he took her hand and said, "You are charming, mademoiselle."

She smiled graciously and moved on to Lady Estelle who commented on her dress. "You must have the best seamstress in London, my dear!" the thin gray-haired woman said.

Mademoiselle merely smiled again, since she was not supposed to be fluent in English. She moved on as Eric introduced Kingston as his father. The actor put on a good show, playing the part of the blustering country squire to the hilt. After they moved on, Eric procured drinks and some food for them, and they stood together in a group.

"The dancing is across the way in the ballroom," Eric told her. "And the gambling is upstairs."

Kingston gazed at the fashionably dressed guests around him and said, "I'll leave the dancing to you young people while I go up and investigate the gaming tables."

"Be cautious," the young major told him with a smile. "The stakes are high here. He would never consent to cover any debts you might accumulate."

The actor bowed. "You may depend on my discretion! I shall put out only a few pounds of my own money and no more."

They left him to enter the brilliantly lighted ballroom. An orchestra played at one end of the big room with its shining hardwood floor. The floor was filled with dancing couples, and in chairs arranged along the sides of the room, there were a number of spectators.

"Do you enjoy dancing?" he asked her.

"When I'm in the mood."

"What about now?"

"I'm terribly nervous," she whispered. "I feel everyone knows I'm wearing a wig and makeup, and they're staring at me."

"If they are staring, it is because of your beauty," he told her. "They don't see such loveliness except on rare occasions."

"I'm sure you're flattering me," she said.

"At any rate let us dance," he replied, leading her out onto the floor. They took their places in a platoon of stately dancing couples.

Betsy thought it strange that she was attending this ball with a man she had been determined to hate. They danced well together, and he made a handsome figure in his evening dress. She knew that many girls would be at his feet if he showed the slightest interest in them. He was striking in his good looks, charming in his manner, and of a fine family. But there was still the shadow of her brother's death spoiling things between them.

The dance ended, and then the orchestra began to play a lively mazurka. They danced one set of the brisk Polish dance, and then she begged off.

She confided to him, "I fear my wig will be askew if I do much of that!"

He laughed. "I doubt it. But I see Sir Humphrey Wood on his way over here to claim you as a dancing partner. If you wish to escape, we'd better go upstairs to the gambling."

Out of the corner of her eye she saw the tall Sir Humphrey gradually coming toward them, halting now and then to speak with a guest.

"Let us hurry!" she urged Eric Walters. "I'm not equal to playing the silent French mademoiselle with him yet."

"Felix Black wanted you to have this experience," her escort reminded her. But at the same time he guided her out of the ballroom and to the winding stairway which led above.

It seemed that all fashionable London had descended on the great house. They passed couples coming down the stairway as they made their way up.

The large room set aside for gambling was at the head of the stairway. They entered it through wide double doors, and Betsy saw it was crowded, with more men than women there. A roulette wheel was drawing a lot of patrons, and there were many other tables which offered games of chance.

Major Eric Walters pointed out a thin dandy of a man talking animatedly with another foppish type. He told her, "The one in the yellow satin suit is Lord Lumley Skeffington, everyone calls him Skiffy!"

She said, "He is surely eccentric."

"He writes plays, paints his face, and perfumes himself so thoroughly that it is a challenge to stand near him."

"His friend is dressed in green," she noticed. "All that he has on is green!"

Eric laughed. "That is Henry Cope of Brighton. He is famous as the green man. He only wears green clothing, and all the rooms in his house of green are painted in the same color. They say he'll only eat green fruits and vegetables. He's more than half dotty!"

"I wonder where George Frederick has gone," she worried, still clinging to the young major's arm.

"I think I see him at the other side of the roulette table," her companion said. "There's such a jam in here, it will take us a little time to reach him."

"It is more crowded than below," she agreed. And the bustle and noise of conversation filled the place. Men were arguing about their betting, the shape of their cravats, and where they'd had their new jacket tailored.

Betsy had led more of a country life and so knew little of the London regency style. The painted ladies and men were a group foreign to her as was their conversation. She was relieved that she was supposed to know no English and so was not required to engage in talk with anyone.

A wiry little man with graying hair passed them and nodded to Eric. "Back in London, my boy!" he commented in passing.

Eric made a brief reply to him, and after he'd passed on, he informed her, "That was Lord Petersham. He is said to own a snuffbox for every day in the year!"

She said, "I have never met such a collection of eccentric people."

"London society breeds them," the young man agreed. As he finished speaking, Kingston left the roulette table looking worried and came over to meet them.

"I hoped you'd be along soon," the actor said. "In the role of your father I have accumulated a gaming debt of twenty-five pounds. I left my IOU. But if you will be so good as to let me have the cash, I'll redeem the paper at once."

Eric sighed. "I remember warning you."

"I could not stand there and make no bet," Kingston complained. "I have to make a good showing as your father."

"Do not feel the compulsion again," Eric said, taking his wallet out and counting the twenty-five pounds and handing them over to the actor.

"Thank you, my boy," Kingston said with feeling. "I shall repay you from my salary." And he went back to the roulette wheel to settle the IOU.

Betsy told Walters, "I think it is time we left. We have made our appearance."

He said, "Are you not enjoying yourself? Surely my company is not all that dull?"

"It has nothing to do with you," she said. "It is just that I'm so terribly nervous."

"Remember you need not converse with strangers," he reminded her. "You are a French mademoiselle and a lovely one."

"I think we should get Kingston out of here also," she added. "He might be tempted to gamble again."

"That is a good reason for getting away," Eric was forced to admit. "I think the fellow is a compulsive gambler."

Betsy was going to reply to this when she saw Sir Humphrey Wood and another man coming towrad them and felt she might faint! It was not the towering Sir Humphrey whom she was afraid of, it was the man walking at his side! Her stepfather, Sir John Cort!

Eric saw her stepfather at the same instant and in a low aside to her whispered, "Your precious stepfather up from the city for a gambling escapade. Don't falter! I'll see you through this!"

Sir Humphrey came up and with a smile on his craggy face said, "Here you are with your French lady! I've been looking for you downstairs."

Eric said, "Mademoiselle wished to watch the gambling."

"And so she shall," their host said. Then he turned and introduced her stepfather, saying, "This is Sir John Cort, a familiar at most gambling spots in London. He's known to be fiendishly lucky at cards!"

Her burly purple-faced stepfather was dressed in a wine jacket, his London best, and he bowed to her and Eric. He said, "I can also be just as fiendishly unlucky. I remember meeting you at Watier's, Major."

"Yes," Eric said, "though I haven't been at the tables as much as usual since bringing my fiancée, Mademoiselle Gaudet, across from Paris. You may speak freely before her as she understands no English."

"Damned fine-looking girl," her stepfather said in his blustering fashion. He poked Eric in the ribs and waggishly confided to him, "Should you tire of her, let me know. I'm staying with Sir Charles Oram at his bachelor flat. Expect to be in town a week or so. A little dalliance would be a pleasant diversion."

Sir Humphrey chided him. "You're much too old for this lovely wench!"

"Do not quarrel over her, gentlemen," Eric protested. "For the moment she is mine, and I have no thought of sharing her with anyone else, I promise you."

Now Sir John Cort began staring at her so fixedly that she felt her cheeks burn, and she lifted the fan she was carrying to partially cover her face. Her stepfather said, "It has just struck me!"

"What, sir?" Eric wanted to know.

"Your mademoiselle has been reminding me of someone, and now I've got it! She bears a faint resemblance to my stepdaughter, Betsy Chapman!"

Sir Humphrey Wood chided him. "There is little or no resemblance. Your stepdaughter is a blonde, and this woman is a brunette. Also this woman is clearly older and more experienced than your Betsy."

Sir John frowned. "That is true. But there is a slight sameness of face. I swear to that." He apologized to Eric. "It happens I have Betsy much in mind. The ungrateful creature ran off after nearly killing Lord Dakin who had come to court her."

Eric said, "That must be the son or grandson of the only Lord Dakin I have met. He is an old, rather senile man."

Her stepfather showed annoyance. "There is only one Lord Dakin, and while he is a man of some years, he is my friend and perhaps will one day be my son-in-law. So I bid you not to talk loosely about him!"

"My pardon!" Eric said humbly, though she could tell by the gleam in his eyes that he had deliberately taunted her stepfather, and he was having a hard time not bursting out laughing.

Sir John Cort moved on in an annoyed mood with Sir Humphrey trailing along. Both men took a stand by the roulette table as Kingston left it. The actor came quickly over to join them and handed Eric the IOU.

Betsy tugged Eric's arm, saying, "I dare not stay here a moment longer. He may have second thoughts and come checking on me."

"Don't panic!" Eric told her. "Let us make a slow and dignified exit, all the while talking to Kingston."

They made their way downstairs where the music and the dancing still went on. Next they sought out Lady Wood who was standing talking to friends near the hallway. She was distressed that they were leaving so early.

"I'm afraid we must go," Eric told their hostess with a smile. "Mademoiselle has a slight headache. I shall take her home to my rooms."

"Where I'm certain you will cure the headache, you naughty boy!" the elderly woman said with an insinuating smile and a tap of her fan.

"Young people in love," Kingston boomed out while Betsy smiled blankly and played to the hilt the French coquette. "We have enjoyed the party and are most grateful!"

"Do come again," their hostess said. "One of the pages will summon your carriage."

As they stood on the steps waiting for the carriage to come around, Betsy gave Eric a glance. His handsome face was shown to advantage in the glow from the torches set out on either side of the door. Kingston, in the role of Eric's father, paced restlessly on the sidewalk, watching for the vehicle.

Betsy told Eric in a low voice, "I think Felix Black did this deliberately!"

"What?"

"Arranged for me to be at this party in disguise since he knew my stepfather would be here," she said in a tense tone.

"No harm done?" Eric said. "You see how excellent your makeup is and what a good actress you are. He didn't recognize you."

"He very nearly did!" Betsy reminded him.

"I was uneasy for a brief instant," her escort agreed. "But Sir Humphrey spoke up at just the critical moment. I was never so grateful for anyone bumbling."

Betsy said, "I'm still sure it was a test."

"Why worry? You passed it with flying colors."

"But I might not have!"

"In that case the game would have been up," Eric pointed out. "I don't think he'll give my mademoiselle another thought!"

She gave him an indignant look. "He wanted to bargain with you for me. As if I were some sort of object! What villainous creatures you men are!"

"He made the overtures," Eric insisted. "And I did nothing to encourage him."

From the street Kingston called, "Our carriage has arrived." He held the door open for her to enter it, along with the handsome Eric. Then the old actor himself stepped inside, and one of the pages closed the door.

The carriage started off as Eric asked the actor, "Did you tell the coachman where to take us?"

"It is the same carriage Black had bring us here," the older man said. "He was waiting in the rear court with some of the other vehicles. I didn't think he needed to be told our destination!"

"You're right," Eric said, settling back. "I'd forgotten."

"No wonder," she observed.

Kingston was in a good humor. "I think we all did well. Especially Betsy! Pulling the wool over the eyes of her stepfather!"

"I nearly died of fright," she said with a sigh of relief. "I was sure he was going to try and take off my wig!"

"He wasn't that suspicious," Kingston said.

"No." The young man seated beside her agreed. "I felt we all played our roles properly. Mine was the easiest since I was playing myself."

She huddled back miserably in the dark carriage as it rolled over the cobblestoned streets in the murky night. The carriage all at once began to gather speed and was being driven at such a rapid rate that she was almost thrown to the floor of it!

"Something strange!" Kingston grumbled as he caught her under the armpits and brought her back to her seat. Now the carriage careened again, and it was generally realized that while they'd been talking, it had increased its speed.

"Slow down," Eric said, lifting the small window flap to notify the driver.

The driver paid no attention, and the carriage rolled on drunkenly as if a madman were at the reins. Eric's face was a study in rage and fear as he threw open one of the carriage doors and attempted to cling to the side and boost himself up to get at the driver.

"Careful!" Betsy screamed, sure he'd be shaken off his perch any moment. Kingston was half on the floor and clinging to the seat.

Eric managed to boost himself to the top of the carriage. There were immediate shouts, and the carriage went on wildly for a moment. Then it was brought to a halt.

A shaken Eric appeared in the open carriage doorway. He said, "That fellow wasn't our regular driver! As soon as I tackled him, he thought of nothing but escaping. He ran off down an alley."

"Where are we?" Kingston asked, looking out with worried eyes.

"In the darkest of slums," Eric said grimly. "He was taking us to some rendezvous to be robbed and likely have our throats cut."

"What now?" she asked breathlessly.

"I shall be coachman and get us away from here before that villain can return with his fellows," Eric said and slammed the door closed.

They heard him clamber up to the driver's seat and cry out to the horses. He was still turning the carriage around when there came hoarse shouting from the street. She looked out and saw four thugs emerging from the shadows and making for them.

But Eric had now managed to swing the vehicle around, and he urged the frightened horses forward at a reckless speed. Once again she and Kingston had to cling to each other and to any part of the inside which offered some secure hold. At last they came back to the gaslit wider streets, and the carriage slowed until they finally arrived at the house in the cul-de-sac which was their headquarters.

Eric tied the reins and opened the door for them. He apologized, "Sorry. But I had no choice but to drive swiftly!"

"What did it all mean?" Betsy asked as he helped her down from the carriage.

"Why were we tossed about in that fashion?" the old actor asked as he straightened out his cloak and hat and joined her on the street.

"At the very least a plan to rob us," Eric said grimly. "Perhaps something more."

"But why pick on our carriage?" she asked.

"And what happened to our own driver?" George Frederick Kingston worried.

"We shall find that out as soon as possible," Eric told them as he escorted them to the door.

It was Felix Black himself who let them in. The old master spy stared at them a moment and asked, "Are all of you safe?"

"Yes," Eric said. "Were you expecting something to happen to us?"

"Come inside," the old man urged them.

"What about the horse and carriage?" Eric asked, glancing back where the horse and carriage waited.

"The driver is already here," Felix Black said grimly. "I'll send him out to look after things."

They followed the bent man in black into his study where the driver was uneasily waiting. He looked at them all in awe, dreadfully ill at ease.

Felix Black told him, "Major Walters brought the carriage back safely. You can go take it to the stables. I'll want to talk to you again in the morning."

"Yes, sir," the man said with a nod. And he hurried out, seemingly happy to escape questioning by them.

Eric watched him leave and then turned to Black with some annoyance. He said, "I had some questions for that fellow to answer."

The master spy waved this aside. "I've taken care of all that." He moved over to her and offered her a chair. "You have had a trying evening, Miss Chapman. Please sit down."

She did so and said, "What did you find out?"

Felix Black eyed them all grimly. "According to the driver he'd settled down inside the carriage for a sleep while he was waiting. He often does this when there is a long wait at night."

Eric asked, "And then?"

"He doesn't know exactly who came after him. He woke with a start as the carriage door was thrown open and someone hit him on the head with something heavy. It knocked him out. When he came around, the carriage had gone. Not knowing what to do, he came straight here."

Eric frowned. "Then it would seem he was not in collusion with the attackers."

"I would strongly doubt it," Felix Black said. "May I ask what happened afterward?"

Eric told him, ending with, "It is only good luck we managed to escape from those villains. It had all been neatly planned."

"So it would seem," the master spy agreed.

George Frederick Kingston had slumped into an easy chair, looking much ruffled, and he demanded, "Why should they have chosen us from all the many carriages at the party?"

Betsy nodded. "Yes. That also makes me wonder. I surely had no jewelry of consequence. Some of the women there were loaded down with diamonds and other precious items."

Eric Walters had been standing leaning against a sideboard, and now he spoke up in a stern fashion, saying, "I think I can supply that information. If I'm not very far wrong, I would say that the opposition to our project has begun, that news of our search for Napoleon has leaked out."

Felix Black's thin, sallow face was clouded with concern. "You have had experience as a secret agent, Walters, so you would be expected to guess. I fear our secret project is no longer a secret. Valmy has been alerted, and what took place tonight was his first countermove."

Eric took a step nearer the old master spy. "Who could betray our plan?"

"Someone in the War Office, I fear," the old man said. "Perhaps the very one who had me discredited and forced my retirement from my official position."

The young secret agent nodded. "I hadn't thought of that. You are probably right. A leak could probably come from someone there."

"The unfortunate thing is we are going to be faced with threats from the start," Felix Black said. He turned to Betsy and the veteran actor and added, "You are now beginning to learn that I'm not paying you highly for ordinary work. There is a great risk involved here."

Kingston frowned, "You're saying there will be other attempts to kill us."

"I would expect so," Black said quietly.

Betsy shrugged. "I assumed there would be danger. It is only that it is beginning earlier than we expected."

"Sooner or later Valmy would have learned we were on his trail," Felix Black agreed. "At least now we know the worst."

Betsy said, "Did you expect my stepfather to be at the party we attended?"

The master spy nodded. "Yes."

"You might have warned me!"

"Then there would have been no test. How did you make out?"

Betsy looked at the others and then told him, "He didn't recognize me, but he did mention that I reminded him of his errant stepdaughter."

"You carried it off!" Black said approvingly. "Excellent."

She eyed him wearily. "After tonight I'm not all that certain I'm equal to being a secret agent."

"You underestimate your possibilities," Felix Black assured her.

Eric spoke up again. "Now that we are under surveillance by Valmy's people, what will our next move be?"

"I think it important that you get away from London as soon as possible," the master spy said.

George Frederick Kingston stared ahead of him bleakly and commented, "Once we're aboard ship, there will be no turning back."

Felix Black eyed him sharply. "It is not my plan to shanghai you into my service. Even after all this, I will free you from any loyalty to me if you wish."

The actor shook his head. "No. I'm in this. I won't back out. Miss Chapman may need a friend."

Betsy smiled at him. "Thank you. But you must not go on for my sake."

"I'm going on because it is not likely I can get an engagement anywhere else," the veteran actor said sadly. "The jobs have been getting scarcer as I've grown older. I need the work and the money."

Eric showed a rueful smile. "I think we three have now found a kind of comradeship. I would say we should be equal to our enemies."

"There are my other agents who will contact you from time to time," the master spy said. "You will not be entirely alone."

"But this will be rather different from my days as a regular government agent," Eric Walters pointed out. "I cannot go running to the nearest consulate for help."

"No. This is my private enterprise. Done against the wishes of His Majesty's government. I can only hope we are able to show that we were right and they were wrong before this is over," Felix Black said.

Eric asked, "Has the timetable been changed?"

"Yes," Black said. "Because of tonight."

"When do we leave for Marseilles?" the young major asked.

"Day after tomorrow. The ship sails in the early morning when the tide is right," the master spy said.

"This is a new arrangement?" Eric suggested.

"Yes," the master spy said. "I have kept this alternate plan open in case something happened—as it did tonight. You will now sail on the *Maria*. It is an Italian four master and not as fast as the other ship I'd planned to use. The chief difference will be you'll arrive in France a few days later than we planned."

"And a few days could make a big difference," Eric said.

"Unfortunate," the master spy agreed. "But it cannot be helped. Now I suggest you all retire. You must be worn out from your experiences tonight."

Eric and Kingston left together to walk to their nearby lodgings. She went up to her room and removed the black wig and the makeup. Not until she had washed and changed into her nightgown did she feel like herself. Playing the French girl had been a challenging experience.

It would be her role from now on. But when they arrived in France, she would no longer have to be silent. She would need to converse with people in their attempt to find out if the dying LaFlenche had really been spirited away to take the place of Napoleon.

That night her sleep was tormented by nightmares. First she relived the mad careening in the carriage, then her dreams fled back to the past, and she was once again in St. Helena, a young girl full of the excitement of meeting a famous figure. She stood on a hillside and watched the exiled emperor and his entourage of a half dozen walk up from the direction of the cliffs overlooking the ocean.

She knew that Napoleon often went there to gaze out at the horizon, chafing at his need to escape. Now he came to where she was standing and his intelligent face brightened and he halted and chatted with her. But he did not discuss the things which he had discussed with her on the island. Now he was warning her not to interfere with his plans, not to oppose Valmy.

"You cannot change my destiny!" he told her in a reproachful tone.

She ran from him in tears, not able to face his strong condemnation. Then she was in a dark wood, and the huge, menacing figure of Parson Midland appeared out of the bushes, and whip in hand he came after her. She cried out in fear, and he lashed her with the whip. She ran, and he followed her, breathing heavily. Then she stumbled over a tree root and sprawled forward on her face and hands. The fat man caught up to her and striving for breath lifted the ugly snake whip again and brought it down across her back!

Betsy screamed with pain, and the scream brought her awake. She stared up into the grayness of the growing dawn and wished for morning—and an end to such nightmares.

When she went down for breakfast, Felix Black was still at the table. As she joined the thin man, he gave her a concerned glance.

He said, "You look weary. Did you not sleep well?"

"I slept badly," she admitted.

"You had an evening filled with strain," he agreed. "I did not expect the attempted abduction. Just facing your stepfather must have been difficult enough."

"I had a great desire to scream at him," she said, "especially when he showed a lustful interest in me and tried to barter with Major Walters for my company."

"Your stepfather is a dissolute man."

"And I gathered from what he said he'd still have me marry that dreadful Lord Dakin, if that old man would have me," she said with disgust.

"So it is still imperative you get away from England," the master spy said.

"I cannot go back home. And I dare not remain in London. So I have little choice."

"This adventure will take your mind from these troubles," the man in black assured her.

She paused over her dish of oatmeal. "Do you expect any of us to return alive?" she asked bluntly.

"Did last night upset you so?"

"I know how near we came to being violently dealt with."

Black stared down at his empty plate. "There is always the chance of death in this rather dangerous business."

"I no longer doubt that," she said.

He fixed his steely eyes on her and said, "But I'm not asking you to do anything more risky than I once undertook as a younger man."

"You were a secret agent?"

"I did not become director of the British service without experience. I rose from the ranks. I started very humbly as an agent."

Betsy said, "You must have shown great talent."

"Let us say I outlived most of my contemporaries in this most dangerous game," he said. "I also have been dedicated. I believe in what I have done."

"This Valmy," she said. "What sort of man is he?"

"Fascinating character," Black said. "A student of history who became an officer in Napoleon's army. He is one of those few who survived the retreat from Moscow. After the defeat of the emperor had changed everything, this Valmy threw himself into politics. He is now leader of a large secret society, and he is also popular with the veterans of the grand army. And there are many of them."

"He can well be the one to rally these groups together in a new cause," she deduced from what had been said. "He cannot be an old man?"

"He is comparatively young. In his mid-thirties and possessed of great charm," the master spy told her. "If you come face-to-face with him, you will not see him as a threat to European peace but as an extremely attractive, intelligent male."

"I shall remember that," she promised.

"Also remember that he is ruthless! The attempt on you last night was only a beginning. He has in his hands a tired and malleable Napoleon whom he hopes to use as a standard-bearer. He will let nothing stand in his way."

Betsy said, "And he has the appeal to take the aging emperor's place when his planned assassination happens."

"That is the plot in a nutshell," Black said. "Then all Europe will have to deal with a young fanatic at the peak of his power. The War Office may live to regret its stupidity if our counterplan should fail."

"We sail tomorrow morning?"

"Yes," the old man said. "You will leave the house tonight and board the ship in darkness. You will be there when she sails. So you have spent your last night under my roof."

"I have felt safe here," she said.

He shook his head. "That is an illusion. Valmy's men can reach anywhere."

"Then you will not be safe!"

"I know I'm needed to head the project," the old spy said. "I shall do all I can to protect myself. And you must keep your pistol close by at all times, and do not forget that you have a special gift with the sword."

"I hardly think Major Walters approves of my fencing."

"That is unimportant," he said. "I have the feeling you and he are beginning to understand each other better."

"I admire him for his courage."

"He has plenty of it."

"And he is a gentleman."

"Without a question."

She hesitated over her teacup. "But there is still that shadow of the past. It keeps a barrier between us."

"I do not think the barrier exists on his part."

She glanced at the old master spy. "You're saying it is all on mine?"

"I believe so."

"I don't agree," she said. "Deep down I'm sure he feels guilt and regret for what happened to my brother. I think I could forgive him more easily if he admitted to error and asked my forgiveness directly."

Felix Black considered this for a moment and then said, "Would you want him to pretend to feel a remorse that he cannot know? He maintains he was not guilty of bad judgment, and knowing him, I doubt if he was."

She sat back in her chair with a sigh. "I fear we are on opposite sides in this."

"I will not belabor it."

"Thank you," she said. "And for my part I shall strive to work with Major Walters as if there was not this trouble between us."

"That is the most I can hope for," the old man said. And he rose from the table. "It is a pleasant sunny day. I have a garden area out back. There are no flowers yet, but you should go out for a stroll and enjoy the sun. It may make you feel better."

"Thank you," she said.

Later she accepted his suggestion. Putting on her cloak and going out through the rear of the house to the brick-walled garden area, she noted that the wall was above her head so it provided good protection against intruders. Not that they couldn't easily scale it if they wished, but at least it gave a degree of privacy.

She was strolling rather aimlessly in the sunshine when she heard a step on the gravel walk behind her. Her nerves on edge, she whirled around swiftly to see who it was. She was relieved to find that it was a friend, Dr. Barry Edward O'Meara.

The doctor's curly brown hair was blowing slightly in the light morning breeze in the garden. He said, "I came to see you before your leaving. So you're sailing in the morning?"

"Yes," she said. "We have had to push ahead our plans."

"So Felix Black told me," the robust Irish doctor said. "I'm worried about you."

She smiled. "Do you think the mission so dangerous?"

"I do," he said solemnly.

"You are a disciple of Napoleon these days," she said. "Your books all praise him."

"I wrote praise of a dead emperor."

"And now it seems he may be alive."

"God save us! Yes," the emotional Irishman said, his pleasant face showing worry.

"If you fear him, why didn't you enlist with us to help find out whether he is truly alive?" she asked.

Dr. Barry O'Meara gave her a strange look. "Perhaps because I have lately come by information indicating he may be alive."

She stared at him. "You know something more than you've told Felix Black, don't you?"

The Irish doctor nodded. "I think he may be in Europe and that he will reign as emperor again."

Chapter Seven

BETSY WAS shocked by her old friend's words. Her lovely oval face clouded. She asked him, "If you think that, why do you not join in with Felix Black?"

The Irish doctor shook his head. "No. I cannot do that. I can never work under him again. But I mean to carry on an investigation of my own."

"To find out the truth about this man, supposedly Napoleon?"

"Yes. I think I can do much better on my own." He gave her a warning look. "But do not tell Felix Black of my plan. He would consider it an act against him."

"Is it?"

Dr. O'Meara shrugged. "Perhaps. But if this man who Valmy has brought forth is truly Napoleon, I will know. And I will warn him that he is caught between enemy forces. I will try and help him gain true freedom."

She frowned. "You don't trust Felix Black?"

"No more than I do Valmy," the Irish doctor told her. "It is my belief that in the end both Black and Valmy will want the former emperor dead. I want to see him alive."

"I think Felix Black means him no harm," she said.

"Do not be too sure," O'Meara warned her. "I have known Black longer than you. When he believes he is right, he is even willing to sacrifice his best friend. As far as he is concerned, the end justifies the means. That was always his policy at the Foreign Office. I think it will be the same now."

"I'm pledged to become his agent," she said.

"I wish you well," Barry Edward O'Meara said gravely.

"We are leaving tomorrow morning," she said. "What about you?"

121

"I shall leave sooner. Perhaps our paths will cross somewhere in Europe."

"They should," she said. "We each have the same quarry."

He nodded. "Who could have predicted this when we were there on Saint Helena."

"I know," she agreed. "I thought Napoleon a gentle sort."

"There is such a side of him, and you brought it out," the Irish doctor said. "But it is not he we have to worry about, but his mentor, Valmy."

"So I understand."

"Valmy is more thirsty for power than the former emperor ever was," the doctor said. "Once Valmy has used him, I'm certain Napoleon will die violently. I want to prevent that."

"So does Felix Black."

"He claims so," O'Meara said hesitantly. "Because I'm not convinced, I prefer to work on my own. But I'll not do anything to hinder you people. I may even be able to help."

"Let us hope so," she said.

"I must leave now," the Irish doctor told her. And he lifted her hand and kissed the back of it gently. "Remember, not a word to Felix."

"He may ask me, I'm sure," she said.

"I count on you," the Irishman said.

She remained in the garden after he'd left her, lost in her thoughts. From the time of their first meeting on St. Helena, she had taken a liking to Barry Edward O'Meara. As she recalled, Napoleon had also liked and trusted him. And all the while he had been spying on the former emperor.

But Napoleon had won him over, so that now O'Meara was his champion. It was possible she and O'Meara were the only two on the British side capable of finding out whether this man Valmy was offering was the real former emperor. O'Meara feared that the others, including Felix Black, might be plotting against the life of his hero. And he could be right.

Yet she was willing to believe Felix Black. In the short while she had known the bent, thin old man, she had come to respect him. He had befriended her and given her an opportunity for a new life full of challenge. When he claimed he wished only good for the fallen French ruler, she was ready to take him at his word. If O'Meara wished to doubt him, it was his own business.

She was still going over all this when the bizarrely emaciated figure of Felix Black came out of the house to walk toward her in the walled garden. When he came up to her, his sunken eyes searched her face.

He said, "So O'Meara has gone. He left without pausing to speak with me."

She said, "Really? He spoke of having an urgent meeting with someone."

Felix Black looked disapproving. "No doubt something to do with his Irish revolutionary activities."

"Is he deep in that?"

"Yes," the old man said. "I might call it his other obsession."

"I think he is a man of principle," she ventured.

"Doubtless!" Black said dryly. "But so swayed by his emotions as not to be always reliable."

"You used him as an agent when you were head of the Foreign Service," she reminded him.

"It did not turn out well," he replied. "And I think I have made an enemy of him. Not that he has shown it in any way. But I fear I no longer have his trust."

"As you say, he is emotional," she apologized for the Irish doctor.

The man in black asked her, "Why did he wish to talk with you?"

"Merely to wish me well," she said.

"That was all?"

"Yes," she said, bound not to break faith with O'Meara. "He knew I was leaving soon."

"But he has not offered his aid in the venture, and he could be of great assistance," the old secret service man said with a hint of anger in his tone.

"I think he wishes to be entirely on his own."

He gave her a thoughtful look. "You're probably right. It comes back to his mistrust of me."

She said, "I think he is torn between the thought that Napoleon may be alive and in need of his help and the idea that the man Valmy has come up with may be an impostor."

"We are all faced with the same quandary."

"But it is more difficult for him," she said, "because of his strong personal feelings for the man."

"What about you?"

She blushed. "I can't deny my fondness for the former emperor. But I do not believe this man is he. I think he died on Saint Helena."

"You may well be right," the old man said. "But if so, it is important we prove Valmy's puppet to be spurious."

"I agree."

"That will be your task, along with the others," he continued. "I will expect written reports regularly."

"Do you plan to come to France when we find out where this man is in hiding?" she asked.

Regret crossed his white masklike face. He said, "I fear my health will never allow that. You must have guessed that I am not a well man."

"You are thin," she agreed. "But then that is the nature of some older men."

He shook his head. "I'm dying slowly of a wasting disease. I knew that before I was dismissed from the Foreign Office. That is why this is so important to me. It will be my last project. I shall most likely be dead before you return to England."

She was shocked. "I'm truly sorry! Are you sure about this?"

"I have the word of my doctor, whom I trust," he said. "I would prefer that you not mention this to the others."

"If you do not wish it."

"It might shake their faith in my ability to carry this through," he said. "I'm certain that I will live long enough to know victory, but perhaps no longer. That will be enough."

Having said this, he left her and went back into the house. She remained standing where she was for a moment, stunned by his revelation. Now that she'd been told, she realized she should have guessed that his condition was grave. But she had no worry that his abilities were in any way impaired by his terminal illness. If anything his desire for victory had been whetted. She was confident he would live to see the project through safely.

Darkness came, and Felix Black gathered with the company of three to give them final instructions and see them to the carriage which would take them to the docks and the *Maria*. They were traveling as lightly as possible with each of them carrying only two bags.

There was a drizzle of rain falling when the old man saw Betsy into the carriage. He held her hand for a moment before she stepped up inside and told her, "I'm placing much of my hope in you, my dear."

"I shall try not to disappoint you," she promised.

"You are on the eve of stirring events. Good luck!" were his parting words.

He bade good-bye to Major Eric Walters and to George Frederick Kingston, and the two men took their places in the carriage with her. As they began the journey through the dark wet night, she glanced out of the window at what would be her last glimpse of London for a while. All she could see were the dull glow of corner gas lamps and a few windows and storefronts dimly lit.

George Frederick Kingston broke the silence among them saying, "The old boy was very serious tonight."

Across the carriage handsome Eric Walters smiled grimly, "Why not? We're on a mission of importance."

"All seems like a play to me," the seasoned actor said.

"You may be faced with reality soon enough," was the younger man's prediction.

Betsay said, "At least we should have some sun in Marseilles. I'm tired of the almost continual fogs and drizzles of London."

"We're on our way to the balmy Mediterranean and who knows what else?" Eric said mockingly.

When the carriage arrived at the wharf, the ship *Maria* was wreathed in fog. All was quiet. A seaman with a lantern greeted them, and they marched up a gangway to the vessel. They were greeted on deck by First Officer Bellini. He spoke with a heavy Italian accent but seemed glad to have them as passengers and promised them they would have choice cabins.

Betsy found herself in a small cabin adjoining a larger one shared by Eric and Kingston. She did not know how this had been arranged, but it was agreeable to her.

She could hear the sound of the waves lapping against the vessel and the occasional movement of its ancient hull scraping against the wharf pilings. It was quiet, and she quickly undressed and got into her bunk and went to sleep. She had only occasional dreams and adjusted well to her new surroundings.

She was awakened by the slight roll of the ship and the sight of daylight coming in through the porthole in her forward cabin. She quickly got up and looked out and saw they were already well down the Thames on their way to the open sea. She then dressed as quickly as she could and went out on deck.

George Frederick Kingston was already on deck standing by the railing and looking rather pale. He tipped his gray top hat to her and clutching the rail asked, "Do you not find the motion disturbing?"

She smiled. "No. I don't think so."

"I fear I do," the old actor said, looking distressed. "In fact I know I shall not eat this morning."

"That bad?"

"Worse, dear lady," Kingston said. "My only previous experience on the water has been in a rowboat on a river. I do not seem to have a seagoing stomach."

"I'm sure you'll be fine as soon as you've gotten used to it," she encouraged him.

He looked more upset than before. "I daren't hope for that, I fear." And he tottered off down to the bow of the ship. It was not a promising beginning for the jolly little man.

She was standing alone by the railing when Eric Walters came up to her. He looked jaunty in a gray jacket and brown trousers. And he wore a kind of nautical cap with a peak. He eyed her with admiration.

"You look very well this morning," he said. "Your yellow dress and bonnet brightens the day."

Betsy smiled. "I'm afraid they didn't have much effect on poor Kingston."

"I know," Eric said, glancing down the deck where the actor was bent over the railing. "I think Kingston has still to find his sea legs."

"I didn't dare confess it to him. But I'm hungry!"

"We shall have breakfast together," Eric promised her, offering her his arm. "I shall take great pleasure entering the dining salon with the loveliest lady on board."

"There must be others!" she protested, taking his arm.

"A mixed lot," he said. "It has all the promise of being a dull voyage. At least I took the precaution of bringing along plenty of reading material."

"I have two of Scott's novels," she said.

"We can exchange volumes," he told her.

They entered the dining salon and found it filled and rather noisy as the various passengers talked loudly and the serving stewards clattered dishes, silverware, and pans about. The tables were set out in boardinghouse style, three long tables which filled the length of the salon. They were fortunate to find one of them with two empty seats at the end.

Betsy and Eric sat across from each other and waited to be served. She saw that he had an ominous-looking Indian in turban and robe seated next to him. The brown-skinned man took no notice of Eric's presence or indeed of anyone else at the table. He ate and drank silently, keeping his eyes on his plate.

Next to her was seated a sour-faced old man with a slightly askew gray wig. He wore a drab brown jacket, light brown breeches, and a brown plaid waistcoat. His jacket and waistcoat were liberally decorated with ancient food stains, and he was greedily diving into a large dish of oatmeal and staining himself anew.

He paused in lifting a spoon from dish to mouth to announce to her, "Good morning, I'm Samuel Jessup, Esquire. I'm delighted to be your fellow passenger."

"How do you do," she said politely, knowing that Eric was watching her with some amusement. "My fiancé, his father, and I are bound for Marseilles."

"Hah!" Samuel Jessup said. "I'm disembarking at Gibraltar. I have business interests there." A splash from his spoon of oatmeal made a new mark on his vest.

She said, "You have made this journey before?"

"Many times," he said in his loud, harsh voice. "And I may say the company doesn't get any better, yourself excluded. I'm accustomed to more genteel companions."

Betsy said, "Did you travel during the war years?"

"Regularly," the strange old man said. "It took more than old Boney to frighten me off the ocean."

"Those must have been stirring times," she ventured.

"They were," he agreed. "But the company was better then." And he put down his spoon and began taking pill cases from his various jacket pockets. He busied himself at this until he had a half-dozen pill cases set out before him. He then began to take pills from each of the cases and swallow them with a gulp from his water glass.

Betsy could not hide her amazement. She stared at him and said, "Are you ill, sir?"

He shook his head, "I'm much attached to physic! My apothecary has gathered a series of the most helpful pills known to man for me. I take them to ward off illness, not to cure it."

She stared at him as he continued to select various sizes and colors of pills and gulp them down. "You must take a great many of them!" she gasped.

He nodded brusquely, pausing between medications. "I take fifty-one pills a day!"

"Fifty-one!" she said, incredulous. "That's more than fifteen thousand pills a year."

"Keeps me vigorous," the old man assured her, a satisfied look on his bronzed, lined face. "Also keeps me strapped for money."

"I should imagine," she said, awed.

"Not to mention what it costs me for mixtures, juleps, and electuaries. I take a great deal of them as well."

She could not restrain a smile. "Then you must have a cure for seasickness."

"I do," he said promptly. "Are you suffering from it?"

"No," she said. "But I have my fiancé's father who is. I'm sure he'd be most grateful if you could bring him some relief."

"I have a special elixir in my cabin," the old man told her as he began closing his pillboxes and returning them to his different pockets. "I shall be pleased to minister to your friend."

The old man left shortly, and she and Eric continued with their breakfasts. She noticed a stout, benevolent-looking curé who passed by and offered both herself and Eric a warm smile.

She told Eric across the table, "You are right. It is a mixed group."

"Many of them are getting off at Gibraltar," he said.

"At least I think I've located someone to help Kingston with his seasickness," she said.

Eric laughed. "Your friend with the pills!"

"Samuel Jessup, Esquire," she told him.

"He must make his apothecary rich!"

"I don't doubt it," she said. "That was a sinister-looking East Indian who was seated by you."

The young man glanced at the empty spot where the Indian had sat and nodded. "Yes. Strange. It seems to me I've seen him somewhere before."

"He has a face one would not soon forget," she said.

"Perhaps I'll remember after a bit," Eric said, still busy with his breakfast.

After the first three days on the *Maria* the ocean became more tranquil and the weather warmer and with more sun. Betsy settled down to the routine of shipboard like a veteran, and Major Eric Walters proved very popular—especially with the middle-aged women returning to their husbands at colonial outposts and having marriageable daughters along. Even George Frederick Kingston began to enjoy the voyage.

Meeting Betsy amidships, he glanced nervously to left and right and confided in her, "That man, Samuel Jessup!"

She smiled. "What about him?"

"I swear he's daft!" the actor complained. "Never an hour passes but he is trying to force some pill or elixir onto me!"

"He wants to be sure you aren't seasick again!"

"I shall certainly be seasick if he keeps at this nonsense," Eric's pseudo father protested. "You shouldn't have set him on me!"

"I'm sorry. I only hoped some of his medicine would help."

"I'm perfectly fine now," Kingston said. "As long as his pills don't make me ill again. I try to drop them over the side, but he watches me like a hawk until I swallow them."

Betsy laughed. "Well, bear up. He'll be leaving us at Gibraltar."

"I may never last that long," Kingston mourned. "And I've been asked to organize a ship's concert and star in it. I plan to do scenes from *Hamlet*! I have always excelled as the melancholy Dane."

Eric had his own cause for laments. He confided in Betsy as they sat out on the deck that afternoon. "I ought to have spread the word we were married rather than saying we are engaged."

She sat up in the boat chair and asked, "Why?"

"Because I've two or three of those women with marriageable daughters after me, that's why!" he said gloomily.

"Surely you can defend yourself."

"It's not all that easy," he warned her. "That Mrs. Gaylin and her daughter, Patricia, trail me all over the boat. It is downright embarrassing."

There was a twinkle in her eyes. "You should be flattered."

"I'm anything but. That Gaylin girl has a face like a colt! You must have noticed."

Betsy nodded. "She seems to resent me."

"That's all part of it," Eric groaned. "And now she's asked me to turn the pages of her music when she plays the pianoforte at the concert Kingston is organizing."

"Surely that wouldn't compromise you."

"You never can be sure," he worried. "That mother of hers watches me all the time."

"Another week should see us in Marseilles."

"And the start of our work," he said. "I'm heartily sick of this voyage."

"I think Kingston is enjoying it."

"Because he's doing the ship's concert. He's putting as much effort into it as he would in a Drury Lane epic!"

She said, "At least it keeps him busy."

Eric scowled at the horizon of endless ocean and said, "Also I'm beginning to feel a little uneasy."

"Uneasy?"

"Yes."

"About what?"

He glanced at her with a worried look on his handsome face. "It's a kind of instinctive feeling with me. I can smell danger before it develops."

"You think we may be in danger here?"

"Yes."

"Some of Valmy's people?"

"Very likely. If they discovered we were traveling on this ship, it would be an ideal opportunity to deal with us. On a ship you are contained. Easy targets!"

She asked, "Whom do you suspect?"

"That Indian for one," he said, "I'm still sure I've seen him before."

"He moves about the ship like a wraith," she said. "He neither speaks to anyone or even looks at them."

"A strange individual," Eric agreed.

"What can we do?"

"Nothing, but wait. I may be wrong. I could be having a bad case of imagination. Let's hope so. Along the way I'm writing my impressions in a long letter which I'll mail to Black when we dock at Gibraltar."

The concert was held the night before the ship was to dock at Gibraltar, the reason being that a number of the passengers would be leaving at this port. A proud George Frederick Kingston had rounded up a dozen or so passengers with talents as varied as imitating bird whistles, singing sad ballads, and playing the pianoforte—plus he was contributing his readings from Shakespeare.

Because both men were involved with the concert, Betsy had to sit by herself. She had no sooner found a chair with a good view than a familiar figure slumped down in the chair next to her. It was none other than Samuel Jessup!

The sour-faced man told her, "I don't like concerts. They give me indigestion."

She suggested, "Then perhaps you shouldn't remain."

"It doesn't matter," he told her. And he took a silver box out of his jacket pocket. "I have two kinds of indigestion pills here. Would you like one?"

"I think not," she said.

"Better consider," he warned. "That Patricia Gaylin is going to play the pianoforte and sing. I heard her this afternoon practicing. She not only looks like a colt, she sounds like one."

"Mr. Jessup!" she reproved him.

"Your friend is a good actor," Samuel Jessup said.

"Yes. He is."

The old man stared at her. "Somehow he don't seem right to be your future father-in-law. Just not the type. You even have a different way of talking."

Hastily she said, "I can explain that. I was brought up by my mother. She was most particular about correct speech."

"I'll venture she was a regular lady?"

"Oh, yes! From a very good family!"

"That explains it," Samuel Jessup said, popping a pill into his mouth. "Your friend talks like an actor, but you can tell he isn't a real gent."

The dining salon filled quickly. The elderly curé in his white collar and black clerical habit came to sit on her other side. The only passenger not present was probably the sinister East Indian.

George Frederick Kingston in a blue jacket and checked trousers and boasting a huge crimson cravat came forward brightly and bowed to the audience. The murmuring among them ceased as the actor addressed them.

"Tonight we have a truly wonderful lot of talent, drawn from passengers and crew, for our ship's concert. We shall begin the evening with a hornpipe danced by Midshipman Murray to the accordion music of Midshipman Trent." He ushered the two young sailors on and stepped back as the performers were greeted with a loud applause.

The dance went well, and the music induced the right mood in the audience. Then an elderly man came on and did his bird imitations. Samuel Jessup groaned aloud during this and brought himself a number of reproachful glances from many seated near him. After that another sailor sang sea chanteys, followed by George Frederick Kingston doing his scenes from *Hamlet*. He was excellent, and when he ended he received a great ovation.

By this time the old curé on Betsy's right had begun to nod off. His chin had drooped and his eyes had closed and he was oblivious to what was going on. Samuel Jessup popped a large pill in his mouth and chewed it with crackling sounds. Then a nervous-looking Eric came out and placed some sheet music on the pianoforte and stood by it. The coltish Patricia Gaylin, looking angular and awkward in a gray evening gown, appeared uneasy before the audience. Her mother clapped loudly in the front row and offered encouraging bravos!

Patricia sat gingerly at the pianoforte and gazed fondly up at Eric with her wide-spaced colt's eyes and then set herself to the task of singing a doleful ballad and playing her own accompaniment. Not only did she seem to go on endlessly, but Eric apparently was having a hard time following her with the music. He made frantic turns and then turned the sheet back again as she came out with a strident, sour note.

Betsy could not watch. She felt dreadfully sorry for him. Finally it came to an end, and there was the usual applause. George Frederick Kingston came forward and thanked everyone and told them refreshments were to be served, so they were not to leave their seats.

Samuel Jessup at once stood up. "I never eat at this time of night," he announced firmly. "And it's time for my late medicine so I must go to my cabin."

Meanwhile the coltish Patricia had linked her arm about Eric's and was braying to him of the wonderful work he'd done in turning her music sheets.

Looking distraught, Eric told the girl, "Excuse me, I must attend to my fiancée."

He then came hastily to her and taking her by the arm, told her, "I need air more than I do food. Let us go outside."

She smiled. "If you like."

In a moment they were out on the deserted deck under a starlit sky. He led her far from the doors of the dining salon to a spot in the bow where they would not be apt to be bothered when the crowd came out from the concert.

He gave a sigh of relief. "I feel safe at last."

She smiled up at him. "You did very well."

"I was a bumbling fool! I turned the pages at all the wrong moments."

"No. I think it was Patricia who lost her place."

"Thanks," he said gratefully. "Her mother seemed to blame me."

"She and her mother will be leaving the ship tomorrow," Betsy said. "That ought to make you breathe easier."

"It will," he promised.

"There are some very pleasant other girls on board if you are interested," she said.

"You know better than that!"

She pointed out, "It would be perfectly natural for you to find one of them worth your time."

"This is not a pleasure trip," he said grimly. "Or don't you remember?"

"Your time is your own on board ship."

"I'm not even all that sure," he replied. "I still have a feeling of danger."

"Nothing has happened yet," she said, gazing up at his handsome face in the shadows.

"We can be thankful for that," he said. "Where is your pistol?"

"I have it locked in my bag."

He frowned. "That's not an ideal place for it should you be attacked."

Her eyebrows raised. "You don't expect me to carry it around with me on shipboard?"

"What if you were suddenly attacked?"

"I don't expect to be."

"That's no answer," he replied unhappily. "I can't seem to make you understand that danger can turn up anywhere—even on shipboard."

She said, "You could, of course, be right. But up to now it has been so uneventful."

"It can always change," he said earnestly. "I don't think you understand yet what you have let yourself in for."

"I know it will be risky after we get to Marseilles."

"It can be risky at any time," he said. "I'm worried for you, Betsy." He took her by surprise by grasping her by the arms and drawing her close to him. "I'm also in love with you."

"No, please!" she protested.

"I can't help it," he said unhappily, "I can't play games any longer. I love you, and I have from the moment of our first meeting."

"Eric!" she pleaded with him to let her go.

He brought her protests to an end by pressing his lips to hers. He kissed her passionately, and she found herself responding despite her determination not to be swayed. It was a reckless, dizzying moment of ecstasy as he held her close and their lips caressed.

"Betsy, my dearest!" he whispered in her ear.

Still in his embrace she said with a tiny moan, "Eric, you know this is wrong!"

"Wrong? How can it be?" His handsome face showed anguish as he gazed at her.

She looked up at him imploringly. "I hadn't planned it this way!"

"Does one plan love?"

"It's being here on the ship together!"

"No!" he said. "Not true. I have been in love with you since that first night in London. Don't you care for me at all?"

He was still holding her, and she leaned against him, tears filling her eyes, her heart pounding so wildly she was sure he must be ware of it. "I didn't want us to fall in love!"

"Because of a fantasy on your part!"

"Call it what you will! It has been real to me!"

"You hated the man you thought caused your brother's death. And when you found that I had been his superior officer, you hated me!"

"I couldn't help it!" she said piteously.

"You know different now," he said. "I was fond of Richard. I was wounded in the same advance in which he was killed. I was a victim as much as he!"

She listened to his tense words and knew that he was right. For too long she had built up this hatred inside her, fueled by the words of someone who had not known the truth about her brother's death. And she had made Eric the target of her desire for revenge.

In a whisper she said, "I understand now. But give me time. Let me work it out my own way."

"You may have all the time you like," he said gently. "Just tell me that you no longer hate me."

She looked up at him. "I no longer hate you, Eric."

"Thank you, my darling," he said. And he kissed her again tenderly.

She remained in his arms for a long, silent period. She somehow felt a great relief. She had known for long enough that she'd fallen in love with the handsome young major and he with her. She had tried to keep a barrier between them, though she was making herself unhappy. Now she had let the barrier down. Their love would have a chance to grow.

He saw her back to the door of her cabin, and they kissed each other good night. She prepared for bed in a happier state of mind than she'd known for a very long while. As a result she almost instantly fell into a deep sleep.

She wakened to darkness and the sound of her cabin door slowly creaking open. A shudder of fear raced through her, and she gazed at the door wide-eyed, not knowing what to do. Very slowly the door inched open, and then she saw a clawlike hand appear!

She screamed, and as she did so, the door was closed and the hand vanished. After a moment Eric and Kingston were knocking at her door.

Eric asked, "Betsy, are you all right?"

"Yes," she said faintly, rising and finding slippers and her robe.

"We heard your screams!" he went on.

"I know." She tied the robe around her and went to the door and opened it.

Eric and Kingston were standing out there in hastily donned trousers and tucked-in nightshirts. She saw there was a businesslike gun in Eric's hand.

He said, "What made you cry out?"

"Someone opened my cabin door. I saw a hand like a claw!" she said in a voice which had a tremor in it.

Kingston said, "Where did this intruder go?"

"I don't know," she said. "When I screamed, he slammed the door and ran off."

Eric looked grim. "That Indian, I'll wager!"

"I can't say!" she told him.

"We'll take a look around," Eric said.

"Be careful!" she cautioned him.

Eric told Kingston, "You stay close to her while I move around a little."

"Don't worry!" the actor said. "I'll be at her side every moment!"

Eric nodded and vanished.

Betsy stood there unhappily and then said, "I'm frightened for him going up there alone!"

"He'll be all right!" Kingston tried to placate her.

"I think we ought to go up there also," she said. "There may be more than one to deal with."

"Eric can defend himself," Kingston said worriedly.

"Please!" she said. "Let us go up!"

He looked unhappy, then shrugged. "If you like. I haven't any weapon!"

"Mine is locked in the bag," she said. "But there isn't time to get it. We can at least scream for help if we see him in trouble! Be there to watch out for him!"

"As you like!" the actor said.

She left the cabin and hurried along the passage to the steps leading to the deck. In a moment she was out in the open with Kingston behind her. She glanced around to see where Eric might be, but he was nowhere in sight.

"No sign of him," she whispered.

Behind her Kingston said, "He may be at the other end of the ship."

"We'll look thoroughly here first," she suggested.

"He may have even gone back down below."

"I doubt that," she said, keeping close to the shadows of the cabin wall and edging along slowly.

All at once she heard a thudding sound behind her. She quickly whirled around and to her consternation saw Kingston collapsed on the floor. Standing over him and smiling at her in a maniacal manner was the old curé! And he had a knife in his hand!

Chapter Eight

BETSY TRIED to scream, but terror had robbed her of the ability to cry out! Just a frustrated, choking sound escaped her lips. The old priest showed a wicked look of satisfaction on his broad lined face, and with the hand with the knife upraised, he straddled the prostrate body of Kingston and came after her!

She automatically turned and fled, racing for a gangway which led to the upper deck. She could hear him behind her, his scudding footsteps and his labored breathing! She kept on and climbed up a ladder to the level above her pursuer. As he came forward to climb up the ladder after her, she saw a strand of heavy rope swinging from the foremast. She grasped the rope and curled it about her and took a few rapid steps back! Then she swung ahead on the rope just as he came up over the edge of the cabin top!

Her slippered feet caught him full in the face, and he let out a cry, threw his hands up in the air, lost the knife, and fell back! He fell all the way to the deck below. And as he lay there, Eric appeared. He stood over the fallen priest, gun in hand.

"Up here!" she cried.

He glanced up. And then she saw she had done him a great disservice. For at the moment of his glancing up to look at her, the priest bounded up from the deck and wrested the gun from his hand. Eric, now aware of his danger, took a step back. The priest was pointing the gun at him, ready to fire!

She screamed again, certain that Eric would be killed. But at that very moment still another figure appeared. The turbaned Indian. He loomed up behind the crouching priest and seized him so suddenly that the gun went off wildly in the air! For a moment the Indian held the squirming priest in the air, and then with great contempt he hurled him over the side!

The shot and her screams had now attracted members of the crew, the captain, and some of the passengers. It was Eric who had to take the captain aside and quickly explain what had happened. While he was doing this, the crew was making efforts to locate the man in the water and rescue him.

The captain was stunned. "You are saying monsieur le curé was a criminal?"

"He was no priest at all," Eric explained. "Just a criminal in disguise."

"But this is most unusual," the captain protested. "I shall have to explain to our owners. Account for this man!"

Eric said disgustedly. "You will get no complaints from any religious order. This man was in the employ of an evil group."

Betsy was at his side. "Kingston is hurt," she said. And she led him to the actor.

Kingston was sitting up now with a dazed expression on his face. "Blighter hit me over the head with something!"

"Are you badly hurt?" Eric asked, helping him up.

"No," Kingston said, rubbing his head gingerly. "Sorry I let you down, Betsy."

"It was no fault of yours," she said.

Eric told her, "You did a lovely job of protecting yourself by kicking him. Then I almost let him kill us both!"

"My fault! I screamed at you!" she reminded him.

"The Indian saved us!" Eric said. And then suddenly realizing, he asked, "Where is the Indian?"

"Back on the other side of the deck," she said.

"Let's find him," Eric said, taking her arm. The three went back to the other side of the ship. The captain was busy directing the crew in their rescue efforts while the passengers still on deck watched with awe.

Seeing Eric, the captain spread his hands and said, "It is no use! We cannot locate him!"

"Too many sharks in these waters," Eric said grimly. "You may as well give up."

The captain nodded and then leaned over the side and shouted to the men in the longboat in Italian. They slowly headed the longboat back to the vessel. It was then that the Indian appeared and silently handed Eric back his gun.

Eric took the gun and stared at the tall Indian. "You saved my life! I'm sure I know you from somewhere."

In a deep voice the Indian intoned, "Raj Singh. I was a member of the secret service at the time of your enlisting."

"Of course!" Eric gasped. "I only met you a couple of times. That's why I couldn't remember clearly where I'd seen you."

"You were extremely careless," the Indian reprimanded him.

"I was," Eric admitted forlornly. "This young lady and I owe you our lives."

"You would do better to thank Mr. Black," Raj Singh said.

"Black!" Betsy gasped. "Did he place you on board to watch over us?"

The Indian nodded.

Kingston said, "And we thought you might be after us!"

"My fault again!" Eric apologized. "I should have known you."

"It was perhaps better that you did not," the Indian said. "I regret I had to act violently. But it was too late to have any choice."

Eric said, "You may be sure the captain will lay no charges against you. That fellow had a gun pointed ready to kill me and then this lady."

"If you will excuse me," the Indian bowed. And he walked away from them.

Betsy watched after his retreating figure. "It seems that Felix Black had some doubts about our safety on board."

"He was right," Kingston said.

"And I surely needed some protection," Eric said. He turned to her. "We'd both have been dead if Raj Singh hadn't appeared.

And no doubt he'd have gotten back to Kingston and finished him after that. Our curé was going to be a busy priest, finishing off three of us in one night."

Betsy shuddered. "I wonder what he thought as he went over the side."

"No time to be morbid," Eric told her. "Let's go back to our cabins and try and get some rest."

Of course it was a vain struggle. She wasn't able to sleep. The unbelievable events of the night kept repeating themselves to her. And soon it was dawn, and the others were getting up. She rose and washed and dressed.

The dining salon was buzzing with gossip of what had taken place the night before and anticipation at reaching the port of Gibraltar within the hour. The excited matrons repeated many different versions of what had happened, most of them far wrong. It was known that Eric and Betsy had been mixed up in the melee, for they were greeted with curious stares.

Samuel Jessup was in his usual place at the table beside her. The old man popped a pill in his mouth and said, "Too bad I took my sleeping tablets last night, or I might have enjoyed the excitement."

"I'd say you were better out of it," she told him.

"From what I've heard, that priest was no priest at all," he said.

"No. He was an impostor," she said.

Jessup nodded. "I tried to talk to him about medicine used in the monasteries, and he turned his back on me. No wonder; he couldn't have known anything about it."

She finished breakfast and went out on deck in time to enjoy the *Maria's* graceful entrance into the sheltered harbor of the fortress town with its great towering cliffs.

The *Maria* was scheduled to remain in harbor overnight, unloading and loading. The harbor was a forest of masts, with the flags of many nations hanging from them. Gibraltar was a free port and attracted shipping from all over the world. The calm blue water of the harbor and its protected location made it a regular stop for many ships.

It had been agreed among them that they would remain on board the ship. There was little to see in Gibraltar, and it might expose them to additional danger if they disembarked. The three stood in conference by the railing as the first of the passengers to leave moved along the gangway from the ship to the docks.

Betsy said, "I see Mrs. Gaylin and Patricia leaving."

Eric smiled. "They haven't even spoken to me since last night. They're convinced I'm some kind of criminal."

"Better for you," Kingston said, grinning broadly.

"Yes. At least I'm no longer regarded as suitable husband material."

"We're all lucky to be alive this morning," Betsy said with a sigh.

"Indeed, that is true," Kingston agreed.

"What I'd like to know is whether he intended leaving the ship here? Or if he had any confederates coming on board to meet him."

She gave a tiny shudder. "That thought doesn't appeal to me."

"We must try to consider everything," was Eric's warning.

The discussion continued, and then Raj Singh came to join them. He strode up to them in his solemn, deliberate way. He said, "You are remaining on the ship?"

Eric nodded. "Yes. We thought it might be wise."

"I'm sure Mr. Black would agree," the Indian said.

Betsy spoke up. "We were wondering about the curé. Was he booked to leave the ship here or at Marseilles?"

"Marseilles," the Indian said. "I have already had that information from the ship's purser."

"So it is unlikely that he has confederates here," Eric said.

Raj Singh studied him with a certain arrogance. "I am surprised that you still do not understand that Valmy has his spies everywhere."

"It's time I should realize it," Eric said unhappily. "I should never underestimate him."

"It does not matter," the Indian said impassively. "I shall be leaving the ship here. My work is done. You will need me no more."

Eric said, "We shan't feel safe after what happened."

"I see no need for your concern," the Indian said in his deep voice.

Betsy assured him, "We shall feel lost without you. And at first we didn't understand. We'd decided you were against us."

The Indian revealed one of his rare smiles. "I hope I may have proven myself."

Betsy said, "You are a brave man and a strong one."

"Thank you," Raj Singh bowed. "If you have any mail you wish to send back to England, I shall be happy to look after it for you."

"I have some reports for Black," Eric said. "To which I must add what happened last night."

"I can wait until until you have finished the report," the Indian said.

"Why are you leaving us at Gibraltar?" Betsy asked.

"Mr. Black's orders are to leave the ship here," the Indian said.

Eric asked, "Are you working solely for Felix Black now?"

Raj Singh nodded. "I belong to Mr. Black's private police force."

"And a good thing you do," Eric praised him. "And now I'd better go and get that report in order for you to take."

The *Maria* sailed from Gibraltar the following morning at dawn. The number of passengers was greatly reduced, and the relatively short sail to Marseilles now took on the appearance of being an uneventful one.

The night before they docked in Marseilles, Kingston arranged another short concert. It was devoted mostly to his readings from Shakespeare. And he induced Betsy to join him in a scene from *The Taming of the Shrew.* She enjoyed memorizing a few lines of the wanton Kate's role so that Kingston could offer a stirring performance of Petruchio. Eric applauded them from the audience

After the concert ended, Kingston remained in the dining salon to receive the plaudits of the passengers. He enjoyed being the hero of the occasion and also welcomed the food which was served. She and Eric preferred to go out on deck for a stroll.

As they walked arm in arm along the deserted deck, she said, "What a gorgeous night!"

"I know," he said. "Such a magnificent show of stars overhead."

She gave him a grim smile. "Not much like the other night—with death threatening us at every turn."

"I could sense that danger developing," the young man at her side told her. "But I entirely missed where it was going to come from."

"At least that is over," she said with a sigh of relief.

"Until we reach Marseilles," he reminded her. "Tomorrow the real task will begin."

"I know. It frightens me."

Eric gave her a thin smile. "At least that's a small improvement. You're beginning to realize this is not all a pleasant game."

"The other night brought me of age."

They halted by the rail, and he gazed at her with loving eyes. "And you have also reached the age of wisdom regarding us."

"I hope so," she said quietly.

"When this chase is at an end, there should be no barrier between us," he said, holding her hands in his.

"My hatred is gone," she told him. "It was wrong of me to let my grief be twisted into a senseless rage at someone else."

"You were misinformed," he said. "Now you know the truth."

She looked up at him. "Now I realize how lucky I have been."

"Lucky?"

"Yes," she said. "You might have been killed along with Richard, rather than merely being wounded. And I might never have come to know you."

"Betsy!" he said with emotion as they embraced.

They remained on deck for a while longer. Then George Frederick Kingston came toward them, a trifle drunk and extremely happy. He demanded, "Young man, what are you doing with my Kate?"

Eric laughed. "Presuming to make love to her!"

"A fine kettle of fish!" Kingston complained with comic overtones. "After I have just made my reputation by my romancing her on stage! You undo me, sir!"

"You forget," Eric said. "Your role in our little drama is that of my father. We must be more careful to stay in character."

"Quashed!" Kingston lamented. "Completely ruined by a younger man with more appeal. Ah, well, that is the way of the world. What must be, must be!" And laughing, he placed his arms around their shoulders, and they all headed to their cabins.

The next morning the *Maria* entered the huge harbor of Marseilles. Long stretches of wharves and cargo docks extended out into the water to take care of the hundreds of vessels of all kinds anchored there. Betsy, standing with the other two in the bow of the ship, was awed by the busy scene. She had never known a harbor so large and bustling.

Eric smiled at her and said, "This has become the second most important city in France. And the greatest port."

Betsy said, "It must have grown greatly since the revolution."

"It has," the young man said. "And it is a city where Napoleon once lived. And where he is still a hero."

"He told me of his early days here," she agreed with a smile. "He brought his family here when he was only a mere army captain."

George Frederick Kingston was studying the city beyond the harbor with its white buildings, green hills, and blue cliffs. The veteran actor said, "That looks like a church on that high cliff!"

"It is," Eric told him. "The church of Notre Dame de la Garde. And not far from it there are the dungeons of the Chateau d'If, where so many were imprisoned and died without ever seeing the sun again."

"Grim business, the revolution!" the actor commented.

"Marseilles has a mixture of every race on earth," Eric said. "And the best bouillabaisse, fish soup, in the world. But do not be deceived, behind its easygoing surface it is a city of massive criminal activity."

Betsy asked him, "Has Mr. Black given us specific instructions about what we're to do?"

"Yes," Eric said. "When we reach the hotel, we will have a briefing session."

Now there came the frantic bustle of disembarking from the vessel which Betsy had come to enjoy. The passengers scattered in various directions, and Eric found them an open carriage which took them up from the docks through colorful winding streets to an inn picturesquely situated on a hill overlooking the harbor.

An elderly man with a gray walrus moustache greeted them. Arrangements had been made in advance, and he now showed them to their rooms. Once again Betsy had a room adjoining that of the two men. Her windows looked out on a garden at the rear rather than having a harbor view. But the room was clean and neat. Only after they had eaten in the good-sized dining hall of the inn did they gather in Eric's room for the promised briefing.

Holding a paper, he addressed Betsy and Kingston who sat in chairs before him. He said, "It is Felix Black's wish that Betsy and you should call on Mademoiselle LaFlenche. She still lives in the family villa, quite alone with servants. She rarely sees anyone, but you must somehow reach her. He suggests that you pass yourself off as father and daughter. And that you, Kingston, are a retired merchant who did business with LaFlenche—buying shipments of dates and oranges from him for the London trade."

Kingston nodded. "I can manage that, old chap. Just so long as she doesn't ask too many questions."

Eric turned to her and said, "You can be greatly interested in the city. And you might casually mention that someone told you Jean LaFlenche looked remarkably like Napoleon. See what her reaction may be."

"If we get to her at all," Betsy said.

"That will be the problem," he agreed.

She asked, "What will you do?"

"While you and Kingston are trying to locate Mademoiselle LaFlenche, I shall be visiting his office and also calling on his lawyer and doctor. It will take the entire afternoon. We will meet here for dinner and a general discussion."

Betsy smiled. "It doesn't sound so dangerous."

"But it could be," Eric warned her again.

She wore her white bonnet and pale blue dress, and George Frederick Kingston decided on a dignified black jacket and gray pantaloons. They hired a carriage to take them to the villa and wait for them there. The driver knew the way and took them through the wealthier residential area of the city. Here it was all gardens, giant shade trees, and fine houses discreetly set in from the road.

When they reached the entrance road to the villa LaFlenche, they got out of the carriage and told the driver to wait on the roadway. Then they walked in the tree-lined narrower driveway to the front door of the white villa. A knock on the door brought a spare, anxious-looking woman in maid's cap and uniform.

She stood warily in the doorway and asked, "What is it?"

In perfect French Betsy said, "My father is a former business partner of the late Monsieur LaFlenche. He has come from

London to pay his respects to the daughter of his old friend. And I have come along as I'm more proficient in French."

The maid glared at them. "Mademoiselle does not receive visitors!"

"We are not mere visitors," Betsy protested. "My father was a friend of her father's."

"It does not matter," the maid said firmly. "My mistress entertains no company!" And she withdrew and slammed the door in their faces.

Kingston turned to her bleakly and putting on his black top hat again said, "Well, I'd say that is the end of that!"

"It can't be!" she protested.

"What can we do? The maid says the woman will not see anyone!"

Betsy's pretty face was troubled under the white bonnet. She glanced around. "There must be some way to reach her."

"We can't break down the door," the actor told her. "It would give a bad impression."

She was thinking. She said, "Let us walk around to the rear of the house."

They did and as Kingston pointed out, "No help in this direction. There's a high brick wall attached to the rear of the house which closes in the big garden area."

Betsy was holding up her skirt a little so she could move through the brush and grass more quickly. She said, "I'll be much surprised if there isn't an opening somewhere in this wall."

"No doubt with an iron gate," the old actor said. "This is a difficult woman to see!"

"That makes it more interesting," was her reply as she continued to move on ahead of him. And after awhile they did come to an iron gate just as Kingston had predicted.

"You see! What did I tell you?" The actor was delighted to have been proven right.

Betsy was staring at it. Then she said, "It is surely agate. But I see no lock on it."

Kingston examined the tall gate and in surprise declared, "You're right! It's not locked!" And to prove his words, he easily moved it inward.

Betsy and he entered the garden area. It was a place of many colored flower beds with a fountain in the middle. She found herself amazed at the elegance of the quiet place.

"Flowers the equal of any London park," was Kingston's comment.

Suddenly Betsy halted, for ahead she saw a woman in black bonnet and dress kneeling by one of the flower beds selecting some blooms for a bouquet. Betsy tugged at her companion's arm and whispered, "Ahead! We must catch her before she goes!"

Kingston nodded and said a quiet, "Righto!" And he let her lead the way to the woman they were seeking.

They reached the woman just as she stood up with some yellow roses in her hands. Only then did she see them and let the roses drop. She looked as if she were going to turn and run away. Kingston at once doffed his hat again and knelt down to gather the roses up hastily and present them to the stricken lady.

Betsy urged her, "Please do not be afraid of us."

Mademoiselle LaFlenche was tall and thin. Her face was stern, and her dark hair was graying. She stared at them in dismay and demanded, "How did you get in here?"

"By the gate," Betsy said. "It was not locked."

The woman's thin lips worked nervously. "What do you want-here?"

"Just to talk to you for a moment," Betsy said.

The woman frowned. "What do you wish to talk to me about?"

Betsy smiled again. "We have come a long way. From London, mademoiselle. And we've made the journey because my father knew your parent and carried on a number of business transactions with him."

Mademoiselle said stiffly, "Then let that be an end to it. You have been misinformed. I see no one."

In friendly fashion Betsy told the thin woman, "You are seeing us, mademoiselle?"

"Because you are intruders!" the woman snapped. "You took advantage of a careless caretaker allowing the gate to remain unlocked."

"I regret we were forced to intrude on you, mademoiselle," she apologized. "But there seemed no other way. We have come such a distance. My father so wanted to pay his good wishes to the daughter of his old friend."

The woman had drawn herself up suspiciously. "My father had no English friends! He hated the English!"

"My father was an exception," Betsy persisted. "You see my father was one of the few Englishmen who had a high regard for the late Emperor Napoleon!"

The thin woman was surprised by this statement. She gave the sedately dressed Kingston a scorching glance. "You were an admirer of the Emperor?"

"Ah, yes, a truly great man!" Kingston said. "Your father and I often discussed him over a glass of wine. That was before the wars began!"

"I doubt if you speak the truth," the thin woman sniffed. "But if you shared my father's high regard for Napoleon, I can only think you were as misguided as he was."

This came as a shock. The woman sounded angry and bitter— as if she had hated the Emperor! Betsy said, "I'm sure we are not making ourselves clear. We much liked Napoleon."

"So did my poor fool of a father!" Mademoiselle said angrily. "And it cost him more than half his fortune! Attempting to restore him to power! Then all was lost at Waterloo!"

Betsy said, "It is evident you did not share your fathers patriotism for the Emperor and all for which he stood."

"It is better now with Louis," the thin woman said.

"But your father so resembled Napoleon," Betsy said. "That may have had something to do with his interest in him."

"It quite turned his head!" Mademoiselle exclaimed with anger. "People would approach him and say, but you are an absolute double of Napoleon! And my father would enjoy it!"

"You feel that was wrong of him?" Betsy asked.

"It was stupid of him," the woman snapped. "Made him an easy victim of those who were trying to bring Napoleon back. Much of my fathers fortune financed the return from Elba."

Kingston said, "But you cannot be bitter. They are both dead now. Both your father and Napoleon!"

Mademoiselle gave him another grim look. "I think my poor fool of a father began to feel ill when word reached him that Napoleon had been stricken with a dread malady. I swear my doting father decided that he was suffering from the same thing!"

Betsy pretended deep sympathy. "He died at the same time as the emperor?"

"He died before him," the thin woman said. "But in the same manner. I think my father willed himself to die. He could not bear to live on without his double. And that is why I had him buried privately without any period of mourning! I hated my father for his madness!"

"I'm sorry, mademoiselle," Betsy said. "We did not mean to touch on tender feelings."

"You have!" the daughter of LaFlenche said sternly. "So now you know the whole sad story and why I have no interest in your parent's mewling about his love for my father and for Napoleon."

"We are truly sorry, dear lady," George Frederick Kingston said in his best manner. "We had no idea what your feeling in the matter might be."

"Well you know now!" she snapped at him.

"And we will impose on you no longer," Betsy said with haste. "Pardon us for opening your grief once again!"

"You forced yourself on me! I bid you leave!" the thin woman said arrogantly, pointing toward the gate.

Kingston bowed. "On the double, mademoiselle!" And he took Betsy by the arm and hurried her out, murmuring, "Let us get away quickly! I have a feeling there are fierce dogs tied up somewhere, and they'll be unleashed on us!"

"You mustn't be so timid!" Betsy remonstrated with him.

But they had barely let themselves out and closed the gate when the angry barking of dogs could be heard in the distance, and a moment later two large hounds appeared and came angrily to the gate, barking and springing up at it!

Kingston eyed the ferocious animals weakly and told her, "At least I was right this time!"

"So you were!" she said, stunned by his prediction coming true.

They made their way back around the fence and out to the road where the carriage waited in the sun. The driver had fallen asleep and had to be wakened and directed to take them back to the inn.

As they rode through the warm flower-scented streets, she asked Kingston, "What did you make of her?"

"Sour spinster!" he said promptly as he sat beside her in the slowly moving open carriage. "A proper vixen!"

"Beyond that?"

"She hated Napoleon and her father's interest in him."

Betsy nodded. "She made that clear."

"Crystal clear!" the actor commented.

"If she was acting, she did very well."

"I think she told us the truth."

"Perhaps," Betsy agreed. "In that case it would explain the strange events surrounding her father's illness. She had always resented his likeness to Napoleon. And finding him dying at the same time as his idol and in the same fashion was too much for her to accept."

The actor said, "That sums it up. She had been fed up with Napoleon and her father being compared to him."

"So she shut him off from friends and visitors and let him die alone. There could have been no great love between those two."

"No love in her for anyone. Mark me!" Kingston said.

"And to avoid any odious comparisons after his death, she had him buried privately," Betsy went on. "It's strange, but it all makes sense when you understand her reasons."

"Robs the whole business of any mystery."

Betsy nodded. "The man who looked more like Napoleon than possibly anyone else had a daughter who resented the likeness and who actually hated the late emperor."

"Be easy for her," the little actor said. "She certainly didn't like us either."

Betsy sat back with a sigh. "I wonder what Eric will say?"

"He'll give us marks for getting to see the woman at all. Wouldn't have if you hadn't stayed at it!"

"It wasn't all that hard."

"Still it needed wits and determination," Kingston said.

She smiled at him. "At least you were right about the dogs."

He chuckled. "The place had the air of a house with ugly dogs guarding it. Lucky for us they were locked up somewhere while we were talking to her."

"She likely had them locked up purposely while she was picking flowers. Those great angry beasts were not pets by any means."

"True," Kingston agreed.

"So we have come up with strong evidence that the whole fable of LaFlenche taking Napoleon's place was wild fantasy."

The actor sighed. "Mr. Black will be sorry to hear that. Ends our project before it begins."

She gave him a sharp glance. "Not really."

"I don't follow."

"There may be someone else impersonating Napoleon. It is not only whether he is actually alive or dead, though that is important, but if we're dealing with an impostor in Valmy's hands, we must unmask him."

"We wouldn't know Valmy if we met him!" the actor protested.

"But we will when the time comes," she said. "Right now we want to match our results with Eric's and see what we have managed."

"Very little, in my opinion," Kingston said.

They reached the inn, but Eric had not returned. This made her a little uneasy. She knew how much she had come to care for the dashing young army major turned secret agent. If he came to any harm, it would be another grim ordeal for her. She had never dreamed that one day she would find herself in love with the man she'd blamed for her brother's death. But fate had played a cruel prank on her.

She hoped there would be no such cruel jests to face. She could scarcely believe she was the same girl who had fled from her quiet home in the country to seek her fortune in London. Already her mother and burly stepfather were faint characters of her past. She could not imagine herself ever returning to such a life, nor ever marrying the lecherous old Lord Dakin!

Now she was a puppet of a mysterious man who had for many years charted the movement of the British secret service. A shadowy figure who had won great battles for England before they were ever fought. An unknown, sinister figure remaining in the shadows of the Foreign Office like a giant black spider, manipulating his agents. And even now as he found himself disgraced and ill, he had embarked on a last great enterprise. And she was part of it!

Her reverie was ended by the sound of knocking on her room door and the welcome voices of Eric and Kingston in an exchange outside. She swung the door open with a smile and let the two men in.

"I was so worried about you!" she confessed to Eric.

"That pleases me," he said, and he bent close and briefly kissed her. Then he moved impatiently to the middle of the room and removing his white gloves said, "Kingston has given me a strange account of your afternoon."

"We were not entirely successful," she said.

Eric stood staring at her, his gloves in hand. "You did get to see the woman though?"

"Yes."

"That was clever of you."

"But she proved a disappointment," Betsy said. "She hated Napoleon and seemingly also her father because of his resemblance to him and his admiration for the Emperor."

Eric looked amused. "I have heard the story from Kingston. Pray sit down and recite it for me as you saw it."

She took a chair and went over the events of their odd meeting with the sour woman. She ended with, "I cannot help but think that all the secrecy surrounding the death of her father was the result of her ugly feelings. I do not think there was any mystery to the death or burial. And I do not think an ailing LaFlenche was spirited away to take the place of Napoleon on Saint Helena."

"Aha!" Eric said, slapping his gloves against his empty hand.

Kingston, who had stood quietly in the background through her recital, now spoke up, saying, "In my opinion Miss Betsy has summed it all up nicely."

"Very neatly!" Eric said with a hint of grimness.

She stared at him. "I'm not sure I follow you."

Eric went on, "You see, the trouble is that your findings don't jibe with my discoveries at all."

"In what way are they different?" she asked.

"In almost every case," he said. "I either found my informants vague or they admitted there was something very strange about the death of LaFlenche. His doctor was no help."

She felt her cheeks warm. "You are saying that I did not do my task well?"

"I talked with the lawyer," Eric said. "He told me much the same story as Mademoiselle LaFlenche told you. Then I went on to interview a business rival. An enemy is often a better source in these cases than a friend."

"And?" she said tensely.

"He told me that LaFlenche had been spirited away. He even spoke of some sailors who claimed they had been on the very boat on which LaFlenche sailed."

"How can that be?" Kingston demanded.

"Did you find anyone who could actually swear seeing LaFlenche placed on a vessel?" she asked.

Eric shook his head grimly. "It wasn't that easy. I have not yet found any actual witnesses to the event. But I have found many who are suspicious and who have heard the rumors of the transfer."

Betsy asked, "And what would you say that means?"

Eric was very solemn as he told her, "I think it means that we have hit on something here. And that Mademoiselle played her role well when she filled you with a pack of lies!"

Chapter Nine

BETSY WAS stunned by the vehemence of the young man who was her fellow secret agent. After a moment's hesitation she said, "So you consider my conclusions completely wrong?"

His tone warmed and he nodded. "Unhappily, my dear Betsy, that is the case. I had it on the word of both the lawyer and the doctor that Mademoiselle LaFlenche was as staunch a supporter of Napoleon as her father."

Kingston raised his eyebrows. "She is an excellent actress then!"

"She very well can be," Eric said calmly. "She knows she is part of a major plan on which a great deal hinges. Her one aim was to throw you off the scent."

Betsy said, "Then you believe that her father was sent to Saint Helena to take Napoleon's place and thus allow the emperor to escape."

"I would swear that the body which rests in that lonely grave on the cliffs of Saint Helena is that of Jean LaFlenche."

"What else can be done to prove this?" George Frederick Kingston wished to know.

Eric said, "LaFlenche was a partner in a shipbuilding company located just outside the city limits. The surviving partner is one Pierre Bartel, and I have arranged through the lawyer of the LaFlenche family to visit Bartel at his office tomorrow. I think it might be an occasion when we could all make a visit together. We will resume our usual roles."

Betsy said, "Do you think this Bartel will be helpful?"

"No," Eric replied. "He will undoubtedly try to disprove the rumors concerning his dead partner. But he may give us some information without realizing it. I wish to make him squirm a little under questioning."

Kingston said, "Mademoiselle LaFlenche surely did not react in that fashion."

"That was perhaps our fault," Betsy told the actor.

"No," Eric said. "You actually had the most difficult assignment. The woman is loyal to her father's memory and to Bonaparte."

"How long do you expect to remain here?" she asked the young agent.

"I'm waiting for some word as to where Valmy may have the former Emperor in hiding," he told her. "And I also have one delicate task to look after."

"What is that?" Betsy said.

He gave her a knowing glance. "I must have a private look at the tomb which holds LaFlenche's coffin."

Kingston looked a trifle upset. "You expect to find something there?"

"I shall be most pleased if I find nothing," Eric told him. "I shall make a raid on the tomb one night very soon. You and Betsy will assist me by acting as watchmen while I enter the tomb."

"Just so long as you don't expect me to visit the regions of the dead," the actor said.

Betsy wanted to know, "Where is the cemetery?"

"Located behind a church in the middle of the city," Eric said. "But it is not in an area frequented much at night. We shall make our visit when the good residents are asleep."

She said, "Won't they be expecting some such move?"

"Possibly," he agreed. "That is why timing is most important in the venture. They might expect us to go there tonight, so we will stay away."

"A rum game!" Kingston grumbled.

"Felix Black expects results from us," Eric told them. "And I intend to see that he gets them."

They had dinner together in the dining hall of the inn, and Kingston elected to remain there over a bottle of wine with the innkeeper. It was Eric's suggestion that he and Betsy should go farther afield.

"It is a port city," he said. "There are bound to be a lot of interesting bistros and cabarets along the waterfront."

Her eyes brightened. "I would enjoy that. Will we be safe?"

"I can think of no unusual risk," he said.

"Then let us go!" she smiled.

They found a carriage to take them down the cobbled, winding streets to the waterfront. Their driver pointed out a café almost directly on the docks which he said offered good entertainment and would not be too rough for a woman's visit.

The rousing singing and accordion music could be heard as they approached the two-story red brick building. At its entrance there were two or three drunken sailors engaged in a loud debate. A torch set in an iron fixture lighted the Café de Paris. When the sailors saw Betsy, they halted their arguing to stare at her with curious eyes.

She at once began to feel apprehensive about their adventure and to worry if she had been wrong in encouraging Eric to take her out for the evening. The café was dark except for a lighted stage and crowded. Waiters rushed about with trays of drinks, and there was loud shouting and laughter! On the stage a much painted young woman in a revealing gown was singing a suggestive comedy song!

"Monsieur wishes a table?" They were greeted by a host so small they could hear him before they saw him. Then he looked up at them from the shadows below with a smile on his huge face. He was a dwarf!

Eric nodded to the little man. "Yes. Find us a corner where we will not be too much noticed." And he gave him a generous tip.

The dwarf, totally bald, and with a round moon face on his misshapen body, grinned broadly. "It will be no problem, monsieur!" And he at once led them past many filled tables in the room to a small empty one within reaching distance of the stage.

Eric accepted the table and ordered some wine. He grimaced at her across the table. "It is not ideal but as good as any."

Her uneasiness grew as she glanced around to see that the noisy, crowded room was filled mostly with men. The few women who were in there were clearly prostitutes, and even the girl entertainer had all the marks of a woman of the streets.

She said, "I'm not sure we were wise coming here."

"We cannot remain contained in our inn," he said.

"But there must be places more quiet," Betsy suggested.

"They would lack the color of here."

"I could well do without this sort of atmosphere," she told him.

The bald dwarf came back carrying a tray in his tiny hands. His arms and legs were weirdly short in relation to the rest of his small body. He lacked the grace of a midget with his oversized head and his odd body proportions. He leered at her as he served her, making her more nervous.

Eric sipped his wine. "It's very good," he said.

She tried hers and told him, "That little man terrifies me."

"The dwarf? He's no different from the average. You must have seen such people before."

"Not as malevolent looking as this one," she worried. "He seems to exude evil."

He laughed. "You're allowing yourself to become needlessly alarmed."

"I hope so," she said, sipping at her wine.

"We are about to have a change of entertainment," Eric said as the girl singer left the stage to much applause.

Now a soldier in full military uniform and fur hat marched on stage. He wore a red jacket with a wide white leather band and belt and blue trousers stuffed in tall black boots. There was a sword dangling at his side as he came stage center and bowed to the audience.

The house at once went wild and began to boisterously sing the "Marseillaise." The soldier had a trim black moustache and a bronzed, stern face with a scar on the left cheek which suggested a saber scar.

"Listen to them!" she marveled.

"The place is full of Napoleon admirers," Eric agreed, looking around. "The spirit of the emperor still runs high in France and especially here in Marseilles. It was a regiment from here which first sang the song and made it so popular!"

Now the soldier was joined on the stage by the grinning bald dwarf in a blue cockade hat slightly askew on his huge head. He was wearing a too large red jacket which almost reached the ground on him to mock the uniform worn by the soldier. And in his hands he held a full-sized sword. His appearance was the cue for the audience to stop singing and start cheering.

She whispered to her companion, "They're evidently familiar to the people here."

"Yes," he said. "They are more popular than the singer."

Now the tall soldier and the dwarf faced each other a yard or two apart, and each drew his sword. It was a grotesque scene. In the glare of the gas footlights the two moved warily, and then the dwarf lunged at the soldier with his sword. He very nearly caught the tall man off guard. The soldier at once struck back, and the dwarf jumped neatly aside to the delight of the audience.

It was a serious struggle between the two. The dwarf was a surprisingly adept fencer considering his size and strength. And he seemed remarkably agile. When the soldier lunged at him with his weapon, the dwarf was invariably not there! They slowed their play and parried for a little with neither one nor the other seeming to have the advantage.

"The dwarf is a genius with the sword!" Eric said in amazement.

"I cannot believe it," she agreed. "Surely his opponent must be deliberately giving him a chance to score!"

"I think not! He seems to be having a hard time in merely protecting himself!"

And it was true. The dwarf seemed tireless, and whenever the soldier let down his guard for a second, the little man toddled forward and shot the sword at him with a lightning thrust. The crowd grew more excited as the curious battle went on, and many were shouting out offers of bets on one or the other contestant.

At last the soldier parried with the little man in a long, difficult exchange. Almost without warning the dwarf made a swift movement with his sword and disarmed his opponent. The soldier's weapon flew through the air and fell onto the stage a distance from him.

This was the signal for a new uproar. Men stood on chairs and tables cheering, and the few women in the place were also lifted up onto the tables where one of them had drawn up her skirts to reveal her shapely legs as she indulged in a wild dance of victory!

The dwarf bowed solemnly to his audience, and then the soldier also accepted the homage of the riotous patrons. The entertainment continued with the accordionist and two violinists taking the stage and playing lively airs.

"What did you make of that?" Eric asked her with a smile.

"A most unusual show," she said.

"We'd have missed it if we'd remained at the inn."

"But perhaps we'd have been safer."

"Are you that nervous?" he asked.

She gave him a reproving look. "You are always the one preaching caution, and yet tonight you seem unduly reckless."

He studied her with loving eyes, and reaching out took her hand in his and said, "Perhaps it is because I'm so much enjoying your company."

"I hope the evening will end as pleasantly as it has begun," she said.

"Do not be a prophet of gloom!" he said.

"All the same I shall feel better when we are safe at the inn," she said. "You should have had the carriage wait."

"I suggested it, but he wasn't interested," he said. "So we'll simply have to find another."

"Carriages will be difficult to find as it gets later," she worried.

"I'm sure we'll locate one," Eric told her.

Reluctantly she allowed him to order more wine. The dwarf did not serve them this time. An elderly waiter took their order and brought them a second bottle of wine. The place never emptied. As soon as one group left, another came. At last it was after midnight, and she prevailed on her escort to leave.

"If we are to be at that shipyard in the morning, we really must go," she warned him.

"Very well," Eric said good-naturedly, his handsome face flushed from the wine. He waved to the elderly waiter and when he came over settled their bill.

They again had to struggle to get out of the crowded cabaret. Men whistled at her as she passed, and some of the street girls made sarcastic comments on her appearance and clothes. She was relieved to emerge in the fresh air of the pleasantly warm night. But as she had predicted, there were no carriages in sight.

Eric refused to be upset. "One should come along soon. The people coming here must have transport."

At his side she suggested, "Most of the men in there are sailors who have walked up from the docks. And the girls are street walkers who live in the district."

"You're probably right," Eric said, concerned for the first time. "Take my arm and we'll walk toward the city as quickly as we can."

She pressed close to the tall, handsome Eric as they made their way along the narrow sidewalks. She had never known a darker night, and the people whom they encountered along the way were anything but prepossessing. A drunken sailor and his girl lurched out of a doorway unexpectedly giving them a scare. Further on a snoring seaman lay stretched out on the sidewalk. A short distance from there a group of drunken, noisy sailors came staggering by and shouted foul words at her over their shoulders.

Eric gave her a worried glance as they kept walking on briskly. He said, "I'm beginning to see you were right. This whole experience has been a mistake."

"There is an evil atmosphere here," she said with a tiny shudder.

"I cannot understand why there aren't any carriages," he grumbled.

"They could be afraid to come here late at night. They might be targets for robbery."

"You're probably right," he said. "I have exposed you to needless danger."

"And yourself as well," she noted.

"I'm not worried about myself," he said looking around in the shadows as they kept walking. "I'm concerned about you."

She said no more. It was evident that he had recovered from his wine drinking and was now soberly seeing their plight as she had from the first. It seemed wrong to continue reminding him of his error. The thing now was to reach the inn safely.

Eric halted with a troubled look on his handsome face. "I hate to say it. But I think we made a wrong turn."

"Where?" she asked in dismay.

"I think back a distance," he said, "I'm almost sure we're going in the wrong direction now. If we keep on this way, we'll be circling back to the docks."

"Anything but that!"

He sighed. "I'm afraid there is nothing for it but to retrace our steps. Perhaps we'll meet someone who can set us straight."

"We don't seem to meet anyone sober enough to give us help," she lamented.

"I know," he sighed.

They walked back until they came to an intersection of the cobbles toned streets at the top of a hill. They hesitated and then took an opposite direction. The streets were deserted in this area and all the houses were in darkness. Betsy almost began to wish to see some of the drunks again. At least they had been company.

As they walked, she suddenly thought she heard a sound from behind them. She tugged at her companion's arm and in a low voice asked, "Do you hear footsteps following us?"

"I don't know," Eric said uneasily.

"I'm sure we're being followed," she worried. "What shall we do?"

"I think you're wrong," the young man said, but his tone was troubled. Then the footsteps became so apparent and so close that they could not be ignored.

Eric unlinked his arm from hers and turned quickly. She also swung around and saw that they had been followed by the man who had performed onstage in the soldier outfit. He was wearing drab, old clothes now, but he carried his sword on a belt at his hip. As they discovered him, he drew the weapon and crouched to attack Eric!

"Look out!" Eric screamed, pushing her aside so roughly she almost fell. Then he drew his pistol and fired at the man.

The bullet missed, and the swordsman lunged at Eric and caught him at the wrist, sending the pistol spinning. She watched and prayed as Eric dodged about. Then Eric sprang at the man and caught him by surprise. There began a grim struggle between them. Soon they were rolling on the ground. Eric twisted the sword from the man's hand and began pummeling him with his fists!

It was not a one-sided struggle! The man fought back savagely, and she saw that Eric had become the underdog. Then the battle began to go Eric's way, and he pounded his opponent to unconsciousness. Rising from the fallen swordsman, he stumbled back, his handsome face dirtied with blood, sweat, and filth from the street. His shirt and jacket were torn, and he seemed at the point of exaustion.

He bent down to pick up the pistol when from out of the shadows appeared the malevolent bald dwarf with a pistol in one hand and a sword in the other. A look of hatred showed on his big, ugly fece, and he fired at Eric. To Betsy's horror the bullet struck Eric, and he fell down near the body of the man he'd been battling with. Now the dwarf chortled gleefully, and stuffing the pistol in his coat pocket, he came at her with his sword on the ready!

Almost automatically she bent down and swooped up the sword which had fallen from the other man's hand. She saw the look of astonishment on the dwarf's face as she thus armed herself. He laughed again, but it was more a rattle of hatred in his throat than a normal sound of laughter.

Betsy took a few steps back to be clear of the fallen two and kept her eyes fixed on her weird opponent. She had no illusions as to the dwarfs ability to manipulate his weapon. He had shown himself to be a master of fencing when he was onstage.

Without warning he darted at her and engaged her sword, attempting to twist it from her by a harsh turn of his wrist. But she was too experienced to be defeated so easily. She disengaged her weapon and moved swiftly back before waiting to lunge at him. She almost caught him, nearly broke through his guard, but he fended her off in time.

She could think of nothing but survival now. It was clear the ugly little dwarf intended to disarm her and perhaps kill her. She could only guess that he and his companion were agents of Valmy out to eliminate them from investigating the facts of the death of LaFlenche!

They parried for a little while and then, as she'd hoped, the ugly little man became impatient. He lunged at her, and as he did so, he stumbled. It was the moment she needed. She did not even think but sent her sword through his chest. He opened his eyes wide in a horrified stare as he staggered back gasping. He still held onto his sword and remained standing as blood began to dribble from his mouth! Then he raised his sword, attempted to come back at her, and fell to the ground with a weird cry, her sword still through him!

She was repelled by what she had done, and yet she knew she'd had no choice. She gazed down at the dwarf with the point of the sword showing through his shoulder blades and with a gathering pool of blood circling him. She was sure she was going to be ill.

But it was a luxury she could not afford at the moment. First she had to check on Eric and see how badly hurt he was. She was alone in this deserted area of the port city with one man dead and not sure about Eric or the soldier. She saw that the soldier was still motionless, and she went and knelt by Eric.

His left temple was bloodied. As she spoke urgently to him and cradled his head in her hands, he slowly opened his eyes and stared up at her in a dazed fashion. Then remembrance returned to him, and he struggled to sit up.

"It's all right," she said. "Just so long as you're not badly hurt!"

With her assistance he struggled to a standing position and gazed down at the soldier and then the dwarf. He gave her a look of disbelief. "Did you do that?"

"Yes," she said. "After he shot you, I picked up the other man's sword and went after him."

"You did well!"

She tugged at his sleeve. "We must get away from here before anyone else arrives."

"Yes. They may have friends. And we want no trouble with the authorities."

Betsy saw the other man stir a little and groan. She said, "Hurry! He's coming round!"

"I can see that," her companion said grimly. He went and found his pistol and then joined her to rush off into the darkness.

She gave him support now and kept him moving as swiftly as she could. Gradually the exercise and the night air restored him to a more normal state.

She glanced up at him anxiously. "Have you lost much blood from that wound?"

"No. The bullet merely grazed me," he said.

She gazed ahead and said, "I think we're coming back to the main section of the city."

And she was right. They recognized a church and then some other official buildings. And by a major miracle a late-night carriage driver appeared, and they were able to hire him to take them back to the inn.

He eyed them warily. "You've not been in trouble with the police?"

"No," Eric said grimly. "A drunken friend went wild on us. He nearly tore us apart as we tried to subdue him."

"All right, monsieur," the driver said, still not certain about them. But he took them to the inn.

A distraught Kingston was waiting up for them, and when he saw their condition, he groaned. "I knew I ought to have gone with you two!" he exclaimed.

"It might only have made things worse," she said grimly. "Get me some water and a clean cloth so I can look after his head."

Eric sat dejectedly in a chair before the last embers of the dying logs in the fireplace. Betsy went about cleaning the wound and was delighted to find that it had been only a minor one. Still it would mean he would have to wear a bandage about his head for a day or two.

He said, "I can't go around with a bandage. I'll seem an idiot."

She was firm. "You must!" she said. "We can't risk your getting an infection."

"Not at this point," George Frederick Kingston said. "We are only just beginning our business here."

"Another night like tonight and we'll be finished," Eric said with a deep sigh. "I take full blame. It was my idea."

She speculated, "Do you think that strange duo were out to rob us or that they were agents of Valmy designated to eliminate us?"

"It's hard to say," Eric worried. "Whatever their motive they meant us no good."

"I'm certain I killed the dwarf," she said. "Do you think we should report the incident to the authorities?"

"Under the circumstances we daren't," Eric told her. "I rather imagine the authorities will be glad to find one or two less thugs for the city to deal with. Swine like them proliferate about every waterfront."

"I shan't sleep tonight," she said solemnly.

Eric rose with his bandaged head. He put an arm around her. "You must try! We have that important appointment in the morning."

He saw her to her door and kissed her tenderly. "You saved my life tonight," he told her.

"Don't let's talk about it!" she protested with a shudder.

"Very well," he said. And kissing her again, he saw her safely into her room. Then he went to join the actor.

She had not been wrong when she'd predicted that sleep wouldn't come to her easily. She sat on the side of her bed and thought about all that had taken place and began to tremble. For a little while her trembling was uncontrollable. She stretched out on the bed and sobbed bitterly.

Tonight she had slain a man! It would forever remain in her memory. True, she'd had no choice since the dwarf seemed intent on murdering both Eric and herself. She had not had any chance to reason, no choice but to try and defend herself. And her training had come to good advantage. She had defended herself with skill, but in doing so she had killed her opponent! She finally fell into an exhausted sleep with her clothing still on as she lay there on the coverlet.

When they all met the following morning for breakfast in the dining hall, she saw that Eric Walters had removed the bandage from his head and brushed his hair over to cover the small wound.

She smiled grimly and said, "You will have your way!"

"It is not wise to show any weakness in the face of the enemy," her handsome companion said.

Kingston sat bleakly without showing much interest in his breakfast. He said, "I have talked with the innkeeper and he tells me a waterfront entertainer was murdered last night. He and a companion were attacked in the street and a sword was driven through him."

Eric listened and innocently inquired, "And what of the companion?"

"He survived though badly beaten," the veteran actor said. "The city is shocked by the incident according to our landlord."

"I doubt that Marseilles is such a stranger to violence," Eric said easily. "At any rate it has nothing to do with us."

"Quite!" Kingston said awkwardly and gave Betsy a furtive glance.

She ignored the glance and said nothing. With the coming of another day she felt less guilty. She knew that it had been a case of kill or be killed. This eased her conscience a good deal.

Shortly after breakfast they left for the shipyard of Pierre Bartel in another of the familiar open carriages. Betsy thought what a king's ransom they would have paid for one the previous night. They were driven out of the city and had a chance to view the colorful countryside with its rich green vegetation and preponderance of white buildings.

The shipbuilding plant was located on the edge of the ocean with the yards located so they could be flooded and the constructed vessel launched when it was completed. There were also ways, built on a downward slant. And when smaller ships were constructed on these, they were blocked in place until the last moment, then the blocks were removed, and the ship actually slid down the way into the ocean.

When they reached the stone building which housed the offices of the shipbuilding yard, they were greeted by an aged male clerk who ushered them into the spacious office of the owner which had windows overlooking the yards below. Pierre Bartel was a portly man with a black beard and a rather bulbous nose. His close-set eyes had a shifty look, and Betsy at once decided she didn't like him.

Eric took care of introductions, naming her as his fiancée and Kingston as his father. The bearded Pierre Bartel was polite but not enthusiastic about seeing them. However, he provided chairs for them and then seated himself behind his desk and proceeded to discuss his partnership with LaFlenche.

He said, "Jean LaFlenche owned fifty percent of the firm, so when he died, I simply bought his shares from his daughter."

"I'm told she is a very solitary person," Eric said to the owner of the shipyard.

"Yes," Bartel agreed. "She was dedicated to her father. Since his death she has become a recluse."

George Frederick Kingston spoke up in his best Mayfair manner and said, "Knew the man slightly. Our friendship was interrupted by the war, of course. But I bought a good many shipments of fruit and other produce of the Mideast through his firm."

Bartel nodded politely. "Jean was known as a good man of business. I was happy to have him as a partner."

Eric said, "He was a staunch supporter of the late emperor, was he not?"

The shipbuilder hesitated and then admitted, "Yes. I guess you could call him that. But then many people in Marseilles felt warmly about Napoleon. Even after his defeat and death."

Betsy ventured, "Do you also believe France would be better with the emperor returned, Monsier Bartel?"

He stroked his beard nervously. "I accept the turn of events which brought about his downfall. One cannot go against history."

"It has occasionally been tried and sometimes with great success," Eric said, studying the man.

"Forgive me, my business is shipbuilding," Bartel said. "I am a poor historian."

"The thing which impressed me when I knew the late Jean LaFlenche was his resemblance to Napoleon," Kingston said.

Pierre Bartel nodded. "Yes. The resemblance was startling!"

"I suppose many people commented on it," Betsy said.

"Yes," the shipbuilder said. "Jean was both amused and pleased to be sometimes taken for the late emperor. It came to be a part of his life."

Eric gave him a direct look. "I wonder if it might have become all of it."

Bartel frowned. "I don't follow you!"

Eric continued, "Surely you have heard the rumors that LaFlenche was spirited away from his sickbed to board a ship for Saint Helena. And that there he took the place of Napoleon. And as a result Napoleon is somewhere in Europe today under the direction of a former army officer named Raymond Valmy, who hopes to use the ailing former emperor to set France ablaze with revolution once again."

The shipbuilder looked more and more uneasy as Eric expounded on for his benefit. He spread his hands and said, "But obviously the story is sheer fantasy! LeFlenche died in his own bed and is buried here in Marseilles."

Betsy said, "We have heard the story is true."

"As visitors you have been deceived by those who enjoy passing off gossip as fact," the shipbuilder said righteously. "No one can be more dead at this moment than Jean LaFlenche."

Eric said dryly, "I question only where he is buried."

"Hard to think of the chap dead," Kingston said in his grand manner.

Bartel eyed them all sharply. He said, "If you have come here hoping for some scandalous story to back these rumors up, you have come to the wrong person."

"That would seem to be clear," Eric said with some irony.

Bartel coughed. "I may say that several reporters from London newspapers have been here following up the same wild story. None of them had any luck with proving it. After a week or two they left disgruntled."

"We do not mean to waste your time," Betsy apologized. "It is just that Mr. Walters, Senior, was a good friend of Jean LaFlenche and wished to learn more about what happened to him."

"He died," Pierre Bartel said.

Eric rose. "I see there is no point in taking any more of your time, monsieur. I thank you for seeing us."

The shipbuilder now looked relieved. He also rose and in a more affable manner said, "It has been most pleasant meeting you. And I insist that you have a short tour of the shipbuilding works of which LaFlenche was a full-fledged partner before you go."

"We don't wish to put you to any further bother," Eric told him.

The bearded man took his black top hat from a hook on the wall, and offering Betsy his arm, he said, "It is no bother. I wish to personally escort you about the yard."

Kingston smiled and said, "I once visited a yard in Liverpool, so I shall enjoy this."

A few minutes later they were being shown the ways, and then they entered one of the big yards where the keel of a sailing vessel was being laid. They were midget figures inside the forty-foot walls which rose on all sides of them. The shipyard owner explained that when a ship was finished and ready to be floated out, ocean water was released into the yard and the outer wall swung away so the ship could float out with ease.

Eric studied the bare bones of the ship's hull in the making. He said, "You are not presently working on this vessel?"

"No," Pierre Bartel said. "We have been asked to complete a ship that's nearly finished. So we have sent all our considerable labor force there until that vessel is completed and launched. But I thought you would enjoy seeing the inside of a yard."

"We have!" Betsy agreed. "Though I found the stairway descent dizzying."

Bartel smiled and glanced toward the open steps up one side of the yard. "It can be frightening when you are not used to it. We cannot spare time to indulge in the frills of a safety railing. The majority of our men are old hands and well used to coming down the narrow steps."

They were still discussing the yard when a man came hurrying down the steps to tell Bartel that he was needed to make some important decision. He excused himself and went up the steps to join the messenger, leaving them in the bottom of the yard. As he climbed the unprotected steps, his figure grew tinier.

Betsy turned to Eric and said, "We've seen all we wish here. We should have gone up to the ground level with him."

"Yes," Kingston said, looking about him apprehensively. "I find it rather disturbing being down here."

"There's no danger," Eric assured the older man. And to Betsy he explained, "I want to ask some other lead questions, and they may not seem so annoying here as they might in his office."

"I see," she said. "So we wait for him to come back down."

"Yes, I think so," Eric agreed. "What do you make of him?"

"He's lying," Kingston said with some annoyance. "I think that is plain."

"I agree," she said. "I'm sure he knows all about the LaFlenche affair and that he is a staunch supporter of Valmy."

"That's the way I see it," Eric said. "There is no question that he is anxious to be rid of us."

"And showing us around down here is just part of that," she suggested.

"Exactly," Eric said. "But I wish to make the best of it. When he comes down again, I'm going to ask him some more questions about the exact time of LaFlenche's death. His answers may be helpful in condemning him."

"Why not put him down as a liar and let it go at that," Kingston grumbled. "He surely can't believe he's deceiving us."

"I have an idea he knows we're seeing through him," Eric said. "That makes him dangerous."

As Eric finished speaking, they were all aware at once of a great roaring sound. It frew louder every second, and she turned to see what was causing it and paled! Coming at them from the ocean end of the yard was a great wave of water! In a moment it would be on them, overwhelming them!

Chapter Ten

"THE SLUICE gates!" Eric cried. "Someone has opened them!"

"We're lost!" Kingston shouted in dismay.

"Come on!" Eric roughly seized Betsy as she stood there frozen by the sight of the growing mountain of advancing sea water coming down on them.

Kingston was already scrambling in the direction of the steps, his top hat gone, his coat streaming behind him as he raced with a speed hardly believable in one of his temperament.

Eric stopped trying to force her along and lifted her up and carried her toward the steps in his arms. He was not able to make the same speed as Kingston with her as a burden. He had only gone a step or two when the water was at his ankles, then at his knees, the roaring horrendous now. And by the time he staggered to the bottom of the steps, the water was waist-high on him.

"Give me your hands, girl!" Kingston cried, bending over from a higher step to catch her hands.

She obeyed him without a word. Passed from one man to the other, she hardly realized what was happening. Then a soaked Eric was clambering up the steps behind her and urging her and Kingston on.

"Hurry!" he cried. "The water is gaining force all the time! It will soon be catching up with us!"

Her fear of the steps without a railing was now behind her. She was terrified of a far worse fate—that of being drowned in the yawning area of the yard! Kingston was literally clawing his way up the steps to freedom.

Sobbing and gasping, she followed the actor with Eric's encouraging cries coming from behind her. They finally reached the safety of the grassy area by the steps. All three of them collapsed on the ground there while they gazed down at the yard now almost completely filled with ocean water.

Kingston gasped. "The mad blighter tried to drown us!"

"He did!" Betsy sobbed in agreement.

"I know," Eric placated them. "This has been no accident, but we dare not accuse him openly. It would do no good in any case!"

"You're going to let him get away with it?" Betsy asked in dismay.

"It is the political thing to do at the moment," Eric said grimly. "One day I will hope to bring Monsieur Bartel to task for what he's done!"

The bearded man was running across the grass to join them with some of his workers following on his heels. He looked shocked as he reached the spot where they were resting. "My good people, I do not know what to say," he said in consternation.

Eric smiled wryly and got to his feet. "Someone made a bad error."

"A ghastly mistake!" Pierre Bartel apologized. "I do not know how to explain."

"You might try!" Betsy said as Eric and Kingston helped her up.

Pierre Bartel removed his top hat and mopped his brow with a large white handkerchief. "It is like a bad dream! I had an inspiration when I came up here. I decided to show you how the yards flood when the sluice gates are opened. A most impressive sight!"

"We witnessed it at close range," Eric said grimly.

"But the stupid oafs opened the wrong sluice gates. I told them clearly yard number one, and instead they flooded number two where you were standing."

"A simple error," Betsy said bitterly. "Yet it nearly cost us our lives."

"I shall make those stupid men suffer for their mistake," the shipyard owner promised. "In the meanwhile what can I do to make up to you for this dreadful accident?"

Eric said, "Have our carriage brought to us as soon as possible. Our tour here is ended. We must get back to the inn."

Pierre Bartel continued to bluster and apologize, but he was hardly convincing. Betsy even thought she saw a smug smile cross his face as the carriage drove off with its three soaked and dejected passengers.

She told the other two, "I'm sure he is laughing at our discomfort."

Eric said, "He would much prefer our having drowned in there. He failed in his instructions."

Kingston stared at the younger man. "You think he had orders to kill us?"

"Yes," the young secret service man said, sitting back against the carriage seat. "And I'm sure he's not the only one out to get us. We are fair game as long as we threaten their scheme."

"I jolly well wish that Felix Black had been down there when the water came flooding in," George Frederick Kingston complained. "He'd know a bit of what we're up against."

Eric said quietly, "He knows about it already. Black was an agent once himself. He has faced every sort of threat in his time."

"Never fancied being drowned like a rat!" the actor said, hunching miserably in his wet clothing.

Betsy gave him a small smile of encouragement. "We will all feel better when we've had a change to dry things."

"This is my best outfit," Kingston said in an injured tone. "Probably ruined!"

As soon as they returned, Betsy had a warm bath and changed into her yellow dress. She had just completed the change and given her clothes to the innkeeper's wife to be dried out and looked after when Eric, also in a dry outfit, came to join her in the hallway of the inn.

"How is Kingston?" she asked.

"Still complaining about his fine clothes being ruined," Eric said with an amused look. "He seems to have forgotten how near he came to drowning."

"What now?"

"We must plan our visit to the tomb of Jean LaFlenche," he said.

She hesitated. "Must we? We have enough evidence to know the exchange took place."

"Checking the tomb is essential. Felix Black demands it."

Betsy shrugged. "I must confess I'm beginning to have some sympathy with Kingston. I almost wish that Felix Black was here to enter that tomb, not any of us."

The young man smiled. "That doesn't sound like you."

"This isn't turning out exactly as I expected."

"What did you expect?"

"That we would be doing the harassing. We would be tracking down the plotters. Thus far we appear to merely be making targets of ourselves. And we are being threatened by enemy agents wherever we go and whatever we do! We are the pursued!"

Eric said, "It may seem that way, but that is only for the moment. The tempo of things will change. And soon!"

"I hope so."

He patted her on the arm. "You have done well. You mustn't falter at this time. I have good news. I have received a message from London from Black. The innkeeper had it waiting for me when we returned."

"What is the message?" she asked eagerly.

"Tomorrow we sail for Naples. That is why it is urgent we check on that tomb tonight."

"Has our passage been booked?"

"No. I will look after that this afternoon," he promised. "There is a continuous traffic between here and Naples. Ships sail every day over the route, and it is only a short voyage."

"Why Naples?"

Eric leaned close and said, "Because at this very moment Valmy is there with Napoleon. It could be your chance to come face-to-face with the emperor."

She was at once excited and eager again. "Do you really think so?"

"Yes," he said. "We do not know their hiding place. But it is somewhere in the city. That is the information passed on to Black."

"So we may not have to wait long," she said.

"No," he assured her. "I'll arrange for our sailing, and tonight we shall visit the cemetery."

Betsy rested for the balance of the day. The innkeeper's wife did a fine job on all their clothing. It was returned to them in the early evening dried and pressed. Even Kingston was satisfied that no harm had come to his precious suit.

They waited until close to midnight. Then the three set out silently from the inn. Fortunately the cemetery was within walking distance. During the afternoon Kingston had located a strong crowbar which Eric deemed essential for the night's work.

Swiftly making their way through the dark and deserted streets, they reached the ancient church and the small graveyard behind it. The uneven ground and the tombstones were bathed in eerie blue moonlight as they went through the cemetery gate in single file.

Betsy had no liking for these places of the dead. The slanted tombstones, worn and crumbling with age, stood sentry duty over thin mounds which marked the last resting places of so many. Scattered among these simple stones were some more pretentious memorials. In several cases there were large tombs with iron doors, unlocked only when a new coffin was admitted to the tomb.

The LaFlenche tomb was the largest of the group. Eric held a lantern in his hand and went down the several stone steps to examine the padlock on the rusted door.

Glancing up, he told Kingston, "Give me the crowbar!"

"You going in there?" the actor asked nervously as he passed the bar down.

Eric said grimly, "How else am I to know if LaFlenche is buried here?"

"Won't be very pleasant if he is. Bodies can't last long in this heat," Kingston worried.

"Please!" Betsy begged him to be quiet.

Eric deftly used the crowbar to break open the padlock. It was evident that he was skilled in the technique and had used it before. This done, he pulled the iron door open. Now he glanced up at them again.

He said, "I want you to stand guard duty, Kingston. Keep your pistol at the ready and watch from a place where you won't be seen!"

"Righto!" Kingston said, taking out his pistol. "What do you say if I post myself beyond that other tomb over there?"

"All right," Eric said. "Just mind you're not seen. And if anyone comes up on us, give us some sort of signal."

"I'll cry out!" Kingston suggested.

Eric nodded. "It will give away your hiding place, but there's no other choice." He turned to Betsy. "I want you to keep watch by the doorway. Also have your pistol ready."

"I will," she said.

He sighed and with a resigned look said, "Now I'll take on the role of grave robber."

A night bird flew overhead, uttering a weird cry. The eerie atmosphere of the deserted graveyard upset Betsy. She stood nervously inside the iron door, just a step within the tomb. Eric had gone on to the rear, and Kingston had taken up his stand behind the nearby tomb.

Eric spoke to her, "Pretty dusty back here. Hard to sort out the caskets."

She turned and saw by the dim glow of the lantern that both walls of the giant, partly underground tomb had shelves. And on these shelves were set out the dust-covered coffins.

She said, "Surely you can recognize the latest addition."

"It has been here so long that it's as dusty as all the others," he replied. "I'll have to find the brass plate. The coffins are all identified with brass plates."

"Hurry!" she said, shuddering.

He glanced at her. "Frightened?"

"Terrified!"

"We were in a worse fix this morning," he reminded her. "We could have ended up as dead as anyone in here!"

"Don't mention it!" she begged him.

Eric moved about a little, examining the coffins on several of the shelves. All at once he let out a small cry of triumph. "I've found it!" he said in a low voice.

"Good!"

"Now we'll get it over with," Eric said between gritted teeth as he pried at the lid of the coffin.

She heard the sound of splintering wood and turned anxiously to ask him, "Well?"

He was holding the lantern. His face wore a strange look. "Come and see!"

"I might faint!" she protested.

"I'll take that chance."

Slowly she made her way deeper in the tomb until she came to the coffin which had been broken open by Eric. She stood back, not wishing to peer in it. She said, "What is the answer?"

"Look!" He took her by the arm and forced her close to the coffin.

Bracing herself, she looked inside and to her utter surprise saw that it was filled with large rocks—weighted down with rocks!

"No body!" she gasped.

"Not a sign of one," he said wryly. "Somewhere along the way the corpse was lost. And I'd say we know where and how."

Betsy said, "Now there can no longer be any doubt."

"None," he agreed. "We'd better get away from here as quickly as we can. Our work is done!"

"For which I'm grateful," she said. She placed her pistol in the pocket of her dress since she would no longer need to stand guard.

"We'll close the iron door by using the crowbar as an emergency lock," Eric said. "Just shove it through the iron brackets."

They emerged from the tomb with Eric still carrying the lantern and crowbar. But just as they stepped outside and were going up the four stairs to ground level, they were confronted by what she at first thought was a shadowy phantom!

"Vultures!" a thin voice accused them. "Grave robbers! Vandals!"

Now she saw that it was none other than a cloaked Mademoiselle LaFlenche, and she was standing covering them with a menacing-looking revolver.

"It's no use, mademoiselle," Eric said, "Your father is not down there! His coffin is empty except for some stones!"

"Liars!" the woman said hysterically, waving the gun from one to the other. "You have stolen him from his grave, and so I shall kill you for the desecration!"

"No!" Betsy pleaded.

The woman made no reply as she fixed the gun on her in terrifying fashion. It was then that Kingston leaped out from his hiding place and grabbed hold of the hysterical woman. He wrested the revolver from her hand, and it went off in the air with a loud report as he did so. Then he clamped his arms around the still struggling spinster.

"What will we do with her?" he shouted.

Eric lifted his voice to be heard above Mademoiselle's continual screaming, saying, "Bring her down here since she's so anxious to join the dead!"

"She's yours!" Kingston called out and shoved the woman down the steps to the entrance of the tomb.

"Foreigners! Murderers!" the thin woman screamed on.

Betsy quickly moved up the stairs and away from her as Eric manipulated the spinster's spare form through the entrance to the tomb and then shut the iron door on her and put the crowbar through the brackets to hold it in place.

He then hurried up to join Betsy and Kingston, saying, "She'll not be heard so well down there!"

"We can't just leave here there!" Betsy worried.

"She'd die!" Kingston agreed.

"I'll fix it," he said. "I'll leave a note with our innkeeper. After she's shouted herself hoarse and flailed the skin from her knuckles, she'll quiet down. In the meanwhile the innkeeper will find my note and she'll be rescued."

"What about us?" Kingston wanted to know.

Eric said, "We shall be on a vessel bound for Naples."

In the tomb below the spinster screamed for aid and rattled the iron door. The three of them ran out of the cemetery in single file again. They did not halt until they were a distance from the place.

Betsy was short of breath from running as were the others. As they paused, she asked, "What now?"

Eric said, "We'll go straight to the inn, pack our things, and leave."

"Our ship to Naples doesn't sail until the morning," the actor reminded him.

"But we can board her tonight. Safer under cover of darkness! And by the time Mademoiselle is free, we'll be far at sea!"

"You won't forget to leave word about Mademoiselle with the innkeeper," she said. "I would not want to see her come to harm."

"Never fear," he said.

They made their way back to the inn and hastily packed. Eric figured out the amount due the innkeeper and wrote a brief note. He left both money and the note in the private office of the inn's owner, on his desk where neither money nor message could be missed. Then they stole silently out into the darkness again."

There was no choice but to walk to the docks. Both Eric and Kingston took turns at helping her with her bags. She did not want this, but they insisted. When they reached the docks, they had to locate a man with a rowboat to take them out to their ship which was anchored out in the harbor. They found one doing a good business taking drunken sailors to their vessels and hired him.

The voyage to Naples was pleasant and short. It gave Betsy a chance to rest a little and forget some of the more unpleasant things which had happened in Marseilles. At least they were now on the trail of the elusive Valmy and his hostage, Napoleon. The vessel reached Naples in the afternoon, and she stood on deck to admire the beautiful setting of the ancient Italian city.

They had gone by the island of Capri which looked for all the world like a great sunbathed giant ship on the horizon. There was Sorrento and high up on the mountainside Ravello. This area of rich green, azure blue, and stark whites was another deceptively calm spot. Politically it had known much turbulence.

Eric reminded her of this as he stood on the deck at her side, studying the busy harbor. He said, "This was once the capital of Napoleon's Kingdom of Naples. His sister Caroline and his brother Joseph held the throne here in turn."

She said, "Caroline was not his favorite. He spoke of her bitterly more than once."

"He felt that she had deceived him and was in many ways his enemy. Like many others Napoleon found his family hostile to him."

"And according to Felix Black he is now here in hiding?" she said.

"That is the last word I had," Eric agreed. "There ought to be a message or a messenger awaiting us in Naples."

The hotel they had selected was more like a grand old castle than a public lodging place. The rooms were large and well furnished, and the restaurant and lobby had the elegance of a castle. Further it had the advantage of being only a short walk from the busiest part of the city.

She'd barely unpacked when Eric came to her room and told her, "I have to go out and try and make contact with another of our agents. Kingston will remain in the hotel to keep you company."

"I should be all right on my own," she said.

"Don't be too sure," he warned her. "The game becomes more dangerous as we near our quarry."

She gave him an earnest look. "You do believe that Napoleon is here?"

"Yes," he said. "That means that Valmy's agents will be all over the place."

"Be careful!" she told him.

He smiled and kissed her. "I think I can take care of myself. I worry mostly about you."

"I'll be all right," she said.

Eric left and she went out on the balcony of her room for a while. Then she became restless. The shopping district was nearby, and she had a few things she wished to purchase. So she left her room and went downstairs to find Kingston seated in the lobby reading a tattered copy of the London *Times*.

The veteran actor rose at once. "I've been catching up with the news from London," he said. "Actually there's nothing new in it for me. This edition was published before we left. I've read it all before."

She smiled, "At least it will bring back facts you knew."

"Covent Garden is having a fine season," the actor said. "The manager here tells me they have many English guests, but I have not encountered any yet."

"It is not the high season," she suggested. "I propose to go out on a shopping expedition to the streets nearby. I felt I should let you know."

Kingston showed concern. "You're not saying you will go alone?"

"Yes. I'll be perfectly safe. It is daylight, and the streets are filled with people. No one will try to kidnap me."

He frowned. "I don't think Eric would approve. Perhaps I should go along."

"It would bore you," she warned him. "And your presence would make me nervous."

Kingston looked hurt. "I was not aware of having this particular effect on you."

"I don't mean your personality. I mean I need time to consider the items I'll be buying, and you would quite properly become impatient. I can manage best alone."

"If you are sure," he said reluctantly.

"I am," she promised. "Now do go back to reading your paper. And if Eric returns before I do, let him know where I've gone."

"Try not to be long," Kingston said with a concerned look on his pleasant face.

She left him and headed out to the narrow driveway which led down to the street. Beyond the walled area of the hotel grounds she found herself caught up in the colorful confusion of the many shops. The people were noisy and friendly and the air warm and filled with the delicious smells emanating from the many food shops scattered along the way.

She spent a long while in a small jewelry shop and then went on to an establishment which specialized in ladies' clothing. She bought herself a needed cape with a hood attached. Then she wandered on down the street.

Unexpectedly a hand gripped her arm and a low voice directed her, "You will show no fear and come along with me!"

She turned in surprise to find that it was a well-dressed elderly man in top hat and blue jacket and brown breeches who had taken hold of her.

She asked, "Who are you and what do you want?"

"I am a friend, Miss Chapman," the old gentleman said. He had a gray moustache, and his face was heavily lined. "I swear I mean you no harm."

"What do you want?" she asked. "And how do you know my name?"

"I'm the messenger of a friend, Miss Chapman," the old gentleman said. "Someone wishes to see you and has asked me to bring you to them."

She held back as they stood on the busy sidewalk with the old man still keeping his grasp on her arm. She said, "I can scream, and someone will come to my aid!"

"There is no need for that," the old gentleman told her. "If you refuse to accompany me, I will let you go free."

She frowned. "How did you know who I am?"

"You do not recognize me," the old man said. "But I have seen you before. On Saint Helena with the emperor. I was a minor member of his entourage on the island."

She stared at him. "I cannot recall you."

"I did not expect you to," he said. "But I had no problem seeking you out. You have not changed all that much since those days on the island."

"Who wishes to see me?"

"A good friend."

She stood there hesitating. And she wondered if it might be Napoleon, himself, who wished to speak with her. If so, she could not miss the opportunity. It might be that while Eric was out making a search for the Valmy party, she was being given an opportunity of contacting it.

She said, "Where is this friend?"

"In a building only a few doors from here."

"You swear on your honor as an officer that I will not be harmed or detained against my wishes?"

"You have my word," the old man said.

She still waited, but she knew she would capitulate to his offer. She would be ignoring the purpose of her quest if she passed up a possible contact with the fugitive Napoleon. She might be able to warn him if she managed to have a personal conference with him. Let him know of Valmy's planned deceit.

"My arm is paining from your grip on it," she told the old ex-officer.

"My pardon, Mademoiselle Chapman," he said, releasing his hold on her.

She stood there knowing she was free; that all she had to do was turn and run back in the direction of the hotel. She doubted that the old man would try to follow her, and if he did, he had only a small chance of catching up to her. Even if he did, she could make a fuss and ask some of the passersby to come to her aid.

But she knew she wouldn't make the escape attempt. She would go with him and see if he'd lead her to the fallen emperor.

She said, "Very well. I'll go with you."

The old man bowed. "A wise decision," he said.

He led her a short distance down the street to a building which held a wine shop on the ground floor. Next to the store front there was an open door leading up a dark flight of stairs.

The old man told her, "We go up here. I will lead the way. It is dark and the steps are not in good repair."

"Very well," she said. And as she followed him up in the darkness, she thought how unlikely a place this was to find the fallen emperor who had known the most luxurious of surroundings for such a large part of his life. He had come back to his early humble days it seemed.

Reaching the first floor, the old man went down a hall which led further to the rear of the building. He halted at a door there and knocked several times in a manner which evidently was a signal. There was a wait, and then the door was cautiously opened.

The old man said, "She is here!" And then he turned to her and said, "Please go in."

She gave him a wary glance and then moved on to the open doorway and into a room whose shades were drawn so that she could see only shadows. The door closed behind her, giving her a feeling of sheer terror.

Suddenly one of the blinds at the window was whipped open, and standing by it, she saw the familiar face and figure of Dr. Barry Edward O'Meara!"

"You!" she gasped.

"And who were you expecting? Felix Black?"

"No."

"Perhaps the emperor himself," the Irish doctor said with a hint of mockery.

"The thought had crossed my mind," she admitted.

The pleasant-faced Irishman said, "I'm sorry it is only O'Meara you'll see this day."

"What do you want?" she asked.

"You must remember Admiral Roche," he said, indicating a man who had been sitting silently in a chair in a dark corner, so motionless she had not noticed him.

Now she gave her attention to the rather frail figure in the chair, and she recognized the black patch he wore on his right eye and the head of curly white hair. He had been one of the trusted officers who had gone to St. Helena with Napoleon. Badly wounded in the wars, he walked with a limp, but he had a handsome face despite the eye patch.

Admiral Roche got up from the chair and bowed. "It brings back nostalgic memories to see you again, mademoiselle."

"Thank you," she said warmly, for she had always liked the man. She felt afraid no longer.

"You were a great inspiration to the emperor," the admiral said. "He missed you when you left the island."

"I missed him," she said.

Dr. Barry Edward O'Meara spoke up in his blustering way and said, "Cannot we not have our discussion in comfort? At least you should sit down, Betsy."

"Thank you," she said and sat in the nearest chair.

Admiral Roche returned to the easy chair he had been occupying and told her, "I had not truly ever expected to see you again."

She said, "Nor I you."

O'Meara told her, "The admiral knows why you are here. That you are an agent of Black's."

"So?" she said.

"I told you I would be here on my own," O'Meara went on to advise her. "And I warn you the city is alive with Valmy's agents."

"That is to be expected," she said.

O'Meara stood before her with a mocking smile on his face. "Tell me, are you still as enthusiastic about being an agent?"

"To be truthful, no."

The Irishman chuckled and told the seated Roche, "You hear that, admiral. She has found out what we all come to know. It is a dangerous and unrewarding business."

"None the less I will see my mission through," she said firmly.

O'Meara lifted an eyebrow. "I see a change in you. Is it possible you have come to love your enemy?"

She said, "I understand the enemy is Raymond Valmy. In that case, I can say no."

The Irish doctor shook his head. "I wasn't thinking of Valmy. I was thinking of Major Eric Walters. Didn't you blame him for your brother's death?"

Her cheeks burned. "That was long ago."

"So I am right," O'Meara said triumphantly. "Walters has won you over."

"I have great respect for him as a colleague," she said.

"Indeed," the Irish doctor said. "And where is he now?"

"Somewhere in the city," she said.

Admiral Roche said, "You have come here hoping to find Napoleon?"

"I don't think that is any secret," she said.

"You've wasted your time," Dr. Edward Barry O'Mears told her. "He is here no longer."

"How do you know?"

Admiral Roche spoke up. "Because we are here for the same purpose. To try and get to him before Valmy pushes him further in this mad scheme."

O'Meara smiled at her bleakly. "It would seem that for all Felix Black's organization, I'm still a step ahead of him."

She said, "I have no comment. I'm here solely because I would like to talk with the former emperor and tell him of his danger."

"We wish to do exactly the same thing," Admiral Roche told her.

"We don't fully trust Mr. Felix Black and his agents," O'Meara went on. "He was never Napoleon's friend in the past. Why should he try to save him now?"

She said, "Because he feels it will also save England from facing another revolution in France and a disastrous war led by Valmy's party. It is known that Valmy has an intense hatred for England."

Admiral Roche nodded gravely. "He is a firebrand. I was always fearful of his political theories. Now, using the emperor, he is especially dangerous."

She asked, "How long since Valmy and the emperor left here?"

"We aren't actually sure," O'Meara said. "We arrived here a week ago, and they had gone by then."

"Where?" she asked.

"We have heard Valmy has a palace in Venice, and that is where they have headed," O'Meara said.

"Venice would make an excellent hiding place," the veteran Admiral Roche agreed. "It is full of dark corners and mystery."

Betsy asked, "Have you talked with anyone who saw the party?"

O'Meara nodded grimly. "Yes. I had a long talk with someone who spent quite a bit of time with them. He is a kind of organizer for Valmy."

"What about the emperor?" she asked.

"Distressing," Admiral Roche said sadly. "He has grown more corpulent. And Valmy has made him grow a moustache. The story is that he has become apathetic and has no heart for this venture."

O'Meara spoke angrily, "It is Valmy who pushes him on. Napoleon is not a well man. And as a final indignity Valmy has saddled him with a bad-tempered mistress who gives him little peace. A scheming widow named Giselle Manton, who was once Valmy's woman friend. Probably still is."

"Undoubtedly," Admiral Roche agreed, "Valmy is using this woman to spy on the emperor and sway him to do Valmy's bidding. It is sad!"

Betsy agreed. "He deserves better than that."

"He has fallen into the worst possible hands," Admiral Roche worried. "If we are not able to rescue him, there will be a major tragedy."

O'Meara nodded. "Our work is far from over now. It is on to Venice."

"We only pray we are not too late, for it is from Venice that Valmy plans to directly move the emperor into France. All the groundwork has been laid for regional insurrections, with a major outbreak scheduled for Paris."

Betsy rose. "I must be going now. I will be missed, and they will worry."

"Walters and that actor," the Irishman said glumly. "I cannot think they will manage all that well."

"I'd rather not think of us being in competition," she protested.

"Wouldn't you now?" O'Meara said with a hint of sarcasm. "Well, let me tell you this. I don't know what Felix Black has in mind. But if we get to Napoleon first, you will never see him."

She sighed. "It is too bad there could not be more trust between us."

Admiral Roche had also risen. He explained, "We fear that in the end Black, like Valmy, means to see the emperor executed. We distrust his plan for sending him to America. We, on the other hand, want to see him free and living his remaining years in comfortable seclusion."

Betsy said, "I know you to be an honorable man, admiral. And I think Dr. O'Meara is sincere. But I believe Felix Back has the best plan, and I will continue to dedicate myself to it."

O'Meara eyed her with some annoyance. "You will remember that the emperor trusted you—that once he showed something close to love for you."

"I will not deny that," she said. "It is the reason I am here in Naples. To warn him!"

"I think Black means to use you as an instrument of the emperor's destruction," O'Meara warned her. "I believe we should make you our prisoner."

"I have put myself at your mercy. I did so because I had an idea I was going to be ushered into the presence of Napoleon. And that I could save him."

Chapter Eleven

THERE WAS a tense silence in the low-ceilinged room with its whitewashed walls. Then Admiral Roche moved over to her, emotion showing on his lined face. The eye free of the black eye patch fixed on her, and he said, "You need have no fear, mademoiselle. We are, as you have said, men of honor. We will not detain you!"

"More the fools we may be!" O'Meara worried.

She smiled at him. "I remember you as anything but a fool. And the emperor relied on Admiral Roche more than on anyone else in his entourage."

"That is why I hope he will listen to me and loose himself from the domination of Valmy," the old admiral said.

"What a story it could make!" O'Meara said. "And I would like to be the one to write it."

"If it goes the other way, the story will be equally hair-raising," Betsy said sobering. "But infinitely more tragic."

O'Meara told her, "You can give Walters the information we've passed on to you. And you can also tell him that we'll be in Venice before him. And we hope to have the emperor safely on his way to real safety before Felix Black can reach out to get him."

"Our motives are identical," she said. "It is too bad you lack trust in us."

"So be it!" the big Irishman said.

"Our man is waiting outside," Admiral Roche told her. "He will escort you back to your hotel."

The elderly ex-officer was standing in the hallway, and she joined him as the door to the room behind her was closed. It was evident that neither the admiral nor O'Meara intended to expose themselves to Valmy's agents or even her own associates. This way they could deny ever having spoken with her.

The old man who was her escort said little as he led her back along the busy street. Her own mind was too filled with troubled thoughts for small talk. The big disappointment was that Napoleon was no longer in the city. And she did not doubt that O'Meara had told her the truth about this. She expected that Eric Walters would also have this information by now.

The gray-haired man bowed to her at the entrance to the hotel and said, "You will be quite safe now, mademoiselle."

"Yes," she agreed. "I thank you."

She went inside and looked for Kingston, but there was no sign of the veteran actor in the lobby. She went on up to her room and left her shopping parcels. Then she searched out the room Eric and Kingston were sharing and knocked on the door. It was several minutes before a sleepy-looking Kingston opened it.

She said, "You've been sleeping!"

"I felt a bit weary," the actor admitted. "I didn't rest well on the ship. I'm still a poor sailor."

"Where is Eric?"

"I don't know."

"Hasn't he returned yet?" she asked tautly.

"No! But he didn't say when he expected to return," the actor pointed out.

"I'd say he's been too long gone!" she worried.

"He was looking for someone. Perhaps he is having trouble locating whoever it is."

"Or he may have found the wrong person," she said with a look of grim meaning.

Kingston ran a hand through his spare hair and for the first time showed signs of concern. "What can we do?"

"Very little for the moment."

"There must be other agents here to help us," Kingston worried. "Eric expected they would be here."

"He may have been wrong," she told the worried Kingston. "Worst of all I've learned that Napoleon is no longer in Naples."

"Then we've made the trip here for nothing!"

"It would seem so."

"What next?"

"That will depend on Eric," she said. "We shall simply have to wait for him."

Kingston's eyes met hers in a look of fear. "What if we don't hear from him?"

"Please!"

"I hate to say it," he worried. "But it is a possibility. Do you know how we can reach Felix Black?"

"Only by the ordinary means of mail," she said, "I have no names or addresses of the agents here. He entrusted all that to Eric."

"Then we could be in a serious predicament," the actor said.

Betsy shook her head. "I refuse to think Eric would walk into a trap."

He gave her a wise look. "You two are in love, aren't you? It has become important to both of you."

She shrugged. "What if it has?"

"Nothing," he said. "It just makes the situation all the more difficult for you."

"We will not give up hope so easily," she said. "We will have dinner, and perhaps he may arrive later."

She went back to her own room and refreshed herself for going down to the evening meal. She had little appetite, but she sensed that Kingston was in a bad state of nerves and she wanted to keep up his courage. She was desperately afraid that something bad had happened to the man she had come to love, but she didn't dare admit it.

She even thought of trying to find O'Meara and the old admiral again and enlist their aid. But she guessed they would have vanished by now. Even if she found that room over the shop, it would be empty. She would simply have to wait and hope.

Dinner proved something of an ordeal, with Kingston saying little. The actor was drinking a good deal, and she feared that he would be no use to her if they should have to set out in search of aid later in the evening. She debated reporting Eric to the authorities as a missing person but decided it was too soon for that.

By the time they left the dining room, George Frederick Kingston's speech was incoherent, and he excused himself for a moment. A distraught Betsy had a shrewd suspicion that he would go straight to his room and fall asleep. He had allowed his fear to make him drink too much; now he was useless to both himself and her.

She stood forlornly in the magnificent lobby of the old hotel, wondering what to do next. Then the problem was solved for her.

The aged clerk left his desk to come to her with a note. He said, "This was left for you while you were at dinner."

Hope rose within her, and she thanked him. As soon as he left her, she quickly opened the envelope to read, "Come at once! I shall be in the Cathedral of the Madonna!" There was no signature, but she could not doubt that it was Eric who had sent the message.

She put it in the pocket of her skirt and debated going up to Kingston and trying to rouse him. But she knew before making the attempt that it would be futile. She must answer Eric's summons on her own. So she quickly got her cloak and went out and hired one of the carriages waiting outside the hotel entrance to take her to the cathedral.

The streets were quiet in the early evening, and the cathedral proved to be on a high hill overlooking a district of well-kept homes. She ordered the driver to wait for her and mounted the imposing steps of the huge stone cathedral.

Two little boys sat on the steps and gave her a defiant look as she passed them. They were ragged urchins and apparently used to playing on the steps. Several old women with shawls over their heads came out of the building, murmuring among themselves, having attended to their religious duties. She went on inside the huge building.

It had great Gothic ceilings which extended forever upward. Huge columns of stone supported the edifice. There were fine murals on the walls and windows of rich stained glass depicting scenes in the life of Christ. It was cool in the shadowed building and quiet. Deathly quiet! No priest was in sight, but in several of the pews there were people kneeling in silent prayer.

She felt like an interloper and wondered why Eric had chosen this place for their meeting. Perhaps because he felt it safe. She stared up at the altar with its gold decorations and white cloth. And then she decided to move along a side wing evidently added onto the large building to hold any overflow on special occasions. There was no view of the altar from this smaller side gallery, but the service in the main cathedral could be heard.

Making her way along in the still darker shadows of this wing, she found her heart beating wildly. She was extremely nervous. The long wait with no word from Eric had taken its toll, and now she was undergoing a further test of her drawn nerves. She moved slowly in the murky atmosphere of the silent gallery, wondering why Eric hadn't shown himself.

Suddenly the whole thing took on a grotesque character in her mind. It was hard to imagine herself so far from England on this wild adventure. Was it really worthwhile? Could Felix Black be trusted? Or was she, as O'Meara had warned, apt to be double-crossed at the last moment. Would she find herself facing death in some dark alley when she was no longer useful to the old secret agent?

Without warning a figure stepped out of the shadows. It was the Indian, Raj Singh. He said, "So you received my message after all."

"Yes. How fortuitous to meet you again. But I thought the message was from Major Walters," she said in a hushed, tense voice.

"I fear not," the Indian said.

"What is happening?"

The Indian drew her aside into the shadows where he had been standing unseen and told her, "I have bad news for you."

"What?" she said, fear tightening her throat.

"Major Walters has been captured by Valmy's men. They are holding him hostage."

"Where?"

"I do not know," Raj Singh said. "He was to keep a rendezvous with me. They sent a false messenger to him, and the messenger, pretending to be from me, led him into a trap."

"How do you know all this and yet not know where he is?"

"My informant lost track of them. But this is known. He was taken out of the city."

"Will they harm him?"

The Indian gave her a strange look. "They may very well kill him!"

"Oh no!" she protested.

"All that will guarantee his life is their hope of gaining some information they do not have from him."

"He can surely deal with them."

"He is clever," Raj Singh agreed. "But so are they. Valmy is daily getting closer to beginning his revolution. He will let nothing stand in his way now."

"The hope then is that Major Walters can delude his captors into thinking he has secret information important to them."

"Yes."

"What can we do to help him?"

"I have been promised word of where he is," the Indian said. "If I get this news, I will take a party to rescue him."

"When will you know?"

"Later tonight," he said. "I wanted you to be aware of what is going on. If anything happens to the major or myself, you must notify Felix Black."

"Nothing must happen to you!" she said brokenly.

"We will see," the Indian said. "If all goes well, I should know by midnight."

"What will I do?" she asked.

"Go out into the hotel gardens at midnight," he said. "Either I will arrive with Major Walters or I will have some further information about him."

"I'll be there," she promised. "You must know that we had been led here on a wild, useless chase. Napoleon is no longer here."

"I'm aware of that," the Indian said. "I have been here for some days—spending most of my time trying to evade the traps which Valmy's men have set for me."

"They really fear us then?"

Raj Singh nodded. "They know if we are able to talk to the emperor, we will be able to dissuade him from Valmy's wild plan."

"I'm beginning to wonder if that is possible."

"It is only the start. We are not alone in this. Our leader is a wise man. He will succeed and so will we."

"I only hope so."

"Do not lose courage," the Indian said. "Now return to the hotel. Wait there and be prepared to meet me in the garden at midnight."

"You may count on me," she said.

"Now go," he told her. "We must not leave the cathedral together. Valmy's men are waiting for me. But it is to be hoped that they do not know about you yet. So you will seem to be just another visitor to the cathedral. They will let you pass."

"What about you?"

"I know of a secret exit which I will use," he said. "I came by that way safely. Do not despair. We may have the major free by midnight."

It was a small hope but the only one offered her. She left the Indian still standing in the shadows and made her way back to the entrance of the cathedral. When she stepped out, dusk was falling and she saw two young men standing on the steps where the boys had been previously. They stared at her with open curiosity. Then one of them made some sort of comment about her and the other laughed.

Pretending not to see or hear them she hurried down to the carriage which still waited for her and returned to the hotel. All during the drive back she was tortured by the news that Eric was now a prisoner of their enemy. She had feared it when he'd been so long delayed in returning. Now there was no doubt of it.

Raj Singh was an agent with superior talents and training. If anyone could rescue the man she loved, it would be the Indian. She dare not let herself think that he could fail. In the meanwhile all she could do was wait and pray that Eric would arrive at midnight.

She debated telling Kingston about the newest development and then decided against doing this. The old actor was probably still in a drunken sleep, and he might prove a hindrance rather than a help. He was plainly fearful of what had happened to Eric and in turn what might happen to them. Better to let him rest until she knew more.

The hours until midnight she spent restlessly in her room. She wondered why Raj Singh had suggested they meet in the garden rather than his coming openly into the hotel and on to her room.

But that would mean he would run the risk of being seen meeting her.

He would actually be leading their enemies to her door, and he would never allow that. So a secret meeting in the garden was reasonable. When it was a few minutes before midnight, she put on her cloak and left her room. Most people in the ancient hostelry were asleep by this hour. The lobby was deserted except for the withered clerk who dozed on the stool by the desk.

She quietly made her way out into the warm dark night and walked swiftly in the direction of the gardens in the rear of the sprawling building. It was equally quiet out there, and the night was cloudy. She followed a gravel path which led between rows of decorative trees neatly set out at intervals on either side of the path.

She had been out there in the daytime and been impressed by the orderliness and beauty of the gardens. Now they were silent, dark, and except for the scent of the flowers, exceedingly menacing. She was expecting to see Eric or at the very least have some encouraging word from him. But she did not feel hopeful. For some dreadful reason the atmosphere of the gardens was poisoned by fear.

Betsy shuddered, and not from the chill but from her growing terror. She began to wonder if she had been wise in agreeing to the rendezvous, if she would really meet Eric there? She had great trust in Raj Singh or she would not have submitted to his idea to meet him in this dark place. Hesitating in the middle of the path, she looked about her for some sign of him.

After a moment she saw him come out from behind the trees. She could see his turban and the flowing robe defined against the night. He came walking toward her stiffly, in an almost mechanical manner which caused her to wonder.

She ran toward him and said, "What is the word?"

Raj Singh looked down at her, his bronzed face stony of expression, and his lips moved; but no sound came out. Then, before she could question him again, he slumped down on the gravel walk at her feet.

She knelt and frantically took hold of him. "What is the matter?" she said, shaking him in an effort to rouse him.

Then she saw the knife sticking in his back and hastily let him go. She knelt there stunned. The Indian had somehow managed to keep his appointment with her, no doubt in an effort to warn her, even though he'd suffered this fatal wound.

She fought her terror and tried to sort out her thoughts. Getting up, she decided to run back to the hotel and summon help in the hope there might still be some life in Raj Singh—though she guessed the odds were all against it.

She gave his prostrate body a final look and then started to run back to rouse the hotel clerk. She'd gone only a few yards when two other figures sprang out of the shadows and blocked her way!

"No!" she screamed, and she turned to run in the opposite direction.

But it was a futile effort! They were on her almost at once. She fell as one of them grabbed her and when she tried to struggle against them, a cloth was placed over her mouth and nose, suffocating her. She made a feeble last attempt to free herself and then passed out.

When she came to, she was stretched out in the back of an open wagon, her wrists and ankles bound and a gag over her mouth. She moaned slightly as the wagon went over some bumps in the road and she was tossed about. She felt cold and ill. Gradually it came back to her!

Raj Singh dead on the path in the gardens and she attacked and captured by some unknowns. They would have to be agents of Valmy. The same ones no doubt who had earlier managed to make Eric a hostage. Perhaps they would be reunited as captives. That at least would be something.

She did not dare to speculate on what her fate might be or where she was being taken. Judging by the road, they were somewhere outside the city. The dust from the dry dirt road rose with the movement of the wheels and made it that much more unpleasant for her.

It was what she might have expected. She'd been told that Naples was alive with Valmy's agents. But because she had never met the mysterious leader of the latest Napoleonic adventure, she had hardly taken the warnings seriously enough. Now it was clear this was not a game that was being played; this was a business of life and death!

The wagon rumbled on for what seemed an endless time. Every so often she could hear voices from the driver's seat, but she was unable to make out what was being said. Her wrists and ankles were paining from the tight bonds around them, and it hurt her to move even a little. This pain was magnified by the jostling of the wagon. Each time they went over a rough spot, she was agonized.

She lapsed into a kind of semiconsciousness, and then she was aware of the wagon halting. Rough voices conversing in Italian seemed to be all around her. The back of the wagon was opened, and she was dragged out by cruel and thoughtless hands. She whimpered with pain!

One of the men lifted her up and carried her like a sack over his shoulder. He walked a short distance and then opened a door and took her into a room lit by a candle. There was a kind of couch in one corner of it, and he threw her down roughly on the couch.

She was faceup and could see his unshaven, coarse face. He wore peasant's clothing, but he had a belt around his waist with a dagger in it.

His smile was mocking as he said, "Not what you are used to, signorina?"

Betsy twisted a little, and the bonds pained her more. She rolled her eyes to express her pain, but she received no hint of sympathy from the man.

He told her, "General Von Ryn has been waiting for you!"

The name of General Von Ryn meant nothing to her, but she assumed he must be one of Valmy's agents. She closed her eyes, and when she opened them again, the man had vanished. In his place there stood in the center of the room an old heavy-faced man with bushy gray eyebrows, shrewd penetrating brown eyes, and a missing left arm. He wore a shabby dark suit. The sleeve on the left was pinned to the front of his jacket in a neat fashion.

She stared up at the imposing figure, and it at once struck her that he was a man of some consideration. His long, weathered face showed character, and there was now concern reflected on it as he studied her condition.

"What have they done to you?" he asked irritably as he came forward to the couch.

Betsy looked up at him with pleading eyes and prayed that he might take some pity on her. The overland journey had been rough, and she was in great pain from the ties binding her.

With a deftness of long practice he reached into his breeches pocket, produced a penknife, and flicked it open. He did all this with surprising speed in view of his having only a single hand. Grumbling to himself, he bent over her and released her ankles, then her wrists. And finally he cut away the filthy gag which had bound her mouth.

He closed the knife and put it back in his pocket, saying, "That should give you some relief."

She managed to speak hoarsely and said, "Thank you!"

"Not at all," he said. "You should not have been treated in that fashion. Move slowly and the circulation will gradually come back to your feet and hands."

"Numb!" she said, trying to move her fingers, and then she raised herself up a little in an attempt to massage one ankle. Her hand was like a piece of ice and refused to function as it should.

"Don't try to hurry it," the old man warned her. "I'm a doctor. I understand these things. And don't panic! You will be all right. The numbness is only temporary."

"A long, terrible journey," she said.

"I'm sure of that," the old doctor agreed. "Let me pour you a glass of water." And he went to the table where a pitcher of water and some glasses had been set out. He poured a glass of the precious liquid for her and brought it over. "Let me touch it to your lips. Your hand may not be alive enough to trust yet."

"Thank you," she said again, more clearly this time. And she eagerly drank from the glass which he touched to her parched lips. The water at once revived her. She felt better and more able to grapple with her situation.

He stood with the half-emptied glass in his hand. "You can finish it later. Better not to drink too much at once."

She nodded, and now she was able to work her fingers, and her feet had some feeling in them. She asked him, "Where am I, and why have I been brought here?"

The doctor's lined face showed a wary look. "I can only tell you a little. You are in a small fishing village on the Adriatic Sea."

"Why was I kidnapped and brought here?"

"You know as well as I do. You are a secret agent operating out of London under the direction of Felix Black."

She stared up at him and said, "And you are one of the Valmy camp."

"So none of this should be a mystery to you, we are on opposing sides it seems."

She stood up with an effort and began to move about a little before his watchful gaze. She said, "What is to happen to me?"

"I'm not sure," the old doctor said. "Probably you will be taken to Valmy. I understand he is interested in you because you were a close friend of the emperor."

She glanced at him with her eyes flashing anger. "Friend enough to warn him away from Valmy and his schemes."

"I cannot argue that with you. I'm glad to see you are recovering from your bondage. We shall try to save you from further indignities."

"You have been kind," she admitted.

"Not at all," he said, though he looked pleased. "My name is Major Lacoste. I spent the most important years of my career in the service of the emperor. I lost my arm in the Peninsular Campaign, but I continued as physician and surgeon. You would be amazed at the skill which I can command at the operating table with one hand."

She went over and filled another glass with water and drank some of it. Then she asked him, "Do you believe you are still serving the emperor?"

"I do." There was no doubt in his reply.

She frowned. "Surely you can't be deceived by a charlatan like Valmy."

"Valmy was a brave soldier in our army, and he is now a political force to respect," the doctor informed her.

"I know nothing of his bravery in the field," she said. "But I do know that he is now undertaking an audacious plan with the real Napoleon or some clever impostor. And that once Valmy has made use of his puppet, he intends to see him destroyed so that he can become the emperor."

Old Lacoste smiled grimly at this. "I expect that is the story your superior in London told you. The truth is that your group has the assignment of killing the emperor."

"And that is what Valmy has made you believe!" she said with a sigh.

"I must believe my leader," Lacoste said. "The only hope France has is to be rid of the weak Louis and have Napoleon back on the throne."

She said, "What about Major Walters? Do you know what has been done with him? I understand your group took him prisoner also."

"I do not know," Major Lacoste said. "And I tell you this sincerely. We work in cell groups—independent of each other."

She said, "But all answerable to Valmy."

"That is correct."

"I was told that General Von Ryn was expecting me. Instead I'm greeted by you."

The old doctor looked rather grim. "You will meet him soon enough. It is his wish that you dine with him tonight."

"Who is he?"

"Valmy's close associate and the head of our unit," Major Lacoste said. "He is a Dutchman. A fairly young officer who rose swiftly. Napoleon has never liked him nor trusted him. But Valmy has found him useful."

Betsy said, "And Valmy makes the decisions now."

She could see a hint of concern on the old man's face as she made this point. Then he made an effort to rationalize this situation by saying, "The emperor is not yet his old self. Saint Helena caused serious problems with his health. He must rely on Valmy."

"And the mistress Valmy has selected for him I"

Lacoste showed surprise. "You know about her?"

"Yes."

"An unhappy choice in my opinion," he said with a sigh. "But the emperor is much alone. He needs company. What better than a lovely woman to divert him?"

"Divert him from Valmy's traitorous intentions," she said. "It is all so obvious. I don't know how you have been so easily taken in."

The old man shrugged. "What other chance do we have? This is our last hope for victory! Many of the old guard like myself are growing too old for action! If we do not restore the glory of France quickly, it will be too late!"

She stared at him sadly. "I can sympathize with you, for I have also known your emperor and came to be fond of him. Perhaps too fond! Your dream is doomed to turn into a nightmare of bloodshed in which the emperor will die along with all your high hopes!"

The doctor bowed. "You are a convincing young woman," he said. "I must close my ears to your arguments. And I warn you not to offer them to General Von Ryn. He will not take them with such tolerance as I have."

"When am I to meet him?"

"Shortly," Lacoste said. "In the meanwhile let me show you to your room so you may freshen up. You will be given the free run of this old house. But do not attempt to go outside. There are sentries all around the place, and they have orders to strike down anyone attempting to leave."

"So I'm still a prisoner."

"With extra privileges," he said. "You should not find it too trying an experience. I'm sure General Von Ryn will respect your sex and youth."

"I expect no more consideration than the average spy caught in my same plight," she said.

"Better not mention that," Dr. Lacoste said dryly. "Now come along."

He led her from the storage-type room where she'd arrived through a dining room where a table was being set lavishly with flowers, lit candles, silver and china and all on a gleaming white cloth. They went along a short hall, and her room was through the first door on the left. It was small, boxlike but had a bed, a commode with a washbasin, and a single plain chair.

"Not elegant," the old doctor said. "But you have all the necessities. When you are ready to dine, you can come out to the dining room. I have no doubt General Von Ryn will have arrived by that time."

She stood staring at the old doctor as he prepared to leave, and she asked him, "You say this Von Ryn will not give me a tolerant hearing. What sort of man is he?"

"Not one of my own favorites, yet I must obey him without question," Dr. Lacoste said. "In the army he was known as the 'White Executioner'."

Her eyebrows lifted. "White Executioner?"

"He was in charge of the division dealing with spies, and he had no hesitance in dealing out the death sentence—whether it seemed justified or not."

"So much for my own hopes."

"I doubt that he will dare touch you," Dr. Lacoste said. "It is my understanding that you are to be taken to Valmy."

"In Venice?" she tried him.

He smiled grimly. "I cannot say." And he bowed and went out, closing the door after him.

So here she was in another outlandish situation. She was not only worried about herself but greatly upset as to what had happened to Eric. He was sure to be dealt with more harshly than herself. On the other hand he was more experienced and better equipped to defend himself than she was. She could only pray that he was still safe.

She could not imagine why Valmy considered her important enough to be taken to him. Perhaps he wanted to try and get her to use her friendship with the emperor to help his cause. It was all terribly confusing. She dare not guess what lay ahead but live only for the moment.

With the limited facilities available to her in the cubicle of a room, she cleaned herself and made her clothing as neat as possible.

Her hair was becoming straggly, and she decided to comb it out and let it fall to her shoulders. It looked better this way.

She remembered that she was expected in the dining room, and so after a little while rather apprehensively she made her way out there. When she arrived in the room with its soft candlelight and fully set table, she found Von Ryn standing with his back to her as he stared into the fireplace. She saw at once that his hair was pure white and also that he was wearing a uniform of white, even his leather army belts were white leather.

It struck her as very strange. And she thought of her first impression of Felix Black, in his black carriage, black suit and top hat! He had seemed a bizarre creature! Now she was to meet a man of white!

He apparently became aware of her presence in the room and turned. She now had a second shock! His face was cruel and his features rather coarse as she had expected. But not only was his hair pure white, so was his skin, and eyebrows. And his eyes were a weird shade of pink!

"Mademoiselle Chapman!" he said with a cold smile.

"You are General Von Ryn," she managed.

"I am," he said, adjusting a monocle in his right eye to inspect her more closely. "They didn't warn me what a beautiful creature you are."

"I fear my role here is that of an enemy, General."

"We will try to forget that for a little," he said. "I suggest adversaries as a better term."

"As you say," she agreed, unable to resist staring at him—this specter in white!

He looked amused. "You think me different? Well, I am. Of course over the years I've adjusted to it. But I can promise you being born an albino is not a pleasant experience. Other children mock you, your health is poor, and you are subjected to much unpleasantness."

"I'm sure you have overcome your early troubles," she said.

"I have," he agreed. "I decided to exploit my being different. It has worked very well. At least people know who I am when they see me."

"You make a distinct and unusual impression."

His eyes met hers. "You do not find me ugly, I trust?"

"Not at all," she said. "You are refreshingly different."

He smiled and removing his monocle said, "Before dinner let us have a drink. I do appreciate that you find me tolerable in your eyes. That should make it easier for us later." He handed her a glass of wine with a significant look of grim amusement that could mean only one thing.

Chapter Twelve

DINNER HAD been a feast of many courses. Now the arrogant Von Ryn sat across from her puffing on a cigar and in a fairly drunken state. He had continued to drink all through the meal and was still at it. She had been careful only to sip the wine offered her.

When the servant waiting on them had retreated after clearing away the dessert, Von Ryn asked her, "You did not like the meal?"

"It was a banquet," she said.

"Yet you did not show enjoyment of it?"

"I am your prisoner."

"So that is your excuse," he said with a sour smile. "You are a spy. You know that I could have you executed at once."

"I do not believe France is at war," she said. "Spies are only given the death sentence when countries are at war. At least that is what I have been told."

"Your information is faulty," he snapped. "In any case the emperor is about to head the new revolution."

"I much doubt that," she told him.

"Do you?" he asked with sarcasm. "Have you any idea what my nickname is?"

"Major Lacoste told me. You are called the 'White Executioner'."

"Correct. And I did not win that title by courting disrespect."

"What do you propose to do with me?" she asked.

He tapped the ash from his cigar, then studied her with frightening pink eyes. "That depends a good deal on you. I have been asked to bring you to our leader."

"Valmy?"

"Who else?"

"I understood your cause was that of the emperor's," she said.

His smile was cold. "Valmy now makes the emperor's decisions."

"Then it is a sad day for Napoleon," she told him.

He did not seem bothered by her words. "Napoleon was finished at Waterloo. But the idea he gave birth to lives on. There must be progress. Thus it follows that a young man, Valmy, must take the role of emperor."

"Have you let Napoleon know your views? That he is merely being used as your stepping-stone to power?"

"That is not necessary. Napoleon does not ask questions any longer. He is a broken man, dependent on Valmy to make his decisions for him."

"Then I think you are introducing a spurious Napoleon. I find it impossible to believe that the man I knew would bow to such an arrangement."

Von Ryn stashed out his cigar. "You will meet the emperor. He is at headquarters. You can find out for yourself."

She rose from the table. "I'm very weary. My ankles and wrists still ache. I would like to retire to my bedroom."

He also got to his feet. "The evening is still young."

"I cannot help that," she said.

"I have a suggestion," he told her, coming around and taking her by the arm. "Let me give you a tour of the place before your retire. I would like to show you my room."

"No!" she said sharply.

The pink, brooding eyes met hers. "You can do as I ask or face a firing squad."

"You wouldn't dare kill me!" she said. "Valmy has made a request to talk with me."

"I can do with you what I will," he replied evenly. "I can tell Valmy you tried to kill me and I was forced to shoot you."

"I doubt if he would believe that."

"I lie very well."

"I do not doubt that," she said.

"You have your choice," he went on. "My room or the firing squad."

She made no reply, realizing this was not an idle threat. He fully intended to kill her if she didn't humor him. She knew he would take her silence as agreement; indeed this was what it was. When she had volunteered to become a secret agent for Felix Black, he had hinted she might be faced with such a moment. Now it was at hand.

Von Ryn's smile was lustful. "My room is down this hallway. You will find it larger than your own. You may spend the night if you like it. It is rather luxurious."

His bedroom was larger and better furnished, its chief feature being a large double bed and a canopy. He closed and locked the door after them. Then he removed his belts and jacket. After that he poured both himself and her another drink.

He ordered her, "Undress! It gives me a certain pleasure to watch a woman disrobe."

She made no reply. She was repelled by everything about him and tried to make herself think this was not real but a kind of grim dream. Slowly she removed her outer clothing and then her undergarments, until she stood before him naked.

He came to her with his pink eyes shining with lust. He whispered in her ear, "Your body is more lovely than your face." At the same time he kissed her and explored her breasts.

She felt no passion quicken in her. She was merely cold and frightened. He kept on whispering endearments and caressing her as he removed the rest of his clothing. Soon they were in bed together, and she felt his thrusting into her. While he was a vigorous lover, she could not offer any response to what she felt to be rape.

When his passion had been satiated, he sat up in bed and scowled at her. "You are like a creature of wax without any life! I have consorted with the kitchen girl here, and I vow her to be a better bed partner than yourself."

Quietly she said, "I did not boast of my accomplishments. This was entirely your idea."

"And so you behaved as coldly as you could," he said with annoyance. "You may have played your cards wrong, young lady. I could have been helpful to you if you had tried to please me."

"I'm not your prostitute," she said. "I'm your prisoner."

"And you can return to your cell!" he snapped. "Go on! Take your things with you! I do not want you here! I shall send for the kitchen girl, and she will spend the night at my side."

She hastily got out of the bed and put on her shift and slippers and carried the rest of her things in her arms. Tears of humiliation in her eyes she rushed out of the room and on to her own tiny quarters. She was spared further embarrassment by the fact she met no one along the way. Alone in her room she threw herself on the bed and sobbed.

A maid brought her breakfast on a tray early the next morning. She ate in her room and then dressed. She had just finished dressing when there was a knock on her door.

Tensely she went and opened it and discovered it was the elderly Dr. Lacoste. He bowed and asked, "May I come in for a moment?"

"Yes. Please do," she said, putting aside the tray and pulling out the plain chair for him.

He waved this aside. "I will not need to sit down," he told her. "I wanted to see if you were all right."

"Yes," she said.

"You saw Von Ryn last night?"

"Yes. I dined with him."

The old man nodded grimly. "So I understand. And he bedded you afterward."

Her cheeks burned. "Did he boast of that?"

"He spoke of it."

"It was not a conquest. It was rape."

"I understand," the veteran doctor said. "You were wise to accede to his wishes. He is not above wanting to have you executed. Best to give him no excuse. I think he derives some sexual satisfaction from ordering people's deaths by the firing squad. I have watched his face as it happened."

"I knew his threat was genuine. But I fear he was much disappointed. I did not prove satisfactory to him."

Dr. Lacoste smiled. "You used a woman's weapon and did it well. He is vain where his bedroom prowess is concerned. Unless he leaves a maid in raptures, he feels he has not been properly appreciated. Your smartest move was to fail him."

"Yes," she said wryly. "He let me know he prefers the embrace of the kitchen maid."

"So let her have the dubious honor of pleasuring him," the old doctor said. "From all that he said this morning, he considers you a cold fish not worth the bother. So you ought to be safe until you are taken to Valmy."

Her eyebrows raised. "Is he a ravisher of his women captives also?"

"He is fond of your sex," the doctor admitted. "And he beds down those who appeal to him."

"Perhaps I can make myself look ugly," she suggested.

He shook his head. "I wouldn't worry about it yet. And it may well be by the time you reach Valmy, he will be too busy with the new revolution to think about women."

"Is the revolt that close?"

"The day has been set," Major Lacoste told her. "We leave here with tomorrow mornings early tide. It is a couple of days transport by vessel to headquarters."

"I do not like what I'm hearing about Napoleon's physical and mental state," she said.

"Perhaps seeing you will be good for him."

"I was his friend, not his mistress. I was little more than a child at the time."

"The emperor needs friends more than he ever did," the old doctor said gravely. "That is why I will not desert the cause."

"It is Valmy's cause!"

He raised a protesting hand. "I have hopes, perhaps they are fantasies. But I believe when the moment of crisis arrives, the emperor will regain his strength. He will rise to his old self!"

"I fear you will be disappointed," she said.

"We shall see," the one-armed man sighed. "I shall keep a protective eye on you. And let me warn you not to annoy Von Ryn further. I believe him to be a little mad."

"Thank you," she said. "I shall attempt to stay quietly out of his way."

Pursuing this thought, she remained in her room most of the day. She opened the small window to let in the sun and air. And mostly she paced up and down the small space trying to think what she might do that she had not done, balancing thoughts of escape in her mind. She knew the house was well guarded, but perhaps between the house and the boat she might make a break or even at the other end of the journey.

She thought of Raj Singh who had given his life trying to warn her. She also wondered what had happened to Kingston. The poor actor would be in a state with Singh dead and both she and Eric vanished. But it was of Eric she thought most. If there had been any doubts in her mind as to her love for him, they no longer existed. She wondered what the sphinxlike Felix Black would say if he were told she had come to truly love the young officer. Perhaps it was what he'd expected.

For it was difficult to know what a master plotter like the thin man in black had in mind. She did not believe, as the old doctor had tried to tell her, that she was a pawn in a game designed to take the life of Napoleon. Felix Black had clearly stated that he wanted the former emperor saved and sent to a safe exile in the United States.

But Edward Barry O'Meara had not believed that. Like Dr. Lacoste, it was the Irishman's view that Black simply meant to discover if Napoleon had escaped for this final adventure and if he had, eliminate him from the earth. She clung to her belief in the word of Felix Black despite her growing confusion.

No invitation to share dinner with him came from General Von Ryn this second night of her being a captive in the old house. She had not expected one, indeed she had hoped she would not hear from him again.

But shortly before seven Dr. Lacoste came to her door, and with a wry smile on his lined face, the one-armed man told her, "I have come to ask you to dine with me. I cannot promise as fine fare as the general offered last night, but on the other hand I shall not expect the sort of payment which he demanded."

She returned the old man's smile. "I shall be happy to dine with you. As long as it will not anger the general."

The old doctor said, "He has left us for the evening. There is a brothel in the next village. He often goes there. I doubt if he will return much before sailing time tomorrow morning."

"In that case I look forward to our dinner," she said.

And she actually enjoyed it. They dined at the same table in a candlelit atmosphere. The food was ample if not as rich as the previous night, and she was able to relax and enjoy it. The conversation was much more interesting.

It turned out that the old doctor was a native of Le Havre on the English Channel and had often visited in England as a youth. He regretted the wars, but he revered Napoleon and his days of service as an army surgeon.

"I lost my arm in a battle with the Austrians," he said, reminiscing over his brandy. "Seventy thousand men crossed the river! We marched over the field where six centuries earlier the first Hapsburgs had battled for their throne."

"It all is still real to you," she said.

"It is," he agreed. "The emperor was there looking after us. It seemed he was everywhere at once. The men worshiped him and so did I. The battle began in earnest in the tall cornfields of yellow! The cavalry rode across the plain under a cloudless sky. Then the casualties began to roll in."

"That would keep you occupied."

"We were near the front line most of the time. So the men hadn't to be brought far. Some of the poor devils were beyond anything but the priest. Others we could help. Fifteen hundred from one division returned, and their strength had been sixteen thousand when they started out."

"So many men lost!" she said, shocked.

"We didn't even think about it," he told her. "I was trying to stop the bleeding in the side of an infantryman when the blast hit us. When the air cleared, I saw the ends of my torn left sleeve. My severed arm was on the ground a distance away!"

"How awful for you!" Betsy said.

"I didn't even realize what had happened: that it was I who had been maimed this time. My helper came to me and stood there in shock. He'd been lucky enough to escape any damage. I swore at him and told him to tie off the stump so I wouldn't bleed to death. I still felt no pain. He did as I directed and then he saw me on my way back to the hospital tent. I collapsed on my way there and had to be carted the last mile."

"And after all that you still had the urge to return to active military service," she said in wonder.

"It is in my blood," Major Lacoste told her. "I felt useless and mutilated. As soon as I was out of hospital, I worked at improving my skill as a one-armed man. I amazed my colleagues at the hospital by my ability to manipulate the scalpel and direct an operation."

"And you did return to the army."

"I had a special audience with the emperor. He gave me a decoration, and I told him that was not what I wanted. When I asked to be allowed to return to front-line service again, he smiled at me and gave his permission. I shall never forget that moment."

"You are a very brave man, Major. Napoleon sensed that."

"He had always been my idol. But after that day my worship was complete. He is my life."

"You long for more battles?"

"I hate war and its battles," he said with a burst of emotion. "But I long for victory, to see the emperor restored to his greatness."

She shook her head sadly. "I fear for you. I fear for both you and the emperor."

"You are a good girl," the old man said. "But you do not understand."

"On the contrary," she said, "I believe that I do. I saw the greatness in Napoleon even as a young girl meeting him only a few times. But the time has passed, if only you could bring yourself to accept that."

"A man lives on his dreams, mademoiselle," the doctor said earnestly. "I cannot give up mine lightly."

"I know," she said quietly.

Her sleep was restless that night, and she was wakened before dawn by the maid arriving with her breakfast tray. Then old Major Lacoste came and told her, "I'm responsible for getting you to the boat. I do not wish to make it too unpleasant for you. So I shall merely blindfold you."

"Is even that necessary?" she asked. "I have no hope of escaping in this strange place."

"I have my orders," he said. "I would be negligent if I did not take certain precautions."

So she was blindfolded, and he led her outside. She was placed in a cart with a lad and another girl. She could not see either of them. But as they chattered back and forth, she gathered that the girl was the kitchen maid who had so caught the White Executioner's fancy that he was taking her along on the vessel with him. The boy was to be cabin boy. Both of them were excited about the prospects of the sea voyage, and neither showed the slightest interest in her. She guessed they had been warned not to speak with her.

The cart was driven off, and she could tell it was only one of a caravan of wagons. She heard the wheels of the others and the voices of their passengers. After some incredibly rough road she could smell salt air more strongly. She knew they were close to the sea. The wagon stopped, and she was helped out.

She stood on the wharf waiting until old Dr. Lacoste came to her. He took her arm and said, "I will personally escort you on board."

And he did. He took her below, and when she was in a tiny cabin, he removed the blindfold from her eyes. He said, "You will stay down here until the ship is well away from shore. I will come and advise you. Then you will have the run of the ship until we reach our destination."

"Venice," she said, for she had been told that was where Valmy was in hiding with the emperor.

The old man's eyes twinkled. "Wherever!" he said.

"That kitchen maid rode in the car with me," she told him.

"I know," the doctor said with a frown. "That is very wrong. Von Ryn should not have taken her away from her village. He will be reprimanded for bringing her on board, and he will likely rid himself of her as soon as we reach port. She will surely end up in some sad straits perhaps even soliciting in the streets."

"Can nothing be done for her?" she worried.

"I will try and arrange something," the old doctor promised. "Perhaps one of the crew will have a sister or mother to take her in as household help. She should not be turned out on her own."

"I agree," Betsy said.

It was more than an hour later that she was notified she could go up on deck. When she made her appearance, the sun was shining and the air was warm and clean smelling. She stood by the railing, her hair blowing in the slight breeze.

She heard young laughter and turned to see that the new cabin boy and the kitchen maid were playing some game of tag on the afterdeck like two mischievous puppies. Her heart went out to the naïve young girl and the fate which might be in store for her.

Moving further forward, she came abreast of the wheel. And as she was standing there, General Von Ryn came out to stand on the bridge. He was resplendent in his usual white uniform, but he was wearing dark glasses. They gave him the look of a blind man.

But he was not blind to her. He came over to her and said, "So you are safely on board, Mademoiselle Chapman."

"Yes," she said, gazing out at the sea.

"You are distant today."

She glanced at him. "Do you wish me to pretend to be friends when we both know it is not possible?"

"I expect nothing from you!" he said harshly. "You will soon be confronting our leader. It will be interesting to know his decision concerning you."

"I expect no kindness," she said.

He gave a short, mirthless laugh. "You had better not, for you will surely receive none. Raymond Valmy is a bad man to have as an enemy."

She said, "Yet the emperor is my friend. I will prevail upon him to have Valmy let me go free."

"Small chance!" Von Ryn gloated. "Valmy makes the decisions these days."

Thinking to turn the conversation from a difficult subject, she countered with, "Are your eyes troubling you? I note you are wearing dark glasses."

He touched the fingers of a hand to the glasses and slightly adjusted them. "People suffering from lack of coloring are troubled by too much light. My eyes pain in the sunlight unless I have something to protect them."

"I did not know," she said.

Happily the captain of the three-masted vessel came along at this moment and took Von Ryn aside for some sort of discussion, and she used the moment to escape. She went to the other side of the deck and later to her cabin.

She dined with Major Lacoste and the captain and first mate in the first mate's quarters that night. It was known that General Von Ryn had taken over the captain's ample cabin and was hosting his kitchen maid there.

The old doctor said, "The sea is calm and the captain thinks it will continue to be until we reach port."

"It is a good season for sailing," the captain explained.

Betsy asked him, "Have you ever left these waters?"

"We have once gone to Gibraltar," the captain said. "But never on to the Atlantic. We have always returned."

Dr. Lacoste said, "If it is turbulent water you're looking for, let me recommend the English Channel. It is rough more than it is smooth. I speak as one who lived near it."

"I prefer it here," the captain said.

When they finished dinner, Betsy and the old doctor went for a stroll on deck. Dusk was turning into darkness and stars were beginning to appear overhead. The vessel was silent except for the creaking and movement of its hull and sails. She rode the waves gracefully, moving up and down like a true queen.

Betsy asked the doctor, "Shall I see you when we land?"

"I hope so," he said. "I would like to be assigned to look after the emperor's health."

"In that case you would remain at headquarters."

"Yes."

"I question that they will give you that responsibility," she said. "You are too honest a man. And you would be bound to tell both the emperor and those around him the true state of his health."

He frowned. "I do not think it will be that bad."

"I'm worried," she said. "But I do hope you will be somewhere nearby. I will not be so afraid."

"I will continue to do my best for you," was his promise.

And she was certain he meant it. In the short time she had known the old doctor, she had come to respect him. She must cling to him until she had escaped from this grim situation. They stood by the forward railing talking earnestly for a long while.

The captain's cabin showed lights through the portholes, and occasionally loud drunken talk could be heard from in there.

Then to the alarm and concern of Betsy and the old doctor, the shouting inside the cabin became more ugly. They could distinctly hear the sound of the young kitchen maid crying.

Betsy turned to the old man. "What do you think?"

"If it goes on, I'll go to the door in a moment," he said grimly. "He must be abusing that girl!"

"Has he done anything else?"

The sound of the girl's crying became louder and then the door of the cabin burst open and she came running out on deck naked. She ran to the railing and leaned against it, breathing heavily, her hair askew, behaving like a frightened animal.

Then Von Ryn came out in his bathrobe, a pistol in his hand. He spoke sharply to the girl, "Stop sniveling and come back in here!"

"No," the girl sobbed, covering her face with her hands.

Betsy was about to rush to the aid of the nude girl when without warning Von Ryn fired the pistol. There was a sharp report, a cry of terror from the girl, and a spreading stain of blood running down between her breasts.

"The scoundrel!" Dr. Lacoste said between clenched teeth, and then he ran forward to where the girl had slumped on the deck. He demanded of Von Ryn, still there with the pistol in his hand, "What have you done, you scum?"

"She wouldn't stop her sniveling! Refused to bed with me!" Von Ryn said sullenly.

The old doctor examined the girl and then looked up and said in a hushed voice, "You've killed her! She's dead!"

"No!" Betsy cried in protest. She had come up to stand beside the kneeling doctor.

Von Ryn smiled coldly and put the pistol back in his robe pocket. "It was her fault! She annoyed me!"

Some of the crew had silently gathered now, drawn by the gunshot. The cabin boy was there, sobbing sporadically, his teeth chattering.

Dr. Lacoste stood up and said grimly, "I regret I shall have to inform Raymond Valmy of this atrocious and needless crime you have committed."

"Tell him what you like," Von Ryn said with anger. "I shall give him my version of it."

The old doctor said, "Sir, you will do me the favor of not addressing me for the balance of the voyage, and I shall behave in a similar way with you."

"What do I care!" Von Ryn shouted. "She was a foul little thing who deserved what she got."

"I deny that, sir," the old doctor said. And to the captain he continued, "I will ask you that this girl be given a proper Christian burial!"

The captain nodded. "I shall look after it!"

"No!" Von Ryn said with hysterical rage. "There'll be no hypocrisy! I'll look after the slut!" And with that he ran to her and before anyone could stop him, he lifted up her still bleeding body and threw it over the side.

Even the common sailors murmured their dissent. The cabin boy ran off sobbing. The captain turned his back on Von Ryn, and he and the first mate walked away.

Von Ryn jeered at her. "Well, you're the only female left on board. Would you like to join me in her place?"

"You are a devil!" she whispered in fervent hatred and turned with Dr. Lacoste at her side. Together they walked away from the mad-acting general.

Lacoste told her in a low voice, "He has always been evil. He managed to get away with his wanton killing when the wars were on. But it is not so easy now."

"He felt absolutely no regrets for what he did," she said in horror.

"There is more wrong with him than being an albino," the old doctor said. "He is tainted with madness, and it is surely getting worse."

"The poor girl!"

"At least it was fast, and she is now at rest," he said. "She must have realized her fate, become homesick, and began to weep uncontrollably so that she was no use to him."

"What now?" she asked in a hushed tone as they stood together in the darkness of the deck.

"I do not think you need fear him," Dr. Lacoste said. "He knows he has to deal with me if he tries to harm you. And he has so far overstepped the bounds of decency that even the captain and crew are disgusted with him."

"He will likely lie to Valmy and escape without any punishment," she said.

"Not if I have anything to say," the old doctor told her. "But Valmy and he have been close. I cannot count on too much."

This proved to be her worst night. She had a fit of trembling when she went to her cabin, and she could not get to sleep. When she finally did sleep, her nightmares were all of the vicious murder she'd seen on deck. The whole grim episode was repeated in her mind!

But in her dreams the crazed Von Ryn stalked her with the pistol in hand. He ordered her to strip off her clothing on deck beside the dead girl, and when she was naked and shivering, he seized her and raped her in full view of the crew and captain! She awoke from this nightmare lathered in perspiration and screaming!

She lay staring into the darkness, unable to believe the kind of inhumanity one person could have for another. She had encountered various sorts of cruelty, but she had never seen the equal of Von Ryn's treatment of the simple farm girl.

Dawn came, and she still sought sleep. She arose with a reeling head and a sense of not having rested at all. When she went up on deck, all was strangely silent. The only person in sight was the man at the wheel. She went across the deck and stood staring at the bloodstained spot where the kitchen girl had fallen.

A voice from behind her said, "Yes. It really happened. There were times in the night when I wondered if it had not been all an evil dream. But it did happen!" It was the old doctor staring sadly at the spot.

She turned to him. "How silent it is. You can almost feel the tension in the air."

Major Lacoste nodded. "The captain and the crew despise Von Ryn. They cannot wait for the voyage to end."

Betsy shuddered. "Nor can any of us. I don't know what evil fate awaits me. But I shall be glad to be free of all this."

The one-armed man gave her a worried look. "I'm deeply concerned for your safety."

She met his look with a frightened one of her own. "You think he may try to force me into his bed again?"

"That is a real possibility," the old doctor acknowledged. "The thing that bothers me most is that I will not be here to protect you."

Her eyes widened. "What do you mean?"

"This morning Von Ryn deliberately brought about a quarrel with me in view of the captain and the first mate. He wants to put the blame for his plight on someone, and he decided on me. He slapped me across the face with his gloves and demanded that I give him satisfaction!"

"Satisfaction?"

He nodded grimly. "I have no choice as an officer and a gentleman but to accept his challenge for a duel. He has also insisted that the duel be with swords rather than pistols."

"But that puts you at a disadvantage," she protested. "With your one arm the only fair contest would be with pistols. And you ought not to be forced into that!"

The doctor shrugged. "It was a deliberate affront on his part. He wants me out of the way so he can tell Valmy his own version of what went on here. And it also means I'm unlikely to live to help you in anyway."

"Refuse the challenge!"

He shook his head. "I'm certain if I do, he will also use that against me."

"When is the duel to take place?" she asked.

"Today. Before the sun sets."

She was thinking swiftly now, and she said, "Is it not possible in a duel to have a surrogate? Cannot you elect, because of your having only one arm, to choose a substitute to act for you?"

"Who could I choose?" he asked. "Who would be willing to go up against an expert fencer like Von Ryn? I doubt if there is anyone on board who can handle a sword except myself and the captain."

Betsy's eyes met his. "You are wrong! I have had the best of training in fencing. By Napoleon's own aides. I will act for you!"

The old man was astonished. "You?"

"Why not?"

"I cannot allow a girl to take my place on the field of honor," he protested.

"I have my own debt to settle with General Von Ryn," she said with grim relish. "I promise you I can defend myself as well as any man!"

"You could be killed!" Major Lacoste pointed out.

"Better to be dead than subject to Von Ryn with you out of the way," she replied. "No, Major, I insist that you allow me to use my ability to protect myself by acting for you."

He stared at her. "You are truly that expert a swordsman?"

"Or swordswoman, if you like," she said with a bitter smile. "But I shall need a pair of seaman's trousers and a shirt!"

Dr. Lacoste speculated on this for a while. He said, "Even if you are defeated, he dare not kill you. He will have to consider satisfaction rendered by his victory, while he would not hesitate to run his sword through me."

"That is why I must act for you," she said.

She had won her point. The old man had chosen the captain as his second, and he took the information to Von Ryn who was said to have been highly amused by the turn of events. In the meanwhile she tried out the doctor's sword and then one offered her by the captain. She found the captain's weapon the lightest and best suited to her.

Word went through the ship quickly and caused a sensation. She and the captain did some practice fencing on the rear deck in the early afternoon. Her purpose was to limber up, but she did not attempt to push herself to her full capability. She feared Von

Ryn might be watching and be able to judge her style of combat too well.

The late afternoon arrived and with it the hour set for the duel. All of the crew came on deck in a sober, tense mood. Hardly a word passed among them. The little cabin boy friend of the girl Von Ryn had murdered was there in the very forefront. Major Lacoste was ready to take care of any wounds which might be incurred. Betsy appeared first in the dark trousers she'd borrowed and a white shirt open at the neck and wrists. The captain was at her side as her second.

Von Ryn appeared next. He wore white breeches and hose, along with a white shirt and vest. He wore his dark glasses and made a striking figure. The first mate was reluctantly at his side to act as his second.

Von Ryn faced her with a contemptuous smile as he said, "I shall not kill you. But in the event I win the match, I shall expect you to join me in my cabin for the night."

Her face was bereft of any expression, and she replied in toneless fashion, "If you bring me to defeat, I will accede to your request."

He laughed harshly. "We could almost forgo the duel by going to my cabin now."

"No," she countered. "You are entitled to your challenge."

The two seconds conferred, and it was agreed that the match take place on the smaller confines of the upper deck. All the spectators were herded to a lower level as the last-minute details were attended to. Then a shot was fired, and they faced each other, swords in hand, crouching for the first thrust.

Still wearing an arrogant smile, the White Executioner made the first aggressive move. They parried for a moment and moved about warily. Then he saw an opening and moved in on her! She saw the attack coming and dodged back, but she somehow stumbled!

Chapter Thirteen

THE POINT of Von Ryn's blade came dangerously close to her, but she swiftly recovered her balance and eluded him. They parried again, moving warily about, and again he made an attack on her, but this time it was he who threw himself off-balance as she dodged. She in return engaged his sword and all but wrested it from him!

There was a roar of approval from the tense watchers on the deck below! A grim look of hatred showed on the face of Von Ryn! He knew now he was up against no amateur opponent. This revelation seemed to urge him on to greater aggressiveness and to taking more chances!

One thrust actually penetrated her shirt at the shoulder and drew a little blood, but it was a superficial wound and she paid it no attention. Instead she studied his technique so that she might find his weak points. He disliked close-in engagement when their swords clashed together, preferring to make wild lunges at strategic moments.

Betsy grimly played on this. Perspiration ran down her temples, and she felt weariness in her sword arm. But she tried to eliminate these thoughts from her mind as she continued her battle against the hated Von Ryn. Then in a brief exchange of their swords his black glasses fell off. He made no attempt to retrieve them and a moment or two later stepped on them as he tried to dodge a lunge from her. His own feet trampled the glasses into broken pieces.

There was no question that the loss of the glasses put him at a disadvantage. It made up for the difference in their strengths. She now pressed him as hard as she could, and when he lunged back, he often missed her widely. Still he had drawn blood from her and was a dangerous opponent!

They circled the deck, crouching and waiting for a new engagement. Then she moved in and almost twisted the sword out of his hand. This seemed to unnerve him, and he jumped back. Finding himself against the railing, he leaped up on it and held the ropes leading up to the masts in one hand to balance himself while he fended her off with the sword in his other hand.

There were shouts of unfair from the crew. But he paid no attention, remaining on his precarious perch and keeping her at a distance with his sword. She moved about warily, waiting for the best moment. The sun was setting and all at once flooded that section of the deck with its dying rays. She sensed this would complicate his vision problems and suddenly lunged at him full tilt. To her surprise he did not block her, and the thrust went through. Her sword pierced his chest!

An astonished look crossed the white face, and blood spurted ruby red across his white shirtfront and vest. As the frozen spectators watched along with Betsy, he dropped his sword, which fell onto the deck with a clatter, looked around blankly, then let go his hold on the ropes, and toppled back from the rail into the ocean!

Betsy stood there breathing heavily, her sword still in her hand, unable to believe that the battle was over. Then she was vaguely aware of the crew cheering and the captain coming over and congratulating her.

Old Dr. Lacoste came to her and said solemnly, "It is settled! He's gone! No one even made an attempt to rescue his body."

She shook her head. "I can't believe it!"

"You have a great talent in fencing," the old man said. "Von Ryn was not your equal. Now you must go below and change. I will see you get a warm drink."

He gave her some sort of sedative, and she slept for several hours. When she awakened, darkness had come. She found it hard to believe that it all had happened. Then Dr. Lacoste came and invited her to dine with him.

They had dinner by candlelight in the same cabin in which Von Ryn had reigned so cruelly. She felt much better about it all, but she could not forget she was still a prisoner on her way to Valmy's headquarters.

She gazed at the old doctor across the table. "My status is unchanged?"

"If you're asking me if you're still a prisoner, the answer must be yes. No matter what I owe you, my first allegiance is the emperor."

"I hope it is not misplaced," she said.

The old man shrugged. "I have explained before. I must take the risk."

"You could let me go and say that I managed to escape on my own," she suggested.

He said, "Even if I could make Valmy believe my story, it would rob you of a chance to meet the emperor again."

"If it is the emperor and not an impostor."

"I'm counting on you to find that out for me," the old doctor said. "That is why Felix Black chose you for this mission."

Betsy said, "If Napoleon is now a broken man, I'm not sure I wish to see him again. I would rather remember him as the great gentleman I knew on Saint Helena."

"I do not think there has been that much change," he said. "It is my hope that my emperor remains strong."

She sighed. "So I shall see Venice, Valmy, and perhaps Napoleon."

"Yes."

"Will I face another Von Ryn in Valmy?" she wanted to know.

"Valmy is a very different sort," the doctor told her. "He has great charm, and while he may be as ruthless as Von Ryn was, he does not show it. I wager you will like him."

"I can't imagine it."

"His personality is hard to explain," Lacoste told her. "You shall judge it when you meet him."

"As Von Ryn's killer will I be much welcome?"

"I do not think the bond between him and Von Ryn was all that great. It is my belief that Valmy feared to force him from the group, thinking he might retaliate and spoil the plan."

"I had almost forgotten I was still in custody," she sighed.

"You will be free until we dock in the morning," the old doctor told her. "And you may rest easy in knowing that I will continue to be your friend."

She smiled across the table at him. "You are a strange old man."

"You think so?"

"Living with your dreams of glory which can never be again."

He sat back in his chair. "Can you blame me? My dreams are all I have. I'm quite alone—no wife, no children. All I have ever had was my emperor and my belief in him."

"I understand," she said quietly.

That night she lay in her bunk a long while waiting for sleep. Her world had a way of changing with confusing swiftness. Von Ryn was no more. At least she was safe from him. And she knew Lacoste would do all he could to help her. The kindly old doctor was her friend.

But Valmy would be quite a different proposition. She feared what he might decide about her. She even worried about a confrontation with the supposed emperor. Would he have forgotten her? It did not seem likely, since St. Helena was not that distant in his past. Yet she could not have made the impression on him which he had on her.

Most of all she worried about Eric Walters and what had happened to him. She missed the companionship she had known with him and the kindly actor. And she missed Eric's presence more than she would have ever guessed. She had come to care for him as she had no other man. If he were dead, she felt she might never love another.

When she finally slept, her dreams were strangely all of London. Again she sat in Felix Black's office and listened to the spare, elderly man question her sharply. She again vowed to serve him and try and discover if Napoleon still really lived. She moved from the room and met Eric in the hallway. He looked infinitely sad, and his wrists were bound. He told her he was on his way to the executioner. She woke herself up protesting this!

Daylight shone through her porthole. And when she looked out, she saw a passing ship. Then her breakfast was brought down, and later the one-armed Major Lacoste appeared looking apologetic.

"We will be leaving the ship shortly," he said. "I must blindfold you again and have you wear a shawl over your head so that it will not be so noticeable to those who may be watching from the docks."

"Is all this caution necessary?" she asked. "What harm if I see where I'm being taken?"

"I would have no objection personally," the old doctor said. "But I must carry out my orders. I'm still a soldier."

"Yes," she said bitterly. "And Valmy is your general."

He looked at her with infinite sadness and said, almost reverently, "No, my dear, I serve my emperor." And he proceeded to blindfold her.

Major Lacoste led her off the boat and to a waiting carriage. She could smell and hear the city, but the blindfold on her eyes allowed her to see nothing. It was an eerie experience. The carriage ride was short, and then she was transferred to a gondola. And it was in the gondola that they finally reached their destination.

Only when she was inside the huge palace did the old doctor remove her blindfold. Liveried servants moved about looking after various duties and the baroque plasterwork and gilded ironwork decorations set the tone for the mansion. Dr. Lacoste allowed her to look into a vast ballroom that shimmered with the dull gleam of gold, then through a series of rooms, one which was especially ornate with delicate red and gold carvings setting off black lacquer panels. The general tone of the palace was white and gold, with floors of black marble mosaic.

He led her up a curving marble stairway with a gilt railing and then along a wide hall with crimson carpeting to one of several tall white doors. He opened one of the doors and ushered her inside. It was a large bedchamber also decorated in crimson and gold, with the coverlet of the bed gold and the canopy crimson with a gold fringe.

"This will be your room," he said. "It is somewhat more comfortable than what I've been able to offer you."

She was awed by the grandeur of it all. "It is truly magnificent!"

"I have a room much like it," he said. "And of course the emperor has his own special apartment below. And Valmy has his quarters on this level. You will be meeting him shortly."

"When will I see you again?" she asked.

"Soon, I hope," he said. "In the meanwhile wash and rest yourself in preparation for your meeting with Valmy."

He left her, and a tiny Italian maid arrived soon with a jug of hot water for her bath. It was hard to communicate with the girl though she seemed bright enough. Betsy enjoyed the luxury of a warm bath and was surprised when the girl brought her a choice of clothing which fitted her very well. It was almost as if her coming had been announced, and they had been able to prepare for her.

She chose a green satin dress with a plunging front. And she was able with the maid's help to put her hair in an interesting updo. Gazing at herself in the mirror, she used the cosmetics offered on the dresser to complete her appearance.

Once dressed, she became uneasy in the room. She wished that Valmy would see her and get it over with. She went to the windows to look out and found them shuttered. She could not open the shutters, so she had to do with lamplight, even though it was not dark. The maid brought her a tray of food which was welcome. And then she waited some more.

It was late in the afternoon when there was a knock on the door, and it was the elderly Lacoste back again. He had changed into a brown coat and fawn trousers and looked rested.

He greeted her warmly and told her, "You are to have dinner with Valmy. I think it an excellent opportunity for you to make a good impression on him."

"I'm growing impatient even though I am a prisoner," she said. "What did he have to say to you?"

"A good deal," the old army surgeon said. "Things are moving slowly to a climax. He plans to move the emperor to Paris shortly to present him in a surprise move."

"Will that not be dangerous? Napoleon still has many enemies."

"But an army of supporters," the old man said. "Valmy has the organizing almost complete. He feels that victory is certain."

"I see."

"Valmy was upset about Von Ryn's death, but he agreed it was perhaps a blessing when I listed the behavior of the White Executioner. So I have overcome that hurdle."

"What is his attitude toward me?" she asked."

"He hopes you will join him in helping to inspire the emperor," he said.

"I cannot promise anything like that."

"He may be able to convince you."

"I doubt it," she replied. "What about my companions. Has he word of them?"

"I'm sure he will go into that when you two meet," Major Lacoste said. "I wish you well."

"I fear I face another ordeal," she worried.

The major made no comment. He left and she remained alone again until another knock on the door came sometime later. It was a footman in livery and a powdered wig.

He bowed and said, "I am to show you to the apartment of General Valmy."

She followed the dignified servant down the hallway and across to another wing of the huge building. They came to a door guarded by two other male servants in livery. The man accompanying her knocked on the door, and they were led inside. She found herself in a high-ceilinged room as ornately finished as all the others. There was a table set for dinner in one corner of it and a desk in another.

At the desk there sat a handsome dark-haired man with a thin, ascetic face. He wore the colorful red jacket of a military man with gold epaulets and other trim. His trousers were blue, and when he stood up to greet her, she saw that he must be over six feet tall.

He came toward her with a smile on his thin, even-featured face. He took her hand and kissed it. He said, "Mademoiselle Chapman. How kind of you to pay me this visit."

"I had little choice," she reminded him.

Amusement flickered in his eyes. "That is true," he admitted.

She asked, "What do you presume to gain by keeping me a prisoner?"

He smiled. "I gain the presence of a lovely lady to grace my rather dull days and nights."

"You know I'm the enemy," she said. "So you cannot much anticipate my company, nor I, yours."

"On the contrary," he objected. "There is such a thing as friendly enemies, you know."

"I doubt we will achieve that status."

He took her lightly by the arm and led her over to the table. "You look exquisite in that gown. I felt it might suit you."

"Where did it come from?" she asked.

"I keep a certain stock here for ladies who may be visiting me," he informed her in the most casual fashion.

She blushed. It seemed she was now in that large group of females. He pulled her chair out, and she sat down. Then he took his own seat opposite her.

He said, "What a remarkable thing that you should have known the emperor."

"I was on Saint Helena."

"Not everyone on Saint Helena knew him, I'm sure."

"They didn't," she admitted. "I happened to be living close by his quarters."

"How fortunate for you," the tall handsome man said. And she could not help but acknowledge that he had a charming, smooth manner—almost too easy.

She said, "Why did you kidnap me?"

He smiled. A servant came and poured them wine. He told her, "Enjoy some wine. You will find it an excellent vintage."

She took the wine and sipped it. Then she told him, "You have not yet answered my question."

"I will counter it with a question of my own. Why did you become an operative of that wily old spider, Felix Black?"

"I needed work."

"And you are opposed to the emperor being returned to his throne?"

"I'm not at all sure the emperor is still alive," she said. "He is supposed to be buried on Saint Helena."

"I will rid you of that notion in due time," was his promise. He was studying her closely. "Have you any idea what a beauty you are?"

"Please!" she protested.

"So you have become a spy," he said, still genial in tone. "You know what happens to spies when they are captured?"

"I would like to know what has happened to Major Eric Walters and George Frederick Kingston," she said.

He looked amused. "Are you so worried about them? But of course, Major Walters is your lover."

She reacted angrily, "I do not think our relationship is any business of yours!"

"You are quite right," he agreed. "I will put your mind at rest. Both the gentlemen you mention are my prisoners."

"They are still alive?"

He nodded. "Being held prisoner in Naples."

"What are you going to do with them?"

He gave her a strange look. "I haven't decided. Perhaps we can work that out later. Black has other agents in Europe trying to block my work. Do you know their names?"

"Only that of Raj Singh."

"He is dead," Valmy said in a bored tone. "And Dr. O'Meara is in Paris being carefully watched by my people. He will be taken into custody soon."

"Why are you so afraid of those of us who knew and admired Napoleon?" she asked.

"Your admiration is for a defeated emperor, not a Napoleon resurgent," he said. Then the waiter came with their first course, and he suggested, "Let us enjoy our dinner. It was prepared especially for you."

She could not resist the food, for by now she was hungry. The wine had also made her pleasantly tipsy. She found it a weird but not entirely unpleasant situation. At least she knew that Eric was still alive and safe.

Over the excellent dinner she said, "Why are you not willing to let the emperor go to the United States and enjoy a quiet life of freedom?"

The handsome dark man said, "Because he is the emperor. It is not right that witless Louis should reign in his place. He wants his power again, not a life of retirement."

"I wonder," she said. "Perhaps you are the one so anxious for power."

Valmy gave her a look of reproach. "One does not cut an eagle's wings and expect him to be happy though unable to fly."

"I fear the eagle in this case is as much a prisoner as I," she said.

"You will meet the emperor in due time," Valmy said. "He has an apartment in this very palace. But I must be sure about you before I allow such a visit."

"I'm not sure he'll recall me," she said.

"I've already spoken to him about you," Valmy said, "and he remembers you very well. It seems some of his officers acted as your fencing teachers, and you proved an apt pupil."

She said, "Did you hear that from Major Lacoste or from Napoleon?"

"From both," he said. "From Napoleon first. He speaks of you with warmth."

"Does he?" she said, not certain that Valmy was telling her the truth. He could very well have made it up, based on what he'd heard from the old major. On the other hand it was possible the emperor had remembered. And if he had, it proved this was truly Napoleon and not an impostor.

Valmy went on, "You proved you have lost none of your skill by your performance aboard the ship which brought you here. You cost me a valuable man in General Von Ryn."

"He was a monster!" she said bitterly.

The dark handsome man laughed. "I agree. But a useful monster. I could assign him tasks which repelled others."

"I do not doubt it!"

He went on smoothly. "At any rate Major Lacoste has pleaded in your behalf. He is one of the true old guard and has the ear of the emperor as well as my own. So you can count yourself lucky."

"Major Lacoste is a fine man," she said.

"Yes, a little old-fashioned in his views perhaps but all in all truly loyal."

She gave the dark man a sharp scrutiny. "I fear you may be leading him astray as you are the emperor."

"Your mind has been poisoned against me by that old spy master, Felix Black. Did you know he has hypnotic powers?"

"I had heard it."

"He has," Valmy told her. "I wouldn't be at all surprised if he had used his powers of hypnosis on you. That would account for your confusion of mind."

Her cheeks burned. "I'm not at all confused."

"Of course you would not think so," he agreed. "But it might pay you to give the thought some consideration. You could perhaps throw off some of your twisted opinions."

She touched her napkin to her lips and placed it on the table. "I consider Felix Black a man of honor. I think he means the emperor only good."

The man across from her frowned. "Your instructions may not have included shooting him at point-blank if the opportunity arrived. But I can tell you some of your fellow agents have been so instructed."

"I can't accept that," she said.

"I will not impose my opnions on you," he said.

She asked, "Have I your permission to retire? I'm weary."

He smiled again, his good humor seeming to return. "Of course. But first let me show you the rest of my apartment." He helped her up from the table and then led her on a tour of the rooms.

The tour came to a halt in a bedchamber which was done with much gold trim like the other rooms. Everything was white and gold with some red lacquer for contrast. The ceiling had an ornate mural in full color of lovers strolling in a garden. The walls were lined with a number of huge mirrors. On every side she saw their reflection at various angles in the mirrors. There was a rich Venetian bed with crimson brocade. This bed was raised up on three steps like a throne and flanked by a pair of torches in the shape of nude maidens bearing baskets filled with tall candles on their shoulders.

"It is a strange room," she said.

He nodded. "It belonged to a prince famous for his amorous conquests."

She arched an eyebrow. "This room has so many mirrors!"

"Yes, it does," he agreed. "The prince has been dead a century. I am the prince here now."

"I understand," she said.

"I doubt it," he told her with a new firmness in his voice. "For I have not yet made my proposal."

"Your proposal?" she echoed, not following his thinking.

"Yes," he said. "You asked me about my plans for you and your two associates, what was in my mind."

"Yes," she said in a small voice.

"I will tell you, Mademoiselle Chapman," he said, his eyes fixing on hers. "I promise Major Walters, Kingston, and yourself freedom and passage back to England if you agree to my condition."

"What is your condition?"

"You remain here this night and for as many nights as I see fit, prior to your meeting the emperor. That you live here with me in this apartment."

She stared at him. "You are asking me to be your mistress?"

"Yes," the handsome dark man said. "I am. I do not think that such a great sacrifice on your part. You have had men before, including Von Ryn. I think you might find me a gentle lover."

"I had not expected this," she said.

"You might have. The arrangement will only be of short duration. We leave soon for Paris. And at that time I will see you and the two others on a Channel boat to Dover."

She gazed directly at him. "Will you give me your solemn promise?"

"I will," he said. "What is your answer?"

"Do I have any choice?" she asked bitterly.

"I will have the maid assigned you sent here and also the items which were provided for you in your room. You can take your ease for a while. I have some matters to attend to. Prepare yourself. I will return shortly."

She stood there stunned after he kissed her gently on the lips and left. She might have known what he planned from the start. He had gradually led her to a point where she could not turn back. So now she was to become the mistress of this handsome dark-haired adventurer! Only because it would mean saving the life of Eric and Kingston.

Could she trust Valmy's promise? She somehow felt that she could. He was not the same sort of rogue as Von Ryn. He had some sense of honor remaining. Yet he demanded that she degrade herself. And if she complained, he would reply that she had let herself in for this kind of experience when she had enlisted with Felix Black.

Her maid came bearing some of the things from the other room. The girl wore a pleased smile as if she felt Betsy had been offered some signal honor. And she supposed in the girl's view she had. For her own part she felt that she was selling herself. But she must do it. There was no other way to save herself and the man she loved.

She bathed again and donned a silken robe brought her by the maid. She suspected the girl had assisted in such preparations before. Then she stretched out on the bed and waited.

When Valmy strode in a little later, he was also wearing a robe. His was of crimson, and she could tell that beneath it he was naked. He came to the bed, sat on it, and leaned down and kissed her again with great tenderness.

"You are so very lovely," he said in a voice husky with emotion.

Then he raised her up from the bed and slowly took the robe off her so that she stood before him naked. He then removed his own robe, and she saw the manly body, well muscled, in the full vigor of late young manhood. He took her in his arms, and she had a glance at their two nude bodies joining in the many mirrors. It was as if the room were suddenly filled with attractive nude couples!

She felt him press against her, her breath came in gasps, his tenderness and his rigidity evoked a mood of passion in herself. She had hoped to keep this restrained as she had when Von Ryn had forced her into his bed. But this gentle approach was entirely different, and she succumbed to his desire!

Soon they were on the bed joined in an ecstatic intimacy! Her soft cries mingled with his murmured words of approval. She had never experienced such a long interlude of passion nor such a stunning climax. At the end they lay side by side, sated and relaxed.

It was then he turned to her and said, "I will ask you something which I have asked no woman before. Will you be my wife?"

"Never," she whispered with tautness.

He turned his head on the pillow to study her as she stared up at the crimson canopy. "I could learn to love you as a wife. I think I love you now."

"I could never love you!"

"Major Walters?"

"Yes."

"Too bad," he sighed. "So I shall only have you for this little while." He reached out and touched her breasts tenderly. "We do so well together! It is a shame!"

Her eyes filled with tears, and she brushed his hand aside and turned her back on him. "I did not mean to behave as I did. I betrayed myself!"

"Never mind, my little mademoiselle," he said softly. "It was good. I am satisfied. I will not give up my hopes. But at the least you will perhaps remember us together one day and think of it with some feeling."

She slept soundly, and when she awakened, he had gone. She got up and the maid came and she bathed and had a breakfast served with silver elegance in the other room. She could not make herself properly accept the events of the night before. She loved one man, and yet she had shared a bed of satisfying passion with another. She had discovered something she had not known about herself, and it frightened her.

She tried to console herself that she was here because it was the only way she could help Eric. But she sincerely hoped that the arrangement would not go on too long and she would not succumb to the desire the handsome Valmy instilled in her.

In the late afternoon her lonely vigil was broken by the arrival of old Major Lacoste. The venerable army surgeon was tactful about finding her in Valmy's apartment. "I was told you were here," he said.

"I was given no choice."

"That does not surprise me," the old man said. "You are a beautiful young woman, and Valmy is an experienced lover."

She looked down. "I feel degraded."

The old man touched her arm. "You must not think about it!"

"How can I help it?"

"Think of the other problems we have," the old man said. "Do not cross Valmy, for he can be as vicious as Von Ryn when he likes."

"I have sensed that," she said. "He has promised to spare the lives of my two associates. Do you think I can trust him?"

"Only as long as you keep his goodwill."

"Which means I must remain here!"

"Perhaps not too long," he told her. "I believe the plan is to leave shortly for Paris. He will not have any time for love affairs there."

For the first time she now gave attention to the old man's mood, and she saw in it something which had not been there before, something close to despair.

Staring at him, she asked, "Has something gone wrong?"

"Why do you ask that?"

"I don't know," she said. "There's a hint of something in your manner—as if you were depressed."

The army surgeon turned away from her and frowned down at the crimson carpet. "I am."

"Tell me!"

"It is the emperor."

"What about him?"

"I was given a brief audience with him this morning," he said.

"And?"

"I was shocked. That woman living with him, rather beautiful in a coarse way, was drunk when I arrived early this morning."

"That is shocking," she agreed.

"A man whose son is the prince of Rome, whose wife was a princess, reduced to living with a drunken slattern!"

"Why does he allow it?"

"He rebuked her in my presence, and she jeered at him. Called him by a foul name! My emperor!"

"Is he truly the emperor or an impostor?" she asked. "This does not sound like the Napoleon I knew."

"Nor does he act like the emperor I revered," the old man said unhappily.

"But he does look and speak like Napoleon?"

"I think so," the old army surgeon worried. "His gray hair and the moustache change his appearance. And he is thinner than when I last saw him. He looks burned-out."

"Perhaps that is a true description!"

The old doctor paced up and down. "I do not know which way to turn. I cannot make up my mind."

Betsy said, "One thing seems clear to me. Felix Black was right. The Napoleon who has returned will be no match against Valmy."

He looked at her over his shoulder. "Felix Black said that?"

"Yes."

"It could be true though I would never have admitted it before," Lacoste said worriedly. "I asked him if he were well and had he any need of my services of a physician."

"What did he say?"

"He said that Valmy had provided him with doctors."

"Valmy has the complete say."

"When I see him, I shall demand that he free the emperor from the company of that drunken woman!" the old man raged.

"Perhaps he wants her there to further demean the emperor," Betsy said. "To make him more apathetic than he is."

"He is surely in a state of apathy if what I saw and heard is any indication."

She asked, "Do you still think your group can successfully place him back on the throne?"

"I'm no longer sure of anything!"

"So what will you do?"

"Speak frankly to Valmy for one thing."

"Do you think that will help?"

"I hope so."

She warned, "You must be careful not to anger him too greatly."

"I know."

She said, "I wish he would allow me to visit the emperor. If there is any sort of recognition of me, I would know he is truly Napoleon."

The old army surgeon asked, "Has he spoken of allowing you to go down below to the emperor's quarters?"

"He promised that I would in due time. I cannot understand his reluctance unless he is afraid I will see this man is not truly the emperor."

"He seemed genuine to me," Major Lacoste said. Then he paused and added, "And at the same time I'm not certain."

"I must try and persuade him to let me visit down there."

"Yes. Keep after him about it."

She gave the old man an anxious look. "If all fails, do you think there is any hope of my escape?"

"The palace is guarded as heavily as a fortress."

"I know."

"There is no danger yet," the doctor assured her.

"But if things grow worse," she suggested.

His experienced eyes met hers. "While I live, I will not desert you," he promised.

Chapter Fourteen

BETSY AND Raymond Valmy lay side by side on the massive bed after a session of lovemaking which had become a nightly routine for them. She knew that he was obsessed with her, and it frightened her. She had also come to enjoy him in a purely physical way. She was hoping to save Eric's life, and she feared that Valmy might decide to break his vow to her. By having the man she loved killed, he would remove the barrier which kept her from being his fully.

She turned to him and said, "It has been ten days, and I haven't been allowed to visit the emperor as yet."

Valmy frowned. "You must be patient."

"I have been," she said. "But I confess it now appears that you are afraid to have me meet him. Is he an impostor?"

"No," he said sharply, sitting up a little so that he could look down on her.

"Then why?"

"He has been unwell. And the woman with him has turned out to be a problem."

"Why not get rid of her?"

"I would, but he refuses to let her go. He is weary of her, but he fears if he lets her go, we will have her silenced so she cannot brag of her conquest."

She stared up into his handsome face. "Would you?"

"Yes. We would have no choice. We couldn't risk her talking at this time."

"When do you go to Paris?" she asked.

"As soon as I have word everything is ready there," he said. "It will begin with a series of political rallies. Our group will storm the people into a fury. Then at just the strategic moment we will appear with Napoleon."

"But he is old and weary, so Major Lacoste says," she pointed out.

The handsome Valmy sighed. "If I tell you something, will you promise not to repeat it to that old surgeon."

"If that is what you want?"

"Swear!"

"If you like."

"Napoleon is dying."

It was her turn to sit up now. "What?"

"He is dying. One of those pranks which fate plays on us. When he left the island, he was pretending illness. But since then he has become really ill—that damn liver disease which has infected so many who lived on Saint Helena."

"My father died of it. In a very short time."

"And Napoleon is slowly wasting away and becoming less able to carry out our plan as the days pass."

"What can you do?" she asked.

"I'm trapped," Valmy admitted. "I cannot hurry the business in Paris. We must wait until the time is right. In the meanwhile I'm having to try and nurse the emperor along."

"The major felt he was ill. He offered his services, and Napoleon refused them."

"He knows that word about him mustn't get out," Valmy worried. "I have doctors looking after him, men whom I can trust."

"What about their abilities?"

"Good enough."

"Major Lacoste seems to have special talents. Why must you keep this from him?"

Valmy gave her a troubled look. "Because Lacoste is of the old guard. The emperor represents everything for him. If he felt Napoleon could not see this plan through, he would abandon it as well. As so would many others of the old army crowd. We need them."

"I see," she said quietly.

He lay back on the pillow and stared glumly upward. "I only needed the emperor for a few months. By that time I would be established in the eyes of the people. Then I could manage without him."

The words bit into her mind. She remembered what Felix Black had told her in London. It was all coming true, though in a rather different way than she had expected.

She said casually, "You never meant to use him long. You planned he should be eliminated so you could take his place."

"But that was different. It threatens everything to have him ill. If he should be unable, to make an appearance in Paris, the whole project is threatened."

"You'd rather have him live to die a martyr by an unknown assassin's bullet and will the throne to you. That was the plan, wasn't it?"

"You witch!" he said angrily, reaching out and grasping her wrist and twisting it until she cried out. "What evil spell did you use to come by that information?"

"It was given to me by Felix Black," she said.

"He's mad!" Valmy said, releasing her wrist. "Your whole theory is mad!"

"I wonder. You will not let me see the emperor. Are you afraid of what I might say?"

"Yes," he told her with a grim smile. "I'll be more careful than ever to keep you apart now."

"You despise my motives and you distrust me," she said. "Why do you want me around you?"

He laughed bitterly. "You have a lovely body."

"There are many as good available to you at any time," she said.

"All right, I'll confess. It is the combination of your mind and body. You have enchanted me. I still want you as my wife."

"You know that is not possible," she said.

He sat up. "Would you not like to be the wife of the new emperor of France?"

She stared at him. "So that is your ambition."

"Napoleon was only a corporal, and he gained the throne. I was a general!"

"And you have the same magic quality, I will not deny that," she said. "But to be a true ruler, one should have more than mere ambition."

"Ambition will suffice for a while," he said. "Later I can develop the other qualities." And he got up and put on his robe and left her naked and alone on the big bed.

His telling her that Napoleon was slowly dying of the same disease which had killed her father had come as a shock. And she could see that Valmy was truly bothered by this unexpected turn of events. The situation had been further complicated by the woman chosen as the emperor's companion turning out to be an unmanageable drunkard. The emperor's desire to protect the woman made it impossible for them to get rid of her.

All was not going as well as Valmy had hoped. And in his musings beside her in the bed he had let drop the plot that had always been his blueprint. He had scheduled the emperor's death when it would do him the most good. Now the unforunate Napoleon might die before they were able to get the plan under way.

Napoleon appearing in Paris and seeming ready to take on the duties of emperor again was imperative to Valmy's scheme. If the emperor were too ill to speak or show himself, the whole plot would be in jeopardy. She must somehow convey the gist of this to Major Lacoste without actually breaking her vow to Valmy.

She was sick of being confined in the apartment. Valmy had gone as far as to unshutter some of the windows facing the ocean so she could have fresh air and sunshine. But he refused to let her leave the apartment or even venture out in his company. She was still very much a prisoner.

Not until the following afternoon did the elderly Major Lacoste come to visit her. When he was sure they were alone, he spoke to her in a low, tense tone, "I am finally convinced that Valmy is an utter scoundrel."

"There is no question he means to use the emperor," she agreed.

"All that Felix Black told you is ture," the old man said bitterly. "I have been deceived. All of us faithful to Napoleon are being used in a crass manner. The emperor himself is but a puppet in all this."

"If he is to be saved, he must be removed from Valmy's charge," she said.

"That will not be easy," the army surgeon worried. "In fact it is probably impossible."

"It should be tried," she said.

"I'll be satisfied for the moment if I can get you free," Lacoste said. "Valmy is planning to move everyone to Paris in a few days. You should escape before the move is made and alert the other agents in Paris to what is going on!"

"The problem is that Major Walters and Kingston are also prisoners somewhere. That is why I consented to live here with Valmy. It's my only hope of saving them. If I run off, he will surely order their execution."

"You cannot let that halt you at this time of crisis," the veteran army surgeon said. "Be sure that they are also making their own escape attempts. They could even be free now."

"You think so?"

"Yes."

Betsy said, "Valmy would never tell me as long as my fear for their safety was keeping me with him."

"Exactly," the old one-armed man agreed. "So you must concentrate on a plan for your own escape. I shall try to help you."

"If I could get out of this apartment, I would try to find the emperor and warn him!"

Lacoste shook his head. "There are guards on this door and at the emperor's door. Guards everywhere! But if you manage to escape, you might in passing be able to get at least a few minutes with the emperor."

She looked at him eagerly. "Have you any ideas?"

"A plan is slowly forming in my mind."

"Tell me!" she urged him.

His lined old face showed concern. "You must not be too impatient," he said. "Let me develop this. It will begin with your complaining of illness to Valmy."

"Will he guess I'm pretending?"

"No. I shall give you a potion which will make you slightly ill, produce the symptoms of a fever without your actually having any."

"And?"

"Then I will ask his permission to bring in a Venetian doctor or two to consult with me on your case. I will explain that the fever is a rare type particular only to Venice, and thus it will take a Venetian doctor to properly understand your condition and treat it."

"It sounds plausible so far," she said.

The old man paced up and down as he planned, his hand on his chin. "I will arrange for the doctor to be your rescuer. Either you will don his dress and escape in this disguise or together with his help we will fight our way to freedom."

"You will come with us?"

"I will have no choice," he said with a shrug. "Once I help you escape, I will no longer be able to remain here. I believe I can do more to help the emperor on the outside."

"I'm sure you can," she agreed. "There is supposed to be a ship waiting off Calais. If we can only get in touch with its captain, the best move would be to somehow get the emperor from Valmy's custody and have him safely transferred to the ship."

Lacoste nodded. "We can work on that next."

"When will we begin?" she said.

"I'll bring you the potion in an hour or so," he said. "Take it and by this evening you should be showing symptoms of a fever."

"What if he has those other doctors looking after the emperor come to see me?" she worried.

"Tell him you don't want them," the army surgeon said. "A female is entitled to her whims—especially when she's been sharing your bed. Tell him you will only see me."

So the project of her escape was set in motion. Lacoste returned with the medicine. She took it as he'd directed, and by the time Valmy returned to dine with her, she gave all the appearance of having a bad fever.

The handsome dark man was upset at once. He asked her, "How long have you felt like this?"

"I started to have a headache and chills this morning," she told him, stretched out in the bed.

He frowned. "This is bad! Especially as we'll be taking off for Paris in a day or two. I have a doctor down with the emperor now. When he finishes examining him, I'll have him come and take a look at you!"

She shook her head on the pillow. "No! No! I do not want him!"

Valmy's handsome face showed frustration. "You must have a doctor!"

"No, I'll be all right!" She groaned and closed her eyes.

"I insist!"

She opened her eyes again and mournfully said, "If I must have a doctor, bring in Major Lacoste. I know him and respect his talents."

"That old man!" Valmy said disgustedly. "I only keep him on because he is popular with the emperor. I do not think him worth anything as a doctor!"

"I disagree," she replied firmly. "And if I'm to have a doctor, it must be Dr. Lacoste."

Valmy was annoyed. "You're being unreasonable! The doctor downstairs is younger and has an excellent reputation!"

"Still I want Dr. Lacoste," she insisted. "I have not asked much of you."

He sighed. "Very well! Since you are so clearly ill, I shall give in to you."

"Dear Raymond!" she said with a weary smile.

He came and sat on the bedside and took her hand in his. "You know how much I care for you. I cannot lose you as we near the moment of our return to Paris. I want you to be well and happy."

"This will pass, I'm sure," she told him.

He summoned Dr. Lacoste, and the old man appeared and examined her. When he'd finished, he told Valmy, "It is a fever. One I cannot name. The city of Venice is known for its several varieties of fever."

Valmy scowled. "How will you treat her?"

"I will do my best," the army surgeon said. And then he added, "If she doesn't respond readily, I would suggest that I be allowed to call in as a consultant one of the local Venetian doctors."

"Why not have one of the doctors taking care of the emperor see her?" Valmy wanted to know.

Lacoste smiled. "They would be no better informed on these Venetian fevers than I. It will take a local man. Several of the priests here are physicians. I might get one of them."

"We must get her well quickly," Valmy said. "We have to make this move to Paris."

"She could be left behind," the army surgeon suggested.

Valmy crimsoned. "That is not possible!" he said in his arrogant manner. "I want her with me."

"Then I have your permission to bring in a consultant if I must?" Dr. Lacoste said.

"Yes. Just so long as you get her on her feet."

"I shall wait until morning," Major Lacoste said. "If she shows no improvement by then, I will seek other help."

Betsy watched and listened to this charade with a pounding heart. It all appeared to be working out well. She did not have to stretch her pretending to seem ill, for the medicine which Lacoste had given her made her feel truly miserable.

Valmy paced about the apartment all evening. He tried to entice her to join him for dinner, but she only took a little broth in her bed. She could see that he was beginning to fear whatever she had might be contagious. After dinner he sat with her a bit, and then he excused himself and told her he would sleep in the adjoining bedchamber. She was left alone in the room with mirrors.

She passed an uneasy night. In the morning he came to see her before he left. The tall handsome man was concerned that she seemed to show no improvement. He said, "I hope that old dog Lacoste is right in his treatment of you."

"Perhaps a Venetian doctor could manage a quick cure for me," she said.

"I have given him permission to try that today," Valmy told her. "I shall not be able to look in on you again until late this evening. I have to go to a town outside the city and make plans for our transportation."

"You will not use the public stages?" she asked with faked innocence.

He frowned. "That would be out of the question. This is a most private mission. We must cross the border into France without the identity of the emperor being discovered."

"I have not met him yet. You haven't allowed it," she complained.

"And I shall certainly not allow it until you are better," he said sharply. "You might infect him with whatever you have."

"I'm sorry," she apologized.

"It is all right," he said stiffly. "I will not kiss you since it is essential I be in good health in the next few days."

"I understand."

"Tell Lacoste to spare no expense or trouble," he went on. "The important thing is that you be ready to travel within the next seventy-two hours."

"Is that when we are to leave?"

"As things stand now."

"I will tell him," she said.

"My thoughts will be with you," he said awkwardly. And then he turned and strode out of the room quickly, with a great deal of relief on his part, she felt.

Major Lacoste came shortly after and made a show of examining her. When the maid had left the room and they were alone, he said in a low voice, "Valmy has left. He will not return until late, and he has taken some of the guards with him."

"He said he was going somewhere to plan the caravan to France."

"This has to be our moment," the old army surgeon went on excitedly. "I shall return later with a priest and a doctor. They will be here to assist in your escape, not attend to your illness."

"I feel very well this morning," she said.

"Excellent," Lacoste said. "You will dress to leave here. Manage it without the maid knowing. Then put your nightgown on over your clothes and return to bed."

"I will."

"Do not be surprised or frightened at anything that takes place," he warned her.

"I shan't," she said.

He reached inside his medical bag and produced a small pistol. "It is loaded and ready in case it may be needed. Conceal it on your person somewhere, and be not afraid to use it."

She took the pistol quickly and hid it under the pillow. "I will transfer it to my dress pocket later," she promised.

"Very well," the one-armed man said, closing his medical bag and picking it up. "I shall return as soon as possible."

As soon as he'd left, she called the maid and sent her to the palace kitchen to get her a warm drink. While the maid was absent, she hastily dressed and placed the pistol in her pocket. Then she donned her nightgown again and slipped into the big bed at the top of the three steps.

The maid returned with her warm drink, and she dismissed her, saying, "I wish to sleep for a little and not be disturbed."

She counted on Major Lacoste and his fellow doctors making their way in on their own. Now began the taut period of waiting. She found it difficult to keep her nerves under control. So much would depend on what happened within the following hour. She had every confidence in the old army surgeon and was sure he had planned carefully.

Where had he found the willing aides to help her escape? Perhaps from among his former army cronies. In any event he seemed to have managed it, and she could be thankful for that. She closed her eyes and pretended to sleep. Then she heard the distant voice of Lacoste as he let himself into the apartment.

She sat up in bed and saw that the old man was accompanied by a thin figure in a priest's robes and cowl of brown. Also with him was a shorter man with a bald head and gray whiskers dressed in a velvet suit. She judged that these were the two doctors he had spoken about. He had mentioned one of them was a priest.

Major Lacoste came over to her bed and smiled at her. "I trust you are feeling somewhat better."

"I am," she said. "And these are the doctors?"

"Indeed they are," the old doctor said. "Let me introduce Father Alberto first. He is a Jesuit and a graduate in medicine."

Father Alberto bowed and in a low voice said, "My greetings, signorina." His face was almost completely concealed by his upturned cowl, and he stood with his hands folded in his ample sleeves.

"And this is Antonio Salvario, one of the best-known medical men in Venice. He also speaks English," Lacoste said with a smile.

The bald man with the whiskers smiled in a friendly fashion, and she felt he had a familiar look. In a high voice he said, "I have spoken a great deal of English, my lady!" And he bowed.

"We are going to try and help you," Major Lacoste said.

"I'm sure you will," she told him. "I dismissed my maid awhile ago so I might sleep."

"Excellent!" Major Lacoste said. And then he opened his medical bag and removed a businesslike-looking revolver from it. He asked her, "Are you ready?"

"Yes," she said throwing back the bedclothes and taking off her nightgown to reveal she was fully dressed. She took the pistol from her pocket and held it on the ready.

"Good girl!" a familiar voice said, and the priest threw back his cowl. She saw revealed the good-looking Major Eric Walters.

"I can't believe it!" she cried. "You escaped and you are here!"

"Later coming to your aid than I planned," Eric said. "But no matter." And he took her in his arms and kissed her.

The man with the whiskers wailed, "What about me?"

She stared at him in delight. "I didn't recognize you! You are George Frederick Kingston?"

"I am," he said. "Also I am Antonio Salvario!"

Old Major Lacoste was smiling. "You see I found you some old friends!"

"You couldn't have managed better," she said. "Now what?"

"We should be able to get out of here. I will tell the guards at the door you are being removed to a hospital on my authority," Lacoste said.

"If they give any trouble, we've guns to reply with," Eric said.

"Let us hope it will not come to that," the army surgeon said. "The blockage will come below. We may have to shoot our way out."

Eric said, "We have a gondola and a man to operate it waiting at the rear door on the canal."

She said, "What about the emperor?"

Lacoste looked troubled. "You may have a moment to speak with him. It would be good if you did. We will see how things go."

"Very well," she said. "I'll go by your advice."

Eric had put up the cowl again so that his face would be hidden. "I say, let us lose no more time," he told them.

Major Lacoste led the way. He spoke a few dignified words to the guard at her door, and he allowed the party to pass. She kept in the middle of the group as they swiftly made their way downstairs to the main hallway.

Lacoste whispered, "Napoleon's quarters are at the rear, the door almost under the stairway."

They turned and went to the rear and then took another left turn to a broad hall which led to double doors at the end. There were two guards with guns and swords at this doorway.

Lacoste and Betsy were ahead. She saw the expression of the faces of the guards at Napoleon's door as they walked steadily toward it. Then one of the guards lifted his gun and aiming it at them, he cried, "Halt!"

It was the signal for bedlam! Eric whipped out a gun and shot the guard down. At the same time Major Lacoste felled the other guard who had his gun raised.

Lacoste said, "This is your moment! Hurry inside!"

Heart pounding, she tried the heavy brass door handle, and it turned. She pulled the great door open and rushed inside. She found herself in a high-ceilinged, richly furnished room. Standing facing her with a look of fear on his face was a gray-haired, shrunken man with a moustache. He wore a shabby blue jacket and trousers, and she had to study him for a moment before she recognized this worn figure as the once great Napoleon.

She fell into the habit of years ago and dropped to her knee in a cursty as she said, "Sir! I am Betsy Chapman from Saint Helena."

His eyes widened, and he seemed more the old emperor. In a hoarse voice he asked, "Why the shooting?"

"To get by your guards, sire," she said frantically. "You have delivered yourself into the hands of a traitor. You are trapped. Your friends wish to save you! A ship waits for you in the Channel!"

Eric thrust his head in the door crying, "More guards coming! We must leave!"

"Valmy is deceiving you, sire!" she cried and then turned, leaving the astonished man staring after her.

The three men had waited for her, and now Eric took her by the arm and rushed ahead. He said, "We may be able to get out the rear before they block us off!"

Major Lacoste cried, "I will act as sentry until you are outside." And the one-armed man took a stand at the end of the hallway.

"He'll be killed!" she screamed.

"Maybe not!" Eric cried. "We can't wait to find out!"

Betsy heard shots from behind and angry male voices. She turned in time to see that Lacoste had been shot down and at least a half-dozen guards were in pursuit of them. They made their way out a cellar door to a small dock and a waiting gondola.

"Help her in!" Eric shouted to Kingston.

The actor helped her down into the waiting gondola as Eric remained behind to barricade the iron door so it could not be easily opened from the inside. The gondolier had the gondola party out from the tiny dock when Eric came running to join them. Any onlookers must have been astounded to see the priest take a great leap and land in the water beside the craft!

The gondolier managed to keep the boat balanced as Betsy and Kingston dragged a soaked Eric out of the water. He now went about removing his priestly robes, and Kingston was busy taking off his bald wig and whiskers. The gondolier was far from the shore when the guards burst the door open and came out to shoot some futile rounds in the air.

"We've made it!" she said. "But Lacoste was shot down!"

"It was he who made our escape possible," Eric told her. "He held them back just long enough to give us time to reach the dock and barricade the door."

"Poor old man!" she lamented. "I hope he wasn't killed!"

Eric looked bitter and pushed his wet hair back from his forehead. "Maybe he didn't care! With the knowledge the emperor is doomed, he lost interest in everything but getting you free."

Kingston said, "It has actually been weeks since we've been together."

"Valmy told me you were both still captives!" she said.

Eric nodded grimly. "So Lacoste said."

The gondolier had taken them along the canal to the mainland. There a black and red stage awaited them. The two men helped her onto the wharf and into the stage. They joined her, and in a few minutes the stage was moving at a fast pace.

"What now?" she asked Eric.

"On to Milan," he said. "Then to Switzerland and finally Paris. We must manage it in record time. We need a few days planning before Valmy arrives with the emperor."

"I saw him," she said in an awed voice.

"What's the verdict?" Eric asked.

"Yes," Kingston said, leaning forward in the seat across from her. "Is it an impostor or the real Napoleon?"

She hesitated. "I believe it is the real Napoleon. I'm almost sure he recognized me."

"Did you have a chance to warn him?" Eric asked.

"Yes," she said. "I told him Valmy was a traitor. That he had escaped Saint Helena only to be trapped by a man mad with ambition!"

"You at least got that much over," Kingston said.

"Yes. Then the guards came, and we had to run for our lives," she said dully. "I don't think it was worth it. We ought to have gone straight out. That way Lacoste would not have lost his life."

"He may be alive," Kingston said.

She grimaced. "If he is, Valmy will court-martial him."

"The important thing is you came face-to-face with this man, and you believe he is the real Napoleon," Eric said.

"Yes," she nodded.

"So we have at least established that feet."

"He has aged and he is ill," she said as the carriage rolled on. "He is suffering the same sort of illness of the liver which killed my father. Many came down with it on Saint Helena."

"Is he well enough to make the journey to Paris?" the actor asked.

"Valmy is worried about that," she said. "Then when I supposedly fell ill, it was the last straw."

Eric gave her a peculiar look; he was sitting close to her and the carriage rocked and swayed, making high speed over the rough road. He said, "You came to mean a great deal to him."

She felt her cheeks warm, and she said, "I dealt with him on the only terms I could."

Eric offered her a smile of understanding. And he reached out and took her hand in his. "I do not question any of it," he said.

She looked at him. "He held the threat of killing you and Kingston over me."

"And all the time we'd escaped," Kingston said. "But then you wouldn't know that. We had trouble finding out where you were."

Eric said, "If Lacoste hadn't become disenchanted, we might never have been able to get you out of there."

"He's a fine old man. And he believes in his emperor. It pained him to see Napoleon ill and nagged by a drunken mistress Valmy chose for him," she said.

"About Valmy?" Eric said. "Do you consider him to be as dangerous as Felix Black painted him?"

"Every bit," she said. "He has a great charm and an ability for leadership. He is also youthful and vigorous and he is mad with ambition. He sees himself as the successor to Napoleon! Emperor Raymond Valmy!"

Eric looked grim. "We may have a thing or two to say about that. And perhaps the emperor will begin to trouble him with a few questions now."

"If he listened to me, it will have made the risk worthwhile," she said.

"Paris is full of agents," Eric told her. "And to top it all, there are the agents of the new empire, the group faithful to Louis."

"They could be the chief hazard for Valmy," she said.

"Yes," he agreed. "We are only trying to get the former emperor out of his hands and see him safely on a vessel bound for America. But the supporters of the new king will want to destroy Napoleon, Valmy, and all his men!"

She said, "As I understood it from Valmy, he is counting on the ordinary people. He thinks when they see the emperor, they will rise up in a new revolution."

Eric said, "The emperor you've described is hardly likely to be a figure to rally round. A sick and weary Napoleon can not hope to inspire followers to the death!"

"And it will mean no less," George Frederick Kingston observed. "This new revolution could be a long and bloody arising."

"I do not think the emperor equal to it," Betsy said. "He has failed greatly."

"It will be a race with time," was Eric's conclusion. "And the sooner we get to Paris, the better."

The stage rode on until late in the evening. She became very weary and slept for a while, her head resting against Eric's shoulder. At least she could relax and feel secure. They finally halted at a small country inn and made arrangements to remain for the night.

The owner was delighted to have customers from the outside world and made a great show of preparing food and drink for them. They sat before a huge, blazing fire in a fireplace that stretched across the end of the room. All the danger and tension seemed far away in this quiet place.

Kingston downed a glass of wine and smiled at her, saying, "I vow your ordeal has left you more beautiful than ever."

"If that is what I must go through to improve my looks, I would prefer to become homely," she said.

Eric gave her a fond smile. "I'm proud of you. You are the one who really brought our end of the venture to a successful conclusion. You have found definite evidence that it is the real Napoleon whom Valmy is bringing to Paris."

"I could not have done anything without your help," she said.

"Had a bad evening when you didn't return that night in Naples," Kingston said.

"I can imagine."

"With Eric and you both gone, I didn't know which way to turn. Then Raj Singh came staggering back to the hotel to let me know what had happened to you," the actor told her.

Excitedly she asked, "So he lived! Did he recover?"

"That Indian is difficult to kill," Kingston said with a broad smile. "I expect we shall be meeting him again in Paris."

Eric spoke up, "I managed to escape from the dungeon in which they were holding me the following night. But by that time you were out at sea."

"It's a miracle that you found me at all," she marveled.

"Valmy's operation is growing. He has so many agents now that he's attracting attention. I was told that someone had taken over that particular palace and placed guards all around it and in it. I deduced it had to be Valmy," Eric said.

"But it wasn't until the one-armed man came to us and offered to get us inside that we had a plan," Kingston said.

"I shall always owe Major Lacoste a great debt," she said with deep feeling in her voice.

Soon it was time to retire in preparation for their long drive the following day. When they went up to their rooms, a discreet Kingston left them alone. And on this night it was Betsy and Eric who shared a bed. At last she was again with the man she truly loved.

Chapter Fifteen

IT WAS raining and the streets of Paris were almost empty of people. Closed carriages and wagons rumbled over the cobblestoned streets and through great puddles of water, sending drops splashing high. Betsy was in one of the carriages with Kingston. She had gone out to do some needed shopping for clothes, and Eric had insisted that the actor accompany her.

She gazed out the window at the drab brick buildings and the storefronts. They all looked good to her. Just to be free was a luxury to be enjoyed after her long spell as a prisoner. She felt that they were near the end of the adventure on which she had embarked so recklessly. And she was anxious to return to London with Eric and lead a quiet married life!

Enough of adventure! Eric had professed an interest in going into a profession. He had a friend engaged in the import business from the Far East who had offered him help. Being a secret agent was not a proper career for a man with a wife. George Frederick Kingston longed for Covent Garden and Drury Lane and the backstage gossip of the theatrical pubs. He was more than ready to resume his career as a small-time actor.

But there was still work to finish! The climax would come when Napoleon was brought to Paris. Valmy must be close to the great capital now. None of them could truly relax until the final act of the drama was played out.

The journey from Venice to Paris had been a long and tiring one. They had been in Paris for forty-eight hours and were living in a modest pension not far from the Champs Elysées. Whether it was being with Eric again and the romantic mood this created in her or whether it was the beauty and charm of the city itself, she was convinced that Paris was an enchanted place.

Eric had to remind her that this languid city of serene beauty had not long ago seen the extravagant cruelties of the French Revolution. It had known the First Empire of Napoleon and was now content under a Louis again, paying homage to a king with the same name as the one they had so grimly beheaded.

Paris was blooming again under the new king. Even in a spring rain such as they were experiencing now, it was a lovely place. She did not want to see it drenched in blood still another time. If Valmy had his way with his planned new revolution, not only Paris but all France would be torn asunder. And after that it could be all Europe in a turmoil for a decade!

Just at the moment they were waiting. They had not been contacted by any of the other agents yet. Eric was worried, as he had expected to meet Raj Singh at the pension. But thus far there had been no sign of the Indian. She glanced across the carriage and saw that the veteran actor was nodding. A lurch of the vehicle, and he quickly opened his eyes.

"I do believe I dozed off," he said apologetically. "Are we near our lodging place?"

"Soon," she said. And she lapsed back into silence again. She was thinking of Valmy and her having been his mistress. Eric had chosen to black this all out and treat it as if it had never happened. She knew that while it was generous of him, it was also an example of the thinking of a secret agent. He considered her survival more important than anything else, and she had managed that.

Valmy had been a proficient lover. Had the circumstances been different, she might have wound up giving her heart to him as well as her body. But because of Eric she had been unable to feel love for the charming adventurer. Yet he had stirred something in her beyond a casual few moments of passion. She knew she would always remember him.

He was that mixture of villain and gentleman which had confused countless maidens from the beginning of the time of romance. She had known him as a lover, and she had also seen glimpses of his dark side when he abandoned every principle to his thirst for power! She much feared that this evil part of his nature would gain full sway as he lived longer, so that in the end there would only be his devouring ambition.

What would have happened if she'd been given positive proof that Eric had been executed? She was not sure. She knew there was a large possibility she might have turned to Valmy in her sorrow and given him her full love. Even knowing that he was not a good man, she would have been satisfied with his charm and knowing that he cared for her.

She tried to imagine what his reaction had been when he'd returned to find her gone and discover the havoc she'd created in her escape. Would he only be angered and frustrated—feel nothing but rage and fear that she would use all she knew against his cause? Or would he feel more? Perhaps the pain of losing someone truly loved? For she felt, despite all, that in his perverse way he had loved her.

"Will you be my wife?" he had pleaded with her.

The words came back to her all too vividly. There had been love of a sort between them, but basically they were enemies. And now they would be pitted against each other once again for the final struggle.

Kingston smiled at her. "A penny for your thoughts?"

"Offer me no less than a pound and I'll tell you," she said with a sad smile.

He grimaced. "Expensive thoughts! I'll have to be content with my own."

The carriage halted before the plain red brick building which housed their pension. Kingston paid the driver and helped her in with her parcels. Their landlady greeted them with smiles and the news that luncheon was ready and Monsieur Walters already at the table.

Later they joined him at the long table in the pension's dining room. He looked tense but managed a smile for them, asking, "How did your shopping tour turn out?"

Kingston beamed at him. "I tell you she has a knack for bargains. You'll be lucky to have her as a wife, my boy."

"I consider myself lucky in any case," Eric said. "But to know that she is a smart shopper as well as a beauty is truly good news."

"Kingston exaggerates," she said. "I just happened to find some very low-priced things I could use."

"Too bad the rain started," Eric said, glancing at her over his plate of delicious-looking sole.

She said, "We were able to get a carriage almost at once, so the rain didn't bother us." She paused, then asked, "Any word?"

Eric nodded. "Yes."

There was something in his tone which warned her of trouble. She said, "Tell me."

He glanced at them. "It is not the most pleasant subject for the luncheon table."

"Please tell us," she urged him.

"Yes. We're not all that delicate," Kingston said.

Eric hesitated and frowned. "You know that I have been expecting word from Raj Singh?"

"Of course," she said. "It's strange he hasn't turned up before this."

"No. It is not," the man she loved said with a grim look on his pleasant face. "Raj Singh was found with his throat slit in an alley last night."

"Poor man!" she exclaimed with sorrow.

"He was trying to ferret out where Valmy was to have his headquarters here," Eric said. "He thought he had a contact. His contact was the enemy. So now he's truly dead."

"A sad loss for our side," George Frederick Kingston said.

"Without question," Eric agreed. "I learned of his death through one of Captain Gray's men who had been with him for a while and came back to meet him only to find him dead."

Betsy asked, "Who is Captain Gray?"

"The skipper of the vessel waiting off the coast to take Napoleon on board," Eric said. "He's a fine American gentleman, if a little impatient."

"Is he here in Paris now?" Kingston wanted to know.

"He's been here several days. He planned to take the former emperor to the coast in the company with several of his men. But he's becoming upset about the long waiting period. Valmy is behind in his schedule."

"Likely because of Napoleon's delicate state of health," Betsy said. "The brief glimpse I had of him showed him to be much too ill to travel far in a day."

"His condition would slow the caravan," Eric agreed.

"So what do we do now?" Kingston asked.

"Wait for Valmy to arrive. I expect further instructions from London before then," the man she loved said.

Betsy speculated, "I wonder what the state of Felix Black's health may be. He was also ill when we left London."

"Not good, I'm afraid," Eric said.

"Thin bloke," Kingston recalled. "Not an ounce of fat on his bones, I would say."

Eric said, "We'll simply have to learn to have that patience which Captain Gray is so short of. We may have a long wait."

After dinner she went up to the room she shared with Eric to read. She was seated by a rose-bowled lamp on a small table enjoying her book when Eric came into the room. She could tell at once that he had something of importance on his mind.

She put aside the book and rose. "What is it?"

"You must come downstairs," he said. "I have asked our landlady for the use of her parlor. We are having a meeting."

"We?"

"Several of us."

"Very well," she said, wondering if he were joking or if others of the secret agents had made their appearance.

They went down the shadowed stairway together. She said, "The rain seems to have ended."

"Yes, it has," he agreed. "We'll probably get some good weather for a few days. Valmy should arrive shortly. He will make better time without the rain."

They reached the parlor door, and he opened it. Inside stood Kingston, Dr. Edward Barry O'Meara, and a dignified man in naval uniform. They all gave their attention to her.

Eric said, "My fiancée, Miss Betsy Chapman, also a member of our organization." He turned to her. "You know O'Meara. This is Captain Gray."

Captain Gray bowed and shook hands with her. He had a weathered, thin face and gray side-whiskers. He said, "I have heard of your beauty, miss. If I had a man capable of carving mastheads, you would adorn my bow."

"That is a most gracious compliment, Captain," she said with a smile.

It was Barry O'Meara's turn to step forward. He said, "I told you we'd meet again."

"I'm glad to see you," she said.

The Irish doctor gave Eric a knowing look and went on, "You'll also be glad to know that thanks to the persuasion of Felix Black, I have come to believe in the sincerity of your group. And I have agreed to work along with you rather than against you."

"That is indeed good news," she said. "We can use such a strong new member after losing Raj Singh."

"Most unfortunate," Captain Gray agreed.

Eric brought a chair forward for her to be seated and said, "Let us all make ourselves comfortable, gentlemen. We have a great deal to discuss."

Dr. O'Meara sat next to her and asked, "Is it true you have seen the emperor?"

"Yes."

"How is he?"

"In poor condition," she said. "He has the liver disease. And he has aged in a shocking manner."

O'Meara shook his head sadly. "And this is the man Valmy would put on the throne!"

"Not so," Eric told the Irish doctor. "He means to put himself on the throne. Napoleon is just his means of getting there."

"So what now?" O'Meara asked.

"I have information Valmy and his group arrive in Paris tomorrow," Eric said. "But I have no idea where his headquarters will be."

"Raj Singh was working on that," Captain Gray said.

"So we must begin again," Eric commented.

Betsy asked, "Since this planned revolution is of much consequence to the present ruler, shouldn't he and his government be informed?"

O'Meara jumped up in anger. "I'm against that! If we can't manage it on our own, then there's no hope. Put Louis and his troops on the alert, and Paris will become an armed city. They will descend on Valmy, and both he and Napoleon will be whisked off to prison and presently executed."

Captain Gray sighed. "If we propose to save the former emperor, it does not seem likely we can afford to notify the authorities here."

Eric said, "The chances are they wouldn't take us seriously if we told them of the threat. They are singularly naïve about such things."

"So we must work alone?" Kingston phrased this as a question.

"I say so," Meara said, siting down again. "If we can get the emperor away from Valmy, it will be like leaving a shell without a fuse."

Eric agreed. "Without the emperor there can be no successful new revolution."

He had barely finished speaking when the door of the parlor opened and a familiar figure in shabby dark clothing came in. It was Felix Black, master spy, thinner even than before and leaning on a stick as he walked feebly to the center of the room.

"Good evening," he said. "I trust my arrival has not upset you too greatly."

Eric rose to greet their leader. "We are delighted to see you!"

"Of course!" Betsy chimed in.

Felix Black smiled in his bleak fashion. "I felt I could not be out at the end of this last chance. So like a veteran huntsman hobbling to his last following the hounds, I have come to Paris."

O'Meara offered him a chair, "Please sit down, sir."

Captain Gray's stern face had even lighted up. "Good to see you again, Black. I'm having a bad time here. That Valmy is keeping us all waiting."

Felix Black seated himself carefully and placed his black top hat on the floor beside his chair. Looking for all the world like a grim schoolmaster, he studied them in turn.

"You've all survived, save Raj Singh," he said. "My congratulations."

"It has been touch and go several times," George Frederick Kingston informed him. "I shall never consider a stage spy drama exaggerated again. More happens in reality!"

The old master spy nodded approvingly. "You have been an apt student, Kingston!"

"Thank you, sir," the actor said looking pleased.

Felix Black fixed his eyes on Betsy. "And so you saw the emperor for a few moments?"

"Only for a very brief time, sir," she said.

"You believe he is truly Napoleon?"

"Yes."

"The report says you found him ill and prematurely old."

"That is true."

"Is he well enough to carry through Valmy's plan?"

"That is hard to say," she told the man in black. "I would be skeptical of any other man. But Napoleon is no ordinary mortal."

Felix Black nodded grimly. "I agree with your judgment of the situation. It is all too likely that he will survive long enough to be shown to the people and to get Valmy in power. Then Valmy can have him executed without anyone aware that he is removing a dying man from his path to glory!"

O'Meara said angrily, "I'd like to get my hands around Valmy's fine throat for just a few moments!"

"I'm sure you would do well," the ailing master spy said. "But the chances of your having that opportunity are unfortunately few."

Eric asked, "What do you think will happen next?"

"Valmy will arrive tomorrow," Felix Black said. "You will pick up the threads which were severed with Raj Singh's death. You will work through the night if need be to learn where Valmy is taking the emperor."

"Yes, sir," Eric nodded.

"You O'Meara will make a round of the taverns where Valmy's agents are known to gather and find out what you can by eavesdropping," Felix Black said.

"Cannot I have a more active role?" O'Meara pleaded.

"You will find your assignment active enough if you should be recognized," the master spy said. "You know what happened to Raj Singh."

Captain Gray spoke up. "My men have picked up word here and there. They say there have been underground political meetings in the back rooms of some of the taverns."

"Valmy's men have been busy preparing the way," Felix Black said.

"What are my duties to be, sir?" Kingston asked.

"Assist Major Walters in any way you can," Black told him. "You two seem to work well together. And now if you will all be on your way, I have some private conversation I would make with Miss Chapman."

Eric rose and Betsy also got to her feet and faced him Concern in her voice, she said, "Do be careful!"

"I will," he promised. "You will be safe here with Black."

"I'll be waiting your return," she said.

They all straggled out, with Dr. Edward Barry O'Meara the last to leave. He offered her a wry look before, he closed the door after him. Now she and the old master spy were alone.

Felix Black tapped his cane on the floor to catch her attention and said, "Do sit down, Miss Chapman."

She sat. Then she said, "What do you want of me?"

His sharp old eyes were fixed on hers. "Several things. Also I have news from England."

She sensed that he had some important thing to tell her. She asked, "What news?"

"Your stepfather is dead!"

"Dead!" she echoed.

"Yes," he said. "I'm certain you will not shed too many tears. Your mother is said to be making a most becoming widow again. And the chances are that your stepfather's timely stroke may have left her with enough money and land to go on living comfortably."

Betsy said, "She surely would not have been able to if he'd lived and gone on gambling. He was steadily wasting away the family fortune."

"Without question," he said. "So though the elderly and lecherous Lord Dakin survives, you need not fear returning to England. Your stepfather will not be around to arrange a match."

"He would have small success if he were," she said with some spirit.

"You have grown in character, my girl."

"I think you may fairly call me a woman now," she said.

"I agree," he said. "And you have put aside your old difference with Major Walters. Indeed I understand that you two now plan to be married."

"That is true."

"What a matchmaker I am," the thin man in black said and then suffered a long and terrifying coughing spell.

When it was over, she said, "You seem not to have regained your health, sir."

"My health is worse," he said "bluntly. "I'm dying. I told you that."

"I remember."

"And so Napoleon is dying along with me," he said with a sigh. "Well, there is irony in that. Better for him to die a natural death in America than to be assassinated by the agent of a man pretending to be his champion."

"I agree. The question now is whether we can stop Valmy without spreading word to the authorities."

"That would spell doom for Napoleon. I would like to save him if I can. My government went back on its word last time. As an Englishman I would like to make that up to him now."

"If anyone can do it, I'm sure you will."

"I'm a helpless old invalid," he said. "But I have done my best work of organizing. I have more agents in my employ than you can guess. I have put my private fortune into this."

"Was that wise?" she asked.

"What difference?" he said. "In a short while I will have no need for money."

"I hope you are wrong," she replied quietly. "We have all come to admire you. And I'm sure the emperor will be grateful if you save him."

"I wonder," Felix Black said grimly. "I'm sure of one thing. He is bound to have better manners than His Majesty, my king."

"He still has a manner. I grasped that even in my brief moment with him. And I'm almost certain that he knew me."

"I'm taking your word we're not dealing with an impostor," Felix Black said. "And that is most important. For if this man were some rogue pretending to be Napoleon, he would use very different methods."

"I have told you what I believe to be true."

He looked at her directly and without warning said, "When you were Valmy's prisoner, you became his mistress."

She was a trifle startled. "Did Major Walters write that in his report to you?"

"Not in so many words. I read it between the lines."

"He knows it to be true," she said, looking down.

"How much hold did he get over you?" the old man asked sharply.

She kept her eyes on the bare boards of the parlor floor. "I fought against being attracted to him. I was not all that successful."

"You were right to give in to him," the master spy said bluntly. "But you were wrong to allow yourself to care for him. I warned you he was a charmer!"

"I know. But I think he really came to care for me. He asked me to be his wife."

Felix Black showed astonishment, an unusual expression on that thin face. He said, "Do you think he meant it?"

"Yes."

"He probably did then," Black said grimly. "Women are usually right about such things."

"He is not all bad, you know."

The master spy leaned forward on his cane. "No one is all bad, not even Felix Black! But Valmy is three quarters a scoundrel and will be wholly one soon. Could you share your life with such a man?"

"Perhaps," she said, "under the right conditions."

"At least you're honest," he said grudgingly. "It is true that good women are attracted to rogues. This accounts for at least half of all marriages."

"I'm well over it now," she said.

"Be firm with yourself," Black warned her. "Your paths could cross again."

"Surely not!" she protested.

"He will be here in Paris tomorrow. You will be assigned to some duty. There is a definite possibility you might have another encounter with him."

"I would prefer not," she said.

"In our world we have to make many compromises," the old spy warned her. "When you became a spy, you were bound by our rules whether you guessed it or not."

"I'm beginning to understand."

"Good!" he said, leaning on his cane and rising with some difficulty. "Now I would suggest that we both have a good night's rest. Tomorrow will be a special day in the history of France."

She asked, "Do you think the riots could begin as soon as tomorrow?"

"Yes. Any time after Valmy and his party get here. The riots and some bombings have already been planned."

She helped the old man up the stairway to the door of his room and bade him good night. Then she went back to the room she shared with Eric and in which she would be alone worrying about him on this special night. Things had happened so swiftly she was having a hard time keeping them straight in her mind.

She had been shocked at the frail state of the old master spy. But there was no worry about his mind not being as active as before or perhaps even more keen. He was now compensating for his loss of physical prowess by honing his keen mind to a new sharpness.

She continued on to her room and prepared for bed. She was in no mood to sleep, her mind filled with fears for Eric.

When Betsy slept, her dreams were troubled. She twisted uneasily in the bed, seeing Eric exposed to all kinds of danger. In one the thin Felix Black entered in his somber garb to inform her that the man she loved was dead. These and other equally disturbing nightmares tormented her.

Then she was rudely awakened by rough hands seizing her and covering her mouth so that she could not cry out for help. She was hastily bound and gagged in the darkness of the room; she didn't see anyone and heard only whispers. She began to wonder if this might be merely an extension of her nightmare, but the physical discomfort she felt told her it was not.

A rope was tied around her, and trussed in a helpless state, she was lowered out the window. Again she was grasped by waiting hands and carried over to a carriage. After she was roughly thrown on the seat of the carriage, it started off.

She sat up and tried to free her hands which were tied behind her but without avail. Her ankles were also bound. Then she became aware of someone seated opposite her in the moving carriage. He reached over and removed the gag from her mouth, and she saw the grim face of the handsome Valmy.

"You!" she gasped.

"You weren't expecting to see me again," Valmy said in his suave way.

"You are not supposed to arrive in Paris until tomorrow." she said, still stunned.

He smiled grimly. "I do not always do what people expect."

"Why have you kidnapped me?"

"Are you so surprised?" he asked. "After what you did in Venice."

"You were keeping me there as your prisoner!"

"You betrayed me," he said harshly. "I offered you my love, and you rejected it!"

Betsy said, "You forced yourself on me!"

"Not content with such betrayal, you went whining to the emperor and attempted to upset him—along with causing the death of Lacoste and some of my best guards!"

"I had a right to try and escape!"

His smile was not pleasant. "And now you are back with your Major Walters! You should be happy!"

"I was!" she said defiantly.

"And you think you will crush my plan!"

"We shall try!"

"You will never succeed," he warned her. "And now that I no longer have any interest in you, I'm going to pay you back for your treachery."

She stared at him anxiously in the shadows of the rumbling carriage. "Where are you taking me?"

"Where you'll be safe!"

"It won't work," she protested. "Felix Black is here in Paris. Your project is doomed, and he is bound to find me."

"I rather doubt that," the arrogant Valmy said. "You have hurt me deeply, and I make a bad enemy!"

"You're mad!" she told him. "And so is your plan! I saw the emperor. He is not well enough to head such an uprising as you intend."

"Leave that to me!" he snapped.

"I have cared for you in a certain way," she went on. "If you turned your talents to some worthy goal, you could truly become a great man."

The handsome Valmy shook his head. "You will not get around me with sweet words!"

"I was not attempting that," she said with some hurt. "I was trying to be honest with you!"

"The uprising will take place, and I shall become emperor in due time," Valmy told her. "And all the while you shall rot in a place without hope and without any relation to the world outside."

Cold fear streaked through her again. And she demanded, "What are you threatening?"

The carriage halted, and he sneeringly said, "You are about to find out, my dear Betsy!"

The ragged coachman came and opened the carriage door, and Valmy leaned over and dragged her out onto the cobblestoned street. It was still drizzling rain and very dark. She screamed for help as he lifted her up in his arms and carried her as easily as he would a child.

He laughed at her continued screaming. They approached a heavy arched door of planks lighted by a torch burning in an iron wall bracket next to it. He pounded on the door, and a small window in it opened. A grimy, wrinkled face appeared to study them with rheumy eyes.

She continued to sob and scream for help while Valmy ignored her and shouted over her clamor, "I'm Monsieur Henri! I have brought my poor sister! It has all been arranged!"

"Yes, monsieur," the old man wheezed. The trap door was shut, and there was the sound of bolts being drawn back. Then the great door opened slowly. Valmy marched inside the dark room which had a heavy stench about it.

After a moment another bent old man came carrying a lantern, his white hair straggling over his shoulders. He bowed to Valmy and paid no attention to her cries for help.

"You have arrived, Monsieur Henri," the emaciated old man said. He held the lamp up to inspect her. "She is very young to be in so sad a state!"

"Hopeless!" Valmy cried. "That is why I have no other alternative but to leave her here with you!"

"We have many like her," the old man assured him. "She will be well treated. We run the place like a regular hospital."

"I'm sure you do," Valmy said, letting her stand on her feet but not untying her ankles. "If we're to let her walk on her own, we will need two husky guards to manage her!"

Betsy cried, "What are you planning? What sort of place is this?"

The old man with the lantern chuckled. "It is a hotel for the mad! A retreat for those who have lost their minds!"

"I'm not mad!" she cried. "He is! He is planning to start a revolt and place Napoleon back on the throne!"

Valmy looked sad and tapped his temple. "You see," he told the old man. "It is too bad!"

"Her madness is obvious," the old man agreed.

"I'm his prisoner! He has kidnapped me!" Betsy sobbed. "I have friends on the outside. I will give you their names. And it is true that he has the emperor as his hostage!"

The old man shook his head. "Shocking!"

"It pains me," Valmy said. "My poor sister sometimes thinks she is the Empress Josephine and at other times Princess Marie Louise."

"We have a Marie Louise here already," the old man said.

"Will you please remove her," Valmy said. "I cannot get away from her quickly enough. I'm horrified to see her in this state."

"I will get the ladies to take her to the women's ward," the old man with the lantern said and hurried off.

When they were alone in the dank brick-lined passage, Valmy turned to her and said, "I have paid them. They will keep you here forever!"

Tears streaked down her cheeks. "You couldn't be so heartless!"

"It is you who proved heartless," he said coldly. "Now you will have time to think about it."

"Please!" she begged him.

He turned his back on her. Then two large rough-looking women came toward her, grumling that their sleep had been disturbed. They seized her roughly and dragged her down the long black corridor while she still screamed for help!

The two halted at an iron door with a grating in it. As one of the women fumbled with the lock, Betsy sobbed to the other, "I'm not mad! I swear! Please let me explain!"

"Slut!" the ugly old woman snarled and gave her a hard slap across the face.

Stunned, she found herself being literally hauled into a big room with cots set out around it. The odor was shocking, and the only light in the place was supplied by two lanterns hanging high up beyond reach on the ceiling.

The women roughly threw her on a filthy mattress and undid her bonds. The one who had slapped her warned, "No more of your screaming! No trying to make trouble! Behave yourself and you'll be treated well!"

"But I shouldn't be here!" she cried.

The other old woman pushed a wisp of dirty gray hair away from the red coarse face and told her, "We hear that every hour on the hour! Save your breath!"

The two women then retreated out the door and locked it. She lay there in shock. Then raising herself on her elbows, she became more aware of the room. All around her in nightgowns were women of various ages and sizes staring at her. Some were obviously demented; others had the look of normalcy but seemed frightened and without spirit.

The horror of the asylum ward came through to her, and she sprang from the bed. Rushing to the iron door, she began to pound on it and scream for help louder than before!

It was a signal for all the unhappy inmates in the room to join her in a chorus of mad screams and sobbing. Some of the denizens of this minor hell began to dance around. Others ran back and forth aimlessly screaming or jumped up and down on their fetid cots! A tiny blond girl actually came up and touched her timidly and then ran off like a frightened animal!

The iron door was thrown open, and the ugly woman came back inside with a whip in her hand. Her lips were moving in rage, and she snarled, "I warned you to be quiet! It seems you must have a lesson!"

"No!" she screamed, retreating toward her cot.

"You will learn to be quiet!" the big woman said, lashing her across the room with the whip, bringing it down in a weird rhythm so that it cut across her face, her back; any way she turned, it bit into her.

At last she flung herself down on the cot and groveled under the still punishing whiplashing. At last the big woman halted the torment and stood above her grimly.

"If you make any further disturbance, you'll get the same, only double!" she warned.

Betsy held her doubled fist in her mouth to stifle her sobs. The room around her had gone silent again. The mere sight of the ugly woman with the whip seemed enough to terrify the mad creatures around her into being quiet. They had learned the rules, and it seemed that she also would have to abide by them.

Her body ached from the whipping. She could barely breathe for the stench in the crowded, shadowy asylum ward. She lay staring bleakly up at the nearest lantern and wondered how soon it would be before she also really became mad!

Chapter Sixteen

BEFORE THE night ended, Betsy became nauseated and vomited over herself and her cot, making the stench about her worse. She tried to clean herself and the filthy mattress with an old rag which she retrieved from the owner of the cot next to her—a fat woman who never moved or spoke but lay on her cot staring up at nothing.

The two big women arrived early with a younger thin woman in tow. The two women guards went about the ward rousing up the patients and ordering them to prepare for the serving of breakfast gruel. The thin woman dished the watery stuff out into tin plates as the patients presented them to her. Betsy did not join the line.

The ugly woman who seemed to especially hate her came and shook her. "Take your place for food!" she commanded her.

"I'm ill," she said weakly. "I don't want any."

"You'll do what I say," the big woman told her, and she roughly dragged her up from the bed and shoved a tin plate in her hand. "Now get in line!"

She obeyed, not wanting to give the woman another excuse to whip her. As it was, her body was covered with welts. She took her place in the shuffling line and held her plate out for the doleful woman to slop some of the sticky gray substance into it. Then she quietly returned to her own bed.

The tiny blond girl with big, frightened blue eyes who had approached her the previous night now came timidly toward her, staring at her.

Seated on her cot, Betsy told the girl, "You needn't be afraid of me. You can come and sit here if you like!"

"I have fits!" the blond girl said in a choked, fearful tone. "They chase me away!"

"I'll risk it," Betsy said wryly. "Would you like my gruel?"

The tiny girl's eyes widened. "You don't want it?"

"No!" And she handed it to the girl.

The tiny girl grasped it as if it were a treasure. Then she sat down on the cot beside her and began to wordlessly gulp down the revolting gruel.

Besty could scarcely believe it—nor any of the other things she saw in the ward. And she knew now what a relentless foe Raymond Valmy was. He had designed a living torment for her, worse than any death! She wondered how long she would remain here in this foul place before she began to lose her own grip on reality!

Would she end up here mad and forgotten? She was sure Valmy would never relent and return for her. And how would Eric or any of the others know what had happened to her? She had been taken from the pension in the middle of the night when all the others were asleep.

What did it matter now whether Valmy staged his uprising and used Napoleon to get power over France? She would never know whether the adventure was successful or not! In time Eric would decide she was dead, killed somehow by Valmy, and he would remember her only with sadness, marry some other girl, and she would then eventually not even be part of his memories.

The tiny blonde finished the gruel and then stared at her. She said, "You're beautiful!"

"Thank you," she replied.

"You were talking about Napoleon last night," the girl said. "There is a woman down the ward who calls herself Princess Marie Louise."

"So I've heard!"

"This is a bad place," the girl went on. "My sickness has gotten worse since my brother put me here. But his wife would not let me live with them any longer. When I had my fits, it frightened her children."

"Surely they would get used to them."

"I don't know," the girl said. "I don't remember them. I feel everything going dark, the fits come, and then I'm on the floor, sweating and ill!"

"Does anyone ever leave this place?" Betsy asked in despair.

"Only when they're dead, and that doesn't take long. It's not healthy here! We had the fever in this ward awhile ago, and more than half died. I wish I'd been one of them!"

Betsy stared at the girl. "You sound as if you meant that?"

"I do," the mad girl assured her. "Then I would be with the Blessed Madonna and the saints who tend to the sick. I wanted to be placed in a hospital run by the nuns, but it was too far away. My brother couldn't bother to take me there. So here I am."

"When does the doctor make his rounds?" she asked.

"Every day," the tiny blonde said. "He'll be here soon. But he can't help you. He's old and mad himself."

"I would expect that kind of doctor here," she said.

"Who put you in here?"

Betsy sighed. "Someone I thought had some feeling for me. I know better now."

The tiny blonde wandered off, and a little later, true to her prediction, she fell down onto the earthen floor in a convulsive fit. This attracted a group of the other women who stood around her in a circle and gleefully commented on her writhings.

Betsy turned away, sickened. A short time later the iron door opened and a portly man with a writing pad and quill in hand entered accompanied by a bent, frail old gentleman with vacant staring eyes. He was bald and had a woebegone look. Betsy at once knew this had to be the doctor.

The two made their rounds of the ward, and she was the last to be visited by them. The old man peered at her and said, "I don't know you. Are you new?"

"Yes," she said, hope rising in her. "I was brought here in the night. And I shouldn't have been. It was the vindictive act of an enemy."

The old doctor stared at her oddly and then consulted with the stout man. They murmured in low voices and after the exchange the old doctor told her, "You were brought here by your brother as being occasionally violent and having delusions that Napoleon is still alive!"

She protested, "That man is not my brother! He is a revolutionary named Valmy! And he means harm to France!"

The vacant eyes showed no interested. He raised a palsied hand to placate her. "You must control yourself, dear lady. Your fears for France are groundless!"

"I have friends!" she insisted. "Will you send a message to them?"

"Only if your brother approves," the ancient doctor said.

"Why must he approve? He is not my brother, and I have to get out of here!"

"Now, now," the old doctor remonstrated. "We can't have you troubling people on the outside. That is why you are here. If you cannot be cured of your madness, at least you will be able to live in peace here."

She jumped up. "But I'm not mad!"

He nodded and smiled weakly. "No madder than the world, I'm sure. But there is some madness in all of us. I advise you to relax, and in due time you will come to enjoy it here!"

"Here in this filthy ward of mad people?"

"Show some delicacy," the ancient one pleaded in his thin voice. "These are your sisters, and I am your doctor. You must show some respect."

"I'm English, and I have a task to do, an important task. I must not be detained here," she told him.

"I understand," he said. "We will discuss it another day. In the meanwhile you must get to know the other ladies here." And with that he and the stout man left the ward.

Betsy sat in stunned silence. Slowly she began to realize there was no hope. This was how it would always be with her. She would remain here and grow filthy and as mad as any of them. Her unkempt figure would become familiar to the guards and doctor. She would be known as the lady who wished to save Napoleon from murder!

She closed her eyes and tried to shut out the shrill wrangling of two of the mad women. She debated how she might kill herself and so make the only exit possible from the dread place. And she was continually haunted by the last glimpse she'd had of Valmy's handsome, sneering face. He had punished her well!

The hours went by, and she still felt too ill to eat anything. Perhaps she would slowly starve to death, or would she become so hollow-eyed and emaciated that she'd finally claw at any wretched scrap of food in the same manner as the others? Hot tears coursed down her cheeks.

She was seated on her cot, her head bent in dejection, trying to shut out the awfulness of her surroundings. She heard the iron door open and then someone come over to her. She raised dull eyes to see who it was.

It was Eric! He gazed down at her in horror. Then he gasped, "Betsy! My poor darling!"

She rose pitifully, almost demented, and begged him, "Take me out of here!"

"At once!" he said. And as she felt the blackness close in on her, he picked her up in his arms.

She was back in their room at the pension. A good wash, some decent food, and a rest of several hours had brought her back to some normalcy. But she knew she would forever be haunted by those hours spent in the madhouse. She could never forget the misery and dejection of the place.

Eric was at her bedside. He said, "You've slept soundly for hours. It is evening."

She reached out and took his hand in hers. "You came when I most needed you."

"I was far too late at that!"

"The miracle is how you knew where to find me," she told him.

"I had no idea at first. Felix Black had a boy watching the house outside. He'd paid the lad to keep an eye on it for the night. The lad fell asleep, but he woke up in time to see you being carried to the carriage. Sure that foul play had taken place while he'd been napping, he ran after the carriage as it rolled through the streets."

"And he followed it to the asylum?"

"Not quite," Eric said. "He wasn't that lucky. He lost the trail at an intersection a block distant from the hospital. But he knew you'd been taken somewhere in that area, for he later saw the carriage returning."

"Then what?"

"Then we began making house calls at every house in the area. At last we found the asylum, and I was certain that was where you'd been taken."

"I'd given up hope," she told him.

"We were too long getting to you," he said. "But it doesn't matter. You'll be all right."

She sighed. "It was the most terrible experience of my life."

"I'm sure of that."

"I shan't forget it."

He looked stern. "Another debt for Valmy to pay."

Suddenly she became alert and asked, "What is going on?"

"Valmy is in Paris."

"I know."

"You would have to," he said wryly. "We have at last located the house where he is making his headquarters."

"Then you'll be able to stop him."

"I'm not sure about that," Eric said. "But he has had a serious reverse."

"What is that?"

"Some member of his own group leaked the word of the planned rebellion to the ruling government. As a result King Louis has called out his troops in strength, and the city has become an armed fortress."

She sat up in be, all excitement. "Then he won't dare go ahead?"

"Not as soon as he planned anyway," Eric said.

"Dr. O'Meara claimed the emperor would be the first casualty if anything like this happened."

"O'Meara is probably right," the young major agreed.

"What is Felix Black going to do?"

"He has called another meeting for eight o'clock," Eric said. "I assume it will be a strategy session."

She turned back the bedclothes and prepared to get up. "I must be there."

"No."

"I'm a vital member of the group."

"Agreed," Eric said. "But you are not well enough to try becoming active again."

"Bosh!" she replied. "I shall be all right. I promise it."

"He won't expect you," Eric warned her.

Expected or not, she dressed and went down with Eric to take part in the meeting. Felix Black was seated and looking even paler than usual. He leaned on his cane for support as O'Meara, Kingston, and Captain Gray stood at various places in the room. When she entered with Eric, there was general surprise and a warm greeting for her.

Felix Black gave her an approving nod. "You are a strong young woman, Betsy. You now know the meaning of not being safe in one's own bed."

"Yes," she said. "I learned it the hard way."

"You also learned the sort of man Valmy is."

"My eyes have been opened," she said.

"Then perhaps it was worth it," the old master spy said. "We can harbor no illusions about our enemies. We destroy or are destroyed."

O'Meara said, "How dare he put you in a madhouse?"

"A crass thing to do," Kingston agreed.

"In America he wouldn't get away with that so easily," Captain Gray vowed. "There seems to be no proper check on officials here in France."

Felix Black said crisply, "We do not have time to commiserate with Betsy or comment on the laws of our various lands. We are here to plan our strategy."

O'Meara said gloomily, "From all I have seen and heard in the streets, this uprising of Valmy is doomed and so is his hope of passing off this Napoleon on the people."

Betsy said, "The impact may be different when they know the emperor has truly returned."

"Louis will have his troops ready with orders to shoot Napoleon on sight," the Irish doctor said with concern.

Felix Black said, "Now the emperor's fete depends almost solely on us. I have a plan."

"I'd like to hear it," O'Meara said with annoyed doubt.

"You shall," the old master spy told him. And turning to Gray, he said, "Your ship is still ready and your men still here in Paris?"

Captain Gray agreed. "Everything is in readiness to take the emperor straight to the coast and on board. Within an hour of his stepping on the ship, we shall sail."

"Excellent," Felix Black said. "Valmy has taken over an old mansion on the avenue Marceau. He is keeping Napoleon there. It is one of those houses with direct connection to the Paris sewers."

"So?" Eric said.

"This must be a small operation," the master spy went on. "It is our only hope of saving Napoleon."

O'Meara warned, "As soon as Louis's men know where they are hiding, they will storm the place."

"Valmy is well aware of that, I'm sure," Felix Black said with a patient look in the stormy Irishman's direction.

"What do you plan to do?" O'Meara demanded.

"I have a plan of the sewer lines and the house. You know these sewers are tall enough for a grown man to walk in. Great caves with a deep river of polluted water running through them. I speak of the main sewer lines, but even those attached to the various houses are large enough for a man to make his way through them."

"They are foul places," O'Meara told him. "The air is not fit to breathe in them. The rivers you speak of are running cesspools with the waste of the city flowing toward the Seine. And the sewers are famous for being infested with a host of aggressive rats!"

"All true," the old master spy agreed. "I do not advocate them as a place to enjoy but a means of us managing our well-deserved victory."

"Go on, sir," Eric encouraged him.

"I propose to send a party consisting of you, Walters, along with Dr. O'Meara and Captain Gray into the sewer by means of another house close by the one Valmy is occupying."

Eric nodded in agreement. "I think I follow you, sir. We shall use the sewer connection with this other house to get into the main sewer line and make our way under the house where Valmy is. Then we can enter it the same way!"

"Precisely," Felix Black said. "Once you get in the house, you will try to reach Napoleon without Valmy knowing, or over his dead body if necessary, and get the former emperor out of the house by the same means. Then Captain Gray can turn him over to his men, and the carriage will take him to Calais."

"It sounds practical," Eric said. "Do you have a plan of the house, sir, with the room marked in which Napoleon is liable to be found."

"I have such a plan," the old master spy said. "But it may not be entirely correct. The man who made it for me used his memory to recreate the plan. He was once a servant in the house."

O'Meara said, "Well, if we are to become sewer rats, let us get on with it!"

Geroge Frederick Kingston demanded, "What about me, sir?"

"I have other plans for you," the old man leaning on his cane said brusquely. And to Eric he said, "You take the others to your room and study the plan for a while. Then arm yourselves well, and I will tell you when to start out."

Eric turned to Betsy. "I will see you before I go."

Felix Black waited until everyone had gone except Betsy and Kingston. Then he said, "How do you feel?"

She said, "I am ready for any task."

"You are sure?"

"Yes."

He said, "I did not ask you when Major Walters was here because he has strong feelings that you have been subjected to rather too much danger as it is."

"He tries to overprotect me," she said.

"That is very likely true," Black said. "But then you should be grateful after your last experience with Valmy."

"I am filled with hatred for Valmy!" she said.

"That pleases me," the old master spy said. "I felt you to be in a dangerous mood before." He rummaged in an inner pocket and produced a sketch and handed it to Kingston. "Do you think you could make yourself up to look like that?"

"Stout chap," Kingston said studying the pencil sketch. "But about my height. And the black whisker is easy enough."

"One of my agents made that sketch," Black told them. "He is holding the original of it prisoner, along with a young woman."

"Indeed, sir," Kingston said. "I'd say I could quite easily make myself up to pass for this fellow. A bit of padding, darken my eyebrows, paste on a false dark whisker, and I think I could pass."

"I hoped you would say that," the man in black said with satisfaction. "The man you are to impersonate is Valmy's cook."

"Indeed, sir," Kingston said with polite interest.

"Valmy takes him with him everywhere, and it is this fellow who prepares the meals of the emperor."

"Jolly important job! Doubt if I'm up to it. Never did much cooking."

"You won't be required to cook," Black said dryly. "Merely look like this cook fellow."

"I can do that," Kingston vouched.

The old man suffered a coughing spell and could not go on for a little while. When he'd finished the wracking session, he looked more ill than ever, and he was trembling slightly.

She rose with concern. "Are you ill?"

He waved her to sit down again. "No. It's over. I've become accustomed to these fits of coughing. Now where was I?"

She said. "You were telling us about Valmy's cook."

"Ah yes," he said. "As you know, most cooks go out in the early morning to the various shops and market for the day. But in the case of Valmy's cook there must be a certain discretion. So he does not go out on his errands until dusk, returning after dark. He always takes a kitchen maid with a basket along with him to carry the goods he selects."

Betsy smiled grimly. "And I am to be the kitchen maid."

"That is my idea," Black said. "A risk! Valmy may try to put you in a madhouse again if you're caught. Do you want to risk it?"

"I wouldn't miss it," she said. "It is probably my only chance to pay him back!"

"And to save the emperor," he reminded her. "That once was your chief concern, and it is still mine."

She sighed. "My desire for revenge seems to have made me forget everything else."

"Revenge can be blinding. One should avoid it. As an example Valmy made a bad mistake in exacting vengeance from you. He made you hate him."

"True," she agreed.

"I have the cook and his kitchen maid in custody," he went on. "And I have the cook's key to the rear door of the mansion."

"Then we should be able to get in easily," Kingston exclaimed.

"As long as someone doesn't spot you as impostors," the master spy said. "In that case all is lost."

Betsy said, "So that is why you will have the others approach by the main sewer."

"Yes. And once you are in the house, it will be your task to make sure that the passage to the sewer is not in any way shut off. Some houses which were on the sewer have since closed the entry off because of the plague of rats."

She nodded. "We can do that."

"If you find it possible, you can try and approach the emperor and tell him that he must deliver himself to the others when they arrive and go with them. It is his only hope for survival."

"I will speak to him if I can and hope that he will believe me," she said.

"He did not have so many beautiful girls as friends on Saint Helena that he should forget you," the old master spy said.

"When do you want us to leave?" she asked.

"As soon as you can be ready."

Kingston rose. "It will take me the best part of an hour to prepare myself."

Betsy said, "I can manage more quickly than that. I'll borrow a maid's outfit and a shawl from the landlady."

Black nodded. "She will supply the items. I have already told her about it."

She smiled. "I wonder what sort of guests the poor woman thinks she has."

"English and quite mad!" the master spy said with a bleak smile. "Come to me when you are ready to leave, and I shall give you the key and my blessing."

"What about the others?" she asked.

"Their departure will be timed to yours," the old master spy said. "I think that between the parties we have a good chance of rescuing the emperor."

"Providing he hasn't been removed before we get there," she said.

"I don't think Valmy dares leave the house with Paris so filled with soldiers. He won't dare attempt his vaunted uprising until he thinks suspicion has eased and the army of Louis's supporters are off guard."

Betsy was standing before the dresser mirror in the bedroom inspecting herself in the maid's uniform when Eric came into the room. She could tell at once he was upset.

He said, "What is this I hear about you and Kingston?"

She smiled. "We're to impersonate the cook and a maid."

"It's too risky! You know how well Valmy keeps his headquarters guarded," he objected.

"He may not have so many now. And in any case Kingston will look very much like the cook. And nobody ever notices a maid."

"No one but the other kitchen help," Eric said. "You might get inside, but that would be it. Someone would be bound to notice you."

She said, "I don't agree. From my experience the guards pay little attention to the household staff."

He stared at her in dismay. "After all you've gone through, you're ready to take another such risk?"

"I can't let Felix Black down now."

"You can if you wish."

"I don't want to. And in any case you'll be nearby. It's not like before. The idea is to have us join forces."

"I'm afraid for you."

She went to him. "You mustn't be!"

He put his arms round her and kissed her tenderly. Then he held her to him tightly. He said, "I can't forget the state you were in when I found you in that madhouse."

"That's over with," she said. "We can't let it spoil our chances."

He sighed. "I see it is no use. Black must have used his hypnotic powers on you."

"I think tonight will end the chase," she told him.

"I hope so," he said, and he kissed her again.

Kingston was downstairs waiting for her. She was impressed by the way he'd disguised himself. He had padded his body so that he seemed at least fifty pounds heavier and the black beard and eyebrows together with a pot hat slouched down over his forehead gave him an entirely different appearance.

He handed her the big shopping basket. "How do I look?" he asked.

"If I hadn't known, I wouldn't have recognized you," she said.

"I have the key," he told her. "There's a pistol for you in the basket. I'm also carrying one."

"At least that gives us some chance."

The actor sighed. "I suppose we'd better get on our way."

"I don't even know the address of the house."

"I do," he said. "We'll take a carriage to within a block of it, then walk the rest of the way."

She asked, "Have the others left yet?"

"A few minutes ago," Kingston said. "I prefer our task, dangerous as it is, to going down in those sewers."

"We may still have to meet them down there," she reminded him.

It was another dark night. But as they rode through the streets of the great city, she was amazed that so many people were about, especially those in uniform. Every so often a group of cavalry would ride by, and she saw clusters of foot soldiers at various corners.

Betsy glanced at Kingston across the carriage and said, "You'd almost think Paris was prepared for siege!"

"That is what Valmy threatened!"

"Someone has spread the word."

"I think they will close in on him soon," the actor said. "It is now just a question of who gets to Valmy first."

"I hope we do," she said. "I still want to see the emperor protected."

"There's a thin line of us to help him now," Kingston said.

"We can still manage it if nothing happens," she said. And at once she knew this was a ridiculous statement. They could manage anything if they were not prevented. The unhappy fact was that the odds of their being prevented were great.

The carriage halted, and they got out. Kingston paid the driver and then told her, "It's over there toward the river."

They walked along in silence, she keeping a full foot behind him as Felix Black had instructed her. This was the respectful distance for the maid to keep from the cook.

As they drew near the house, Kingston told her over her shoulder, "That's it! Directly ahead!"

"We must go to the back door."

"Yes," he said. And then he halted suddenly and in a nervous voice whispered, "Do you see what I see?"

She stared ahead in the near darkness and then began to make out the blurred figures of soldiers milling about in the street in front of the house. There were also some mounted officers riding among them.

Betsy gasped. "It looks as if they're ready to make an attack on the house."

"If they do it at once, we're out of it," Kingston said.

"I think they're just preparing," she ventured. "We can't lose any time. We ought to go straight in now and try and get to the emperor before they smash down the front door and overflow the place."

"I don't like it," Kingston worried.

"We can't turn back."

"What if we're caught in there, and they take us for being one of Valmy's crowd?"

Betsy said, "I don't think even then they would stoop to shoot mere servants. And that is how we're dressed."

"Will they take time to find out?"

"I think so," she said. "Don't be so nervous."

He eyed her grimly. "You're a wonder to be this calm after all you went through."

"I have you with me this time," she said. "They caught us before by ticking us off one by one."

They made their way around to the back of the shuttered mansion, half expecting to find military men there, but there were none. They were all congregated in the front. It was as if they felt the rear door was of no concern.

Her heart pounded wildly as Kingston fitted the key in the door and opened it. They both entered the vestibule as quietly as they could and moved on to the kitchen. They found themselves in a large room completely empty at the moment.

He whispered, "What now?"

She drew her pistol from the shopping bag and held it ready. At her side George Frederick Kingston glanced around him, then moved slowly forward toward the front of the house with Betsy close by him.

The place gave her a strange feeling. There seemed to be no guards around at all. Then suddenly from behind them there came a harsh voice.

"What are you two up to?" the voice demanded.

They turned and found themselves looking at a tall stern man in butler's uniform with a large revolver in his hand pointed straight at them. He stared at them and said.

"You're fakes! She's not the maid and you're not the cook! Drop those guns!"

There was nothing else but to drop the weapons. He quickly picked them up and dropped them in the basket. Then with the basket on his arm he backed slowly into the big kitchen again. He nodded to them, "Come along! Move smartly!"

They did what he told them. And he moved slowly to a corner of the kitchen and opened a door to a medium-sized closet. He stood close to the door and jerked his head as he instructed them, "You two in there!"

She felt a true feeling of despair along with her fright. Once they were locked in the closet, they would be at the mercy of Valmy. She made a move as if to step inside, then instead shoved hard against the butler and caught him by surprise so that he stumbled back into the closet with the revolver in one hand and the basket in the other!

Betsy swung the door closed as the man inside began to hammer on it. She cried to Kingston to turn the key as she pressed all her weight against the door. Kingston turned the key, and the butler was caught in his own trap!

She said, "That's that!"

Kingston grasped her by the arm. "He fixed us just the same!"

"No one seems to be hearing him," she said, ignoring the clamor the butler made as he pounded at the door.

"I don't mean that," Kingston told her. "He has our weapons! They were in the bloomin' basket!"

"Oh!" she said groaning. Then, "Never mind, we shall have to manage without them."

"We won't get far, I know that," Kingston whispered fiercely.

She whispered back, "maybe we can snatch a weapon from the next one who comes by!"

The frail man stared at him, saying, "I should have listened and known better," he turned and let Valmy direct him toward a door along the rear hallway.

They moved to the big stairway at the front of the house. Outside the sound of the gathering army group could be plainly heard. It meant they would be attacking soon. And there was this eerie silence and the great house was seemingly deserted. She glanced toward the doors to the right, large double doors, and from behind them she heard voices suddenly in an urgent dialogue.

She gave a signal to Kingston to crouch in the shadows under the stairway so as not to be seen. She also took a place beside him, scarcely daring to breathe!

The double doors opened, and Valmy came out in a mood of angry tension. He cried, "We have no choice! It must be the sewers!"

Behind him came the frail-looking gray-haired man whom she remembered from Venice: Napoleon, even more thin and ill looking than he had been. The former emperor was wearing a dark jacket and white breeches in his familar style.

Now he faced Valmy and said, "I cannot do it! It is beneath my dignity! I have not come all the long way to Paris for this!"

"Damn your dignity!" Valmy said in a frenzy. "Don't you understand? They are outside about to attack the house and take us prisoners. The king's army! All my guards have deserted me! There's no hope but the sewers!"

"Then go," the worn former emperor said. "I shall stand my ground. The king will give me the honorable consideration of which I'm entitled!"

"Fool!" Valmy cried. "You will come with me!" And he whipped out a pistol and pointed it at the emperor.

By this time the clamor from outside was so loud that the noise of the butler trying to escape from the kitchen closet could not be heard.

Soon after Valmy escaped with his prisoner, she motioned Kingston to emerge from their hiding place. She raced across to the room from which the two had come to try and quickly find a weapon of some sort. A hasty glance showed nothing. And then she saw it as it lay on a polished table near the door. A sword in a sheath! And she recognized the sheath and knew it to be the emperor's sword!

She seized the sheath and drew out the sword and joined Kingston again. "All I could find," she told the astonished little actor. "We must hurry after them!"

"He'll kill us if he sees us," Kingston quavered.

"One of us, perhaps," she said. "The other must finish him."

They ran down the hall with the splintering of the front door and the shouts of incoming soldiers in their ears. They found the door open through which the emperor and Valmy had vanished. She led the way, eyes alert on the shadowed stairway as they descended, sword at the ready in her hand.

Kingston was breathing hard behind her. "Caught between them!" he gasped.

"This way," she said as they reached the cellar.

Ahead was an open trap door, and there was a ladder leading down to the sewers from it. She turned to Kingston and told him, "I'll go first!"

Chapter Seventeen

BETSY STEPPED gingerly off the ladder and tried to adjust her eyes to the near darkness of the dank sewer. Then Kingston came down after her. A short distance ahead they saw the glow of a lantern.

She whispered, "That will be them. Trying to make their way to another house and escape!"

"It's Valmy wants that, not Napoleon!" Kingston whispered in return.

"I know," she said. "Watch your step!" she warned. For at that point the tunnel narrowed, and there was only a platform of perhaps two feet running alongside the poisonous-looking sewer water.

She pressed close to the slimy side of the tunnel, and Kingston did the same. Slowly they gained on Valmy and his distinguished prisoner. All at once the platform widened again to about four feet.

Ahead Valmy said, "We should be able to find an entrance to a house about here!"

"I will go no further!" his captive said, facing him sternly.

"You're right! It is the end of the road!" Valmy sneered and he lifted his pistol and fired at the man on whom he had pinned all his hopes.

The former emperor received the bullet direcly in the area of the heart. Blood poured out over his waistcoat, and he fell back into the polluted stream of sewerage and vanished.

Betsy watched in awe, and a great rage surged up in her. "Traitor!" she cried! And she lifted the emperor's sword.

A surprised Valmy turned around quickly and aimed his pistol to shoot her, but she was too quick for him. She was close to him and the emperor's sword was through his chest as he pressed the trigger of his weapon. The pistol went off with the bullet harmlessly spending itself in the wall of the tunnel.

Valmy's expression was one of sheer horror as she withdrew the sword from him. He lifted his hands as he tried to hurl some imprecation at her. Then blood spurted out from his mouth, and he tottered back to join his victim in the sewer stream.

Kingston was at her side, panting, "I didn't think you'd manage!"

She was staring at the dark stream of the sewer. "I had to," she said, her own breath coming with difficulty. "I had to do it for Napoleon and for myself!"

It was then the voices of Eric and the others came to them from far along the sewer tunnel. She turned and touched Kingston on the arm.

"Down that way!" she said. "We'll meet them."

He nodded and started along the dark tunnel. She held the bloodstained sword in her hands for a moment and then she tossed it into the polluted river. She picked up the lantern which was on its side but still burning and followed Kingston.

They joined with the other group within a few minutes. Eric took her in his arms and said nothing for a time. Then he began to question her as they stood there—a forlorn little squad in the dank tunnel under the Paris streets.

"What happened?" he asked.

"Valmy killed him," she said. "I finished Valmy with the emperor's sword. They're both somewhere there in the river of sewerage!"

Eric gave a small gasp of dismay. "Felix Black will be unhappy."

"There was no other way," she said.

They found a passage to the surface and then took a carriage back to the pension. Captain Gray was to return to his ship at once, there being no reason to delay his sailing any longer.

O'Meara left them at the door of the pension. He seemed in low spirits as he told them, "I will make my way back to England on my own. It has been a sad night for me."

"For all of us," she said, touched by his sorrow.

"Not the same for any of you," the Irishman said looking away. "I had great hopes for him. I always believed." And giving her a last look which could have been one of reproach, he walked off into the darkness.

Kingston stared after him indignantly, "The nerve of the man! You'd almost think he was blaming us for what happened."

"He's a romantic," she said with a small tremor in her voice. "He has to blame someone!"

Eric shook his head. "It is you who are the romantic! He's a stubborn firebrand of an Irishman! They're never to be satisfied!"

They went inside and were greeted by a long-faced landlady. She said, "I'm glad you have come. Monsieur Black has suffered a severe attack. The doctor is with him now. I do not know!"

Betsy felt panic. "He was ill before we left."

"Let us find out how he is," Eric said.

They all three went swiftly up the steps and were greeted by a sober-looking little man carrying a medicine bag. He looked at them and said, "You are his friends?"

"Yes," she said. "How is he?"

"He has not long," the doctor said sadly. "He should be dead at this moment. But somehow he has revived a little."

Eric asked, "Can he be moved?"

The doctor shrugged. "It would be dangerous. I cannot say. I will come by again in the morning."

He went on his way, and led by Betsy, the three filed into the softly lighted room. The candle on the bedside table showed a motionless Felix Black in bed, his face the same color as the white pillow. Apparently he heard them and opened his eyes.

"Well?" he asked in a low voice.

She had tears in her eyes as she took his hand and said, "Later. We can talk about it later."

"Now!" he said in a firmer voice, and his eyes were fixed on her.

Briefly she told him. "They are both gone! Somewhere in the waters of the great sewer. The army broke in afterward but too late to come upon them."

"Good!" Felix Black said. "My own little army completed the task." His voice still terribly weak, he went on. "And it was proper that he was avenged. Avenged with his own sword!"

Eric spoke up. "You must not talk, sir. You are very ill!"

"I have been dying for a long time," the old spy master said. "The time is close. But not yet. Tomorrow we begin our journey home. I wish to have the game end in Fetter Street. In England."

Betsy asked, "Are you able to travel?"

The old man smiled bleakly. "I shall make the journey. And you, Kingston, sit with me a little. I dislike being alone tonight."

"Yes, sir," the actor said with emotion and drew a chair up by the master spy's bed.

Felix Black closed his eyes. Betsy and Eric left the room silently. She turned to the man she loved and tearfully asked, "Will he manage it?"

Eric smiled sadly. "He will. Have you ever doubted him?"

"No," she said huskily. "Nor you!" And she pressed close to him, and their lips met.